Miss Austen INVESTIGATES

THE HAPLESS MILLINER

Miss Austen INVESTIGATES

THE HAPLESS MILLINER

A NOVEL

JESSICA BULL

UNION SQUARE & CO.
NEW YORK

UNION SQUARE & CO. and the distinctive Union Square & Co. logo are trademarks of Sterling Publishing Co., Inc.

Union Square & Co., LLC, is a subsidiary of Sterling Publishing Co., Inc.

ISBN 978-1-4549-5180-3
ISBN 978-1-4549-5181-0 (e-book)

For information about custom editions, special sales, and premium purchases, please contact specialsales@unionsquareandco.com.

Printed in Canada

2 4 6 8 10 9 7 5 3 1

unionsquareandco.com

Cover design by Will Staehle/Unusual Corporation
Interior design by Kevin Ullrich
Images: Rawpixel (house); Maisei Raman/Shutterstock.com (hand)

For Eliza and Rosina, my obstinate headstrong girls

The eight children of the Reverend Mr. George Austen and his good lady wife, Mrs. Cassandra Austen (née Leigh), listed in order of their birth, by a partial, prejudiced and ignorant *family* historian.

1. **The Reverend Mr. James Austen (b. 1765):** The eldest—an accident of birth he regards as divine providence.
2. **Mr. George "Georgy" Austen (b. 1766):** Before I could write, or speak, he taught me how to talk with my fingers.
3. **Mr. Edward "Neddy" Austen, later Knight (b. 1767):** My favourite. For it's only prudent that one's wealthiest brother is one's favourite.
4. **Lieutenant Henry Austen (b. 1771):** Beastly. The most horrid brother who ever lived.
5. **Miss Cassandra Austen (b. 1773):** The sweetest, kindest, most gullible of creatures.
6. **Lieutenant Francis "Frank" Austen (b. 1774):** Young, tenacious, away at sea a lot.
7. **Miss Jane Austen (b. 1775):** Come now, do I really need an introduction?
8. **Midshipman Charles Austen (b. 1779):** *See* Frank.

CHAPTER ONE

Hampshire, England, 11 December 1795

By moonlight, Jane hitches up the hem of her muslin gown and darts across a neatly scythed lawn. The fireworks are over but the musky tang of gunpowder lingers in her throat, and the din of a raucous crowd rises above the efforts of the string quartet performing in the Tudor mansion behind her. It is nine o'clock and the ball has hardly begun. Jane, accompanied by two of her elder brothers, James and Henry, arrived less than an hour ago but already the finest society in all of Hampshire are tipsy and braying at each other over the melody.

As she crosses the manicured garden, Jane crouches behind each colossal tower of yew to check for onlookers. Her heart pounds at the ruinous prospect of being spotted. God forbid she is caught sneaking away from the party unchaperoned. Her feet are cold, and damp is seeping through her shell-pink silk slippers. They were made for pirouetting on polished mahogany, not dashing across frosty grass.

Her breath turns to steam. The bare branches of a laburnum reach out like the bony arms of a great skeleton but she races on regardless. Tonight she and her clever young man will come to their agreement. He will make her an offer of marriage, she is sure of it. Which words will Tom select for his purpose? *My dearest Jane, you must allow me to tell you . . . Miss Austen,*

I offer myself to you . . . She will listen carefully and commit each phrase to memory. It could prove useful the next time one of her heroines receives a proposal.

Flickering lamps guide her path to the glasshouse. She presses down gently on the door handle, yet it creaks and the hinges groan as she slips inside. Exotic orchids perfume the misty atmosphere and she touches a hand to the back of her head. Her maid coiled her chestnut hair into a passably elegant chignon, with ringlets framing her face. If her curls turn to frizz, her brothers will guess where she's been, and report her to their mother.

A lean figure steps out from behind a desert pine. He is fair with distinguished features, and instantly recognizable in his ivory swallowtail coat. "Mademoiselle."

The deep timbre of his voice dissolves Jane's heart and propels her toward him. Pausing just out of his reach, she gazes upward through fluttering eyelashes. "It was most wicked of you to lure me here alone."

His bright blue eyes sparkle and his mouth curls into a seductive smile. "You understood my message, then?"

"I understand you perfectly, Monsieur Lefroy." Jane's gaze locks on his lips and she lets herself be gathered tight into his arms. His mouth hovers over hers, and she tips her head back to accept his kiss. She is almost, but not quite, as tall as he. Their relative statures seem designed to aid their *amour*. Glued together, they stumble into a row of shelves. Beside Jane, a terra-cotta pot tumbles and smashes at her feet. Dark earth spills across the clay floor tiles. She breaks free, stooping to pick up the tangle of roots and placing the plant carefully back inside its damaged pot.

Tom bends down on one knee, cupping her face in his palm. Is this the moment he will propose? He directs her eyes back to his. "Leave the wretched weed, Jane. It doesn't matter."

"But I must! We are guests—it's only respectful." Jane's heartbeat returns to a regular rhythm as she places the orchid back on the shelf beside its neighbours. She fingers the tall stem, lined with papery chartreuse flowers, until the plant looks as if it was never disturbed. Tom kicks shards of terra-cotta beneath the cabinet with the toe of his dancing pump. "Besides, someone will know we've been in here . . ."

He silences her protests with kisses. Slowly, he peels one kid leather glove down her arm and pulls it free. Jane presses her naked palm to his, their fingers interlacing. Through half-closed eyes, she watches the condensation form rivulets and slide down the walls of the glasshouse, and waits for the strings to strike up again. A drop of moisture falls to the floor.

"Wait. Something is wrong. I can't hear the music." She reaches for the nearest pane of glass, rubs a spot clear and squints through it. The doors of the great hall are open to the terrace. Guests are standing about, heads bent together. The dance floor is clear.

Tom releases her, straightening. "You're right. It's too quiet. Sir John can't be making the toast already—not so early in the proceedings."

"I expect Mrs. Rivers is hounding Lady Harcourt and the baronet to make the announcement. Jonathan Harcourt is the most eligible bachelor in all of Hampshire. Sophy Rivers will be champing at the bit to be congratulated on their engagement. I'd better get back. James and Henry will be looking for me. I bet them half a crown, weeks ago now, that Sophy would be the one to snare him."

Tom's shoulders sag in defeat. "You go ahead. I shall follow."

"We can meet again, afterward?" Jane is reluctant to let the moment pass without resolution of their future together. The glasshouse is the perfect setting for Tom to declare his intentions toward her. Yet if her family discover her missing from the ball, she risks having her limited freedom curtailed even further. "Back here. As soon as the dancing strikes up again?"

Tom offers her a rueful smile. "Go, then. Give me a few moments to compose myself."

Jane flushes as she turns toward the door, pressing her fingers over her lips to prevent herself from laughing.

"Wait!" He waves her glove at her.

She runs back into his arms, giggling freely. She would look a fool returning to the ball with only one glove. Her brothers would be furious if they guessed she'd lost it in an amorous tryst with a young man so recently of her acquaintance. As much as James and Henry seem to approve of Tom, Jane is their little sister, and it's their duty to guard her virtue. A lady's reputation is her most precious asset. Especially a young lady like Jane, who has scant enough resources to recommend her.

She reclaims her stolen token, leaning in for one last kiss before heading out into the night. Tom may not have proposed, but from the look of wonder in his eyes and the passion in his rapturous kiss, Jane is certain of his most ardent affection for her.

The enormous studded oak doors to the great hall of Deane House are wedged open. Heat and light radiate from the crush of well-heeled guests inside. Jane hesitates, staring down at the grass stains on her slippers and along the hem of her best muslin gown. Cassandra, Jane's elder sister, to whom the gown officially belongs, will be most vexed. But Cassandra cannot reproach Jane for ruining her gown, or for her wanton behaviour with Tom in the glasshouse, because she is not here. In preparation for joining her new family, the Fowles, Cassandra is keeping Christmas in Kintbury with her fiancé.

Hence, Jane is playing fast and loose with her virtue to secure a fiancé of her own, lest she become the only one of the Austens' eight children to remain at Steventon Rectory. She cannot imagine a fate worse than to be a spinster all her life, forced to play nursemaid to her ageing parents in their dotage. She fills her lungs with one last breath of cool night air before she slides inside.

Below the vaulted oak ceiling of the Elizabethan hall, more than thirty families mingle and murmur to each other. Heavy-lidded ladies whisper behind fans, while gentlemen frown and shake their heads. Surely they cannot have discovered Jane's impropriety already. With her back to the tapestries, she side-steps along the edge of the throng. Above her head, enormous torches, placed at intervals, burn brightly in their iron sconces. On the balcony, the musicians drink and chatter, their instruments silent, laid across their laps.

Snatches of conversation float in the dense air: "An incident . . . Sir John called away . . ."

Thank Heaven. Something other than her own misdemeanour must have disrupted the evening; one of the party will have knocked over the punch bowl or dropped their spectacles into the soup tureen. Poor Sir John and Lady Harcourt, having to put up with such behaviour from their guests.

Sophy, the eldest of the Rivers sisters, and the rumoured object of Jonathan Harcourt's affections, sits on a sofa, staring at the dazzling white roses on her shoes. Really, she could muster up a little more enthusiasm. What any of the Rivers girls, with their insipid beauty and thirty thousand pounds apiece, might have to frown about, Jane does not know. Especially Sophy—who has apparently ensnared the most sought-after bachelor in the county, and wears a diamond choker with, in her usual style of modesty, an ivory cameo of herself dangling from it.

Yet Sophy's grey eyes are hard, and the corners of her mouth turn down. She must be anxious to have the matter publicly squared away. It is a precarious position for a young lady to be in, her good name attached to a gentleman, without the protection of having taken his in return. The widowed Mrs. Rivers stands over her daughter, making up for Sophy's moroseness by yapping loudly. The late Mr. Rivers's fortune was built on cotton, but his widow favours silks and furs. Tonight she is resplendent in black bombazine trimmed with sarsenet.

Across the hall, Jonathan Harcourt's rangy frame is swallowed by the door to the main wing of the house. Perhaps he is already repining the prospect of attaching himself to the daughter of a brazen parvenue. Jonathan has only just returned from his Grand Tour of the Continent. Jane likes him all the better for his having been away, but not so much that she wishes *she* was his bride-to-be.

Jonathan and his elder brother, Edwin, were Jane's father's pupils, and spent their early years living alongside her at Steventon Rectory. She has the same problem with all the single gentlemen in her locality. Having seen far too much of them as schoolboys, she cannot quite bring herself to view any as a potential lover.

Her interest is only ever piqued by newcomers, such as the delectable Tom Lefroy. And perhaps Douglas Fitzgerald, the young clergyman-in-waiting, who is having his ear bent by Mrs. Rivers. The hall is crawling with clergymen, but none quite like this one. He is the natural son of Mrs. Rivers's brother-in-law, Captain Jerry Rivers. Captain Rivers owns a plantation in Jamaica and has sent Mr. Fitzgerald home to England to be educated.

The young man is extremely tall and striking, and wears a silver peruke, which contrasts with his deep brown complexion.

Jane will find James and Henry and reassure them that her behaviour befits a young lady of her station. Then, as soon as Sir John has dealt with whatever incident has taken place, and the string quartet take up their bows, she will dash back to the glasshouse to hear Tom out. She smiles to herself as she snatches a crystal goblet of Madeira wine from a passing footman and takes a long sip, attempting to quench her thirst. It is served warm, and tastes of orange peel and burnt sugar.

James stands at the rear of the hall. He is lean, and lofty, dressed in ecclesiastical apparel, his shoulder-length curls dusted with powder. His features are a distorted reflection of Jane's own. The Austen siblings all have the same bright hazel eyes, high forehead and long, straight nose, with a small mouth and full pink lips. James is the eldest—an accident of birth he regards as Divine Providence.

"There you are!" He pushes his way through the sea of people toward her. "Where have you been? I've searched for you everywhere."

"I went looking for a fresh glass," Jane lies, holding up her wine as evidence. "I didn't want to be caught empty-handed when the speeches were made."

James rubs the back of his long neck. "I'm not sure there will be any toasts now."

"Why? Has Jonathan made a last-ditch attempt to escape the marital noose?"

"Don't be ridiculous, Jane. Jonathan wouldn't dare disappoint his parents so. Not after . . ."

Edwin. Five years previously, Jonathan's elder brother, Edwin, was thrown from his thoroughbred stallion on the eve of his marriage to the daughter of a duke. He died instantly, simultaneously breaking his neck and his parents' hearts. The tragedy heightened Lady Harcourt's already nervous disposition. Even now, she grips the arm of a footman, twisting her head toward her guests so that her monstrous coiffure wobbles like a freshly set jelly.

"Where's Henry?" Jane surveys the crowded hall. If the incident is serious, she dearly hopes her brother is not caught up in it. Henry should be easy to spot. Of those assembled, almost all the ladies are in pale gowns while the gentlemen wear dark blue or black. Only Tom Lefroy bucks the trend by masquerading as English literature's most affable rake, Tom Jones, in his frightful ivory coat, while Henry has been strutting around like a peacock in his scarlet regimentals.

James grimaces. "Last seen dancing with the amiable Mrs. Chute."

Mrs. Chute is six-and-twenty, with a lively character and a handsome countenance. She is recently married to a rich old man who shuns company and will not, therefore, be in attendance. It is infuriating that Henry does not have to guard his flirtations as closely as Jane does.

From across the room, Tom flashes Jane a rueful grin, making her flush with warmth. He must have slid into the hall immediately after her.

Behind James, the door to the house swings open once again, and Mrs. Twistleton, the Harcourts' housekeeper, slinks through it. With her almond-shaped eyes, black silk dress and white lace cuffs, she reminds Jane of the Austens' best mouser—the smallest cat in the yard has black fur with white paws. She sits in the sun all day licking her claws and waiting for her next kill.

Mrs. Twistleton grabs the butler's arm. As she mouths a few words into his ear, the man's eyes bulge and his face pales. What disaster could have befallen the Harcourts to cause their usually stony-faced butler to lose all outward sign of composure? Jane slides her wrist through the crook of James's arm, suddenly grateful for the familiar shape of her brother beside her.

The butler recovers himself and rings his brass bell, calling in a crisp, high-pitched voice: "Ladies and gentlemen, is there a doctor in attendance?"

A gasp reverberates through the hall. The local physician staggers up from his seat, red-faced and swaying, then falls hard on his well-padded backside. Jane tuts. He's clearly in his cups. Mrs. Twistleton lifts herself on tiptoe to speak into the butler's ear. He recoils. She raises her dark brows and nods.

The butler stares at her open-mouthed, before giving the bell another shake. "Do excuse me. Ladies and gentlemen, is there a—a clergyman present?"

Nervous laughter ripples through the crowd. More than half of the men here are members of the clergy. Hampshire is overrun with them.

James spreads his arms wide, then lets them fall to his sides. He just so happens to be the man of the cloth standing in closest proximity to the servants. "I should go. Will you be all right?"

"I'll come with you." Jane passes her half-empty goblet to a nearby footman. "Just to check it's not Henry."

The crease in James's brow deepens as he hastens toward the door. Jane follows. She'll make sure that Henry hasn't got himself into any trouble, then slip away. Hopefully, all is not lost, and Tom will have another opportunity to declare himself before the night is over. She tries to catch his eye before she leaves, but he turns his back to her as he is pressed into the milieu.

James reaches the entrance to the main wing of the house at exactly the same moment as Mr. Fitzgerald. They bump shoulders. Mr. Fitzgerald may not yet have his Geneva bands, but the soon-to-be clergyman is most eager to perform his priestly duties. He blinks, bowing from the waist to signify that James and Jane should proceed. Beeswax candles flicker in their brass sconces, throwing light and shadow over the oil portraits lining the walls. From within the paintings, generations of Harcourts stare at her coldly. Jane recognises the same long face, beaked nose and pointed chin as the current titleholder and his son. The housekeeper's and Mr. Fitzgerald's footsteps echo close behind.

They emerge into the grand entrance hall. A weighty chain suspends a brass chandelier from the double-height ceiling. Scores of candles illuminate the oak paneling and the ornate carved staircase leading to the upper floors of the mansion. Henry stands guard in front of a small door left ajar in the paneling. With his feet planted hip distance apart, his right hand resting on the handle of his glinting sabre, he is dazzling in his officer's finery. The double-breasted scarlet jacket shows off his tall figure, and the gold epaulettes sit well on his broad shoulders. In protest at the powder tax, he's cut his chestnut hair short—giving himself a raffish air. He looks so much like a tin soldier that Jane wants to laugh with relief at the sight of him.

"What's happened?" asks James.

But Henry remains silent, his face uncharacteristically grim. He nods to Mrs. Chute, who sits opposite on a blood-red damask sofa, sobbing into a handkerchief. A housemaid kneels at her feet, proffering a green glass bottle of smelling salts. A younger maid stands by, with a mop dipped into a bucket of soapy water. She is a small round girl, with broad features and a thick neck. Her complexion is ghostly, and she is trembling.

The pale gold ostrich feathers of Mrs. Chute's headdress bob and weave as she blows her nose. "I had no idea she was there. I almost tripped over her."

Jane places a hand to her throat. "*Who* is in there?"

"Damned if any of us know." Sir John Harcourt stamps up and down the Turkey runner. Beneath the sausage curls of his fat-bottomed peruke, his complexion is puce. He has always made an imposing figure, with his great belly and flapping jowls. Tonight he is especially threatening.

Henry steps aside. "I'm afraid we found a . . . well, a body."

James pushes open the door. He balks. Jane sidles up beside him, squinting into the room. It is a small closet. There is a ghastly metallic smell coming from inside, like a butcher's shop. On the floor, from the light spilling in from the hallway, Jane can just make out a chintz-patterned skirt. It is heavily stained with a dark substance. Two brown laced shoes poke out from beneath it. They are ladies' shoes, with a well-worn leather sole.

"I wouldn't." Henry places a hand on Jane's upper arm, lightly restraining her.

Mr. Fitzgerald edges past with a lit taper. He kneels beside the skirt, throwing light into the cramped space.

Jane catches bile in the back of her throat.

It is a young woman—her arms flung wide, her pallor ashen and her features frozen in abject terror. Her mouth gapes, and her glassy eyes stare blankly. Blood congeals at an enormous gash in her temple and puddles around her on the floor.

"Dear God." Jane takes a step back, but she cannot tear away her eyes.

Mr. Fitzgerald stoops, placing his ear to the woman's chest, listening for her breath. After a few moments, he lays two fingers on her neck, then shakes his head. "May the Lord, in his forgiveness, grant her eternal peace," he says softly, stretching his thumb and forefinger over her face and attempting to close her eyes.

He falters. Her eyelids are stuck fast.

Withdrawing his hand, he bows his head and makes the sign of the cross. As he does so, candlelight flickers across the lifeless form and a spark of recognition stirs. Jane lets out a high-pitched scream. It is so unlike her that even she is shocked by it. Her knees buckle. She clings to James's lapels for support as she stares at the familiar face.

It must have been early October, for the chill was not yet in the air, when Jane first saw the woman's delicate features. She had traveled to Basingstoke with Alethea Bigg, and stumbled across the milliner, Madame Renault, perched upon a wooden stool in the marketplace. On a table covered with green baize cloth, Madame Renault had arranged a few straw hats and several delicate lace caps. Her clothes, while not fashionable, were neat and clean. She wore a chintz gown with a gold and pearl chain tucked into the bodice, and one of her own lace-trimmed caps over her dark hair. Jane considered buying a gift for Cassandra. Some of the caps were so fine, they would make a pretty headdress for a bride.

But, as usual, Jane's vanity overcame her good intentions. She bought one of the straw hats for herself instead. She had meant to try it on for a lark, but she looked so very well in it. Jane tried to negotiate on the price by saying she didn't think she'd brought enough and would have to come back for it another day. Madame Renault shrugged, indifferent. In broken English, she explained she spent most of her time working to order and rented the stall only when she had stock to spare. She couldn't guarantee when, or even if, she would be in Basingstoke again. She might be persuaded to take a commission, if she had time.

Alethea thought the milliner arrogant, but Jane was so impressed by her confidence that she paid her the full twelve shillings and sixpence. Evidently Madame Renault knew the value of her artistry and trusted her handiwork to be in demand. How liberating to belong to a class of women who could openly take pride in their work.

The encounter lent Jane the audacity to imagine herself sitting behind a stall in the marketplace, with all of her manuscripts neatly copied out, tied between marble boards and resting on green baize . . .

Now, she places her fist to her mouth, biting back a sob as she stands transfixed by the milliner's brutally battered corpse.

James's arms circle her shoulders. "Come away, Jane. Don't upset yourself."

"But I can't. I know her."

Everyone looks at Jane expectantly.

"Then who the devil is she?" Sir John thumps his fat fist on the mahogany sideboard. "And what's she doing lying dead in my laundry closet?"

Jane slips out of James's hold, stepping into the doorway the better to see the woman's blood-spattered face. She must be certain before she says anything.

Mr. Fitzgerald holds the taper beside the woman's cheek, and Jane is overcome by weariness. Everything has changed.

The evening is no longer one of frivolity. She will not receive her romantic proposal or enjoy any more secret kisses with her lover in the glasshouse tonight. "Her name is Madame Renault. She was a milliner—I bought a hat from her in Basingstoke market."

Henry nods, as if this information tells him all he needs to know. "I've sent for the parish constable. The magistrate is expected anyway, for the ball."

Mr. Fitzgerald covers Madame Renault's face with a blanket, tucking it around her shoulders with care, as if it might keep her warm even now.

James steers Jane toward the main entrance. "Come, let me help you into the carriage and take you home. This has been a terrible shock for all of us."

As Jane stumbles toward the door, she cranes her neck to take one last look at Madame Renault. A fresh wave of nausea comes over her at the pool of blood seeping into the blanket Mr. Fitzgerald had used to cover the corpse. How could such a monstrous act have been committed, here, in the midst of such gaiety? Violence and murder have no place in Jane's safe, staid little world. And yet there Madame Renault lies, bludgeoned to death by someone who, by all accounts, cannot be too far away from where Jane is standing. Who, among Jane's society, could have carried out this heinous crime?

CHAPTER TWO

The morning after the ball, Jane skips up the two steps from her bedroom to the landing, and rushes down the narrow staircase into the kitchen, then hops up to enter the family parlour. Steventon Rectory is a higgledy-piggledy construction, its very layout revealing the history of a dwelling haphazardly thrown together over the previous two centuries. Jane dressed with haste, in terror that Tom might be an early riser. Surely he will call on her today. His declaration was sorely interrupted, and he must be as desperate for her answer as she is to hear the terms of his proposal. God forbid he should complete the mile-and-a-half walk from Ashe Rectory, where he is staying with his uncle, the Reverend George Lefroy, before Jane is ready to receive him.

Several chestnut tendrils escape from Jane's plait and the laces of her canary-yellow gown hang loose. Sally, the Austens' maid, hums softly as she places a tray of dirty crockery on the table and moves to assist Jane with her drawstring neckline. Within the parlour, the whole family are gathered and a blaze burns in the redbrick fireplace. In the centre of the room, Jane's mother, Mrs. Cassandra Austen, sits at an old-fashioned cherrywood table, covered with a plain linen cloth and laid for breakfast. Mrs. Austen holds steady a wooden bowl of stewed apples as Anna, James's infant daughter, leans precariously out of her high chair to get at it with a spoon.

Mr. George Austen, Jane's father, studies yesterday's newspaper, which a kindly neighbour drops off once he's finished with it. James reads a different section of the same broadsheet. Mr. Austen has divided the newspaper in half, allowing James to peruse the advertisements and the gossip, while he scrutinises the naval reports for any mention of His Majesty's Ships *Glory* and *Daedalus*. Both vessels were last reported off the coast of the West Indies, and each carries the extremely precious cargo of a younger Austen boy. Twenty-one-year-old Frank and sixteen-year-old Charles are both on active service with the Royal Navy.

Technically, as his father's curate for the nearby village of Overton, James has his own home. But since the tragic and wholly unexpected death of his young wife, earlier in the year, he's found solace in returning to the nest. He may sleep and preach in Overton, but he takes his meals and leaves his laundry at Steventon. Eighteen-month-old Anna is always at Steventon, in the care of her grandmother. It used to break Jane's heart when she cried for her mama. It is almost worse now that she has stopped doing so.

"I'll have that, thank you." Mrs. Austen prises open Anna's chubby fist to remove a small glass medicine bottle. "Who left it lying around?"

Sally dips an apology as she tucks the bottle into the folds of her apron. Jane doesn't point out that it was Mrs. Austen who had left the medicine on the table. Sally was already in bed by the time Jane got home and broke the news of the horrific incident to her enrapt parents. Mrs. Austen had retrieved the bottle from the locked medicine cabinet and all but forced a drop of laudanum on Jane for the shock. Jane had clamped her lips shut and stoutly refused the tincture. Her wit is the sharpest weapon in her armoury. She will not have it blunted. When Tom calls, and surely he *will* call today, he'll ask Jane to make the most important decision in a young woman's life. Perhaps the only important decision she'll ever make by herself. How could she have faced such a prospect, had her mind been reeling from the aftereffects of a laudanum-induced haze?

"Did I miss Henry?" Jane pulls out a chair, scraping the wooden feet over the quarry-tiled floor. The walls of the snug room are lime-washed and adorned with horse brasses and cross-stitched samplers, which do little to absorb the noise of her rowdy family.

James nods as he shakes out his half of the paper. "He shot off back to Oxford first thing this morning." Henry is a student, another Hampshire lad destined for the clergy, but with the imminent threat of an invasion of Jacobins from across the Channel, he's volunteered for the militia. Being Henry, he somehow arranged for his regiment to be stationed just outside Oxford, allowing him to continue his studies while simultaneously serving king and country.

"That's a shame. I wanted to talk to him before he went." Jane pours herself some tea from the black basalt teapot. She hasn't slept well. Every time she closed her eyes, Madame Renault's sunken cheeks and gaping mouth appeared, as if her death mask was imprinted on Jane's eyelids.

As a rector's daughter, she's seen plenty of corpses. The poor of the parish cannot afford their own coffins. They arrive for their funerals wrapped in their shrouds, borrow the communal box for the service, then are tipped out of it into the freshly dug earth to be buried. From the window of the stagecoach, she's even seen the remains of highwaymen, wrapped in chains and suspended from gibbets at the crossroads. Their decaying bodies, oozing with maggots and swarmed by flies, are prominently displayed near the scene of their crimes to deter others from replicating their sins.

But looking into the face of a woman whose life had been so recently, and so unjustly, snuffed out was an entirely different experience. One Jane already knows will haunt her for the rest of her days.

"I expect he feared old Mr. Chute might challenge him to a duel over his wife's virtue if he remained at home any longer," says Mr. Austen, without looking up from his broadsheet.

Jane chokes on her tea at the prospect of geriatric Mr. Chute calling out young Lieutenant Austen. She pictures the old man dropping his walking stick to reach for his pistol, and toppling face-first onto the grass.

"It's not funny, Father." James peers over the top of his half of the newspaper. Despite their late night, James is already clean-shaven and fastidiously dressed.

"You need hardly explain that to me." Mr. Austen takes a sip of his tea. He wears a russet banyan over his clerical robes, and his bright white hair pokes out from a matching cap. "I'll be forced to sell up to keep Henry out of the Marshalsea, if Mr. Chute sues for crim con."

Jane gulps some tea, scalding her throat. For the middling classes, divorce is so difficult and costly as to be nigh impossible. And, since a married woman has no property or wealth of her own, the only recourse a wronged husband can take toward an adulterous wife is to sue her male partner for "criminal conversation." Strictly speaking, the term refers to seeking compensation for the devaluation of property. In the eyes of the law, a wife's status is only moderately higher than that of a favoured horse. Both can be whipped and worked to death, but only one can be legitimately slaughtered when it has outlived its usefulness. It is a most distasteful truth to acknowledge.

"Perhaps that's why Mr. Chute married the girl." Mrs. Austen is tall and spare, with an aquiline nose she believes to be evidence of her aristocratic bloodline. "In hope of her tempting some wealthy young buck into a sordid affair, so he could reap the damages." She runs a damp cloth over her granddaughter's chubby cheeks.

Suits for criminal conversation have become so lucrative that men have been accused of encouraging their wives to flirt with wealthy acquaintances, intending to catch them in the act. Mr. Chute is far too rich to bother with such a tiresome scheme, but he is the type of man who is always hungry for more.

It is just as well Jane's current heroine, the diabolical Lady Susan, is a widow, and therefore not susceptible to such humiliations in a court of law. Instead, at the flick of Jane's pen, Lady Susan is free to wreak havoc on the male sex. There is a certain irony in that it is only by submitting to, and then outliving, her husband that a woman can ever achieve true freedom.

"Then why on earth did he let her anywhere near Henry?" Mr. Austen places his teacup back in its saucer, aligning the handle at exactly three o'clock. "He should have set her in the direction of Jonathan Harcourt."

"Mrs. Chute would have no luck with Jonathan," says James. "He's hardly likely to be tempted away from Miss Rivers, is he?"

Mrs. Austen flattens her lips. "Sophy's a nice enough girl and I imagine her dowry will be most welcome, even to the Harcourts . . ."

Jane's teeth itch at her mother's description of the ambitious heiress. Sophy was born almost a full year before Jane, arriving keenly on New Year's Day 1775. Despite the narrow gap in age and close proximity to one another since the Rivers family settled at Kempshott Park more than a decade ago, upstart Sophy has never been particularly *nice* to Jane.

Anna makes a grab for Mrs. Austen's lace cap with her apple-encrusted fist. "But I always hoped Jonathan would meet someone who would help him come into his own. Someone like you, Jane." Mrs. Austen attempts to bat away Anna's sticky hands.

"Me? I'm sorry, Mother, but that ship has already left port. Unless you'd like me to whisk Jonathan up to Gretna Green, and have him pledge his troth to me in front of a blacksmith before the religious ceremony takes place?"

"I didn't mean he should marry you, only someone *like* you." Mrs. Austen disentangles Anna's fingers from the frill of her cap. It is so well spattered with stewed apple that it matches her stained cotton pinny. "A more independent-minded young lady, who wouldn't let his parents intimidate her."

Unsure whether to be flattered or insulted, Jane butters her toast and spoons some of her mother's homemade raspberry jam on top. "So, has Henry ruined all our good names?"

"Hardly," says James. "The grisly discovery rather overshadowed Henry's indiscretion. We managed to put it about that Mrs. Chute stumbled across the body, and Lieutenant Austen went running to her assistance only *after* he heard her scream."

"How gallant of him." Jane smiles.

"Indeed." James frowns.

"What a commotion. I wish I'd been there now." Mrs. Austen sighs. Anna dips her spoon into her stewed apple and flicks it at her grandmother.

Jane chews her toast. "I said you should come."

"Out of the question. It's far too cold. My constitution would never withstand it." Mrs. Austen plucks the little girl out of the high chair and sits her on her knee. "Besides, we couldn't leave darling Anna."

"Darling Anna?" Jane leans over to ruffle the wisps of golden hair on the baby's head. "You never minded leaving us. We were all still living with Dame Culham at twice her age."

Having a troop of schoolboys to look after, and a farm to run, had meant Mrs. Austen had delegated the daily grind of motherhood when her children were very young. Once weaned, all of the Austen babies were handed over to a dry nurse in the village and barred from returning to Steventon Rectory until such time as they could make shift for themselves.

Mrs. Austen purses her mouth. "Jane, we visited you every day."

Jane smiles sweetly. "Oh, how thoughtful. Did you leave a calling card if we were out?" Jane has heard her mother's explanation for the unusual practice a thousand times. Given how much time and energy Anna commands, now she resides at the rectory, Jane cannot fault her mother's reasoning. Yet neither can she help feeling a little resentful at having been ejected from the family home during her earliest years. Especially as it is unlikely that one member of the Austen brood will ever be able to live independently. George "Georgy" Austen is Jane's second eldest brother. At the age when children typically learn to walk and talk, Georgy became prone to the violent fits that interrupt his mental capacity and exhaust his body. He has never learned to form words but, like a true Austen, he does not let that prevent him from making himself understood. Before Jane could write, or even speak, Georgy taught her how to talk with her fingers.

He's ten years older than her and, in her childish naivety, she could never have imagined that she would move up to

Steventon Rectory while he remained with Dame Culham at the cottage. But Georgy's struggle to comprehend the most everyday hazards—such as a coach and six hurtling along the highway toward him, or why a dip in a leech-infested pond was inadvisable—and his medical needs mean he requires constant supervision.

In fairness, Mr. and Mrs. Austen tried several times to bring him home to live with his brothers and sisters. But after a terrifying incident when they feared they'd lost him down the well, they agreed Georgy should remain under the more watchful eye of his nurse. It's probably for the best, and Georgy is very happy in the village, surrounded by his friends and neighbours. But the thought of him excluded from the rectory, despite the family's best efforts to keep him close, weighs heavy on Jane's heart.

These days, more often than not, it is Georgy who pays the house calls. He comes and goes as stealthily as a hawk to visit his sisters while avoiding his ever-anxious mother. His favourite trick is to appear in the Austens' kitchen, without ceremony, to help himself to Sally's legendary gingerbread (sometimes it's so spicy, you'd think she'd exchanged the ginger for mustard) before the rest of the family have a chance.

Mrs. Austen sucks in her cheeks and glares at Jane, while Mr. Austen merely chuckles. James puts down his newspaper to peer out of the window. A compact figure, in a pot hat and mud-brown cape, is plodding along the lane. "Is that Mary Lloyd?" he asks.

Jane exhales audibly as she nods.

Usually, Cassandra and Jane form a congenial foursome with Mary and her elder sister, Martha. Cassandra's and Martha's sweet dispositions balance their younger siblings' tartness. But Martha, who is cousin to the Fowles, has accompanied Cassandra on her jaunt to Kintbury, leaving Jane and Mary to rub along together throughout the Christmas season. It is just deserts for all the jolly outings Jane and Mary have spoiled with their bickering. If Cassandra and Martha weren't so infuriatingly good-natured, they would be having a raucous laugh about it at this very moment.

Sally opens the front door and ushers Mary into the family parlour.

Mary lingers at the entrance, staring at the toes of her walking boots. "Do forgive me. Am I interrupting your breakfast?"

As a girl, Mary suffered from smallpox. Her scars have faded, but she remains prone to sickness and can be painfully self-conscious . . . mainly in the presence of James. Even more so since he became a widower. He is Jane's tallest, darkest and most brooding elder brother.

Mrs. Austen slides the breadbasket along the table. "Come in, dear. Would you like some tea?"

Mary's cheeks flush. "I don't want to intrude. I came to fetch Jane."

Mrs. Austen leans on her hands, pushing herself up from the table. "Nonsense, you're not intruding—"

"Fetch me for what?" Jane speaks over her mother.

Mary takes a shaky step closer to James. "Uncle Richard is asking everyone to go to Deane House to help catch the murderer." Mary's uncle, Richard Craven, is magistrate for the county. She peeps up from under the shallow brim of her hat. "Oh, Mr. Austen, I heard you were called to pray over the dead woman's remains. How dreadful. It must have been simply awful for you."

Jane and her family stare at each other in confusion, before awareness dawns that Mary is addressing James, rather than Jane's father.

James blusters, "Well, I . . ."

Jane suspescts that Mary would not be so impressed if she had seen how James paled at the sight of Madame Renault's slain corpse. Or, rather, knowing how deep Mary's blind devotion to James runs, she probably would. "I'll pop up there later," she says.

Mrs. Austen tuts. "You mustn't keep Mr. Craven waiting."

Jane stares at the dregs of her tea. She's adamant Tom will be on his way to see her. If she leaves now, who knows when they'll have another chance to speak? He may even think she's avoiding him after the way she disappeared from the ball. According to Cassandra, a gentleman needs a great deal of encouragement to make such a declaration. Cassandra had had to paint the most flattering watercolours of Mr. Fowle, with lovebirds in the border for goodness' sake, before he finally took the hint and popped the question. "It's just . . . I'm awfully tired this morning. I didn't sleep very well, you see."

"Well, I did warn you . . ." Mrs. Austen folds her arms across her chest.

Mary's chin wobbles. "But you must. I heard you identified the dead woman."

Jane fiddles with the handle of her teacup.

James looks up from his newspaper. "If you're hanging around waiting for Tom Lefroy to call, you needn't trouble yourself. He'll be joining the search party, out looking for the scoundrel who did this—as will all the other able young gentlemen hereabouts."

Jane has done her best to keep to herself her tryst with Tom. Not that she doubts her family will approve. While Tom isn't yet established, he's fantastically bright and hardworking. He's not yet twenty but has already graduated from Trinity College Dublin and is planning to study the law at Lincoln's Inn. It might take a while before he and Jane can actually get married, but she's confident her father will give the match his blessing. With a little persuasion from Jane and her mother, anyway. Even so, Jane is far too proud to let anyone, apart from Cassandra, know quite how earnestly she is anticipating Tom's declaration.

"How do you know that?" she asks.

"Because the parish constable was asking for volunteers. He told me Lefroy had already signed up."

"When?"

"First thing this morning while you were struggling to sleep." James smirks. "I'll be gone as soon as I've finished my breakfast. If you like, I could tack up Greylass and loan you my hounds. You could have a go at hunting Lefroy down."

Jane scowls at her brother.

James hides behind his newspaper, his shoulders shaking.

Greylass is Cassandra's pony. In theory, Jane can ride, but she'd rather not. Especially since she hasn't tested the theory since she came off a flighty mare at the age of twelve. "Does that mean they've identified the culprit?"

James lets the corner of his newspaper fall away as he frowns. "I think not."

"Then how will you know whom to look for?"

James shrugs. "We'll round up any vagrants, all the usual undesirables."

"Wait there, Mary. I'll fetch my bonnet."

If there is even the slightest chance it will help identify the actual killer, and save some other poor soul from being falsely accused, Jane must tell Mr. Craven everything she knows about Madame Renault. She owes it to the murdered woman to seek justice. It was selfish of her to want to stay at home. And if Tom is not going to call today, at least it will give her more time to compose a less obviously enthusiastic answer. A young lady must preserve her modesty, after all.

CHAPTER THREE

Jane approaches the gates of Deane House, nodding in acknowledgement to a steady stream of acquaintances walking in the opposite direction. Mary must have issued her uncle's orders far and wide on her way to Steventon Rectory. Well-to-do families, merchants and servants mill about on the swept gravel drive. One of Jane's father's most devout parishioners dabs her eyes with a handkerchief, while the farm labourer beside her clenches his jaw and mutters to himself.

Jane presses her hand to the stitch in her side. She scaled the hill from Steventon at a brisk pace, the song of the robin in the hedgerow making up for the lack of chatter between herself and her companion. "Tell me, Mary. How does your uncle think inviting the entire county to view Madame Renault's corpse will help in his investigation?"

"Don't be dull, Jane. Everyone knows the souls of murder victims linger. They can't pass on into eternity until they have tried to communicate the details of their fate to the living."

"I see," Jane nods despite her scepticism. She is keen to have the business of speaking to the magistrate over and done with, in the hope that Tom might call in at the rectory on his way back from the manhunt, although that doesn't sound very romantic. Now, as Jane stands before the half-timbered façade of the Tudor mansion, her spirit plummets at the prospect of returning to the scene of the crime. "And has your uncle apprehended many murderers in this way?"

"Perhaps not." Mary marches ahead, bouncing up the stone steps toward the double doors of the entrance. Deane House is all angles and sharp edges, with black beams and steeply pitched roofs. Even the glass in the windows is sharpened to a point, with crystal lights shaped into diamonds. "He's mostly called out to look for poachers, and I don't suppose game birds have souls."

Jane falters, picturing Madame Renault's arms flung wide and the dark puddle of blood around her ashen face. "You go on. I'll be with you shortly."

"What is it? Are you ill? You look a little green."

"I just want to catch my breath."

Mary shrugs and ducks inside the open doorway.

Once she's gone, Jane closes her eyes to dispel the sudden sensation of dizziness threatening to overtake her. When she opens them again, she spies a familiar rump poking out from the shrubbery. She follows the path toward the rustling while regaining her equilibrium. From the oriel window jutting out of the first floor, directly above, Lady Harcourt's pinched features and beady eyes stare out from behind the criss-crossed lines of lead. Jane raises a hand in greeting, but the woman's brittle body remains motionless.

Apparently, Lady Harcourt is in no mood to welcome the tourists trooping through her home. And why should she be? To lose her eldest son, Edwin, in such a sudden, tragic accident, and for Jonathan's betrothal to be marred by yet another brutal, senseless death must be unbearable.

Jane waits patiently for the owner of the rump to finish whatever he's doing in the bushes. After a few moments, he stands and turns to face her. He has the same height and attractive features as all of her brothers, but a slightly tubbier frame and is more casual in his attire. He does not ride and hunt as the others do, and he rather enjoys his food. "Why, Georgy! What on earth were you doing in there?"

Georgy's eyes light up and his face splits into a wide grin. He reaches for her hand, grasping it with both of his own, and shaking it vigorously. When he finally releases her, he puts one hand to his mouth and makes a gesture of biting into something.

"You want a biscuit?" Jane asks.

Dame Culham once worked for a deaf family in Southampton, and taught Georgy the extensive litany of hand gestures he uses to communicate. Subsequently all of the Austen children became fluent in talking with their hands by sheer proximity to their brother, even if Georgy enjoys catching them out occasionally by introducing new signs of his own invention. Jane is sure he could have learned to read, if only her mother and father had had the time and the patience to teach him.

"Well, you won't find one in there, will you? Silly poppet."

Georgy makes the same biting gesture, only more animatedly.

Jack Smith comes running from behind the house. Jack is Dame Culham's son. He's a few months younger than Jane. When he spots Georgy, he puts his hands on his knees and pants for breath. "Miss Austen." He wheezes, taking off his felt hat and clutching it to his chest. "I really thought he'd slipped away from me this time."

When Georgy was one-and-twenty, Mr. Austen had hired Jack to be his professional caretaker, accompanying him on his adventures and doing whatever he could to keep him out of trouble. Jack was only eleven but, from the start, he performed his role with admirable gravity and has never faltered in his dedication to his charge during the decade since. In order to keep his humours in balance, Georgy must eat and sleep regularly—something he is wont to forget if left to his own devices.

Jane points to the naked roses beneath the oriel window. "I found him scrabbling around in the bushes." What could Georgy have found so fascinating? So late in the year, only the swollen red rosehips remain on the shrubs, and there is nothing but soil on the ground.

"Oh, Georgy. What am I to do with you?" Jack laughs, replacing his hat. "I'll have you on leading strings if you're not careful."

Georgy makes an entirely inappropriate gesture, leaving Jack in no doubt as to what he'd do if he ever dared to treat him so.

"I think he's hungry," says Jane, in an attempt to excuse her brother's ill manners.

"Hungry, Georgy? Why, we've only just breakfasted." Jack throws his hands into the air. "I suppose you heard about the awful business here last night?"

Jane shivers. "Yes. Dreadful."

"We came up to pay our respects. Mother was called in to lay the poor woman out, you see. Georgy was next to me at one minute, but when I looked back, he was gone." Jack smacks his palm against his forehead.

Georgy scowls at him. It is fair to say that at the time Mr. Austen appointed Jack, Georgy was completely bemused to find his de facto younger brother had somehow become his keeper. For much of the time Georgy treats Jack as a willing accomplice, and they have fun gadding about the countryside together on foot, but for the rest, Jack is an irritant that Georgy must shrug off—like a horse trying to swat a fly with its tail.

But Jane can still hear an echo of her mother's ear-splitting cry, the moment she realized young Georgy was missing from

Steventon Rectory. Jane and the other small children ran around the farm, like decapitated chickens, desperate to find him. When there was no sign, Mrs. Austen took it into her head that Georgy must have climbed into the open well. He was always dropping pebbles into it, waiting for the splash of the stones hitting the water fifty feet below. Mr. Austen sped to the barn for a length of rope while James tore off his clothes, ready to climb in after his brother.

Thank God Henry came galloping back with Georgy (who had wandered almost five miles along the lane to Kempshott Park where Mrs. Rivers's cook had once slipped him an unauthorized macaroon) before they had finished tethering the rope to a nearby oak. To this day, that quarter of an hour when her brother was missing remains the longest of Jane's life.

"That's our Georgy for you. He does like to wander." Jane rubs Georgy's upper arm. She is gratified to hear that Madame Renault has been shown due respect. Perhaps returning to the scene of the crime will not prove such a trial. Although it is unclear how anyone can look for clues if the body has been moved. Even allowing for Mary's assertion that Madame Renault will be attempting to commune with all and sundry from beyond the grave.

"And don't I know it. Come, Georgy. Let's go down to Deane Gate Inn and see if Mrs. Fletcher has any of her pies ready yet. You know she always puts by the best one for you." Jack holds a palm flat and draws a circle above it with the first finger of his opposite hand.

Georgy's eyes widen. He nods eagerly and repeats the gesture.

Jack tips his hat toward Jane, the hint of a blush creeping into his cheek. "Good day to you, Miss Austen."

Jane watches them walk away, big Georgy in his blue-black woolen frock coat, and smaller Jack in his humbler suit of brown worsted cloth. A sweet ache forms in her chest for the pair.

She remembers when she and Jack were not quite so furiously polite—as children they chased each other about and shared secrets in Dame Culham's old dirt-floored cottage.

Inside the entrance hall of Deane House, Jane's throat constricts at the sight of the laundry-closet door. It is closed, absorbed back into the oak paneling. The Turkey runner has been removed, and the scent of vinegar and beeswax pervades the air. The hallway, and presumably the inside of the cramped closet, has been scrubbed clean. All traces of Madame Renault's violent death have been washed away.

Jane tightens her jaw. The authorities are going about this wrongly. It's understandable the Harcourts should wish for all reminders of the terrible incident to be erased, but Mr. Craven is a fool if he thinks anyone will be able to interpret the identity of the killer from the shiny parquet flooring. If achieving restitution was as easy as waiting for a message from the dead, no crime would go unpunished, and the great mysteries of England's past would be resolved. Between the two princes slaughtered in the Tower of London, you'd think at least one would stir himself to pass on a message as to the whereabouts of their remains.

Mrs. Twistleton's treacly voice floats from the landing at the turn of the grand staircase where she stands next to a bust of Edwin Harcourt mounted on a marble plinth. "And did you not think him a very handsome gentleman, miss?"

Mary is beside her, eyes drilling into Jane as Mrs. Twistleton seductively caresses the stone form of the Harcourts' late son. The bust is not a convincing likeness of the exuberant young man Jane once knew. The jaw is slack, and the cheeks are gaunt. But, then, it was carved according to a plaster cast of Edwin's death mask. Sir John, deep in grief and heartsore that no portrait existed of his eldest son to add to the family gallery, commissioned the work after his death.

"I am sure *I* know none so handsome." Mrs. Twistleton rakes her fingers over the marble curls of Edwin's hair. Her manner is affected, as if she's performing a Shakespearean soliloquy. "I didn't arrive at Deane House until after the tragedy. But it is said he took after his father, and I can certainly see the resemblance."

"Jane, there you are." Mary is no stranger to grief. Her own little brother had not survived the smallpox epidemic that had stolen her looks, but even she is not morbid enough to make a spectacle of his death mask. "Are you ready to view the corpse now?"

The butler enters, his mouth turned down as if to underscore the sombreness of the situation. "This way, if you please." He directs the ladies down a narrow flight of stairs, into the basement, and along the corridor.

Mary tucks her arm into Jane's, hissing, "Had you heard that Mrs. Twistleton used to be an actress?"

"You shouldn't say things like that, Mary. People might mistake your meaning."

"Oh, no. I mean she was a prostitute."

"Ahem." The butler coughs into his hand as they reach a closed door. "Mrs. and Miss Rivers are with . . . the deceased at present. When they have completed their inspection, you may proceed. Mr. Craven asks that you note any observations and disclose them to him before leaving."

"Of course." Jane nods. The butler bows and strides away along the corridor. Jane tuts, lowering her voice. "Honestly, Mary, where do you get these stories from?"

"Me? Why, the ones you write are even more salacious."

"Yes, but at least I don't pretend mine are true."

"Ssh . . ." Mary places a finger over her lips as she presses her ear to the door. Raised voices float from within. Jane tiptoes closer and leans her cheek to the smooth wood.

"What a disaster," moans Mrs. Rivers, in her distinctive London drawl. "How could your fiancé have let this happen?"

"Don't call him that, Mama," replies Sophy. "We are not betrothed, not formally, and you do me no favours by behaving as if we are."

"But you will be. Just as soon as this matter is resolved."

"We shouldn't rush the Harcourts, lest we risk appearing heartless."

"Heartless? What about my heart?" Mrs. Rivers shrieks. "You were on the brink of being acknowledged as Jonathan's fiancée. This match is everything your father and I ever wanted for you. You'll be a future baronetess."

"Strictly speaking, Mama, the wife of a baronet is simply a *lady*. Only a woman who holds a baronetcy in her own right can be a baronetess, and I believe there's only ever been one of those."

Jane and Mary fight to suppress a snigger. From Sophy's tone, it is obvious that her symmetrical features are arranged in their usual expression of smug condescension.

"That's quite enough of your impertinence, young lady. I should have seen you well married years ago. The Lord knows you've had plenty of offers. Mr. Chute would have taken you off my hands gladly when you were seventeen. But, no, you wanted to wait for someone younger, and now I've let you delay for far too long. Five more minutes and you would have been settled. Instead, this unfortunate wretch turns up dead and ruins everything."

"You cannot blame the murdered woman, Mama. It is hardly her fault," says Sophy.

"You're right. It's yours. The whole accursed mess is down to you. If you hadn't talked Lady Harcourt and me out of placing the announcement in *The Times*, insisting we wait until you could have your big day, none of this would matter. The betrothal would be official and you'd be halfway up the aisle by now."

It is true. Jonathan Harcourt's thwarted proposal has left Sophy in a romantic limbo. Her reputation demands that he settle the matter immediately. Yet, as Sophy herself says, it would be most indelicate to have her happy news tied forever to the slaughter of another.

"Perhaps it would be best if we gave the Harcourts some time," continues Sophy.

"No. That's the last thing they need. I'll speak to Lady Harcourt, ask her to press Jonathan. You'll be married by the end of the year."

"But anything might happen before then, Mama."

"What might happen, Sophy? Tell me!"

Jane locks eyes with Mary, both straining to hear what Sophy is so afraid of, but dead silence persists from the other side of the door. It would be utterly humiliating for Sophy if, during this enforced period of cooling off, Jonathan changed his mind and his much-anticipated proposal never materialized. The thought of it is almost, but not quite, enough to dissolve Jane's long-held animosity toward her.

As her association with Mary Lloyd proves, Jane is willing to be friends with any young lady in her locality—but Sophy has consistently snubbed all of Jane's overtures of friendship. The Rivers girls keep company only with the rich or titled, preferably both. It wouldn't feel such a slight if Sophy were as vulgar as her mother, but Miss Rivers is cold perfection. She is the most accomplished young lady Jane has ever met. Infuriatingly,

Sophy shows little passion for any of the musical and artistic pursuits she has mastered. Only once has Jane seen her mask of composure slip. Last year, when Sophy joined the Boxing Day hunt with Jane's brothers, a wilder, more headstrong side of her character emerged—she galloped alongside the men and leaped hedges in hot pursuit of the terrified fox.

"Must you be so obstinate?" Mrs. Rivers rallies. "Can you not see I am trying to do what is best for you? Jonathan is a man of unquestionable breeding. Marry him, and you'll have a title and a respectable husband. What more could you want? Are you really so determined to remain a thorn in my side, threatening to taint the family with scandal? How are your sisters supposed to find husbands of suitable pedigree if you behave like this?"

Half a beat later, the door handle turns. Jane and Mary spring back as Mrs. Rivers glides out. The widow lifts her nose into the air and gazes straight ahead. Sophy shuffles after her, pressing a lace-trimmed handkerchief over her mouth and nose. Jane and Mary bob a curtsy, but the ladies pass without acknowledging them. Mary ducks inside the room immediately, but Jane pushes back her shoulders and pauses on the threshold for a moment before following her inside.

The Harcourts have moved Madame Renault's body from the laundry closet to a boot room. The walls are lined with shelves, crammed with polish and brushes. The milliner's slim figure is laid out on a hard wooden workbench in the centre. Her corpse smells faintly of lavender and is dressed in a plain white cotton nightgown, covered to the chest in a slate-grey blanket. Her dark hair has been brushed smooth and is fanned out around her head. The wound at her temple has been bathed, and her colourless face scrubbed clean of any trace of blood.

Two tarnished silver shillings press down on her eyelids, keeping them shut, but her mouth remains stubbornly open.

She could be asleep, except for the dent at her temple and over her left eyebrow. It is almost as if she is a wax doll, held so close to the fire that part of her forehead has melted away. Jane wants to scream at the injustice of it.

How is it possible that, in a supposedly civilised society, a young woman can be robbed of her life in such a violent way? What hope is there for Jane, for any woman, if this crime is allowed to go unpunished? At their brief meeting, Jane recognised a reflection of her own pride in the milliner's haughty manner. And now here Madame Renault lies, in a borrowed nightdress, laid out for the entire county to gawp at and speculate as to the cause of her untimely demise. She would be furious to know her corpse was being handled with such indignity.

"Dear Lord, it's *her*." Mary gasps, placing both hands on her cheeks.

"You knew her, too?"

"I met her in the covered market. It was only yesterday morning. Oh, this is so unfair."

"I know." Jane rests her palm gently on Mary's wrist.

"No—it's not that. I gave her ten shillings to make me a straw bonnet."

Jane freezes, staring at Mary open-mouthed.

"What?" Mary blinks. "It's a lot of money and I don't suppose I shall ever see it again."

"Absolutely. And very well you'd have looked in such a bonnet, too. Like the Queen of France herself." Mary brightens. "With her head in a wicker basket," Jane finishes.

Mary's chin wobbles. "Must you be so cruel?"

"Me? You're the one who thinks *you're* the victim here." Jane gestures toward Madame Renault, lying lifeless on the workbench. Jane would feel the loss of ten shillings keenly, too, yet she hopes she'd have the compassion not to lament it so publicly when the debtor's fate is vastly more dire.

She turns her shoulder to Mary, fixing on Madame Renault's face: the long dark eyelashes, the dainty nose, the pale lips. Her gaze lingers at the dead woman's bare throat. There is a very faint line of torn skin on one side of her neck.

"Wait." Jane grabs Mary more firmly by the wrist.

"What is it? Can you sense her spirit? Is she present?"

"What? No. It's just—" Jane clasps her own throat. "When I met her in the market, she was wearing a necklace. It was long, like a guard chain, looped twice around her neck and tucked into her bodice."

Mary leans forward, comparing both sides of Madame Renault's neck. "So she was. I noticed it, too, and assumed she was hiding a Catholic bauble. You know what these foreigners are. And, look, is that a scratch? Could it have been torn off, do you think?"

Jane pictures the necklace. It was yellow gold, very thin and interspersed with seed pearls. "It must have been valuable."

Mary nods. "Did she still have it, last night, when you identified her?"

Jane shuts her eyes, recalling a clear image of Madame Renault lying in the closet. "It was dark, and there was so much blood . . . but, no, I'm sure she didn't. We should tell your uncle."

Mary spins on her heel. "Yes. I'll ask him what I should do about my ten shillings, too."

Jane grinds her teeth, suppressing the urge to shoot another barb at Mary. Once she's alone with the corpse, she says a silent prayer for Madame Renault's spirit to be at peace. She doesn't hold out much hope. Despite her doubts about Mr. Craven's investigative methods, if some villain had stolen Jane's life, she'd make damn sure to linger in this earthly realm until she'd haunted the blackguard into repentance.

Back upstairs, Jane steels herself to talk to the magistrate. She'll make sure he knows about the missing necklace, and has noted the mark on the corpse's neck, then prevail on him to take a more empirical approach to his investigation. Casting his net aimlessly over the countryside will not achieve justice for Madame Renault.

Mr. Craven loiters in the entrance hall, beneath the giant bronze chandelier, talking quietly to Mrs. Twistleton. He is a stern-faced man, ambling toward middle age. The leather buttons of his hunting suit stretch tight over his bulbous girth. A sheen of perspiration covers his cheeks, and his nose has the consistency of a cauliflower.

With Mary's scandalous assertion fresh in her mind, Jane takes a proper look at the housekeeper. Mrs. Twistleton must only be in her early thirties. With her dark brows and ash-blond hair, she is certainly very striking. She makes a great show of listening to every word the magistrate says by nodding earnestly.

"Mary, child, what are you doing here?" Mr. Craven snaps, as they enter.

Mary's lip quivers. "You said everyone should come and see if they could spot something that might help."

"Yes, but I didn't mean you."

"Sir." Jane steps forward. "I am Miss Austen . . ."

Mr. Craven pulls at his collar. "Let me guess. Another thrill-seeking young lady? This is not a theatre. A very serious incident took place here last night."

"I know that, and I want only to help. I knew Madame Renault, you see. In fact, it was I who identified her body."

Mr. Craven peers at Jane through heavy-lidded eyes. His bushy eyebrows are black, threaded with silver. Drawn together, they are as foreboding as storm clouds. "Out with it, then."

"She wore a necklace. It's missing, and there's a mark on her neck."

"Is that all?" He takes a pocket watch out of his waistcoat, flicks open the silver case and checks the hour.

"It was a long, yellow-gold chain—"

"With seed pearls. I know. Your friend Miss Bigg has already enlightened me. Now, I've spent long enough standing about in conversation with young ladies. I should be with the search party, bringing this villain in."

Jane's mouth falls open. "What do you mean, 'bringing this villain in'? Are you saying you know who did it?"

Mr. Craven continues to fiddle with his pocket watch. Jane turns to Mary, but Mary will not meet her eye and the tips of her ears are bright pink. She is clearly mortified at being chastised by her uncle in front of Jane, and unwilling to question his methods.

"It's no mystery." Mr. Craven slips his watch back into his pocket. "Sir John informs me his estate has been plagued by a gang of trespassers. One of the vagabonds must have used the distraction of the ball to rob Madame Renault of her necklace, leaving her for dead. It wouldn't surprise me to learn she had been associating with them. Damned French, always up to no good."

"But that makes no sense." Jane digs her fingernails into the palms of her hands.

Mr. Craven flattens his lips into a thin line, causing them to disappear beneath his broom of a moustache. "Excuse me, young lady?"

"I said your theory makes no sense." Jane taps her fingers against her thigh as she speaks. "If the murderer was a passing thief, why pick Madame Renault as his target? I'll admit her necklace looked valuable, and it appears to have been torn off, but here's the thing. There were women here last night who were *dripping* with diamonds. With such riches on offer, why would anyone risk the gallows for a paltry gold chain?"

Mr. Craven tips back his head, letting out a hollow laugh. "Miss Austen, the criminal mind is not guided by logic. If you'd served as a magistrate for as long as I have, you'd know that a hardened villain simply seizes whatever opportunity he can."

"Again, your theory is weak." Jane's voice is terse, and her head is starting to pound. "Have you ascertained why Madame Renault was here at Deane House? She's unlikely to have been a guest, after—"

"Jane," Mary interrupts. "I'm quite sure my uncle knows what he's doing."

"I expect she was here to assist." Mr. Craven looks to the housekeeper.

"I'd never seen her before, I swear it." Mrs. Twistleton lays a hand across her bosom. "That is to say, she wasn't here as part of the household staff."

"See?" says Jane. "She was an artisan, a craftswoman, not a scrub."

Mr. Craven gives a half-hearted shrug. "So? It was a celebration on a very grand scale. I expect there were tradesmen and -women coming and going all day. What do you say to that, Mrs. Twistleton?"

"Oh, certainly, sir." Mrs. Twistleton drops her hand to her side, nodding eagerly. "Leagues of them, in and out all day. I couldn't keep track of them all."

"Indeed, wine merchants, cooks and the like. But Madame Renault sold straw hats," Jane explains. Mr. Craven is still peering at her, eyes narrowed and mouth half open. He has not grasped the significance of her words. "No one wears a bonnet to a ball. There is no obvious reason for her to have been here. Is there, ma'am?"

Mrs. Twistleton takes a step backward. "Well, I—I wouldn't want to speculate."

"Miss Austen, really." Mr. Craven raises his voice by several octaves. "I've a murderer to catch. I haven't the time to stand around discussing ladies' fashions."

"But can't you see? You must look beyond the obvious, interrogate all possibilities, to reach the truth. It's like lifting the veil in *The Mysteries of Udolpho*."

"The mysteries of what?" Mr. Craven splutters, beetroot blotching his already pink cheeks.

"It's a novel, Uncle, by Mrs. Radcliffe," Mary pipes up. "Naturally, I haven't read it."

Jane narrows her eyes at her friend. So far, Jane has had the opportunity to read *Udolpho* only once. She had recommended that Mrs. Martin add the novel to her circulating library, and the librarian had kept it back for her to take out first. Since then, Jane has tried to borrow it again several times, but it's always on loan to a "Miss M. Lloyd, of Deane."

"Enough! This is no time for young ladies to be gadding about unchaperoned. This country's going to the dogs, I tell you. Come, Mary, I'll escort you back to your mother." Flecks of spittle fly into the air as Mr. Craven takes Mary by the arm. "Miss Austen, if you've any sense, you'll go home and stay there until we've caught the scoundrel."

Mary throws Jane a look of panic as her uncle steers her toward the door. Jane stiffens. It might be highly improper for a young lady to be caught sneaking off at a ball, and Jane submits cheerfully to being chaperoned on trips to Basingstoke, but her freedom to roam the familiar countryside unmolested is never curtailed.

"Impudent, ignorant fool," she mutters under her breath, once she and Mrs. Twistleton are alone. "A gang of trespassers. How convenient for Sir John to come up with such a story. And what does the fact she was French have to do with it?"

"Now stop right there, Miss Austen." Mrs. Twistleton's pretty features harden. She is a different woman altogether, now Mr. Craven has left. "It's not for you or me to contradict the baronet. These are his ancestral lands, and he knows them better than anyone."

Jane startles at the housekeeper's transformation. "But is it not rather odd? I haven't heard of any strangers in the vicinity lately, have you?"

Mrs. Twistleton grabs Jane by her elbow. "Come along, Miss Austen. I'll see you out." Jane is too shocked to protest as she is ushered speedily toward the front door. Once she is through it, Mrs. Twistleton slams it behind her.

She stands on the doorstep, in a state of agitated confusion. Why is everyone so ready to swallow such an obvious cock-and-bull story? Mrs. Twistleton is dependent on Sir John for her living. She must feel obliged to defend him, but Mr. Craven should have no such reason for partiality. He is clearly blinded by obsequious deference to the baronet. Enough. Mr. Craven has left Jane with no choice. If he will not investigate Madame Renault's murder with due diligence, then Jane must—lest the magistrate's incompetence allows the young woman's killer to walk free.

CHAPTER FOUR

As Jane trudges along the driveway, toward the immaculate white doors of Manydown House, perspiration gathers under her arms and she could die of thirst. The grand manor is a good three-mile walk from Deane House. She fixes her eyes on the wisteria running across the wide, red-brick building. It is sadly gnarled at this desolate time of year. Mr. Craven might have ordered Mary to her nursery, like a naughty child, but Jane refuses to be cowed. She was perfectly safe walking here on the main road in broad daylight, especially with half the county out searching for the murderer. Her stomach is rock-hard, and she started at every approaching vehicle along the way, but she must waste no time in launching her own investigation.

She'll begin with Alethea Bigg. Jane and Alethea had met the milliner at the same time and, so far, Alethea has provided the magistrate with the single clue he has to go on. Before Jane reaches the Grecian-style portico, the butler opens one of the double doors. Alethea steps out in a bright purple gown, which clashes beautifully with her auburn hair.

"I saw you from the window." Alethea holds a hand flat to her brow, shielding her yellow-brown eyes from the harsh sunlight. The layers of her gauzy skirt flutter in the breeze so she resembles the mast of a ship speeding through the waves. "I'll send for tea, shall I? You are utterly bedraggled!"

"Why, thank you, Alethea." Jane enters the house, shrugging off her cloak. "May I say you are a slattern this morning, too."

Alethea titters, letting the insult glance off her in the way of a woman who knows she is beautiful and genteel. She leads Jane through the marble-tiled entrance hall, making graceful taps with her slippers while Jane stalks behind in her walking boots.

They enter a drawing room that looks out over the manicured parkland. Alethea flops onto a duck-egg blue sofa. "What are you doing tramping around the neighbourhood alone? Haven't you heard that a murderer is on the loose?"

"That is exactly why I'm here." Jane rests in a wingback armchair, beside the gentle flames flickering in the Carrara marble fireplace. The room is light and airy, papered in chinoiserie and perfumed with crystal bowls of rose-scented potpourri. As Jane shares the infuriating details of her encounter with the magistrate, a footman brings in a lacquer tea tray, and places it on the low table between them.

Alethea pours from a Japanese teapot. "Mr. Craven was much the same with me, I'm afraid." On the glazed porcelain, women in kimonos wander among pagodas, while a snow-tipped mountain rises behind them. The tea things are all of a set, decorated with gilt, and so thin they are almost transparent. "Once I had told him about the necklace, he dismissed me entirely."

"You noticed it, too, then, when we met her in Basingstoke?" Jane picks up her cup and saucer, declining Alethea's offer of cream. She prefers her tea black with sugar—if there is any. At Manydown, she can help herself to a whole lump with no admonishment for her gluttony.

"It was so unusual, with all those dear little seed pearls. But I agree, it was a mere trinket compared to the jewels the ladies at the ball were wearing."

"Exactly." Jane retrieves some sugar, using the tongs, and plops it into her tea. She stirs it, the silver spoon rattling against the edge of her cup, until the crystals dissolve. "Did you see the size of the diamond baguettes in Lady Harcourt's tiara?"

"Oh, no, those were obviously paste." Alethea wrinkles her freckled nose.

"They were? How could you tell?" Jane sips her tea, too thirsty to let it cool. It is so sweet, she winces. How odd that Lady Harcourt would choose to wear paste rather than genuine jewels. Perhaps she is so accustomed to her ancestral collection she's grown weary of them.

"It's all in the lustre." Alethea flutters her long white fingers. "Now Sophy's choker, that was definitely real."

"Of course it was. Did you know her dowry is said to be thirty thousand pounds?"

"Yes, and she must have been wearing most of it. Tell me, Jane, why are the nouveau riche always in such a hurry to fritter away their wealth?"

"Alethea," Jane splutters, "you're hardly descended from William the Conqueror."

"No." Alethea fingers the single strand of pearls at her throat. "But I do have excellent taste."

It is not just for the sugar that Jane is happy to tramp the four miles out to Manydown. Alethea's observations are almost as sharp as her own. "It's left Sophy in a bind, though, hasn't it? She's not formally betrothed, yet everyone knows the anticipation of it is the very reason the Harcourts hosted the ball."

"I expect she'll be most eager to have the matter settled as soon as decently possible. But what an ominous start to a marriage!"

"Yes." Jane replays the conversation between Sophy and her mother. Something is niggling at her. If Sophy is at all nervous about Jonathan's constancy, it's odd that she pushed for a public proposal where anything could, and indeed did, go wrong, rather than settling the matter once and for all with a newspaper announcement. She lowers her voice, feeling as much of a chatterbox as Mary. "This morning, at Deane House, I overheard Mrs. Rivers accuse Sophy of dragging her heels over making their engagement official."

"How dare she? The uppity miss. I hope she wasn't trying to put Jonathan off. She won't do any better than him, even with all her father's money."

Jane suppresses an impish grin, having successfully provoked her friend with the gossip. Alethea and Jonathan are the same age, and there was a time, before Edwin died and Jonathan departed for his grand tour, when Jonathan was considered to be Alethea's suitor. If there is anything unsavoury in Jonathan's attentions, Alethea will know. "Why didn't you marry him, then?"

Alethea's jaw drops in mock outrage. "Dear Jonathan, he was never *serious* in his intentions toward me."

"Yes, he was." Jane balances her cup and saucer on her knee. She's long sensed a more interesting story behind Jonathan's unsuccessful proposal, but Alethea is always so guarded about her romantic interests. "I heard that was why he fled to the Continent, to mend his broken heart."

"He went to the Continent to study art."

"And to get away from some saucy upstart?"

Alethea falls back on the sofa, clutching a hand to her chest and giggling. "Oh, Jane! You are awful. But why the sudden interest in the past? All that was years ago, best to leave it buried."

Jane slips her cup and saucer back onto the tray and rises from her seat. "I'm just so rattled by poor Madame Renault's death. My mind is everywhere."

"Just like the rest of you, then?" Alethea tuts.

Jane wanders over to the long windows, gazing out at the park. On a hillock in the distance, a herd of deer grazes on the patchy grass. The white-spotted does clump together, while a veteran stag stands a few feet apart. His body is lean, and his giant antlers are too heavy for his frame. The tips are broken to a sharp point, where he has been bested in a fight. A younger, more muscular buck ambles up beside him, antlers intact. He will displace his father, come summer.

"Don't you think Mr. Craven should be questioning all of us, looking into what everyone was doing that night, and finding out why Madame Renault was even at Deane House, rather than looking for strangers hiding in the hedgerow?" Jane muses.

Alethea knits together the thin red lines of her eyebrows. "You're not suggesting one of the guests had anything to do with her murder, are you?"

Jane shrugs. "I don't know. That's the point, surely. No one can be ruled out as a suspect, not until we know who did it."

"He is the magistrate. I'm sure he knows best."

"Any fool with enough land can be a magistrate." Jane slumps down into her chair. "Think of my brother Neddy."

Edward "Neddy" Austen is the third eldest of Jane's brothers. It's just as well he was the one to be adopted by their wealthy Knight relations—he's neither as clever as James and Henry nor as tenacious as the younger Austen boys.

"Jane! Is no one safe from the lash of your tongue?"

Through the window, the deer are on the move. The veteran stag lifts his head, sniffing the air for predators, while the herd of does strolls casually behind him. "Any fool but a woman, that is." Jane folds her arms across her chest.

It is a landowner's duty to keep the peace by volunteering as a magistrate. Neddy frequently complains about the irksome task of dragging a man to the altar to marry the mother of his bastard lest responsibility for the child fall upon the parish. Or extracting an oath of allegiance to the Crown from a recusant Catholic. Some magistrates, like Mr. Craven, are more enthusiastic about the role and take on more than their fair share of work. All are appointed on the basis of sex, rank and wealth, rather than merit or, Heaven forbid, the extent of their legal training.

"Well, that's men for you, always underestimating and riding roughshod over us," says Alethea. "Why any woman would willingly subject herself to being ruled by a man is beyond me."

As the daughter of a clergyman, it is incumbent upon Jane to argue that holy matrimony is the highest state of being—if one can snare the right partner. Jane's mother and father are well satisfied in each other's company, even after all these years. And Cassandra is positively gleeful at the prospect of being wed to her longtime sweetheart, Mr. Fowle. But Jane's friend seems not to have considered this prospect. Perhaps it's because Alethea's mother died when her children were young, and her father remains a widower, setting no example of marital bliss for his children to aspire to.

"Mr. Craven hardly listened to a word I said," Alethea continues, flicking crumbs of sugar from her skirt. "Not until I mentioned the missing necklace. Beastly man. He was even more dismissive of Hannah. She tried to show him where Madame Renault was found, but he shooed her away, like a stray dog."

"Hannah?" As far as Jane knows, there were no Hannahs at the ball last night. But, as all but the closest of confidantes in her polite society refer to each other as Miss or Mrs. with their surname, there may well have been scores. Jane can only claim the title "Miss Austen" when Cassandra is not present. Being addressed as "Miss Jane" is perhaps the only thing she won't miss when her sister abandons her to become the unfortunately named "Mrs. Fowle."

"One of our maids." Alethea picks at a loose thread on her gown. "We lent her for the evening. Lady Harcourt can never keep her servants for long. She's always trying to poach ours."

Jane taps a finger against her lips. "May I speak to her?"

"Hannah? If you like."

"I would. Very much. Mr. Craven may have refused to listen to what she has to say, but I'm most eager to hear it." A maid would have access to whatever went on behind the scenes at Deane House. Hannah will have seen and heard more than any of the guests.

Alethea raises her eyebrows, forming two red crescent moons above her eyes. "In that case, I'll send a footman to fetch her." She picks up a small brass bell from the table and gives it a tinkle.

When Hannah pokes her head around the drawing-room door, Jane recognizes her as the small round girl who was standing in the Harcourts' entrance hall with a mop and bucket the previous evening. She is very young, fifteen or sixteen at the most. She wears a mobcap and a pewter-grey gown, with a starched apron pinned to it. Her face is puffy and her eyes are red. She must have been crying all night.

Alethea flaps her hand, beckoning the maid to enter. "Are you quite all right, Hannah?"

"Yes, miss." The girl grips her apron, kneading it as she edges slowly into the room. She stands on the Turkey rug with her back to the fireplace.

"Don't look so worried. You have done nothing wrong. Miss Austen and I just want to ask you some questions." Alethea crosses one leg over the other. "Now, Hannah, who do you think murdered that poor woman?"

Hannah's eyes widen and her mouth falls open.

"You can't ask her that!" Jane scoffs. "She won't know—you don't, do you, Hannah?"

Hannah takes a shaky breath, stepping backward. Her skirt swishes dangerously close to the fireplace. "No, miss, I swear."

Alethea pouts. "You ask the questions, then."

An awkward silence hangs over the room. Hannah is obviously deeply affected by her ordeal, and now Jane is about to cause her to relive it. "Have you worked for the Harcourts before, Hannah?"

"Yes, miss." Hannah nods, her voice thin. "They always make me go—the other servants here at Manydown, I mean."

Jane sits forward in her seat. "Why is that?" She ducks her head, trying to meet Hannah's eyes. Behind them, she sees a haunted look. Hannah knows something about the murder, something that is making her tremble with fear hours after she had left the scene.

"Well, no one really wants to go to Deane House, and I'm the newest here . . ." Hannah's gaze wanders about the room. She looks everywhere, except at the ladies.

"Oh." Alethea frowns. "I thought you girls were always glad of the chance to earn a little extra. Is it Sir John? He can be rather bullish."

Hannah shakes her head vigorously. "No, miss."

"What is it, then?" Alethea asks, but Hannah's mouth remains clamped shut.

"There's no need to fret," Jane assures her. "Whatever you say, we shan't repeat it outside this room. We're just trying to understand what happened to Madame Renault. You want her killer caught and punished, don't you?"

Hannah's eyes bulge. "Madame Renault? Was that her name, the dead woman?"

Jane nods. "You didn't recognize her then? She wasn't working at Deane House that day?" Mrs. Twistleton had confirmed the milliner hadn't been there to work for the family, but perhaps Hannah saw her with one of the other merchants.

Hannah blinks, tears brimming in her red eyes. "No, miss. I'd never seen her—not until they called me in to clear up the mess."

Jane inclines her head, trying to impress her sympathy on the girl. "Oh, Hannah, that must have been truly awful." If no one saw Madame Renault during the day, perhaps her body had remained hidden in the closet for some time. "Had you any occasion to enter that little room before? Earlier in the day, perhaps?"

"Yes, miss. I got there at noon, and my first job was to make up the beds in the east wing. The Rivers party was due to stay overnight, in case of frost. They arrived early and dressed at Deane House. I went straight to the closet to fetch the sheets. Later I went back to find the table linen to make up the great hall."

"And you're sure Madame Renault's body wasn't there on either occasion?"

"No, miss." Hannah glances at Jane askance. "I think I'd notice a dead woman at my feet while I was trying to work."

Jane forces back a smile. Hannah is clearly no fool. "That must mean Madame Renault was killed after you left the closet for the second time." There was so much blood around the dead woman's wound, it would have left a trail if she'd been killed somewhere else and moved. "What time was it when you went back for the table linen?"

"I'm not sure. After four, because the light had already faded and I needed to borrow a lamp to make sure I took the right cloths. Lady Harcourt can be very particular, and I didn't want to get in any trouble." Hannah takes a step closer to Alethea. "Please don't make me go there any more, miss. I'll not sleep for weeks, thinking about that poor woman. I never want to set foot in that cursed place again as long as I live."

"Of course not. We'll keep you to ourselves in future. And we'll let you go now, won't we, Miss Austen?" Alethea reaches out to pat Hannah's hand, fixing Jane with a pointed look. "Tell the housekeeper I said you're to take the rest of the day off. Try to sleep."

Jane tries to meet Hannah's roaming gaze one last time. There is something on the maid's conscience, she's sure of it, but however hard she tries, Hannah will not meet her eye.

"Yes, you should rest. Unless there's anything else you want to tell us? Anything at all that you think might help?"

Hannah grips her apron so hard that her knuckles turn white. "They made me clean it." A green tinge creeps into her complexion as she sways.

"The floor? Yes, I could smell the vinegar when I visited this morning. It looked like you'd given it a good scrub."

"The floor . . . and the bed-warming pan. That's what the villain used to knock her down." Hannah's voice cracks. She places a hand over her mouth. "There were bits of her skin and her hair stuck to the copper and they made me . . ." She retches, her body convulsing as she spits a mouthful of bright yellow bile into her apron.

"Oh dear . . . We'd better call for a maid." Alethea picks up the small brass bell and rattles it urgently.

Jane draws her hands into tight fists. By declining to talk to the maid, Mr. Craven had missed his opportunity to narrow down Madame Renault's time of death *and* stood idly by while a child was forced to clean the murder weapon, destroying vital evidence. It's obvious he is not competent to run such a serious investigation. Left to him, Madame Renault's killer stands a very good chance of slipping the net.

Alethea insisted on sending Jane home in her father's coach. But as soon as she reaches Steventon village, Jane thumps on the ceiling and tells the coachman she'll walk the rest of the way to the rectory. As the carriage recedes, she marches along the main street, waving to the weavers, spinners and farm labourers who make up her father's congregation, heading for the last house, at the edge of the village, where she spent the first three years of her life. For it was Dame Culham, not Mrs. Austen, who had held Jane's hand as she took her first wobbly steps, whooped with delight when she passed water into the chamber pot and taught her how to say her bedtime prayers. And now Jane wants to know what, if anything, Dame Culham can teach her about Madame Renault's death.

A woven hazel fence surrounds the thatched cottage Jane's former nurse shares with her son, Jack, and Georgy. The house is bigger, with an extensive garden, and in far better repair than the other, humbler, dwellings in the row. To the rear stands a half-built pigsty, which Jack has been assembling with discarded bits of wood. Georgy ambles around the vegetable patch, watching the hens as they claw and peck at the freshly raked beds. Jack is beside the woodpile, splitting logs for the fire on a stump with an axe. The sleeves of his coarse linen shirt are rolled to his elbow, and the muscles in his forearms are taut as he brings down the blade.

"Good day," Jane calls from the gate.

Georgy grins, waving with both arms.

"Miss Austen." Jack reaches for his hat. His cheeks flush as, fingers brushing against his dark curls, he realises he's not wearing one. "Twice in one day. This is a pleasure."

Jane smiles, releasing the latch on the gate to let herself in. "I was sorry to hear about the Terrys' sow, Jack."

Over the last couple of years, Jack has shown signs of aspiring to a more lucrative living than caring for Georgy. He even visited the blacksmith to enquire about an apprenticeship. Thankfully, for the Austens anyway, no other significant opportunities have materialized. It would be nigh impossible for Jane's father to find a more suitable companion for her restless brother. Jack's latest scheme to boost his income involved investing in a sow to breed. Unfortunately, before he could find the money, Squire Terry realised the animal was already in pig and decided to keep her for himself.

Jack gives a weary shrug, refusing to meet Jane's eye. "Oh, something else will come up." The sow is all Jack has talked about for weeks. He'd planned how he'd forage enough to feed her, and which of his neighbour's boars might be a suitable mate.

"I wanted to ask, have you noticed any strangers hereabouts lately?" Jack must walk a good ten miles a day, keeping sight of Georgy. If any unfamiliar persons are loitering in the area, the pair are bound to have come across them.

Jack rakes a callused hand through his hair. "Strangers?"

"Yes. Anyone camping in the woods, say?"

"Oh, no. The Romany have been traveling these roads for centuries, and they've their own customs. They won't be back in these parts until spring, for the Wickham horse fair."

"Right. And you haven't heard of any others passing through?" Jane shifts her weight to one foot, squinting at Jack in the fading sunlight. "Only, Sir John told Mr. Craven he was troubled with trespassers in the woods behind Deane House."

Jack shakes his head. "Georgy and I often go rambling that way, but I can't say as we've seen any camps. I'm sorry, Miss Austen."

Dame Culham nudges the side door of the cottage open with one hip, a basket of kitchen scraps in her hands. She is a comely woman, in her mid-fifties. Her complexion is clear and brown, and there are deep laughter lines around her dark eyes. "Here you are, Georgy. Will you give these to the hens, my lovey?" She falters at the sight of Jane. "What're you doing here?"

"Good day, Nan. It's nice to see you, too." Jane uses the Austen children's pet name for their nurse. According to the parish register, she is Mrs. Anne Culham, but as infants, their little mouths struggled to pronounce either Anne or Mrs. Culham—and no good would come of them calling her "Mama."

"I suppose you'll be wanting to come in." Dame Culham hands the basket to Georgy, before stepping back inside. "How's your mother?"

Jane follows, savouring the homeliness of the warm kitchen. It is modest, but tidy, full of mismatched bowls and shabby furniture Jane recognizes from her childhood. Bunches of herbs hang from the oak beams of the low ceiling, and a steel cauldron is suspended by a chain over the flame in the inglenook fireplace. "As unpredictable as ever, I'm afraid."

Dame Culham wipes her hands on her smock. "Is she drinking the dandelion and burdock tea I made up for her?"

"No. I believe she still prefers bitters." Jane pulls out a hard-backed chair and sits at the scrubbed-pine table. The surface is dusted with flour, and an earthenware bowl sits in the centre, draped with muslin.

Dame Culham wraps some suet in brown paper and secures it with twine, then places it in a rusted tin. "Then what does she expect?"

Jane pulls at the fastenings of her cloak, letting it fall loose around her shoulders. "Indeed."

Lavender flowers stand out against the muted greens of sage and thyme, strung upside down to dry above the fireplace. Jane pictures Dame Culham sprinkling a pinch of the dried petals into warm water, and dipping in a cloth to wash Madame Renault's body as tenderly as she once blotted the grit from Jane's grazed knees.

Dame Culham smacks her lips. "Out with it. Why are you here?"

Jane tilts her head to the side. "Must there be a reason for me to call?"

With a wooden spoon, Dame Culham pokes at the steaming contents of the pot over the fire. "I'd say there usually is."

She's boiling a neck of mutton with rosemary. Jane doesn't need to look inside the cauldron: she can tell from the aroma. Her stomach growls. "How's business, Nan? Have you attended many births of late?"

"Aye. I was called out last night, in fact."

"All went well, I hope?"

"As was God's will." A curl, at the nape of her neck, has worked its way loose from her headscarf. At one time, Dame

Culham's hair was the colour of caramel. Now it is shot through with silver. When had that happened?

Jane bites her lip. "I expect in your line of work you must have had to accustom yourself to it. Death, that is."

"We'll all have to accustom ourselves to it at one time or another, Jane."

"Yes . . . but you must have had to perform some rather distressing tasks." Jane runs her fingertip over a knot on the surface of the table. "Laying out Madame Renault, at Deane House, perhaps."

"Here we go." Dame Culham rests her fists on the shelf of her wide hips. "How did I know you'd be after idle talk about that poor girl?"

"I'm not gossiping. It's just they haven't caught the killer."

"And I expect you imagine you can do a better job of hunting him down than the magistrate."

Jane straightens, her shoulder blades brushing against the wooden rungs on the back of the chair. "Why not?"

"No reason." Dame Culham wipes her cheek with the back of her hand. "No reason at all. I always said, of all the Austen children, you'd be the one to do anything you wanted. If you could fix your wandering mind to it, that is."

Jane continues working at the knot in the table, her fingertip pressing deep into the groove. "So, what can you tell me about Madame Renault?"

"Naught." Dame Culham turns her back to Jane, furiously prodding and poking at the mutton bone with her wooden spoon.

"You don't need to shield me from anything. It was I who identified her."

"Of course you did."

"We tried to shut her eyes, but they wouldn't close. Why do you think that was?" Jane understands some of how the body declines in the days and hours following death, but as a midwife, Dame Culham will be an expert. Her steady hands bring life into the world, just as they prepare a body for its final journey back to the earth.

Her shoulders rise and fall. "I expect it was too late. She'd gone stiff already."

"And how long does that usually take to happen?"

"Depends. A few hours, sometimes several."

Jane thinks back to Hannah's testimony. "So, if Madame Renault wasn't in the closet at dusk, but by ten o'clock she'd been dead long enough for her body to have stiffened, it must follow that she was killed between four and seven in the evening."

Dame Culham locks eyes with Jane over her shoulder. "I suppose . . . unless she was moved, afterward."

Jane pictures the enormous pool of blood around Madame Renault's head. "No. She had bled too freely. Moving her would have made an almighty mess. And she had been hit with a bed-warming pan, which I expect originated from the laundry closet."

Dame Culham releases a deep breath, her bosom deflating. "Well, as much as I'd caution you to mind your own business and stay out of trouble, not that you'd ever listen to me . . ." she frowns, casting deep lines into her usually cheerful face ". . . I hope you discover who did it, I really do, Jane. When I think of those poor souls, left to perish in such a wicked way . . ."

Jane leans forward, elbows on the table. "Those?" Dame Culham is so tight-lipped, she rarely misspeaks. Was someone else killed? Surely Jane would have heard about it already, if that was so.

"I meant *her*. That Madame Renault." She waves the wooden spoon, sending spatters of broth across the hearth.

"Then why did you use the plural?"

"The what?"

"Why did you say 'those poor souls'? As if there were more than one?"

"Oh, Jane, you and your questions." Dame Culham casts her eyes up to the wooden beams stretching across the low ceiling. "Do you know, it pained me to send your brothers and sister back to your mother—but when she came for you, my head was glad of the peace!"

Jane pouts and dips her chin. She looks up at Dame Culham through her lashes, as Henry sometimes does when he talks to women.

Dame Culham huffs. "She was expecting. I'd say about five months along. Satisfied?"

Jane's entire body sags. So, it wasn't just the milliner who was killed: the innocent life growing inside her was extinguished, too. Poor Monsieur Renault. Has anyone told him of his wife's brutal death yet? What if Madame Renault has other children? How will they cope without their mother? It is too painful to contemplate.

Horses' hoofs clatter outside in the street. Dame Culham peers out through the leaded glass. "What the devil are they doing here?"

Through the window, Mr. Craven jumps down from his black mare. Mr. Fletcher, the proprietor of Deane Gate Inn, and the parish constable, pull up in an open wagon.

Jane's stomach tightens. The magistrate and the constable together can mean only one thing: they've come to arrest one of the villagers for the murder.

She follows Dame Culham outside.

Mr. Craven is in the garden, talking to Jack and Georgy. Mr. Fletcher climbs out of the wagon and approaches the open gate. He is a big man, with a bent nose, which looks as if it was broken in a fight some time ago.

Jack scowls. "I'm telling you, Georgy don't know nothing about no necklace."

Mr. Craven narrows his eyes and steps toward Georgy, addressing him directly. "Mr. Austen, several witnesses claim to have seen you this morning at Deane Gate Inn, flaunting a woman's necklace. I demand you show it to us, at once."

All of Jane's muscles tighten. Why is Mr. Craven talking to Georgy in such sharp tones? Surely he cannot think her brother knows anything about the murder. She tears across the grass, inserting herself between Georgy and the magistrate. "Mr. Craven, what is the meaning of this? There is no need to speak to my brother like that."

Mr. Fletcher saunters into the garden. He points to his own neck and draws a semicircle over his chest. "Come on, Georgy, show us your pretty necklace." He smiles encouragingly. One of his front teeth is missing. "The one you showed me, while Jack was fetching your pie."

Georgy grins. He delves a hand into his breeches and digs around. When he opens his fist, he is holding something shiny. It is a yellow-gold guard chain, interspersed with seed pearls.

Jane sways as if the ground beneath her has tilted.

"Ah, Miss Austen. How convenient." Mr. Craven glowers at Jane from beneath his bushy eyebrows. "Would you look at the necklace your brother is holding, and tell me if you've seen it before?"

Jane swallows. "I—I have." The words are thick on her tongue.

"On whose person?"

A cold shudder runs through Jane's frame. "Madame Renault's, when I met her in the market . . . But this makes no sense. There must be some mistake."

Mr. Craven jerks a thumb at the cart. "Get him into the wagon." Mr. Fletcher pushes up the sleeves of his coat. His arms are as thick as ham hocks.

"Oh, God help us . . ." Dame Culham stands hip to hip beside Jane. "No, no, this ain't right. He wouldn't hurt anyone."

"Out of the way, Mrs. Culham." Mr. Craven places his hand on the top of her arm. But she doesn't need to get out of the way. Behind the women, Georgy ducks and slips out of the gate. He climbs up into the wagon, smiling as he dangles Madame Renault's gold chain before the parish constable.

Jane sprints to the gate. "Wait! Where are you taking him?" Beside her, Jack scissors-steps over the willow fencing, reaching the wagon before she does.

Mr. Craven mounts his horse. "Winchester County Gaol."

Jane's heart beats in her throat. She cannot let Mr. Craven take Georgy away. What will her mother and father say when they learn she allowed this to happen? Her dear, sweet, guileless brother. She must protect him at all costs. "Winchester? Please, stop. Georgy couldn't have done it."

Jack grabs onto the wagon with both hands, as if he could prevent it from rolling away with his raw strength. "At least let me go with him! He ain't used to being by himself. And you'll need me there, if you're to understand what he's trying to say."

Mr. Craven exhales loudly but makes a curt nod and Jack leaps into the cart beside a grinning Georgy, who is still proudly holding Madame Renault's chain. The delicate gold links glint in the sunlight.

Dame Culham grips Jane's shoulders, digging her strong fingers into Jane's flesh and shaking her out of her dismay. "Run, Jane. Go and tell your father they're taking our Georgy away. Quick as you can."

Jane gulps. This cannot be happening. Mr. Craven cannot be taking Georgy away to charge him with Madame Renault's murder. Not Georgy—he is the gentlest of souls. White spots blur Jane's vision. It's as if someone is holding a pillow over her mouth and nose. She can hardly breathe.

From the wagon, Georgy smiles, waving merrily at Jane as the horses lift their hoofs and the wheels creak into motion.

This is all wrong. Jane must stop this. She *must*. But how?

CHAPTER FIVE

Jane stands at the window of the family parlour with a knot in her stomach, watching for her father's return from Winchester. Over the past couple of nights, ever since Georgy's arrest, visions of her brother in leg irons and manacles have plagued her restless sleep. Her eyes sting and her throat aches with the relentlessness of her concern for him.

Once, when she was a little girl, Jane had asked her father why Georgy was not like the other Austen children. Mr. Austen frowned and told her firmly that Georgy was exactly as God intended him to be, and it was not Jane's place to question the Lord's design. Jane was cross, annoyed on Georgy's behalf that he could not form his words or his letters. Mr. Austen gave a resigned sigh. "Yes, but we have this comfort. In his perpetual innocence, Georgy *cannot* be a bad or wicked child."

When Mr. Craven had asked Jane if she recognized the necklace and to confirm whom it belonged to, it hadn't occurred to her to lie. Now she would do anything, anything she possibly could, to spare her brother.

As soon as Henry received his father's message, he begged his commanding officer for leave and rode all the way home from Oxford in one stint. His horse, an enormous piebald stallion named Severus, looked half dead when they arrived at the rectory, poor thing. Now Henry can't keep still. He paces up and down in front of the hearth in his shirtsleeves, wearing a track on the already threadbare rug. The tall, dark figure of James, in his clergyman's outfit, stands motionless beside the fireplace. At the table, Mrs. Austen wraps her arms around herself and stares at the sputtering flames as if they might provide a solution to her woes. Anna, bereft of attention, wails and bangs her fists on her high chair.

Eventually, as the cold creeps into Jane's bones and the white sky turns lavender at the edges, Mr. Austen plods along the lane on his faithful steed at the pace of a man condemned.

Mrs. Austen pounces on him as soon as he is through the front door. "How's our boy? Is he eating? Has he slept? Tell me, truly." She grapples her husband out of his greatcoat, throwing it to Sally.

The maid brushes away the fine powder of snowflakes, then hangs the heavy woolen garment on a stand near the fire to dry. Sally has not yet served the Austens for a full twelvemonth, yet her face is etched with despair.

"He's confused, frightened, vexed at being kept within doors." Mr. Austen seems a decade older than he was when he departed. His back stoops and the vertical lines in his cheeks carve even deeper. "They wouldn't grant bail, but I've arranged for him and Jack to board with the governor, in his own home. It's attached to the prison. His wife will cook and care for them both."

"We can't let Jack stay with him," says Mrs. Austen. "It's too much to ask. One of us should go."

Henry and James exchange a loaded glance. Jane can tell exactly what they're thinking. Frank and Charles are on the other side of the world; Neddy can't risk embroiling his benefactress in scandal; Henry is committed to the army; and James has his congregation, not to mention motherless Anna, to think of. None of Georgy's brothers are in any position to go to gaol with him.

"We could send Jane, I suppose." Mrs. Austen gestures toward her superfluous daughter. "It's not as if she's doing anything vital here."

"We are not sending Jane." Mr. Austen's colour rises. "Watching over Georgy is Jack's living, always has been. He was insistent he remain. If we were to dismiss him, the poor lad would think we somehow blame him for allowing Georgy to get into this scrape."

James grips the chunky oak beam stretching across the brick fireplace to form a rustic mantelpiece. "They can't seriously think our Georgy is capable of taking a life?"

Jane steps forward, circling her father. "And he'll have an alibi, surely. He's never left alone."

Mr. Austen drags his palm over his tired face. "Not usually, no . . . But on that particular evening, Jack was out running errands when Dame Culham was called to an unexpected delivery. Twins, apparently—they came early. Georgy was already asleep, worn out from one of his long walks and with a belly full of pound cake." He makes a hollow laugh. "So, Dame Culham thought it safe to leave him for a few hours."

"Right," says James. "But that doesn't mean they can convict him of murder."

Mr. Austen slumps into the battered leather armchair beside the hearth. "No, and they haven't charged him with murder." A flicker of hope rises in Jane's breast. Mr. Craven must have realized this has all been a terrible misunderstanding and, at this very moment, be arranging for Georgy's release.

"They have him on the hook for the theft of the necklace," Mr. Austen continues. "And since it was clearly in his possession . . ."

Mrs. Austen lets out a strangled cry. Jane presses her eyes closed to prevent tears from falling. The theft of any item worth more than twelve pence is treated as grand larceny—a capital offence. Occasionally, sympathetic jurors might purposely devalue stolen goods by a few pence, or even shillings, to spare the defendant from the death penalty. But Madame Renault's gold necklace, with its many seed pearls, will be worth a small fortune—several hundreds of pounds. A judge would never allow a jury to perjure itself by grossly devaluing such an item. If Georgy were to be found guilty, he could hang for this crime.

James rests both hands on the mantel, arms shaking. "What are we going to do?"

"Find a lawyer to argue his case. Gather as many witnesses as we can to attest to his good character . . ." Mr. Austen trails off, but his mouth remains open.

Jane places a tentative hand on her mother's shoulder. "Shouldn't we explain about Georgy's difficulties? It wouldn't be fair to make him stand trial."

Henry folds his arms. "Have him declared a lunatic, you mean?"

Mr. Austen frowns. "No, they'd pronounce him guilty by default and lock him up in an asylum. If you knew what those places were like, Jane, you wouldn't suggest it. A beast in a menagerie would attract more compassion." His voice grows louder and more urgent as he continues, "Besides, Georgy's *not* insane. He knows right from wrong. Since the day he was born, despite his many challenges, he's fought to live as dignified a life as possible. And I am not condemning my own son. Not now, not ever."

Jane clings to her mother, as Mrs. Austen gulps back sobs. Henry bashes the side of his fist against the wall. He knocks a sampler askew, leaving a mark in the plaster. "If only he could tell us where he found the damn thing."

The sampler is Cassandra's handiwork. Jane is more than proficient with a needle and thread, but what is the point in sewing words when writing in pen and ink is so much faster? Beneath the alphabet and the row of numbers, her sister has cross-stitched "Trust in the Lord with all thine heart; and lean not unto thine own understanding."

Jane wishes Henry had put his fist through the proverb. "But did Georgy *find* the necklace?" she asks. "What if someone, the murderer perhaps, gave it to him to throw the authorities off his own scent?" Jane's stomach lurches at the realization that someone might have set out deliberately to place Georgy in danger.

Henry is hugging himself by the elbows. "Actually, that's a good point. Everyone knows our Georgy is guileless enough to accept such a gift without suspicion. And, of course, he wouldn't be able to explain where he got it from."

Mr. Austen closes his eyes and shakes his head. "Jack and I did try to persuade him to elaborate, but it distressed him even more."

Anna lets out a sharp cry. Jane abandons her mother to lift the baby by her armpits. Anna stiffens her little body, so that Jane must wrestle her fat thighs and rigid toes out of the high chair. Her downy head smells of warm milk and home. "When will they try him?"

There are black shadows beneath Mr. Austen's eyes and his voice is grave. "The next assize is set for the first week of February."

Jane tries to swallow, but it's as if a large piece of flint is blocking her throat. If the Austens are to save Georgy's life, they have a mere seven weeks to do so. Serious crimes, such as theft, are dealt with only once a year, when a judge descends on Winchester and appoints a jury of twelve men. Over the course of two or three days, they hear the backlog of cases and clear out the gaol. Those found guilty are marched out of the courtroom and hanged before a jeering crowd.

"We can't just trust in the law to prove Georgy innocent. We must find out what really happened to Madame Renault, and prove it, before it's too late," she says.

James and Henry blink at her. Mrs. Austen twists her sodden handkerchief between her fists. Jane can tell by their pained expressions that the agony of Georgy's predicament is clouding their usually razor-sharp minds. They are like stunned mice, rescued from the cat but too stupefied to make their escape.

Mr. Austen releases a deep breath. "That poor woman. I volunteered to bury her, too, before all this happened with Georgy. Have arrangements been made for the ground to be dug? It'll be hard work, in this frost."

James nods. "It's been done, Father."

"Why are *you* burying her?" asks Jane. "The church at Ashe is a stone's throw from Deane House."

Mrs. Austen often complains her husband is too obliging for his own good. He is the type of clergyman who returns a new mother's sixpence after he has churched her and will baptize a natural child without pressing for details of the errant father. Jane loves him all the more for his kindheartedness, and suspects that, secretly, her mother does, too.

Mr. Austen holds up his palms. "The good Reverend Mr. Lefroy seemed reluctant, so I offered my services. I didn't think the Harcourts would want a reminder of the incident on their doorstep, either."

Jane flinches at the mention of Tom's uncle. In all the horror of dealing with Georgy's incarceration, she has barely registered that Tom still hasn't called. She must get a message to him. Now, more than ever, she needs his help.

"Are you certain you still want to conduct the service?" asks Henry.

"Why wouldn't I?" Mr. Austen looks about the room. To refuse to bury Madame Renault now would imply the family has something to be ashamed of—further implicating Georgy in the crime. "The unfortunate woman must be laid to rest. It is not her fault our Georgy has somehow embroiled himself in her case."

"That's very Christian of you, my dear." Mrs. Austen takes her husband's banyan and cap from Sally and hands them to him wearily. The maid goes to the sideboard to fetch a glass of port.

"That's what I thought, until Sir John offered to pay for the arrangements." Mr. Austen stands to poke his long thin arms through the loose sleeves of his robe and settles his cap on top of his bright white hair. Once seated, he takes the glass from Sally, nodding his thanks as he sips.

"He did? But why would the Harcourts pay?" Henry pauses in his pacing, giving the rug a moment's respite. It was once a bright red, woven with Moghul motifs. Now it is a sun-bleached coral with only traces of faded geometric fronds.

Mr. Austen shrugs. "I suppose Sir John feels somewhat responsible for her. She died in his home, after all."

Jane winces at the casual way in which the men have agreed between them the details of Madame Renault's burial. It is as if the milliner's corpse is an inconvenience to be dealt with, rather than the remains of a person who deserves to be laid to rest with Christian solemnity.

She jiggles Anna in her arms. The baby's eyes are drooping, but every time they close, she jerks herself awake again. "What about her people? Do they not want her buried closer to them, in Basingstoke?"

Mr. Austen furrows his already deeply grooved brow. "I'm afraid no one has come forward to claim her. Not so far, anyway. I arranged for a notice in the local paper. Perhaps one of her acquaintances will see it."

Jane grips Anna tighter. She pictures Monsieur Renault, fretting over the whereabouts of his pregnant wife—then reading the details of her brutal murder in the *Hampshire Chronicle*. What a devastating way to receive the news. He may not even speak English. That could be why the story hasn't reached him yet. Perhaps the Renaults had only recently arrived in England. Monsieur Renault may have relied on his wife to translate for him. Please, God, let someone break it to him before the funeral so that he may bid his wife and unborn child a final adieu.

Mr. Austen points to his greatcoat on the stand, dripping melted snow onto the quarry tiles. "That reminds me. I dropped in at the Wheatsheaf Inn on my way back and collected the post."

Henry digs around in the pockets, retrieves a handful of letters and distributes them around the room. One is addressed to Jane.

Recognizing the elaborate penmanship, Jane balances Anna on her hip and grips the note between her teeth, using her free hand to break open the seal. "It's from Cousin Eliza."

"Eliza?" James and Henry say at once. The pair stand a little taller.

Eliza de Feuillide is the daughter of Mr. Austen's late sister, Aunt Phila. Since the death of Eliza's husband, a French nobleman, executed by the new regime, she has been staying with friends in Northumberland. It is odd for Jane to think of her gregarious cousin in mourning. Eliza is always gay, no matter how life contrives to make her sorrowful.

"She says she's desperate to keep Christmas with her family, and we should expect her here at Steventon on the twentieth of December." Jane reads the letter aloud, while Anna grabs the paper, tugging it toward her mouth.

James examines the tired cuffs of his shirtsleeves. "But that's less than a week away."

Mrs. Austen rises from her chair, pressing her fists into her slight waist. "It's too late to put her off. By the time our message reaches Northumberland, she'll already have left. Not that she'd let us. If Eliza knew Georgy was in trouble, she'd insist on coming anyway to do whatever she might to help. Jane, come with me. We need to air the linen and make up a bedroom."

Jane places Anna in James's outstretched arms. He cradles his baby daughter to his chest, while Jane grips her sausage-like wrist and peels her tiny fingers from the letter.

Her spirit rises at the prospect of Eliza's company. Jane's audacious cousin escaped the insurrection in France, survived the Mount Street riot in London and even bested a highwayman. If anyone will know how to go about solving a murder, it's Eliza.

CHAPTER SIX

The sixteenth of December 1795 is Jane's twentieth birthday. Tom still hasn't called, but Jane remains sanguine, as she's invited herself to luncheon with her dear friend and Tom's aunt, Mrs. Lefroy. She expects Tom fears that it would be insensitive of him to ask Jane's father for her hand while Georgy's fate hangs in the balance. All the same, he *might* declare his intentions to Jane herself, especially since it's her birthday. The scandal of Georgy's arrest will not have put him off. He's a more faithful fellow than that. Or so she hopes.

Accordingly, Jane dresses with great care. She suffers the dreaded curling irons rather than relying on the buoyancy of her natural waves, and gives herself permission to borrow Cassandra's cornflower-blue gown. Jane has her own gown, made from the same bolt of cotton, but since she has not taken as much care of it, the colour is washed out.

In the Austens' family parlour, her mother and father sit at the linen-covered table in their dressing gowns and caps. A red-cheeked Anna chews her dimpled fist in her high chair, and James crouches before the fire with a piece of bread on a toasting fork. A chill runs through the rectory, despite the blaze in the grate.

Mrs. Austen forms a strained smile, baring her teeth but failing to turn the corners of her mouth upward. "Many happy returns, dear."

"Thank you, Mother." Jane sits, pouring herself a cup of tea: black but, alas, there is no sugar. In the centre of the table a large parcel is wrapped in brown paper. Rather than pleasure, Jane is awash with guilt. How can her mother and father celebrate the day of her birth when another of their children's lives remains in peril? "But you shouldn't have. Not in the current circumstances."

Mr. Austen peers over his newspaper, directing his gaze toward the parcel. "It was already done. Besides, we must go forth with as much normality as we can muster. The Lord in Heaven knows Georgy is innocent, and our family has no reason to be ashamed. Sticking to our usual routine, insofar as we can, is the only way to survive this turmoil."

In the past, Jane has been guilty of judging her parents as coldhearted for their stalwartness in the face of difficulty. Now, she has more sympathy for their pragmatism. The constant dread over her brother's plight is like a stone weighing heavy in her chest, but weeping and wailing in her bedchamber all day will not save Georgy. She must maintain a cool head if she's to catch a murderer. "I suppose you're right."

James releases his toast from the fork, burning his hand on the bread as he pushes it onto his plate. "Ouch." He blows on his fingertips and shakes his hand from the wrist. "Aren't you going to open your present, Jane? It's not like you to be so restrained."

Jane pushes aside her tea and pulls the parcel toward herself. "Well, I'm almost a grown woman now. A most refined and rarefied creature. One more year, and I'll have reached my majority."

The gift is heavy. Hopefully, it isn't a tambour frame for embroidery, or some such nonsense. She takes care untying the string and unfolding the paper. She will not tear it—even brown paper is expensive and Jane never misses an opportunity to reuse it.

Under the paper she finds a wooden box, the varnished grain too fine for it to be a mere container. There is a diamond-shaped locking mechanism and brass handles on either side. The lid is attached with hinges. She opens the box like a book. The parts are wedge-shaped, so it forms a slope—a writing slope.

Jane places one hand over her mouth. The box has transformed into a portable writing desk topped with dark green leather.

"Well," says Mr. Austen, "do you like it?"

She shakes her head, in a state of disbelief at her dear father's thoughtfulness—not to mention his generosity. "More than I can possibly say."

On her travels to visit the Austens' extended family, Jane has stared enviously at gentlemen in the dining rooms of various coaching inns making use of their portable writing desks. Since the very first time she saw one, she's dreamed of having her own. Inside the box are several cubbyholes, containing a small glass jar of ink, a miniature silver pot of setting powder, sheafs of paper cut to size and even a penknife to sharpen her quill.

Jane's father hasn't simply given her a wooden box. It is a means of carrying everything she needs to compose her stories wherever she goes, safely locking away her ideas until she's ready to share them.

Mrs. Austen tops up the teapot with scalding water from a copper kettle. "We thought you could keep *Lady Susan* in there. Then you'll have no excuse not to get her finished, wherever life takes you. The Lord alone knows where that will be."

"God's teeth." Mr. Austen's elbows are as sharp as pins as he shakes out the pages of his broadsheet.

Jane has found two little keys inside one of the internal compartments and is too busy locking and unlocking the small drawer of her new desk to ask her father why he swears. She slides the drawer in and out of the box, holding the brass handle and peering within, as if something might have appeared there by magic.

Mrs. Austen blows the steam from Anna's wooden bowl of rice pudding. "What is it, dear?"

"It's Madame Renault—the news of her demise has made it all the way into *The Times*."

James freezes, butter knife in the air. "Oh, good God. They've not mentioned Georgy and the necklace, have they?"

It's difficult to comprehend how anyone who has met Georgy could believe him capable of harming Madame Renault but, in the unscrupulous hands of the London press, he'll be made into a monster.

Mr. Austen peers at the article. "No, they refer to no one by name. It's in the society pages, focusing on how the gruesome discovery of a robbed and murdered woman marred the betrothal of a future baronet and a cotton heiress. Everyone will know to whom it refers, of course. Sir John will be spitting venom."

"As will Mrs. Rivers." Mrs. Austen's refined features have taken on a careworn look, and there are dark circles beneath her usually bright eyes. "Not quite the entrance into high society she was hoping for." She offers a cup of warm milk to Anna.

Anna grabs her grandmother's wrist and sends the milk splashing across the table.

Jane places a protective arm around her writing box and draws it closer. "If it's in the newspaper, they should be appealing for witnesses, not publishing the details of Madame Renault's death for titillation." She slams the lid of her box and secures it with the key. "This is infuriating. Mr. Craven is going about his investigation wrongly. It's clear she wasn't killed as part of a robbery. Not a premeditated one, anyway."

Mr. Austen inclines his head. "How so?"

Jane keeps her palms flat on the lid of her writing box, grounded by the texture of the smooth, solid wood. "Because a professional thief would carry his own weapon, something like a knife or a pistol. He wouldn't need to use one of Lady Harcourt's bed-warming pans. Would he?"

"It could have been an opportunist," says Mrs. Austen. "A fellow trader, who spotted the necklace and was too sorely tempted to resist? It may be that they tried to lift it without her noticing, but she cried for help? If the thief meant only to silence, not kill, her that may explain why he discarded the evidence. The necklace was too obvious for an amateur to dispose of."

"That doesn't make any sense, either." Jane is irritated by everyone's willingness to accept the motive for the crime at face value. "Why choose *her*? And in the Harcourts' linen closet, of all places?"

Mrs. Austen shivers, wrapping her dressing-gown tighter around her shoulders. "Who knows? That poor maid you told us about. It must have taken her an age to get the bloodstains out of the floorboards, never mind returning the copper to a shine."

Jane takes a deep breath. "This is exasperating. There must be a way in which we can identify the real culprit. Then Mr. Craven will have to drop the charges against Georgy."

Her family stare at her, stunned into an unusual silence.

James leans forward, resting his elbows on his knees. "But, Jane, we're doing everything we can. We've scoured the countryside for miles around, but so far we've found no trace of the trespassers. They must have fled the county. We must widen the search—involve some of the Sussex landowners in case the ne'er-do-wells are making for the coast."

Jane grits her teeth. There were no strangers camping on the Harcourts' estate. Why would Sir John want people to believe there were? She's growing suspicious about his motives for fabricating such a story, and her recollection of Mrs. Twistleton leaping to the baronet's defence rattles her even more.

Mr. Austen rubs his eyes. "Well, if my cleverest child cannot work it out, what hope have the authorities?"

"That's gracious of you, Father." James rests his chin in his hand. "But, I admit, it has me foxed. They couldn't have covered their tracks completely. Did you look at the letter I drafted for the lawyer? Neddy's confirmed he's happy with the arrangement, and to send the invoice straight to him."

Mr. Austen shoots Jane a lightning-fast wink, bolstering her bruised heart. "I did, James, thank you. I'd say it's ready to go."

Jane stares into her lap, trying to conceal her smirk. Once, when she was alone with her father in his study, he had declared one of the smartest tricks she played was to allow James to believe he was cleverer than her—so that she might more easily outwit him.

Madame Renault was killed before seven o'clock in the evening. Jane has checked the invitation to the Harcourts' ball: guests were invited from eight onward. Which means the murder took place at a time when far fewer people were in the vicinity than she had originally thought—the Harcourts, the Riverses, the servants and the tradesmen. This knowledge significantly cuts down her list of suspects. Now, all she has to do is examine each and every one, and trick the murderer into revealing himself.

* * *

Ashe is just under two miles from Steventon. It is a good walk on a fine day, and one Jane has done many times—although never before with a murderer abroad. Despite her determination not to let the villain steal her personal liberty as well as Madame Renault's life, she hastens her step and startles at every rustle in the hedgerow. By the time she reaches St. Andrew's Church, her heart beats faster than that of a dormouse. Not wanting to appear flustered when she meets her secret lover for the first time since their amorous encounter in the glasshouse, she forces herself to amble through the churchyard to recover her composure. The tombstones are more elaborate than those at St. Nicholas's, but they are covered with the same mottled lichen and balls of furry green moss.

Mrs. Lefroy opens the door to Ashe Rectory and pokes her gold-turbaned head outside into the pale sunlight. She has reached middle age, but is an excellent horsewoman and the exercise maintains her graceful figure. "Come in, Jane, come in . . ." Jane wonders if she and Tom will ever achieve the same relaxed air of refined hospitality as his aunt and uncle. She certainly hopes so.

The Lefroys have improved their home in much the same way as they have enriched Hampshire society with their cultural panache. The once tired red-brick building now boasts an elegant façade in the Palladian style, and ivy creeps beneath the freshly painted sash windows. Jane steps over the threshold and follows her hostess, surreptitiously glancing around for signs of Tom. His top boots are not in the rack, and neither is his coat hanging from the row of brass hooks. Mrs. Lefroy pads along the narrow corridor in her sumptuous paisley robe toward her best parlour, which she refers to as her "salon." It is papered in a green trellis design, filled with imitation French furniture, and lined with bookcases.

Tom is conspicuous in his absence.

"Is Mr. Lefroy not joining us?"

Mrs. Lefroy takes Jane's basket, so she may remove her cloak and bonnet. "George is out, organizing the poor relief for the winter," she replies, referring to her husband, the Reverend George Lefroy.

"No, I meant Mr. Tom Lefroy."

"Tom?" Mrs. Lefroy lifts her long white fingers to the base of her throat. "Why would he be joining us?"

Jane lowers her head, feeling her face slacken. "Oh, no reason." If Tom has not shared the news of their mutual infatuation with his family, he cannot be serious in his intentions toward Jane. Perhaps he's avoiding her on purpose and ran away when he saw her coming, either because he's horrified at the prospect of being tied to a woman whose brother has been charged with grand larceny or he never really liked her. Jane grasps the back of an armchair to steady herself, then moves around it and collapses into the seat.

Mrs. Lefroy turns away, placing Jane's basket on her mahogany sideboard. "Foraging for sloes? Are you making cordial?"

Jane wrinkles her nose. "What? Oh, no—ink."

"You're managing to write then? Under the circumstances?" Mrs. Lefroy perches on the edge of a chaise longue.

"No, not really. But I thought a good long walk in the fresh air might help clear my head." Jane flexes her frozen feet toward the fire. She's been trying to further *Lady Susan*, but she couldn't even manage a note to Cassandra. She began a letter to her beloved sister, but instead of her usual cheery roundup of the village gossip, she found herself scrawling:

Steventon, Wednesday, 16 December 1795

My dearest Cassandra,

Who could have killed the hapless milliner, Madame Renault?

There the letter stands, at only two lines. Unfinished, resting on the green leather top of her portable writing slope, at home on her dresser. Beside it, the straw hat she bought from Madame Renault is displayed on a wooden stand, whittled for her by Frank. The stiff vellum invitation to the Harcourts' ill-fated ball is propped up against the mirror.

"It must be dreadful for all of you." Mrs. Lefroy pats Jane's hand. "My husband has already volunteered to stand as a character witness for Georgy, but you must let me know if there's anything else we can do to help."

Jane forces her lips into a semblance of a smile as she stares at the oak fireplace. Garlands of grapes and Etruscan urns are carved into the surround. On the mantel, a brass carriage clock ticks away the minutes and hours. "Thank you, I will."

The room fills with the potent scent of coffee as a maid brings in a floral Staffordshire pot on a tray and places it on the side table. Mrs. Lefroy closes her eyes as she breathes in the aroma. "Your poor mother. How is she coping?"

"I don't know. But she always seems to."

When she was younger, Jane thought her parents immune to the never-ending series of misfortunes that constantly befell them. Through all their setbacks—illness and bereavements within the extended family, farming disasters and their ongoing struggle to bring in enough money to cover their expenses—they made an excellent show of carrying on in good humour. Now, she can perceive their distress over Georgy etched into their faces and in the slow drag of their step. Their stoicism may know no bounds, but it takes its toll.

Mrs. Lefroy leans forward, pouring thick black coffee into two small cups. "And that unfortunate woman—I went to see her laid out."

Jane wraps one of her hard-won ringlets around her finger and tugs it straight. "Madame Renault."

"Yes, may she rest in peace. Lady Harcourt is devastated, too. She had such high hopes for the evening, and to have it end in such tragedy . . . She put her heart and soul into organizing that ball. She was the most animated I've seen her in years. You know how stupefied she usually is. And who can blame her? She's been through so much. What with losing Edwin, and all of Sir John's *indiscretions*." Mrs. Lefroy tuts. "Jonathan coming home and settling down is the one bright spot on her horizon."

Out of the corner of her eye, Jane studies Mrs. Lefroy's curled lip as she sips from her coffee cup. Could there be any truth in Mary's salacious gossip about Sir John's housekeeper? If he had indeed invited a fallen woman to manage his household, it would certainly explain Mrs. Twistleton's blind devotion to him. "Oh, yes, all of Sir John's indiscretions," Jane responds. "Heavens, his drinking, too . . ." Mrs. Lefroy tsks ". . . and his gambling . . ." Mrs. Lefroy strokes her throat, as Jane goes in for the kill, ". . . not to mention Mrs. Twistleton."

"Ugh . . . *Mrs.* Twistleton. Why Sir John feels the need to behave so beneath his poor wife's nose is beyond me. It's one thing for him to act the libertine while he's in Basingstoke, but to bring the hussy to Deane House and dishonour his marriage vows under his own roof! Lady Harcourt would be mortified if she ever found out. The despicable man—he has no compassion at all for his wife's frayed nerves."

Jane straightens, eyes wide. "Are you saying Sir John is bedding his housekeeper?"

Mrs. Lefroy gasps, her fingers flying to her mouth. "Jane, you little minx! What have I said? Sometimes you seem so much a matron that I forget what an innocent you are. Don't let your mother know I told you that rumour, I heard it from my hairdresser, and she's the most terrible gossip. It's all conjecture—I should never have said a word."

Despite herself, Jane is laughing. If Mrs. Lefroy was the murderer, Jane is confident she'd have the truth out of her in five minutes flat. "I won't. Even if I did, she'd accuse me of letting my imagination run wild, as usual." But even as Jane wipes away her tears of mirth, she shudders.

Her father preaches a tired old sermon warning of the slippery path to ruin and destruction. If Sir John and Mrs. Twistleton are guilty of fornication, what other sins might they have committed? But neither could have any reason for wanting Madame Renault dead. Not unless the milliner had recognized the pair from Basingstoke and threatened to expose their arrangement. It is a sobering thought.

For the rest of her visit, Jane probes Mrs. Lefroy for more details of Sir John's philandering and Mrs. Twistleton's true character. But Mrs. Lefroy is wise to Jane's tricks and refuses to indulge her young friend in any more unsubstantiated gossip, steering the conversation toward literature instead.

One of the reasons Jane enjoys her visits to Ashe Rectory is that she is granted unfettered access to the library. Before she leaves, Mrs. Lefroy presses *Evelina* into Jane's wicker basket.

Jane has read the novel several times, but evidently her friend knows that the familiar text will bring her comfort—even in this period of great distress. When her host opens the front door, Jane's heart gives an unexpected surge. There, loitering among the viburnums, is a familiar, lean figure.

"Ah, the delightful Miss Austen." Tom Lefroy presses his hat to his chest and bows. By daylight, he is less of a fop and more of a sportsman, in his blue-black double-breasted frock coat and top boots. "Have I missed your visit? In that case, you must allow me to escort you home."

Mrs. Lefroy puts a hand to her chest. "I could have the carriage brought round?"

"Oh, no, thank you. It's a lovely day, and I don't want to put you out." Jane exchanges a tacit smile with Tom, then walks through the garden gate into the churchyard. The sunlight glints on the granite headstones.

Tom hurries after her. "And it would be my pleasure." As soon as they enter the lane, Tom offers her his arm. Jane slips her hand through the small gap between his elbow and his muscular frame. They are so close that their hips bump and her entire body tingles. "I was sorry to hear about the unpleasant business with your brother. I hope your mother and father are bearing up under the strain."

"Thank you." Jane chews her lip, wondering how best to solicit his legal advice. The situation is rather more than a spot of "unpleasant business" and she needs Tom's brilliant mind to help to resolve it. "They're as well as can be hoped for. But it was a dreadful shock for all of us. I keep expecting to wake up and find it's all been a horrid nightmare."

"I can imagine." He shivers, as if casting off something nasty. "So, have you missed me?"

Jane keeps her eyes on the path. "Missed you? Why? Were you absent? If you were, I dare say I didn't notice," she teases. Leaves of all different shapes and shades of brown, from pale gold to deepest chocolate, scatter the lane. Jane presses their outline into the earth as she walks.

"I had to return to town to do some business for my great-uncle Langlois. He's to be my sponsor at Lincoln's Inn, so I'm at his mercy. But he assures me I'm at liberty now. Until February, at the earliest."

A warm sensation bursts forth in Jane's chest. Tom will not be disappearing again. By February, they are sure to have settled their future between them. "So, you're a gentleman of leisure."

"Yes, indeed. You must send me more of Lady Susan's correspondence. She has me completely enthralled."

Jane is accustomed to receiving compliments for her stories from those she loves. She's been causing her friends and family to grow wide-eyed and shriek with laughter for as long as she can remember. But Tom is the first person, outside her immediate family or the handful of friends she's known for most of her life, with whom she has ever dared to share her work. "I can't say I'm surprised. Lady Susan is the most accomplished coquette in all of England."

Tom catches her elbow, pulling her backward. "Oh, I'd say she has competition for that title."

A great oak spreads its bare branches over the path, cocooning Jane and her lover in its protection. Tom glances around, then draws her into his warm embrace and brushes his soft lips against her own. Every nerve ending in her body stirs. She has longed for this moment since last they parted. Now that it is finally here, she wishes she could suspend it in aspic and hold on to it forever.

As Tom pulls away, his lips form a rueful smile. "What have you been doing while I've been gone? Apart from receiving your many admirers, of whom I expect I'm at the end of the line." He walks on a few steps. "Scribbling all day?"

Jane remains rooted to the spot. "Not really. As I said, I've been preoccupied with my brother Georgy's predicament. I wish there was something I could do to help." She stares at Tom, willing him to provide the answer.

"I admit I have been pondering his case and, well, I doubt you'll like what I have to say . . ." Tom pauses, hands on his hips and staring at the sky while he waits for Jane to catch up. "But my advice would be to avoid a trial by having him committed."

"Committed?"

"Yes. He's not quite right, is he, your brother?" Tom taps a finger against his temple.

Jane had made the same suggestion to her parents but, from Tom, the idea of having Georgy declared a lunatic sounds utterly heartless. No wonder her father rejected it outright. "I did raise the possibility, but my father said it would be pronouncing Georgy guilty by default. And that an asylum would be even worse than gaol."

A large muddy puddle, spanning the width of the path, lies before them. Tom, protected by his top boots, splashes through it. "In that case, the only other option is for your brother to plead guilty to the theft, and throw himself on the mercy of the court. There are no guarantees, but providing you draw a sympathetic justice, his sentence may be reduced to transportation."

Jane lifts her skirts and picks her way carefully over the roots of the great tree to follow him. "Transportation?"

"Yes, he'd be shipped to a penal colony, probably Australia, and obliged to remain there for up to fourteen years."

"I know what transportation means but . . ." Jane hesitates. Georgy cannot be trusted to wander out of the village by himself without coming to grief. She cannot countenance how he would survive being forcibly removed to Botany Bay for more than a decade. With his medical complaints, it is doubtful he'd survive the passage.

"I know it's not ideal, but it's the best I can come up with. If your brother goes to trial and pleads innocent, and the jury finds him guilty—which, given he clearly had the necklace in his possession and no credible explanation for how he came by it legally—they're certain to do, then . . ." Tom's handsome features turn sombre. "By God, Jane, I hope I'm not the first to break this to you but . . . it'll be a capital sentence. There's no doubt of it."

"They'll hang him for a necklace?"

"For anything worth more than a shilling."

Jane casts around for a shred of hope. She knew all of this—but listening to Tom spell it out in stark legal terms makes it all the more horrifying. "But don't juries sometimes adjust the value of articles stolen to spare the defendant from the gallows?"

"By a few pence, not hundreds of pounds. No justice worthy of the name would allow it. It's perjury."

"But it's not fair."

"It's the law, Jane." Tom stretches his arms out by his sides. "Your best bet is to avoid the case going to trial by having your brother declared insane."

"No, that's not our best bet. It's not even a bet—folding before the game has begun." Jane takes a breath, struggling to suppress the irritation in her voice. "Our best bet would be to discover what really happened to Madame Renault, so that we can clear Georgy's name."

"Who?" Tom gazes at her. His face is blank.

"Madame Renault. The milliner found dead at the ball. The woman whose necklace my brother is accused of stealing. How is it possible you don't even know her name?"

He smacks his palm against his forehead. "Oh, right. Yes, I think I heard it mentioned."

They walk along the main road in awkward silence. Several carriages and a few riders on horseback pass, meaning Jane must desist from holding his hand. Instead, she sneaks sidelong glances at him. "Do you know why Madame Renault is to be buried at St. Nicholas's rather than St. Andrew's? After all, Ashe is much closer to Deane House."

The cold has brought warmth to his pale complexion and his blue eyes are bright against the clear sky. "I expect because my uncle doesn't wish to stand at the grave of a papist pauper. More fool your father for volunteering to do so."

"She wasn't a pauper. She was a merchant. And I thought you, of all people, would show more tolerance than that, given your lineage." Tom may have been born in Ireland, but he is descended from a long line of French Huguenots.

"Exactly. I'm inclined to show any Catholic the same tolerance they showed us when they drove us out of France."

Jane looks at Tom. She studies the features she's grown to admire, dreamed of even: his fair hair, the proud curve of his cheekbones, and his enticing lips. The only sound comes from the sheep bleating in the nearby field. What does she know of his true character? Who is the young man behind the handsome face and easy charm?

After they pass through the village of Deane, and turn into the lane toward Steventon, Jane takes a sharp breath. "Aren't you intrigued to find out who killed her? You're hoping to be called to the bar, after all."

Tom narrows his eyes. "It's the magistrate's job to identify the culprit and press charges. A barrister focuses on developing the argument to be used in court, convincing the jury, beyond a shadow of doubt, that the defendant is guilty—or otherwise."

Jane frowns, her body sagging. She expected more of Tom. She has pictured them poring over the problem together, interrogating it from every angle until they find a solution. As her brother, Georgy deserves more of Tom's attention than this. "That's just it. Georgy's not guilty."

Tom glances over his shoulder. "But how do you know that?"

Jane halts, winded. "Georgy isn't a thief, and he certainly isn't capable of harming anyone."

"But how can you prove it? Isn't it possible he might have done it by accident? Not knowing his own strength?"

"Tom! You've never met him." How can Tom be saying such dreadful things about her brother? They've reached a fork in the lane—one way leads to the heart of Steventon village, the other to the rectory.

"I didn't mean it like that." He holds up his hands, as if defending himself from a blow. "I'm playing Devil's advocate, showing you how a lawyer thinks. These are the arguments that will be put to your brother in court. If your family is determined to let the case go to trial, you must be prepared if you're to have any chance of defending him."

Jane speaks through gritted teeth: "He didn't do it."

"I'm not saying he did. Please don't be vexed with me. I may seem unfeeling, but really I'm trying to help." He takes

Jane's hand, slipping a finger inside her glove to stroke her wrist. His eyes, the colour of the sky on a hot summer's day, drill into her own. "It's a shame we never finished our talk at the ball."

Is this it? Is he finally going to ask Jane's permission to speak to her father? "No, we didn't."

"Let us see if we can find an unlocked barn. There must be one around here. Then we can conclude our conversation."

Jane lowers her head. Her heart is as heavy as a sack of flour. "I think not." Dallying with Tom after dark, in the glasshouse at the ball, where everyone was drinking and making merry, is one thing. Sneaking into a barn, in broad daylight, where her father's labourers might see her and report her to her mother, is quite another.

Besides, after Tom's callous words, Jane's in no mood for making love.

"Good day to you, Mr. Lefroy. Thank you for escorting me home. There's no need for you to take me any farther."

"Jane!" Tom calls after her. "Miss Austen!"

But Jane turns on her heel and marches onward to the rectory without looking back. Tom is clearly too confident of her affection. Perhaps reminding him she has the option of walking away from their entanglement will encourage him to work a little harder for her hand.

1. To Cassandra Austen

Steventon, ~~Wednesday 16 December1795~~
Thursday, 17 December 1795

My dearest Cassandra,

Who was it, really, who killed the hapless milliner, Madame Renault? Please don't waste any ink admonishing me not to involve myself in the investigation. If you don't know by now that to do so would only serve to make me all the more determined, you've not half the wit I credit you with. It is right and proper that Justice should be lauded for her poor vision—but her servant, the magistrate, ought to possess keener sight. If Mary's dim-witted uncle is too foolhardy to understand that our Georgy cannot so much as swat a fly without lamenting the unnecessary bloodshed, it falls to me to tear the scales from his eyes. And poor Madame Renault, her body ill-used and her precious life stolen before her time, I fear her spirit will not rest until I uncover the murderer. But who, in our circle of acquaintances and beyond, could have committed such an atrocity, beloved sister, and why?

- A witless thief (witless indeed, to rob a humble merchant while allowing the women of quality to retain their jewels, and then to forgo the bounty altogether)

- Mrs. Twistleton (once a woman has fallen prey to sin, is it ever possible for her to recover herself?)

- Sir John Harcourt (licentious adulterer turned killer to protect his good name?)

I know it will cause you unbearable pain to consider any of our friends or neighbours guilty of this act of depravity. You, who see the glimmer of good shining through the blackest of hearts and pray for repentance from the most tarnished of souls. But I also know you will share my unshakeable faith in Georgy's innocence, and therefore I beg you to undertake this scrutiny alongside me. Please take extreme care not to let anyone else read this letter. In fact, after your eyes are done with it, rip it to shreds and feed it to Mr. Fowle's pigs.

Yours affectionately,
J.A.

PS I have already apologized profusely about your sprigged muslin. Please don't be so churlish as to hold a grudge. Really, with the tragic circumstances in which the Harcourts' ball ended, you should be thanking me for having avoided any bloodstains along the hem.

Miss Austen,
Rev. Mr. Fowle's,
Kintbury,
Newbury.

CHAPTER SEVEN

Funerals are public rather than private affairs. Therefore it is not customary for well-bred Anglican women to attend. Which is why Jane is bundled up in her cloak with her back pressed against the sturdy red trunk of the ancient yew in the graveyard of St. Nicholas's Church. Its enormous evergreen branches sprawl around her, providing an excellent vantage point to spy on the proceedings without being caught. She was hoping to spot Monsieur Renault among the crowd of mourners. However, as her father leads the procession out of the small flint church, Jane counts a pitiful total of five men following him, of whom two are her brothers, James and Henry.

Her heart aches as she realises there is not one among the remaining three mourners who owns to knowing the dead woman during her lifetime. Sir John clings to his son's arm for support, but Jonathan Harcourt's eyes wander and he stumbles, catching his foot on the grass. Mr. Fitzgerald is stiff, his chiseled features betraying no hint of emotion. Jane recalls the would-be clergyman's air of preternatural calm at the discovery of Madame Renault's slain corpse. Was that because he already knew what he would find, having left his victim bleeding to death while he dressed for the ball? As a member of the Rivers party, he was close at hand when the milliner was murdered, but what reason could he have for wanting her dead?

The pallbearers carry the coffin to a corner of the graveyard, stopping short of where the parish poor are buried. Madame Renault has her own box at least. She will not face the indignity of being plunged into the cold earth wrapped only in her shroud. Jane's father utters a few words at the graveside, but she is too far away to hear them.

Perhaps Sir John will pay for a headstone. Is it guilt or pity that motivates his generosity? Jonathan takes a handkerchief out of his breast pocket and presses it to his eyes. Sir John glares at him and Jonathan sniffs, screwing the cloth into a ball and placing it back inside his coat. Poor Jonathan has always been a sensitive soul, a quality his bullish father clearly detests. He must take after his more anxious mother, as he was forever bursting into tears at the other schoolboys' taunts. He'd even cry when Mrs. Austen returned from the henhouse with a headless chicken dangling from her side. Silly, really, since he tucked into his dinner with as much gusto as all the others.

During the ceremony, Mr. Fitzgerald bows his head low, and Jane's brothers are typically placid. As the sexton tips the first shovelful of earth onto the coffin, Sir John grabs his son's arm and hauls him toward their crested carriage. Jonathan is dazed, but his father has him scrambling across the lawn. Sir John is a deplorable brute, certainly, but does that mean he's capable of taking a life?

Mr. Fitzgerald unties his black hunter from the lich-gate. Once mounted, he taps the horse's rump sharply with his crop and sets off along the lane. Meanwhile, Mr. Austen and James retreat into the flint church. Henry saunters past Jane in the yew, coming so close that the branches bend and rustle. He disappears through the rusty iron gate in the flint wall surrounding the churchyard.

Once the mourners have gone, Jane disentangles herself from the arms of the ancient tree and crouches low. It is too late in the year for flowers, but she finds a sprig of holly with blood-red berries. The sexton rests against the handle of his shovel, mopping his brow with a dirty rag, as Jane launches the holly into the freshly dug hole. It lands with a thud on the lid of the coffin.

She grinds her teeth, silently promising Madame Renault that her short life will not be forgotten. With God as her witness, Jane swears she will find whoever wielded that bed-warming pan, rescue her brother and ensure that the murderer pays for his crime. The villain has already deprived Madame Renault and her unborn child of their lives. Jane cannot let him steal Georgy's, too.

After she has recited her prayers, and her more vengeful oath, Jane follows Henry through the gate leading directly onto the Austens' private land. She crunches along the stony path between the ramshackle outbuildings, passing the feed barn and the henhouse. As she reaches the stable block, a shadowy figure obstructs her peripheral vision.

"Argh!"

Vicelike arms grip her waist, spinning her into the air. The wrists are enclosed in mustard-yellow cuffs, attached to blood-red sleeves. Brass buttons dig into her abdomen. Jane slaps and kicks behind her with all her might—but her spirited defence only encourages her captor to swing her with greater velocity, deflecting her blows.

It is Henry, the buffoon. He must have been lying in wait.

When he finally puts her down, Jane thumps his shoulder. "You scared me half to death, you monster."

"Oh, I see." Henry laughs off her assault. "But you may sneak around, watching us?"

"You knew I was at the graveside?"

"I know your tricks." He smiles, his eyes sparkling with mischief. "I taught you most of them."

"You rogue, you gave me such a fright." But Jane is laughing too, wiping tears of mirth from her cheeks while she presses a hand to her breast, trying to ease the palpitations of her heart. "You're beastly, the most horrid brother who ever lived."

Henry puffs out his chest. "But I'm still your favourite."

"No." Jane continues to laugh. "You're not. That's a lie. I've never liked you at all."

"Then who is?"

Jane is pensive. "Neddy. For it's only prudent that one's wealthiest brother is one's favourite."

Henry grins, offering Jane his arm. "Fair enough. Neddy's my favourite, too, for exactly the same reason."

Jane hangs onto Henry's elbow, and they walk side by side down the hill toward the rectory. The sky looms ash-grey above them, and the rolling hills stretch into the horizon. Their only company is the livestock. Her mother's bantams and galinies wander the yard freely. Some of the hens walk beak to the ground, tail feathers in the air, as they scratch at the earth with oversized red claws to expose their prey. Others fluff up their feathers and dig bowl-shaped dents in the soil to bathe in.

Jane wonders what her brother made of the impersonal nature of Madame Renault's funeral service. Beneath all his bluster lies a sympathetic heart. "That was a pathetic affair, wasn't it?"

Henry rakes a hand through his cropped hair and stares at the sheep, bleating as they huddle together for warmth in the windswept field. "The poor woman. Can you imagine not having a single friend willing to stand at your graveside?"

Jane clutches her brother tighter. "I can't believe no one came. What about her family? Her husband, even?"

"We don't know what kind of life she led. If she was involved with the vagrants camping on Sir John's estate . . ."

"You don't believe that, do you?" Jane looks up at her brother's profile, gauging his reaction as she speaks. "I don't see why there's any good reason to suspect trespassers. James still hasn't found any evidence of a camp—despite what Sir John told Mr. Craven. In fact, it's making me rather suspicious as to why Sir John would put about such a story."

Henry's eyebrows shoot up. "You think Sir John killed her?"

Jane falters. She doesn't want to be reprimanded for slandering the neighbours. Or laughed at and labeled a fantasist. "Not *necessarily*, but he should be investigated alongside all others. Did you know he has a rather . . . tawdry arrangement with his housekeeper, Mrs. Twistleton?"

"Does he now? The old goat. Who did you hear that from?"

Jane lets out an exasperated sigh. It is just like Henry to be more interested in gossip than in calculating what might lie behind such a sinister deed. "Never you mind. We must scrutinise everyone who was about when Madame Renault died. I've already told you why I believe she was murdered at least an hour before the guests arrived for the ball. That leaves the Harcourts, their servants, the tradespeople and even Mr. Fitzgerald." Jane counts each of her potential suspects on her fingers. "The Rivers party arrived early, to dress . . . and Mr. Fitzgerald was rather stoic at the discovery of Madame Renault's corpse. Don't you think?"

Henry grimaces. "Yes, but I assumed that might have more to do with the horrors he must have witnessed as a child. Growing up in Jamaica cannot have been easy. Did you read that pamphlet I left you?"

"Not yet, but I will. I promise." It is noble of Henry to give everyone the benefit of the doubt, and under normal circumstances she'd admire him for it. But right now nothing is normal, and, to Jane's mind, all of her acquaintances are guilty until proven innocent. "Why don't you speak to him? And Sir John? See what you can find out."

Henry slouches, placing his hands on his hips. "Jane, if either of them killed the woman, they're hardly likely to admit it to me. Are they?"

"But you have to. *I* can't—it would be improper for me to approach them. Do gentlemen not share confidences, as ladies do? Invite them both for a game of cards, and see what you can get out of them." It is frustrating for Jane to conduct her investigation at arm's length. How is she to make any progress when propriety governs her so closely she must hide under the branches of a tree?

Henry throws up his hands to the sky. "Mr. Fitzgerald, perhaps. But with Sir John's rules of play, I'd go bankrupt before he so much as shared the name of his tailor."

"He's a bettor?"

"Aren't all gentlemen?" Henry scoffs.

"You're not."

"I would be, if only I could afford it."

"Hmm . . ." First whoring, and now high-stakes gambling. Sir John's "good name" is flimsier by the day. "What about Jonathan Harcourt? You two were friends at school."

"Hardly."

It's true. The Austen boys are a rowdy bunch—always restless to be outside competing with each other at some violent sport. Whereas Jonathan would sit and paint quietly for hours once he'd finished his lessons. He probably had more in common with Cassandra or Jane than with any of their brothers.

Henry rubs his jaw. There is more than half a day's stubble running along it. His commanding officer would reprimand such unkemptness, but Henry's standards have slipped since he came home. "It's much more likely she was killed by one of her associates from Basingstoke. She was a milliner, after all."

"And?" Jane stares up at him, waiting for an explanation.

Henry raises an eyebrow. "They have a . . . certain reputation."

"Do they? As what?" Jane is flummoxed. She's never known Henry to look down his nose at the merchant classes before.

"Well, as ladies of . . ." he purses his lips, spots of colour blotching his tight cheeks, ". . . negotiable morality?"

"But Aunt Phila was a milliner, wasn't she? Before she went out to India and married Mr. Hancock?"

Henry smirks. "Yes, I believe she was."

Jane punches him, harder this time, on his upper arm. "You don't think that's why Madame Renault was at the ball, do you? For a rendezvous with a gentleman?"

"I've no idea why she was there. I wish I'd never opened that closet." Henry rubs his arm and narrows his eyes at his sister.

"Ah, yes . . . You never did explain to me what you were planning to do in there with the amiable Mrs. Chute."

Henry gives Jane his best hangdog look. "Come! I'll race you back to the house." He breaks into a run. The chickens cluck and scatter in lopsided flight.

Jane chases him. "You're the one with negotiable morality . . . Lieutenant Austen!"

CHAPTER EIGHT

A post-chaise rolls along the lane between Steventon and Popham. Jane, who has been standing at the window surveying the horizon for its arrival since breakfast, dashes out of the rectory, closely followed by both of her brothers. Eliza pokes her upper body out of the side of the carriage. She is a mother and widow in her mid-thirties, but to look at her girlish face and pert figure, you'd think she was a newlywed of five-and-twenty. Eliza's star shines so brightly, other women sometimes resent being dulled by comparison. Not Jane; she's always happy to bask in her cousin's glow.

"My Steventon darlings, how good it is to see you!" Eliza cries, as the driver slows the carriage to a halt. Her miniature three-cornered hat, with its black lace veil, is set at such a jaunty angle, it somehow belies the sobriety of her half-mourning dress.

Already, Jane wishes she could spirit Eliza away from the rest of her family and consult her in private about her investigation into Madame Renault's murder, but also about Tom. He hasn't called since he walked Jane home from Ashe, but he left her a note—concealed behind a loose flint in the wall of St. Nicholas's Church and marked for a "Miss Weston." Ever since Jane had had the temerity to ask Tom if he wore his frightful light coat in deference to the fictional Mr. Jones, he has addressed her in writing as the sweetheart of the famous foundling, rather than "Miss Austen."

Presumably he takes this precaution to protect Jane's good name in the event of the note's discovery. Never mind that she has assured him, at length and on several occasions, there's no need for this disguise as, having loosened the flint herself with her penknife, she's certain nobody else knows of it. However, Tom is clearly enjoying the tomfoolery. Amusing as it is, Jane cannot help but reflect that her suitor really ought to have chosen a more fitting exemplar of consistency to imitate.

Madam,

Since you have made a prisoner of my heart, I beg you to withhold from passing judgement on the folly of my lips until you have lent ear to my appeal. Pardon my presumption, and my offences. In this case, the argument was spoken with the intent of being of assistance: it is only by rehearsing the accusations that will be made by others that I can shore up your defence. Be assured, however, that no misery on earth can equal mine while I think myself guilty of adding to your distress. Therefore, I bid you, fly back into these arms, which are ever open to receive you.

Your devoted servant,
Thomas Jones

Jane hasn't yet replied. As churlish as it may be for her to continue to punish Tom for his callous words after he has apologized, she can think of no other way to spur him into proving his love for her—by coming up with a better way to save Georgy and by making his intentions toward her public.

From the window of her carriage, Eliza touches her gloved fingers to her cherry-red lips and flings her arms wide, throwing her kisses indiscriminately over the Austens, all their sheep and even Squire Terry's bull, which lives in the field at the top of the lane. She wears her hair lightly powdered and pinned up at the back, letting three large curls escape to drape artfully over a shoulder. Jane wondered if, like Henry, Eliza might have dispensed with the formality of powder by now. She has always been at the forefront of fashion. Perhaps James is right, and powdered hair will remain de rigueur, despite the mounting powder tax. Jane, a simple country girl, has never bothered with it. They might be first cousins, but Eliza is a different species of woman entirely—*she* once danced in the same room as Queen Marie Antoinette.

James and Henry jostle each other to help their glamorous visitor descend. James wins and claims the privilege of holding Eliza's dainty hand as she climbs down from the post-chaise, revealing a black silk stocking and an elegant court shoe. The heel is at least two inches high, and the silver buckle sparkles with jewels.

A flushed James bows low before Eliza, while Henry reaches into the carriage and scoops up her son. At nine years of age, Hastings remains fair and pretty. His rosy cheeks have even grown quite fat. He suffers from a similar phlegmatic complaint to Georgy. Hastings, too, is prone to convulsions, especially when cutting new teeth. However, with his mother's perseverance, clever Hastings now lisps away in French and English, and has even learned his letters. What would Georgy be capable of if he had been the only child of such a devoted mother? Jane brushes away the thought. Her parents did their best.

Over tea, Mr. Austen relays the news of Georgy's predicament to an increasingly distraught Eliza while Mrs. Austen bites her handkerchief and swallows her sobs. They sit in the best parlour—the slightly larger room reserved for visitors—which looks out onto the garden. The walls are papered in yellow, adorned with small oil paintings on tin and a set of French agricultural prints. James and Henry sit at either side of their guest, on the cramped sofa, while Mr. and Mrs. Austen enjoy an armchair each. Jane perches on the arm of her father.

Eliza flaps her hands about her rouged cheeks. "Oh, this is wretched, just wretched. My poor Georgy. Please, I beg you, tell me what I can do to help? Have you engaged a lawyer?"

Jane scowls. "The law couldn't give a fig about our Georgy. We must discover what really happened to the dead woman. I've been making some discreet enquiries—"

James sighs. "Not now, Jane. Can't you see you're upsetting Eliza?"

Eliza sniffles, kohl-stained tears rolling down her pink cheeks.

Mr. Austen pats Eliza's small diamond-clad hand. "Please don't fret, dearest niece. James has indeed engaged a lawyer, and Neddy is insisting on covering the expense. A fellow in Winchester, whose son I taught here at the rectory."

Jane's shoulders drop. It's no good trying to enlist Eliza's help while the rest of her family are present. James might convince Eliza it's best left to the authorities, or Henry will make fun of Jane for attempting to solve the crime. Her mother and father are entirely deaf to Jane's pleas that they work together to unveil the truth. Without Cassandra's presence, there is no one Jane can trust to support her. Now Anna is the only one to take her seriously, staring up at Jane with doleful eyes as Jane whispers her theories on who killed Madame Renault while rocking the baby to sleep. No, Jane must bide her time and tread carefully to bring Eliza to her side.

Eliza presses a lace-trimmed handkerchief to her eyes, smearing it with black kohl. "What a tragic turn of events. I'm so sorry to have intruded at such a distressing time."

Hastings sprawls on the Turkey rug, playing peekaboo with Anna. The little girl is delighted with her new companion and giggles madly every time his excited face appears from behind his hands.

"Eliza, you are family." Mr. Austen's eyes are misty as he grips his niece's hand. It is almost four years since Eliza's mother, Jane's Aunt Phila, succumbed to the ravages of cancer of the breast. Since his sister's death, Mr. Austen's reunions with his niece have become poignant. "You are always welcome, in good times and in bad."

Eliza pouts prettily and places her hand over her uncle's.

Anna has worked herself up into such a frenzy, she hiccups. Her startled face amuses everyone.

"And poor Jonathan Harcourt and Miss Rivers, to have such a terrible scandal attached to their union." Eliza crumples her handkerchief between her hands.

Jane folds her arms across her chest. "How inconvenient of Madame Renault to be killed at Deane House, and ruin Sophy's big moment," she says. "Apparently, it was her idea to forgo a newspaper announcement and instead have Jonathan ask for her hand publicly at the ball, no doubt so she could laud her stratospheric social advancement over the rest of us. She'll be regretting it, now he's left her dangling."

Jane recalls Sophy's anxiety over Jonathan's constancy.

You'll be married by the end of the year.

But anything might happen before then, Mama.

Why is Sophy so rattled? Is it possible the milliner witnessed an indiscretion on her part and was there to extract money from Sophy for her silence? With all her solo horseback riding, Sophy has had plenty of opportunities for an ill-advised dalliance.

"Maybe she's in no rush to marry old piss-the-bed Johnny," says Henry.

"Ew." Mrs. Austen removes her sodden handkerchief. "I should hope he's grown out of that by now."

"Poor Jonathan." James shakes his head. "Remember how he'd flinch whenever Father looked at him crossly for forgetting his participles?"

Henry interlaces his fingers behind his head and stretches out his long legs, crossing them at the ankle. "He was even more afraid of you, Mother. He'd practically faint with fear any time he put his elbow through his shirt."

"Dear Jonathan." Mrs. Austen sighs. "He was an anxious boy. I expect it's his artistic temperament."

Eliza inclines her head. "And she was a French milliner, you say?"

Jane nods. "I met her when I bought a straw hat from the market in Basingstoke."

Eliza's brown eyes glitter. "May I see it?"

"Certainly." Jane leaves the room, with Eliza treading fast on her heels.

Long ago, Jane and Cassandra agreed to share a bedroom so they could keep the tiny chamber next to it as a "dressing room." Really, it is their private sitting room, but it is so small it would make a mockery of the term to call it so. Jane creaks open the door, inching past her pianoforte, piled high with music and notebooks. Eliza squeezes in behind her. The walls of the small chamber are covered with light blue white-sprigged paper, and matching blue striped curtains hang at the windows. Along the brown-carpeted floor, Cassandra has arranged her watercolours and her workboxes in a neat row.

Once inside, Eliza clutches both Jane's hands and peppers her face with kisses. "Oh, my sweet little Jane. It's so good to see you. And you've grown into such a beauty."

"Hardly." Jane winces. She glances into the mirror over her dresser. Eliza's kisses have left her dotted with rouge—as if she's caught some terrible pox.

"It's true. Just look at your graceful figure, your sweet features, your dazzling eyes . . ." Eliza cups Jane's cheek in her hand. "I don't think I've met another family as blessed in appearance, as well as temperament, as the Austens." Eliza cocks her head and raises a manicured eyebrow. "And I hear I'm not the only one who thinks so. I demand you tell me everything about your Irish friend immediately."

"How do you know about my 'Irish friend'?"

Eliza taps one side of her delicate nose. "I have my informants." Her eyes dart to the dresser, where Madame Renault's lace-trimmed hat sits proudly on its wooden stand. Jane's writing slope is open and her latest letter to Cassandra, with her list of suspects, rests on the green leather top. Behind it, the invitation to the Harcourts' ball is gathering dust. "Is this it?"

"Yes. Yes, it is." Jane holds her breath. The hat is one of the finest things Jane has ever owned, but she fears Eliza will dismiss it as provincial or outmoded. It is a simple bergère shape, but the ivory lace band, which goes over the top and falls down either side, is beautiful. It has a heavy textured pattern, featuring swirling flowers and leaves intricately joined together.

"This is very nice." Eliza lifts the hat from the stand. She balances it on one finger and gives it a twirl, examining it from all angles. "But it's not French."

Jane frowns. If Madame Renault turns out to be plain Mrs. Reynolds, and Jane has been swindled out of her twelve shillings and sixpence for an ordinary English hat, she's not sure she wants to know. "Are you certain?"

Eliza fixes Jane with a steely glare. "I know my lace, Jane."

"I didn't mean to imply—"

"And this is exquisite." Eliza runs her fingertip over the band. "Look, do you see the way the threads have been knotted together to form the design? The French no longer bother with such painstaking traditional methods. No, they buy machine-made netting and stitch the pattern onto it. This is too fine to be French. I'd say it was Brussels lace."

"Brussels?" Jane pictures the wooden globe in her father's schoolroom. Brussels was part of the Austrian Netherlands, but that was before the new French Republic had begun to annex its neighbours.

"I'd stake my fortune on it." Eliza lets the lace band run over the back of her hand like water. "Where in France did Madame Renault tell you she came from?"

Jane is silent for a moment. "I don't think she ever did. What with her accent, we just . . ."

"Assumed?" Eliza tuts. "Oh, *ma chérie*, you will have to work harder than that if you are to catch a murderer." She picks up Jane's unfinished letter to Cassandra by one corner. "This is your list of suspects, I presume?"

"Well, I wouldn't say that. But they're people I'd like to speak to in connection with my enquiries." Jane bites her lip, waiting for Eliza's rebuke; she had allowed herself to be carried away.

Instead, Eliza perches straight-backed at one end of Jane's piano stool. "Very good. Now, tell me everything you can about each of them. I want to know exactly what they stood to gain by Madame Renault's death."

"Should I not leave it to the magistrate, then? I've tried enlisting my brothers to help, but I'm afraid they think me foolish."

Eliza lifts her dainty chin. "Jane, if I had left it to my husband or the authorities to protect me from the mob raging through France, I'd quite literally have lost my head." She taps the empty space on the seat beside her. "Now, come along, we have work to do."

"Well," says Jane, "when you put it so . . ."

Eliza is right. She has proved herself right. Jane's audacious cousin fled France with her young son at the first hint of insurrection. She persuaded her husband, Captain de Feuillide, to join her in England. But when the Jacobins threw his friend, an elderly marquise, into gaol, the gallant captain insisted on returning and even attempted to bribe the Committee for Public Safety to release her. In the event, *he* was charged with treason and executed.

Eliza does not entrust her fate, or the fate of those she loves best, to the clumsy hands of others—and neither will Jane.

CHAPTER NINE

Over the next couple of days, Jane interrogates the neighbours under the guise of paying seasonal social calls with Eliza. Her task is made significantly easier by the presence of her lively cousin. Henry and James, who are perfectly content to let their sisters tramp about the countryside on foot, insist on driving Eliza everywhere in the carriage. Since the Countess de Feullide has been a regular visitor to Steventon all her life, she receives an enthusiastic welcome from the Austens' wide circle of acquaintances. There is not a respectable household in England that would refuse entry to a countess, even if her title is French. The neighbours return Jane's calls, inviting her and the convivial countess to call again until, at last, the entire neighbourhood is thrown into confusion and no one can find anyone because they are all out calling on each other.

At Kempshott Park, Jane plans to flush out whatever secrets the Rivers family may be harbouring. She's briefed her accomplice on her intended three-pronged attack: as well as questioning if the Riverses saw or heard anything out of the ordinary before the other guests arrived, and investigating potential connections between Sophy and the victim, she wants Eliza to probe into Mr. Fitzgerald's past. He is essentially a stranger. Throughout the long decade in which the Riverses have been the Austens' close neighbours, Jane had heard no mention of a "Mr. Douglas Fitzgerald" until he was introduced a few weeks ago as Captain Rivers's natural son.

The usually frosty widow, Mrs. Rivers, invites Jane and Eliza into her sitting room and insists they warm themselves before the rocaille fireplace, with its ornamental carved shells and scrollwork. The room is swamped in tassels and fringes, and every possible surface has been pasted with gold leaf. Mrs. Rivers gestures toward a mahogany sofa, inlaid with porcelain. Instead of taking a seat herself, she flaps her hands and turns in circles. "Where can Sophy have gone? She won't mean to offend."

"I'm sure she'll be along shortly." Jane smiles, especially enjoying the widow's deference to Eliza as her social superior. The Riverses are so shallow, Jane could wade through the lot of them without a single splash on her petticoat.

Mrs. Rivers does not offer refreshment, but as their previous visit was to the Terrys' farmhouse, Jane has had her fill of plum pudding and lukewarm tea.

The second eldest Rivers girl (whose name might be Claire—Jane cannot remember and it is well beyond the point in their acquaintance when it would be appropriate to ask) sits in the corner, working on a sampler. She frowns as she pulls a silk thread through the stretched linen. "I don't know, Mama. She's probably plotting with Douglas."

Mrs. Rivers flushes scarlet. "Hold your tongue, Clara! How dare you imply your sister is behaving in an unseemly manner."

Clara's—not Claire, Jane muses—mouth falls open. She looks like an unspoilt version of Sophy: she has the same fair hair and orderly features, but without the practised smirk. "What? I only meant they're always whispering in corners." Clara turns to Jane and Eliza. "They imagine they're too good to associate with the rest of us."

Mrs. Rivers flicks a hand dismissively. "Hush, child. Enough of your nonsense."

The door to the drawing room opens and Mr. Fitzgerald saunters through, a small black leatherbound book tucked under his arm. He already dresses as a clergyman, albeit one with a far better class of tailor than either Mr. Austen or James can afford. His black coat and breeches are hewn from the finest wool, and exquisitely tailored close to the shape of his long, muscular frame.

"Miss Austen. What a pleasure." He bows from the waist.

"Mr. Fitzgerald. This is my cousin, the Countess de Feullide. I don't believe you've been introduced?"

He bows again, even more gracefully. "Your ladyship."

Eliza swivels in her seat, presenting Mr. Fitzgerald with the best view of her pert figure. She has explained to Jane how, in profile, a lady may arch her back and lift her bosom to appear at her best advantage. Now Eliza sweeps her gaze up and down Mr. Fitzgerald's Corinthian physique, practically caressing him with her lashes.

Jane presses her lips together. If Mr. Fitzgerald is not careful, the coquettish countess will take her fan from her reticule and signal coded messages of seduction.

Mrs. Rivers drums her fingers on the mahogany sideboard. "Clara, go and find your sister."

Clara huffs, tossing her embroidery into the sewing basket at her feet. "What's the point? If she's not with *him*, she'll be in the stables, reeking of fresh horse, as usual."

"Clara!" Mrs. Rivers screams.

Clara thumbs her nose at her mother as she leaves. Mr. Fitzgerald tries not to betray his amusement as he takes a seat at a bureau in the far corner of the room.

Eliza tosses a bouncy curl over her shoulder. "Tell me, Mr. Fitzgerald, what brings you into Hampshire?"

"Family, ma'am. The same as you, I expect?"

Eliza smiles politely, baring small white teeth. "And will you be staying long?"

Mr. Fitzgerald opens his book, licking a finger and turning the pages. "That all depends. I'm hoping to be ordained in the new year."

"You're to become a clergyman. How delightful." Eliza grazes Jane's ankle with the pointed toe of her shoe. "Don't you think so, Jane?"

Given she's fortunate enough to live in an age of such rapid philosophical and scientific advancement, Jane cannot understand why so many young men, her own brothers included, settle for becoming clergymen. But she was raised to display superior manners so instead of replying, "Not really," she simpers, asking, "What was it that made you choose the Church?"

"If a man must have a profession, I'd say shepherding souls is the best one to have." Mr. Fitzgerald's features remain impassive. "Wouldn't you?"

"And must you?" asks Eliza, getting straight to the point. "Have a profession, that is?"

"Indeed I must, ma'am. My father is very generous, but there's a limit as to how far he can go in making me independent."

"Ridiculous." Mrs. Rivers hovers behind her nephew. "What is the point in a man amassing such a fortune if he can't pass it on to his son?" She places a hand on his shoulder. "He has not given up yet, Douglas. You know that. Your mother won't allow him a moment's peace until the matter of your inheritance is settled. We'll show those interfering cronies at the assembly. How dare they tell Captain Rivers what to do with his own money!"

Mr. Fitzgerald finds his place in the book, holding it open with both hands. "Please, Aunt. May we leave that matter to discuss in private?"

"There's a legal impediment to you inheriting?" Jane asks. Is it because Mr. Fitzgerald is Captain Rivers's illegitimate son? That can't be right: there can be no entail on new money.

"There are some . . . obstacles to overcome, yes." Mr. Fitzgerald squares his jaw. "So, it's best I prepare to make my own way. My father has a connection in Cumberland who might have a living to offer, but nothing is settled yet. In truth, I'd like to tour more before I settle down."

Mrs. Rivers yawns. "Show the ladies your watercolours, Douglas."

"Please, Aunt. Don't force me."

"Really, Douglas. Why do you think Captain Rivers spent all that money on your education? If you want to be accepted as a gentleman, you must make yourself more agreeable."

Jane's toes curl in her walking boots. Mrs. Rivers really is as gauche as they come.

"Well, I'm sorry to disappoint my father, but I feel it's only fair you write to him immediately and let him know my artistic skills are severely lacking. You should advise him to withdraw me from society immediately, to avoid further embarrassment. Why, Clara thought my mountain vista was a plate of gelato."

"*Gelato*?" asks Jane.

Mr. Fitzgerald shoots her a lopsided smile. "Excuse me, it's the Italian word for *ice cream*."

"Oh, from the Latin for *frost*." Jane giggles, almost as girlishly as Eliza, but in her mind she's tracing her fingers over her father's wooden globe. Given that most of Europe is closed to travelers, due to France's aggressive attempt to expand its empire, what route could Mr. Fitzgerald have taken to reach the Italian Alps? And might it have involved passing through Brussels?

"Exactly." Mr. Fitzgerald holds up his book. "May I read you a poem instead?"

Jane squints, trying to read the gold lettering from across the room. If she's not mistaken, it is *The Poems of William Cowper.* Jane hasn't had the opportunity to enjoy much Cowper, as her father's collection of the poet's verse is usually tucked into Henry's kitbag rather than sitting idle on the bookcase. She resolves to seek out Mrs. Martin's copy, from her circulating library, so that she can judge for herself whether the poet is worthy of these young men's adulation.

"If you must." Mrs. Rivers slumps, as she studies the elaborate cornicing that decorates the plasterwork ceiling.

Mr. Fitzgerald clears his throat.

"'Twas in the glad season of Spring,
Asleep at the dawn of the day,
I dream'd what I cannot but sing—"

The door flies open and Sophy bursts into the room. "Miss Austen, your ladyship. I'm so sorry to have kept you waiting." Her cheeks are so full of colour, they rival Eliza's rouged features.

Mrs. Rivers glares at her. "What's happened to your hair?"

Sophy puts a hand to her coiffure. "Nothing."

"It's flat." Mrs. Rivers narrows her eyes. "You had it styled only this morning. I know you like that French woman, with all her scandalous stories, but the curls should hold for longer than a few hours."

Sophy turns her back on her mother, gazing out of the window across the park. "I went for a quick ride. That's all. My hat must have smothered it."

Mrs. Rivers crosses the room, fluffing up Sophy's ringlets. "Again? Sophy, must you? I assured Lady Harcourt you'd given up horseback riding. It's such a dangerous pastime, and hardly fit for a wife and mother. You'll have to desist once you're married, so you may as well get used to it now."

Jane taps her ring finger. This is the perfect moment for Eliza to bring up the ball. Eliza coughs into her fist. "Congratulations, Miss Rivers. I hear wedding bells are imminent."

Sophy's head snaps toward the ladies on the sofa. "Thank you, ma'am. But the sentiment is premature. No announcement has been made."

Mrs. Rivers lets out a heavy sigh. "Must you stand on ceremony, dear? Everyone knows the betrothal is forthcoming."

Sophy balls her hands into fists. "These things are important, Mama. We wouldn't want to embarrass the Harcourts. I'm not engaged, and you do me no favours by implying I am."

"I heard about the terrible incident at Deane House." Eliza launches into their well-rehearsed routine. "It must have been dreadful for you."

"Awful. Just awful." Sophy touches the ivory cameo on her necklace, as she shakes out her newly fluffed ringlets.

"Jane and I were wondering if you might have seen or heard anything in the hours before the ball began."

Sophy grips her cameo tighter. "Anything?"

"Anything that might help explain what happened," says Jane. "You dressed there, I believe. Were you upstairs all afternoon?"

Sophy's eyes flicker toward Mr. Fitzgerald. He dips his chin and fixes his eyes on the pages of his book. "Why, yes. We all were."

"Was anyone with you? Your maid, perhaps?" asks Jane.

"What is this?" Sophy sneers. "Have you come to wish us a merry Christmas or to accuse me of murder?"

"Nothing of the sort." Jane recoils. "I wondered if you might have witnessed something that could prove useful, that's all. Or if you recognized the woman?"

"Recognized her? From where?"

"Basingstoke covered market."

"B-Basingstoke?" Sophie erupts into laughter, as if Jane has made a fantastic joke. Which is not unusual, except this time, Jane cannot imagine what she's said that's so funny. "Basingstoke? Did you hear that, Mama?" Mrs. Rivers snorts. Even Mr. Fitzgerald appears to be struggling to maintain his composure. "Oh, Jane. You are droll. I'm sure *you* pick up some very pretty little things in Basingstoke covered market, but it's hardly Lock's of Mayfair, is it?" Sophy tosses her head. "Oh, no. We furnish our wardrobes in town at the start of every season."

Jane's cheeks blaze brighter than the sun. Beside her, even Eliza is speechless. At this point, in all of their previous interviews, the conversation has turned toward expressing sympathy for the dead woman. A few ladies admitted to recognizing her description, and one of buying a cap. No one else has shamed Jane for her paltry dress allowance or for her parochial taste in fashion.

But Sophy's grey eyes are hard as ever. She is unmoved by Madame Renault's fate. Mrs. Rivers sidles up beside her daughter. "Why don't you play something for us, dear?"

"Certainly, Mama." Sophy swishes triumphantly over to the pianoforte. "What would you like? One of Cramer's études?" She interlaces her fingers, stretching her hands over her head. The fitted sleeves of her gown reveal the shape of her arms. The many hours she spends on horseback have given her an unusually toned figure for a young lady. If Madame Renault went to Deane House with the intention of soliciting money from Sophy, perhaps because she had witnessed something that might cause the Harcourts to regret their association with the Riverses, then Sophy certainly possesses the strength and the vindictive temperament necessary to have wielded the bed-warming pan that killed the milliner.

Sophy lifts the lid of the instrument, narrowing her eyes at Jane. "Or I could play one of those *Irish* melodies you're so taken with, Jane?"

Jane's face burns with the intensity of an iron rod held to a furnace. From the supercilious expression on Sophy's face, it's evident she's referring to Jane's infatuation with Tom. She must have witnessed the pair walking together while she was out riding. Or one of Jane's brothers might have let word slip.

No. It will have been Mary Lloyd who set the rumour going. Jane has tried to keep private the extent of her feelings for Tom, even from her friends and family. The only person she told explicitly was Cassandra, who is in Kintbury with Martha Lloyd, who writes to her sister, Mary, every day.

With a sinking feeling, Jane realises she didn't explicitly ask Cassandra to keep her confidence. In fact, she had been rather boastful of Tom's attentions. The secret will have remained safe only until the return of the post.

But Sophy is clever, for it is a double-smart—a reference to an earlier humiliation, too. At Jonathan's welcome-home party, Jane had entertained the company with several tunes from *Moore's Irish Melodies*. Afterward, Sophy praised Jane's playing generously. Too generously. Jane is confident in her abilities, but also conscious of her limitations as a mostly self-taught musician. When Sophy finished lauding Jane's "charmingly simple style," she flexed her fingers, sat down and promptly delivered her own virtuoso performance. It was mortifying.

No wonder Jonathan had never looked twice at Jane, not that she'd have wanted him to. Not after she'd met Tom, anyway. But Jane must have seemed a complete simpleton, while Sophy fooled everyone into believing she was generous and accomplished. She sits in silence, fiddling with her gloves and fuming, while Sophy plays the familiar arrangement with her irritatingly light touch and lightning-fast fingers.

Afterward, Jane makes her excuses, then she and Eliza scuttle out of the manor house. They will lick their wounds in private and formulate a new plan to interrogate Sophy and Mr. Fitzgerald. But if Sophy's vehement protestation of her innocence was aimed at removing herself from Jane's enquiries, she has failed. Now, more than ever, Jane would like to see her rival carted away in disgrace.

2. To Cassandra Austen

Steventon, Wednesday, 23 December 1795

My dear Cassandra,

Yes, I'm very sorry but you really must keep Christmas with the Fowles as planned. Take heart that you can do nothing more to further Georgy's cause in Steventon than you can in Kintbury. At this moment, your place is with your fiancé. Heaven only knows how long it will take young Mr. Fowle to reach St. Lucia and back. He could be away for as long as two years, and you're sure to regret passing up any opportunity to dawdle away the hours with your sweetheart once he's gone. Besides which, with all the to-ing and fro-ing to Winchester to check on dear Georgy, my father says he can't actually spare anyone to fetch you. Now, who could have killed the hapless milliner, Madame Renault? With the assistance of our visiting countess, I have expanded my list of potential suspects to include:

– Sophy Rivers (could the milliner have been hiding one of smug Sophy's secrets under her many hats? Sophy swears they never met, but perhaps she doth protest too much?)

Accuse me of basing my suspicions on no more than my distaste for our neighbour, if you must—but I think I have a good eye for a murderess. Your prayers are greatly appreciated, but my mother bids you also spy on Mrs. Fowle's kitchen maid and obtain the receipt for her fish sauce. The one in port wine, with the anchovies. Apparently, it's Georgy's favourite, and keeps very well in a bottle.

Everybody's love,
J.A.

PS When you have finished reading, fold this letter into a boat and set it sailing down the river Kennet.

Miss Austen,
The Rev. Mr. Fowle's,
Kintbury,
Newbury.

CHAPTER TEN

On Christmas Eve, James drives Jane and Eliza to Basingstoke in the carriage. He offers to accompany the ladies, to carry their purchases and escort them from shop to shop, but Eliza persuades James that it would be polite for him to call on the town's clergy while she and Jane perform their "feminine errands." For, by now, Jane has exhausted all of the Austens' respectable contacts and is still no clearer as to who murdered the milliner. And it would be impossible for her to begin investigating the seedier side of Madame Renault's life if her most protective elder brother was present to police her every move.

Despite Henry's warnings about what she might find, it is time for Jane to examine exactly how Madame Renault made her living. As Sophy pointed out, in such humiliating terms, Basingstoke is hardly the metropolis. And Madame Renault was a merchant—she lived her life in the public sphere. It is unfathomable to Jane why none of her people has come forward. If she has to question everyone in the small town, until she finds someone who will own to knowing the milliner in life, she will.

Once they have thrown off James, the ladies head straight to the covered marketplace. They show the stallholders Madame Renault's lace trimming, asking if they recognize it or remember its maker. Unfortunately, Basingstoke is packed with seasonal shoppers buying trinkets to give to their loved ones, and dried fruit and nuts to add to their festive feasts. The merchants do not appreciate being distracted from their bustling trade. Most claim not to recognize the distinctive lace and never to have heard of a "Madame Renault."

Tired of being ignored and jostled by the crowds, Jane takes a break from her detective work to visit the haberdashery. As the haberdasher wraps her and Eliza's purchases, Jane tries again and strikes lucky. The surly shopgirl imparts that, although she's by no means sure, she believes "the girl with the foreign-looking hats" rents a room at the Angel Inn.

Jane knows the inn well. Or, rather, she knows the assembly rooms on the first floor of the labyrinthine, timber-framed building. Once a month the Angel Inn hosts a ball and Jane is rarely absent. In fact, she is planning to attend the next on New Year's Eve. She hopes the iridescent gold ribbon she's bought to adorn her pale gown will attract Tom's attention, in the same way a lit candle draws a moth. Eliza, in her infinite wisdom about matters of the heart, claims the intimacy of dancing can prompt a gentleman to complete the final steps of courtship.

Several days have now passed since Jane last saw Tom, but she has accepted his groveling apology with the good grace of the angelic Miss Weston, and their furtive correspondence has resumed with alacrity. His words still sting, but Jane knows she has a sore spot where Georgy is concerned. All of the Austen children do. The schoolboys at Steventon Rectory, and even the village children, learned the hard way that none of Jane's brothers would tolerate any mockery of Georgy. Even Cassandra has been known to pick up a stone to defend him. If only a bloody nose or a thrashing with a branch could save him now.

Jane clutches Eliza's arm tightly as they follow Mr. Toke, the proprietor of the Angel Inn, to a quiet corner of the common dining area on the ground floor. It is a grubbier side of the inn, which Jane has never encountered before. Working men crowd the dining room, dipping bread into wooden bowls and drinking ale from pewter tankards. The smell of unwashed bodies and overboiled cabbage is stifling.

Happily, Eliza is characteristically unperturbed. "So, was she here? The milliner? It's imperative we find out where she was lodging."

Mr. Toke wipes his hands on his stained apron. "Yes, she was here. Came in August, harvest time. Sharp woman. A bit above herself but never any trouble. When she disappeared, we assumed she'd done a moonlight flit. But then Sir John sent a message and, well . . ." He exhales loudly. "My wife was most aggrieved to hear how she died."

Jane holds her basket tight to her chest. "So were we."

Mr. Toke scratches his silver whiskers. "We were about to hold a sale of her belongings to settle her debt. Not that a few old bobbins would have covered it. But Sir John said to send him the invoice. He's a good 'un, the baronet. My most esteemed patron, he is."

Again, Sir John's generosity nettles Jane. First, he pays for the dead woman's funeral. Now he promises to clear her debts. There must be a reason for such philanthropy. Sir John is a responsible landlord, but not a lavish one. She can point to several cottages on the Deane estate whose roofs are in dire need of rethatching.

And no one has mentioned Monsieur Renault.

Perhaps Madame Renault's husband was not lodging with his wife in Basingstoke. He may be somewhere else, working or taking care of their children while she was sending him money from the sale of her hats or other, less reputable, employment. What if Monsieur Renault does not know his wife is dead?

Will Jane be the one to impart the dreadful news to Madame Renault's loved ones?

"Can her husband not pay?" Jane asks.

Mr. Toke frowns. "No husband. Told us she was a widow. Expect he was killed in the fighting. So much of it about, on the Continent."

Jane lowers her eyes to the scuffed floorboards. The war in Europe has claimed Eliza's husband, a proportion of her fortune, and her son's inheritance. Jane is heartsick every time she thinks of Frank and Charles patrolling the Caribbean Sea for enemy vessels.

She counts back the months. If Madame Renault was five months pregnant when she died, she must have conceived in July. The baby could have been her husband's, imparted before he died and she sought refuge in England.

Or Monsieur Renault might already have been dead—or never existed at all. Perhaps Madame Renault was drawn to Basingstoke by the father of her illegitimate baby.

Jane shuffles closer to Mr. Toke, and out of the way of a passing serving girl holding a wooden tray laden with overspilling tankards of ale. She fears her cloak will retain the odour of the inn for days. "Does that mean her personal effects are still here?"

Mr. Toke wipes a greasy hand through his thinning grey hair. "Yes, miss. None of the maids will go in her room. Silly doves think it's haunted. I'm waiting on Sir John to settle. Then we'll pack her things and send them on."

Jane's breath hitches in her throat. "May we look at them?"

Mr. Toke wrinkles his tired features. "I shouldn't really, miss." Without speaking, Eliza dips into her pocket and extracts a handful of silver coins. They chink as she drops them into

Mr. Toke's outstretched palm. He tucks the money into the front of his apron, digging into the furthest reaches of the flap. "Well, just for a few moments. What harm can it do?"

The ladies follow Mr. Toke into the courtyard, up a dark, narrow staircase, along a cramped passageway, then down a few steps until they come to a series of doors. The confusing jumble of entranceways and differing levels is oddly reminiscent of Steventon Rectory.

Mr. Toke takes a bunch of keys and unlocks a garret overlooking the stables. It is about the same size as Jane's dressing room but appears much larger on account of it being so sparsely furnished. Flaking pink plaster covers the walls. A wooden crucifix hangs from a nail above a bed. A neat, patchwork quilt is stretched smooth over the mattress and tucked in at the corners.

Eliza motions to a worktable, where a short length of ivory lace is pinned to a wooden board attached to a pillow. "I told you, Brussels lace."

The unfinished edge of the floral design dissolves into two dozen cotton threads. Each length of cotton is wound tightly around a separate wooden bobbin. It is clearly highly skilled work. Every few inches of the intricate pattern must have taken Madame Renault hours to complete. How beautiful the lace would have been, if only she'd had the chance to finish it.

Eliza picks up a straw hat from a small pile. It is similar to Jane's, but without the lace, it is dull and ordinary. "She must have bought these already made and added the lace herself."

Jane steps into the centre of the room and slowly spins around, looking at every corner. "So, she wasn't a milliner, then." Jane is overwhelmed by the dizzying sensation of being closer to Madame Renault than she's ever been, yet farther away at the same time.

Eliza balances the hat back on the pile. "Not a milliner, and not French."

Mr. Toke stands in the doorway. "Have you seen enough, ladies? I got customers need feeding and watering."

Jane spots a familiar book on the bedside table, next to a rosary made up in plain dark wooden beads. It is the very copy of William Cowper's poems that she resolved to borrow from the circulating library. She opens it to find a plate glued to the inside. "This isn't hers. It's from Mrs. Martin's collection. Shall we return it for you?"

"I should wait for Sir John to see to it."

"You could. But I doubt he'd thank you for running up a fine." Jane holds up the open book, displaying Mrs. Martin's distinctive library plate.

"Take it. Now, you'd best be off."

Jane slips it into her basket. "How often does Sir John call in here?" Mr. Toke's tongue lolls in his mouth. "You said he was your most esteemed patron. How often does he frequent your establishment, and what does he do here?"

"Oh, fairly often. He and his gentlemen friends rent a private room for card nights. Or if there's a cockfight happening, he'll drop in and have a flutter."

So, Henry was right. Sir John is a gambler. All gentlemen gamble, but only one with difficulty in controlling his urges would place a wager on something as uncouth as a cockfight.

Jane eyes the single bed. *Milliners do have a certain reputation. . . .* Technically, Madame Renault wasn't a milliner—but she was a woman living on the fringes of society, and she must have been desperate for money. At five months, she'd feel the quickening and know she was due to give birth, hampering her ability to support herself. Could her circumstances have made her desperate enough to try to extract money from Sir John? Either through blackmail, or via an arrangement with the licentious baronet? "Does he keep a room here?"

Mr. Toke takes a step backward. "Excuse me, young lady?"

Eliza clamps a hand over her mouth.

Jane presses on: "Or does he keep a room for someone else here, perhaps?"

"What are you insinuating, miss?"

Jane's cheeks burn, but she must know the truth. "I'm not insinuating anything. I wondered, with Sir John being such a regular customer and Madame Renault lodging here, if they might have bumped into one another. Were they acquainted, do you know?"

Mr. Toke yanks the door wide open, and steps behind Jane, driving her toward it. "I don't like the tone of your enquiry. I'll have you know this is a respectable establishment. We earn our crust entertaining the finest families in the county, not turning a blind eye to vice. Now, it's time for me to escort you off my premises."

Back on the windy street, Jane's face is on fire as she flicks through the book. How dare Mr. Toke accuse *her* of impropriety? She has no time for delicacy; it's been nearly a fortnight since the murder and neither she nor the magistrate is any closer to discovering the culprit. There must be a reason why Sir John is taking on Madame Renault's obligations, and Jane is willing to bet the contents of her pocketbook that it's a nefarious one.

Eliza watches Jane leaf through the pages as she buttons her lavender redingote to her throat and shivers with the cold. Wedged toward the back of the small volume, a thin slip of paper looks as if it was used as a bookmark.

Jane squints at the strange marks and numbers. "Oh, it's just a receipt."

Beneath her veil, Eliza arches an eyebrow. "Did you think it would be a love note from Sir John?"

Jane tucks the receipt into her pocket, resolving to study it properly. Rows of numbers have always taken her longer to decipher than lines of words. "Why else is he paying for everything? And when did Madame Renault's husband die? I told you, Dame Culham said she was expecting, about five months along." Deep in Jane's gut lies a suspicion that identifying the father of Madame Renault's baby will unlock the mystery of her death.

Eliza slides her arm through Jane's. "Oh, *ma chérie*. One does not *always* need a husband to make a child."

Jane tuts. She was raised on a farm, not in a nunnery. "I know that, Eliza. I may not be as worldly as you, but I'm not a complete dolt."

CHAPTER ELEVEN

Mrs. Martin operates her circulating library from her husband's apothecary shop in London Road. Jane was most excited when she launched her enterprise as, by the time she'd reached the age of fifteen, she'd read everything she cared to in her father's collection. She hopes Madame Renault's reading record might reveal more of her life and possibly her death, although Jane hates to ponder what impression of her own character someone might gain if they could see the scandalous volumes she's borrowed from Mrs. Martin over the years.

A bell tinkles as Jane pushes open the glazed door. The shop smells sweet and peppery, fresh and musty all at once. Mahogany shelves and glass-fronted cabinets line the walls from floor to ceiling. The majority are crammed with glass jars, oddly shaped bottles and earthenware bowls containing every known remedy in the modern world. Mrs. Martin's collection of books takes up only part of one wall.

Unlike a private library, the bindings do not match, the books of an irregular size and in various states of repair. Some are new, bound in glossy black leather with gold lettering on the spine, while others are cracked along the edge or held together between two marbled boards with twine.

Mr. Austen and Mrs. Lefroy built their libraries by selecting texts that promised to enlighten the mind or contain at least some literary merit, while Mrs. Martin's only consideration is popularity, which makes for a wonderfully varied selection. Every time Jane peruses the shelves, she fantasizes about discreetly placing *Lady Susan* among the volumes. Anonymously, of course; she has no wish to become a pariah. Copied out in her best handwriting, in one of her smart vellum notebooks, the work would not seem so completely out of place among Mrs. Martin's hotchpotch collection. Then Jane would linger at the apothecary's counter, and listen to the first truly unbiased reviews of her writing. Would the good people of Basingstoke be appalled or enthralled by her heroine's antics? Perhaps both.

"Oh, Miss Austen," Mrs. Martin calls, from behind the counter. She is a genial woman in her late thirties and wears a lacy pinafore over her red spotted gown. "All my Mrs. Radcliffes are out, I'm afraid. Can I interest you in something else?"

"I'm not borrowing today, Mrs. Martin, but returning. We found this in the deceased Madame Renault's room at the Angel Inn." Jane holds up the book. "On second thought, may I keep it for a while?"

"So, it *was* that poor girl who was killed." Mrs. Martin presses her lips together and shakes her head. Her dark blond ringlets bob around her temples. "We read about it in the *Hampshire Chronicle*. Still, I prayed it wasn't true. She spelled her name differently, you see."

Mrs. Martin dips below the counter. She reappears, hefting a thick leatherbound ledger onto the surface. She flips open the book and turns it sideways so Jane and Eliza can see it, too. On the first page is a long list of all her subscribers. Jane reads her own name, along with Cassandra's and Mr. Austen's near the top. Despite claiming to have no time for reading, Mrs. Austen devours everything her husband and daughters borrow as soon as they leave it unguarded.

Jane holds her breath as Mrs. Martin runs her finger down the list, until she reaches the last entry written in fresh black ink: *Madame Zoë Renard*. "I must have misheard." Jane berates herself for her carelessness. Her misspelling might well be the reason none of Madame Renard's acquaintances attended her funeral. "She said her name only once. And with her accent—she placed such emphasis on the first syllable."

"And she was bludgeoned to death, they say? Out at Deane House? Oh, my, whatever is the world coming to?"

Jane's heart aches as Mrs. Martin dips her quill into an ink-pot and strikes through Madame Renard's name.

"Small lady, yes?" Jane places her hand flat beside her cheek-bone. "She made lace and decorated hats. Occasionally hired a stall in the marketplace. In fact, I think that's one of her caps you're wearing."

"Yes, it is." The back of Mrs. Martin's hair is tucked into a neat cotton cap, trimmed with a pretty frill. The heavy lace design of swirling flowers and leaves is similar to the pattern on Jane's hat. "We came to an agreement that would pay her subscription."

"We're meant to be running a business, not furnishing you with the latest French fashions," Mr. Martin calls, through the open door of his laboratory at the rear of the shop. He stands at a pair of scales, carefully balancing lead weights on one side and a fine light brown powder on the other. The apothecary is at least a decade older than his wife, but similarly well kept, with neatly trimmed side-whiskers and a starched apron over his linen shirt and waistcoat.

Mrs. Martin crosses her arms and rests them on the counter. "Never mind him. Go on. What were you saying?"

Eliza removes her glove to run a finger along the lace of Mrs. Martin's cap. "It's Brussels lace. Finer than French, even. Did Madame Renard ever mention where she came from?"

Mrs. Martin straightens. "No, she was very quiet. Kept herself to herself. She liked to borrow poetry. Nothing trashy. None of those Gothic novels you're so fond of, Miss Austen." The librarian flicks through the ledger to the page reserved for the borrowing records of "Miss J. Austen," so she may add the details of her latest loan. Above it, Jane's crimes against refined taste in literature are listed in date order.

Despite herself, Jane cringes. She shouldn't be embarrassed in front of Eliza. As well as listening rapturously to snatches of *Lady Susan*, her cousin has spent the evenings regaling the family with the half-remembered plots of the scandalous novels she read in France. There is one in particular, entitled *Hazardous Encounters*, or similar, which Jane would love to read. "May we see what Madame Renard borrowed?"

Mrs. Martin thumbs through the pages to the back of her ledger. "She hadn't time to borrow much. She only joined in October, after I met her in the market. We began talking over the cap, you see. I couldn't understand her thick accent. She told me she was still learning English and could read it better than she could speak. So, I mentioned the collection and, the next thing I knew, we were making an arrangement. She liked the Cowper. Renewed it several times."

Jane's body grows heavy at the image of Madame Renard reading poetry alone in her garret bedroom. But she couldn't have been entirely alone; someone sired her baby. Mr. Toke would not give up the name of her lover, but perhaps Mrs. Martin had spotted her out and about with a man. "Did you know any of her acquaintances?"

Mrs. Martin blinks. "I never saw her walk out with anyone."

"No one? Not even a gentleman friend, perhaps?"

"She wasn't that type. She came across as very well-bred. She was so hoity-toity, I wondered if she might be one of those unfortunate émigrés. A lady fallen on hard times perhaps. The dancing instructor at the Angel Inn is an exiled French count and there's a very good hairdresser who claims to be a *ci-devant vicomtesse*, whatever that means."

Jane grasps Eliza's forearm. If Captain de Feullide hadn't been such a gallant, he would have been included among those "unfortunate émigrés." Instead, he was guillotined and thrown into a mass grave. "I should buy some magnesia for my mother while we're here."

Eliza's arm trembles, but her voice is perfectly composed. "And I'll take a tincture of liquorice and comfrey for my little boy. He suffers terribly with phlegmatic complaints."

Mr. Martin makes up their order. While he's busy, Mrs. Martin takes out a publisher's catalogue and solicits Jane's advice as to which "trashy" volumes might prove the most popular with her subscribers. Among the titles listed, Jane is most excited to spot *Camilla*, a forthcoming publication by "the author of *Evelina*." She resolves to persuade her father to subscribe to this himself, so they may have their own copy for the rectory library. She'd rather not rely solely on Mrs. Martin—lest she is forced to wait for Mary Lloyd to finish with the book before she can read it. With *Camilla*, Jane advises Mrs. Martin to purchase an intriguing new novel in three volumes called *The Monk*, which purports to be utterly terrifying. They search for an English translation of *Hazardous Encounters*, but it is not listed by that title, and Eliza cannot recall the name of the author. Mr. Martin comes through to the shop and places two small glass jars on the counter, next to an oversized pestle and mortar.

Eliza smiles sweetly. "Did Madame Renard purchase anything from you, sir?"

"Not that I recall." Mr. Martin inserts a cork stopper into the neck of each jar and seals it with wax. Eliza's innocent smile could be drawn on with rouge. "Nothing for her ladies' complaints? A tincture to restore her courses, perhaps?" Jane admires the way her cousin keeps her face completely impassive, as she asks the apothecary if Madame Renard had requested pennyroyal, or some other herb which might bring on a miscarriage.

Mr. Martin furrows his brow. "Definitely not. That I wouldn't be likely to forget."

The bell tinkles as the shop door opens, cutting short Eliza's interrogation of the apothecary. The ladies move along the counter, allowing Mr. Martin to deal with the new arrival. "Another bottle of black drop? I gave you one only a few days ago."

Jane catches the customer's profile out of the corner of her eye. She's an attractive woman, with ash-blond hair and strikingly dark brows. The woman answers, in a honeyed voice, "If you'd be so good, sir."

It is then that Jane turns and recognizes her as Mrs. Twistleton. She is wearing her usual black silk dress beneath an emerald-green velvet cape.

"Tell your master he must be careful with this tincture." Mr. Martin wags a finger. "It can be harmful in large quantities."

"It's neither my place nor yours, sir, to question the baronet. And if you cannot complete the order, I'll advise Sir John to take his custom elsewhere." She lifts her chin, staring Mr. Martin in the eye.

The apothecary holds her gaze for a few uncomfortable moments, then releases an audible sigh and returns to his laboratory.

The corners of Mrs. Twistleton's full mouth turn upward slightly. "I'll take some rose water, too," she calls to Mrs. Martin, barely glancing at her.

Mrs. Martin sniffs. "Rose? Are you sure you don't mean lily of the valley? That's Lady Harcourt's usual scent."

"How observant of you," says Mrs. Twistleton. "The rose water is for me. You can put it on a separate account. It might be my mistress's favourite, but I find lily of the valley rather old-fashioned and cloying. Don't you?"

From the curl of Mrs. Martin's upper lip as she makes up the housekeeper's order, Jane guesses the librarian is party to Mrs. Twistleton's chequered history. It must be galling for her and her husband to defer to such a woman in her new cloak of respectability. Once Mrs. Twistleton has retrieved her purchases and tucked them into her basket, she turns to the door. Jane lunges for it, grabbing the handle and yanking it open before she gets there.

Mrs. Twistleton flinches. "Miss Austen, I didn't see you there."

"Mrs. Twistleton." Jane keeps to the housekeeper's side as she slinks out onto the street. "Have you a few moments? I wanted to ask you about the terrible incident at the ball. I'm trying to identify the murderer."

Without slowing, Mrs. Twistleton pulls her hood over her head. It is trimmed with fox fur. "I must hurry. I need to catch the coach back to Deane. Besides, you know full well who the murderer is. You heard Mr. Craven. It was one of the vagabonds trespassing on the estate."

"But have you seen any evidence of a camp? The search party found no trace of anyone sleeping in the open." Jane hurries to remain in step. "I know he claimed not to, but do you think there's any possibility Sir John recognized the dead woman?"

Mrs. Twistleton rears back, her features twisting. "Look here, Miss Austen! None of us at Deane House knew that poor wretch. I know your brother's been arrested for thieving her necklace, and it's only natural you'll want to shift the blame, but that doesn't give you the right to make spurious accusations. Don't you dare go about questioning Sir John's word. Do you hear me? Now, good day to you. I've a coach to catch." The housekeeper spins around and marches away, while Jane remains rooted to the spot.

Eliza's hurried footsteps catch up with her. "Where did you run off to? We were questioning the librarian."

Jane fixes her eyes on Mrs. Twistleton's cloaked figure, receding along the crowded street. "That's Sir John's housekeeper *and* his kept woman."

Eliza's eyes widen. "You suppose she knows something?"

"She does! She hissed and spat at me, like a feral cat, when I asked if Sir John might have recognized Madame Renard."

"Might she have grown jealous over her paramour? Viewed Madame Renard as a rival, perhaps?"

"I don't know . . ." Jane doesn't want to be naïve, but Mrs. Martin's description of Madame Renard as a proud young woman chimes with her own impression of the unfortunate lacemaker. Try as she might, she can't imagine Madame Renard abandoning herself to Sir John. Rather than dallying with him, perhaps she witnessed some indiscretion between him and his housekeeper. Despite Mr. Toke's protestations, the Angel Inn would be a convenient venue for the baronet to indulge in other vices, as well as gambling. "Maybe it was merely her appearance at Deane House that led to her death. Mrs. Twistleton might have panicked, thinking Madame Renard was about to report her true character to her new mistress. Lady Harcourt would have been sure to dismiss her, leaving her with neither a keeper nor a livelihood."

Eliza's rouged lips form a perfect O. "You consider that the housekeeper might have killed Madame Renard?"

Jane shudders. The trip to Basingstoke has left her feeling in need of a good scrub in a hot bath. "I don't know. I'm trying to imagine all the possible versions of Madame Renard's story and examine them beside the facts to see which fits. Sir John and Mrs. Twistleton could even have done it together. Perhaps Madame Renard found out about their arrangement, and was so desperate for money, she tried to blackmail them. But they decided it would be more expedient to remove her."

Eliza puts a hand to her throat. "Goodness, Jane. The way your mind works, I'm glad *I* wasn't here when it happened. Heaven only knows which of my private affairs you might have unearthed to accuse me of damnable dealings."

Jane tucks her arm into her cousin's, bending toward Eliza so that their foreheads touch. "As well you should be. I wouldn't put anything past *you*, Countess."

CHAPTER TWELVE

On Christmas Day, Mr. Austen leads the service at St. Nicholas's Church. He steps into the pulpit, breathes on his spectacles and rubs the lenses clean with his handkerchief before reading aloud from the tattered copy of the same sermon he's given on Christmas Day for the last ten years. Nobody minds. What it lacks in originality, it makes up for in brevity. The small crowd of weavers, spinners and farm labourers who have gathered to worship in the damp and draughty church are as eager to get back to their firesides and enjoy their rare day of leisure as Jane is. That being said, she feels wretched that they are celebrating the festive season while Georgy is trapped in gaol for a crime he didn't commit.

To assuage her conscience, she's been trying to decode the receipt she found in Zoë Renard's library book in the hope it might help prove her brother's innocence. Unfortunately, the writing is so bent over and blotted, she can make neither head nor tail of it. She resolves to share it with her family. Perhaps one of them will be able to read it. After all, they are experts at deciphering her untidy scrawl—even when she writes in haste, chasing a story as it unfolds in her imagination.

The family gather in the best parlour as Sally prepares the yuletide feast. Jane and Mrs. Austen wear their finest pale morning gowns with pink Persian petticoats. Eliza is in ash grey, which is only a shade or two more sombre. The waistlines of her cousin's dresses are creeping ever closer to her bust. Jane is not sure what to make of this new fashion, except the shorter stays Eliza wears underneath look much more comfortable than Jane's own undergarments.

First thing that morning, Henry had traveled to Winchester and back to visit Georgy. He does his best now to assure the family that Georgy remains in good spirits and is being diligently attended to by the prison governor and his wife. In the interest of objectivity, Jane had previously asked Henry and James to obtain a more specific alibi from Jack while they were at the gaol. Alarmingly, they are yet to report back with a credible answer.

Jane gnaws her thumbnail. "Did you ask Jack where he was on the night Madame Renard was murdered?"

James, sitting beside Eliza on the sofa, scratches his cheek. "He can't vouch for Georgy, as he was running errands."

Jane cannot quite bring herself to consider her childhood playmate as a potential suspect, but she is growing mildly concerned that, even when pressed, Jack continues to be so vague. "I know that, but can anyone vouch for *him*?"

Sally, who is carrying a tray of lemon sorbets to the table, loses her footing. She manages to catch most of the glasses, but two slip through her fingers and crash onto the floor. Mrs. Austen rushes to her assistance before Anna can reach the broken glass.

James gapes. "Jane, you're not accusing Jack Smith of having anything to do with Madame Renard's death. Are you?"

"No . . . not explicitly." Jane's cheeks grow warm. "But it is only fair for everyone to account for themselves on the evening she was killed. If only so that they can be ruled out of the investigation."

"Now, Jane," says Henry, leaning against the mantel for warmth, "Jack's looked after Georgy all his life. The man is as wretched about this as any of us."

Jane's family stare at her as if she's sprouted an extra head, with horns. It goes against her instincts to question Jack, but examining all possibilities is the only way she knows to find the truth. "I'm only saying—"

Mr. Austen's voice is uncharacteristically stern. "Jane, Jack Smith had nothing to do with what happened to that woman. He's a good, Christian soul."

"I know that—"

Mrs. Austen interjects, after handing Sally a dustpan and brush. "He's one of the family. And he never grumbles about his responsibilities. Why, he never even made a fuss when your father refused to advance his wages."

"He asked for a loan?" Jane's stomach plummets. No, it's not possible. Even if he was desperate for money, Jack wouldn't sink so low as to take something that didn't belong to him.

Mrs. Austen nods. "Yes, to buy the Terrys' sow. But we explained we couldn't afford to. Not with Christmas coming up, and your sister's wedding to plan for."

"When was this, Papa?"

Mr. Austen rubs his eyes. "I don't know. A couple of days before the ball, I suppose."

Her parents are too blind to see it, but Jack has been trying to strike out on his own for years. What if he had tired of "waiting for something to turn up" and decided to take what he wanted instead?

If he *was* the thief, it would explain how Georgy had come by the necklace—he would have found it among Jack's things. But for Jack to commit murder? Surely not. Unless none of it was planned, and he had worked himself into a blind panic. As her mother suggested, the culprit could have been an opportunist who meant only to rob, not kill his victim. "Then, do you not see why it's especially important to establish where he was that night?"

"Jane!" Mr. Austen snaps, making Jane and her mother jump. "I'll not have you flinging accusations about. You are playing a dangerous game."

Jane is winded. She has always taken her father's support for granted. "I'm simply investigating all possibilities."

"That's as may be, but you cannot point the finger at our friends," says Mr. Austen. "We don't want to see another innocent man condemned. If you're not careful, you'll start a witch hunt."

"Of course. I'm sorry, Father. I promise I'll say no more about it." Jane lowers her head, clawing at the skirts of her gown. She would not have to nag her brothers to interrogate Jack if she could question him herself. "Please will you take me with you, the next time you visit Georgy?"

The room is silent, apart from Anna's babble and Hastings's footsteps as he chases the toddler around the sofa. It is humiliating for Jane to have to rely on others to ferry her about. It means asking their implicit approval for every move she makes.

Sophy has the right idea on that score. It must be liberating to be such a confident horsewoman, coming and going as she pleases. The knowledge that she'll come into her own enormous fortune one day cannot hurt either.

James looks to Mr. Austen. "Well, Father?"

Mr. Austen covers his eyes with a palm. "As long as she promises to behave herself, she may go."

Jane gives a curt nod. She wants to see Georgy, of course she does. But if the others lack the stomach to ask Jack where he was that night, she must. It is painful to imagine that he might have been involved in any way with the death of Madame Renard, but until she knows the truth, Jane will not rule anyone out of her investigation.

Over the next hour, vivacious Eliza coaxes the Austens into levity by strumming her guitar. All the family join in with "Nos Galan." The countess performs a duet with James and Henry in turn. Jane has never seen her brothers so keen to display their musical talent. They have reasonable singing voices, but neither possesses the dedication required to become a truly accomplished musician. Especially Henry, who, in his youth, was known to alternate his instrument with each passing week.

The paper chain that Jane and Hastings constructed together reaches all the way across the beam over the dining-room table, despite Anna's attempts to destroy their handiwork. Of course, the decorations are not as plentiful or as artistic as those Cassandra would have produced if she were there. If Eliza and Hastings weren't present, Jane doubts she would have mustered the energy to bother at all. With Georgy in gaol, a Puritans' Christmas would have felt more fitting.

Jane wonders how Tom is enjoying his Christmas feast with the Lefroys. It's bound to be a more civilized affair, with more meat and fewer interruptions from the children. Is that the standard of dining he will expect once they are married? Or will he be happy with the Austens' more chaotic style of domestic harmony?

"Which turkey are we having?" she asks, as soon as grace has been said. Sally serves all the different dishes at once, becoming more red-faced and closer to tears with every plate she sets beside Jane's centrepiece of evergreens. Really, with the extra guests, they should have hired another girl to assist her for the day.

Mrs. Austen settles Anna and Hastings at the far end of the table, away from the fireplace. "The black spotted one."

"Oh, I rather liked her," says Henry. He sits opposite Jane and the other women, on a bench with James.

Mr. Austen takes his seat at the head of the table. "I expect you'll like her all the more with some plum pudding and melted butter sauce."

"True." Henry heaps his plate with roast beef, potatoes and, most unwisely, in Jane's opinion, Jerusalem artichokes.

Mr. Austen hands the carving knife and fork to his eldest son. "Would you mind, James?"

James jumps at the opportunity to stand in as paterfamilias. "Certainly, Father." He unbuttons his cuffs and rolls up his sleeves to below the elbow. Eliza passes round the jug of white wine. Everyone fills their glasses, while James huffs and puffs over the enormous boiled bird.

"Would you like me to grab my sabre and lend you a hand?" Henry teases.

A sheen of sweat forms on James's brow. "No, no. I shan't let the old girl get the better of me."

Jane turns to her mother, who is busy filling the children's plates. "Have you ever taken black drop?"

Mrs. Austen tucks a napkin under Hastings's chin. "Yes, I have. Terribly strong. It brought on the most frightful expulsions—"

Jane holds up her hand. "That's quite enough information, thank you."

Mrs. Austen twists to face the adults and takes a sip of her wine. "Why? Were you thinking of trying some for your restlessness?"

"Certainly not. You know how laudanum addles my brain, and I can't stand to be stupefied. We bumped into the Harcourts' housekeeper in town. Apparently, they consume rather a lot of it up at Deane House."

Mrs. Austen places her wineglass on the table. "I expect it's for Lady Harcourt's nerves. Caroline's always been of a rather . . ." she purses her lips, ". . . nervous disposition. And the disaster at the ball couldn't have helped."

Jane shakes out a napkin and settles it over her lap. "How much would one take, typically, to steady one's nerves?"

"I don't know. A drop or two a day?"

"So, she shouldn't be getting through a whole bottle in less than a week? Not on her own?"

Henry swallows, emptying his mouth. "Good heavens! I'd say that's enough to put down an entire squadron."

"And you were wrong in your licentious insinuations about Madame Renard, as we now know her. We have it on good authority, from Mrs. Martin, that she was a respectable woman. She wasn't even a milliner, as it turns out. She was a lacemaker, unless lacemakers happen to have a similar reputation to milliners . . ."

Henry gulps. His Adam's apple brushes against his starched linen cravat.

"What do you mean, 'a similar reputation'?" Eliza sets down her glass.

"No." Henry coughs, cheeks reddening. "As far as I know, lacemakers tend to be sweet old ladies."

Eliza leans across the table. "But what kind of reputation do milliners have?"

"Go on, Henry." James smirks. "You're a man of the world. Pray tell us, what kind of reputation do milliners have?"

Henry takes a swig of his wine and shoots a pointed look at Jane.

Mrs. Austen straightens. "This is hardly a conversation we should be having in front of the children."

Jane glances at Anna and Hastings. "They're not listening." At the far end of the table, Anna is cramming squashed-up bits of potato messily into her mouth. She squeezes them so tight, the fluffy white insides poke through the gaps between her fingers. Hastings is wearing his best short jacket and his golden curls rest on his shoulders. He sits motionless with his hands in his lap as he stares into the middle distance. It's as if his body is present, but his mind is entirely elsewhere.

"Hastings . . . Hastings?" Eliza shoots up, sending her chair crashing to the floor behind her.

The little boy's eyes roll into the back of his head, leaving just the white. He twitches. His body spasms and jerks and his head is thrown up and down. As his torso stiffens, he knocks himself against the table. Eliza scrambles to him. But Henry, who is closer, catches Hastings as he's propelled into the air by the frenetic movements of his own body. Hastings thrashes wildly as Henry gently guides him onto the Turkey rug.

"Quick." Mrs. Austen grabs a silver spoon. "Get this into his mouth, before he bites his tongue."

Eliza bares her teeth. "Get away, you'll choke him!" In an instant, Jane's cousin is transformed into a tigress protecting her cub. Eliza drops to her knees, as Hastings twitches, his little body jerking across the floor.

Mr. Austen removes the napkin tucked into his collar. "Oh, good God." James stares, open-mouthed. He is frozen, with the carving knife and fork still in his hands. Anna turns scarlet and wails. Mrs. Austen scoops her out of her high chair. She presses the baby to her chest, squeezes her eyes closed and turns her face away from the scene.

"Ssh." Henry holds up his palms as he crouches beside Eliza and Hastings. "It's all right, it's all right."

But it's not all right. Eliza's eyes are red and brimming with tears. Foam bubbles on Hastings's lips as he shakes and shudders. Henry grabs a velvet cushion from the sofa. Eliza screams in fright as he slides it beneath her son's thrashing head. "Shush . . . I'm not going to touch him, I promise. It'll pass. We'll just wait for it to pass."

And Jane remembers. The hardest thing about having Georgy at the rectory was not his wandering or that he couldn't speak. All of that was fine, really. It was the sudden seizures. They came out of nowhere, like the invisible hand of a malicious demon taking hold of her brother and shaking him with such terrible violence. There was nothing her parents could do to prevent the fits, and no way of stopping them once they took hold. Just like Hastings, Georgy's body became racked with jerks and spasms. Jane would stare in horror until finally the movement became less fraught and the gaps between the twitches lengthened. Then Georgy would lie in their mother's arms, shivering with his hair slick against his forehead. He'd be exhausted and confused for days afterward.

Every time it happened, Jane fretted they lost a little more of Georgy. His comprehension lessened, and the sounds he'd learned to form on his tongue would retreat. Until, she feared, one day they'd lose him altogether.

With an aching lump in her throat, Jane stands. She creeps closer to Eliza, kneels on the carpet and grasps her cousin's hand. Eliza slumps to her side, resting her head on Jane's shoulder.

Jane smooths her other hand over Eliza's fashionable coiffure. She reaches inside her pocket for her handkerchief and presses it to Eliza's cheek.

"Hush now, Henry's right," Jane whispers, as Eliza chokes on her sobs. "It'll pass, it always does. We just have to let it pass."

Later, when the full moon hangs in the night sky and there are wisps of snow in the air, Jane takes a dish of tea up to the back bedroom where Eliza and Hastings are staying. She knocks gently on the door and nudges it open with her foot. Hastings is fast asleep in the centre of the double bed. His cheeks are red, and his lips form a perfect bow. At peace and by candlelight, he is the picture of a cherub. Eliza sits in a nearby chair, staring at her son with a face as colourful and swollen as her carmine-pink quilted dressing-gown. She has brushed out her hair and left it loose around her shoulders. Without the powder, it is close to Jane's chestnut shade.

"I brought you some tea." Jane holds out the dish.

Eliza tries to smile, but it does not reach her dark eyes. She lifts her trembling hands and Jane gives her the dish, keeping her hands over Eliza's until it is safely balanced on her knee.

"How is he?" Jane draws a three-legged stool from the dressing table and sits beside her cousin.

Eliza's long dark eyelashes throw shadows over her drawn cheeks. "Oh, you know. He'll be fine, he just needs to rest."

"Does it happen often?"

"Not so much, any more. Every time I pray it's the last. Then, with any slight cold, or a change in the weather . . ." Eliza's voice cracks. She places her fist in her mouth. "I tried to make sure he was wrapped up for the journey, but it must have been the draughty carriage ride that brought it on. What about Georgy?"

Jane lowers her gaze. It is the question she never dares to ask her father or her brothers when they return from Winchester. The prospect of Georgy suffering one of his seizures on a dirty gaol floor in front of strangers is too much to bear. "I don't think so. Not any more."

"That's good." Eliza takes a sip of her tea. "Ew . . . How much sugar did you put in this?"

Jane winces. "We've just got a new loaf, and Mother said it would be good for the shock. Perhaps I should have found you some black drop instead."

Eliza manages a small but genuine smile.

Jane tucks a hand inside her skirts and rustles around until she finds the receipt in her pocket. She takes it out, placing it on her lap and smoothing the wrinkles in the delicate paper. "I've been puzzling over this. The handwriting is difficult but I can make out the date and something about two pieces of jewelry." She hands it to Eliza, hoping to distract her cousin from her seemingly never-ending maternal concerns.

Eliza sets her tea on the dresser, holding the receipt beneath the dim glow of a tallow candle.

30 August 1795

One lady's chain, 18ct, pearl	*36 gns*
One gent's ring w intaglio	*14 gns*
Total:	*50 gns*

3 November 1795
Received

"You see? It sounds like her chain, which Georgy somehow got hold of, and a gentleman's ring. Possibly a signet ring, inset with an engraved gemstone. But it makes no sense. Why would

Zoë Renard be laying out money on jewels and at the same time working her fingers to the bone and living so humbly at the Angel Inn? And look at the price she paid." Jane taps her finger to the column of figures on the right-hand side of the note. "You haven't seen the chain, but it's exquisite. With all the pearls, I'd have thought it would be worth several hundreds of pounds. But here it says she paid only fifty guineas for the ring *and* the necklace."

Eliza turns it over to examine the other side, holding the worn paper dangerously close to the flame as she peers at the writing. "I don't think it's a receipt. Not from a jeweler, anyway."

Jane tilts her head, trying to follow Eliza's reasoning by studying her features. "But it must be. I've read it a hundred times and those are the only words I can make out."

"But look . . . there's another date, the third of November. And is that 'Received' written underneath?"

"Yes. That must be the date she received the jewelry after placing her order in August. Perhaps the amount is so low because it was merely a deposit."

"No. It's as you said. She wasn't the kind of woman who would have had either the means or the inclination to buy baubles." Eliza brandishes the note in the air. Her dark eyes glitter. "This isn't from a jeweler, it's from a *pawnbroker*. Madame Renard must have pawned the necklace and the ring in August, possibly to pay her rent at the Angel Inn."

"Oh . . ." Jane falters. She's never owned any jewelry, let alone pawned it. "Is that why the amount is so low?"

Eliza sucks the air through her teeth. "When people are desperate, they'll take whatever they are offered. I wonder how she found the money to retrieve the items. She couldn't have sold that many hats.

"Why wouldn't she sell the jewelry in the first place? She'd have got much more for it, wouldn't she?"

Eliza shrugs. "The pieces might have had sentimental value to her. The necklace could have been an heirloom."

"Yes. And the ring . . ." Jane stands, bouncing on the balls of her feet. "The ring, Eliza. It's a gentleman's ring! A love token, given to her by someone she cared deeply about—the father of her unborn baby, surely."

Eliza holds a finger to her lips, glancing toward her dozing son.

"Forgive me," Jane whispers. "She must have come to Basingstoke looking for him, because she was desperate and carrying his child. And when she found him, *he* gave her the money to reclaim the jewels."

Eliza folds the note, passing it back to Jane. "You're getting carried away."

A sudden lightness floods Jane's frame. It's the same euphoric feeling as when a new story unravels in her mind. "The ring is a clue. An actual clue—the first decent one we've stumbled across. No one has mentioned a ring."

"Because the thief made away with it?"

"That's possible, yes. Although, if Mother is right, and the thief discarded the necklace because it linked him to the murder, why keep the ring? An intaglio would be even more identifiable." Jane puts her hands to her waist and rocks back and forth, deliberating all the different turns this story might take. "It would have made more sense to sell the necklace and plant the ring on Georgy."

"You're correct there. Gold and pearls are easy enough to pass on."

"What if the thief didn't steal the ring—because Madame Renard wasn't wearing it when the incident took place? Suppose the gentleman who gave it to her took it back after she reclaimed it from the pawnbrokers."

"Why would he have done that?"

"Because he didn't want anyone to know about their connection. Did he? Otherwise he'd have come forward to mourn her." Jane shivers at the recollection of Madame Renard's lonely funeral. "It's one thing for an English gentleman to give a woman he met on the Continent his ring, quite another for her to show it off here. Basingstoke is a small town. There are only so many established families in Hampshire. A signet ring, especially one bearing a heraldic crest, might be recognized."

"It could be in her room, with the rest of her possessions."

"No. Don't you remember? Mr. Toke said the sale of her belongings wouldn't be enough to cover her rent. The owner *must* have taken it back to protect his identity."

Eliza lays the back of her hand on Hastings's forehead. "Well done, *ma chérie*. But please don't wake my boy. He needs his rest."

Jane's chest is about to explode. She wants to rampage through the county, checking the fingers of every gentleman she passes. "But don't you see? If we find the ring, we find her secret lover. And who better to lead us to her murderer?"

3. To Cassandra Austen

Steventon, Thursday, 31 December 1795

My dearest Cassandra,

If you bid me look after my mother one more time, I shall accuse you of thinking me unsympathetic, which cannot be true. As you know, I am a most astute observer of my mother's complaints and list them to you—indexed by humour and physiology—in every other letter. Back to the more pressing business of who killed the hapless ~~milliner~~ lacemaker, Madame ~~Renault~~ Renard. It was not a fancy man—she was no milliner, in either sense of the word. But my net of suspicion is further cast over:

- Jack Smith (was it a robbery gone awry? I doubt it—but Mother says we shouldn't rule out an opportunist thief, and I must admit it's the simplest explanation for why Georgy had the necklace.)

As to why she was here at all, could she have been lured to Basingstoke by the owner of a gold signet ring with an engraved gemstone? And, if so, how am I to find the gentleman in question?

I have no idea how my cornflower-blue gown ended up in your valise instead of my own. It must have been Sally's lackadaisical approach to maintaining our wardrobes. I shall reprimand her most severely on your account. Tear this letter into strips, dip it in flour and water and use it to fashion yourself a papier-mâché bridal hat. I'm confident you will look most fetching in it.

Your affectionate sister,
J.A.

Miss Austen,
Rev. Mr. Fowle's,
Kintbury,
Newbury.

CHAPTER THIRTEEN

The year ends on a crisp, cold, clear night. The moon is waning, moving into its last quarter, but bright enough to light the country lanes as Henry and James take turns driving to the New Year's Eve celebration at the assembly rooms of the Angel Inn. Jane sits inside the carriage with Eliza, staring out of the window at the flickering stars strewn across the inky sky. Deep inside, she longs to connect with the blithe young woman she was before she followed her brother into the Harcourts' laundry closet and discovered Zoë Renard's slain corpse. But how can she, when dear Georgy remains in such peril?

Instead, she'll soothe her conscience by doing what she can to save her brother—dancing with as many gentlemen as possible, while discreetly examining their hands for a signet ring inset with an engraved gemstone. If she can find the father of Madame Renard's unborn baby, he may be able to point to her murderer. Only once her mission is accomplished will she allow herself to stand up with Tom so many times that the tongues of the local gossips will wag faster than the tails of James's hunting hounds when they see her coming with a juicy bone.

Eliza dabbed rouge on Jane's lips and cheeks, and some of her French perfume behind her ears and along her throat. Her cousin rouged Sally's face, too, making the maid smile for the first time since Christmas Day. Sally has been so down in the mouth that Jane fears, in her distress over Georgy, her mother has neglected to give the maid her due. It is customary to tip household servants on Boxing Day so Sally is bound to have been expecting something. Jane resolves to rectify the matter as soon as she can, if only to encourage Sally to be more careful when dressing Jane's hair.

Without Cassandra to govern her sense of propriety, Sally made freer than ever with the curling papers and tongs. The maid's touch is far from gentle, and her sense of style is anything but restrained. As a result, Jane's hair is arranged so that her chestnut locks explode into a profusion of corkscrews from the crown of her head. Eliza wrapped her cousin's new iridescent gold ribbon around Jane's pale gown so many times that the waistline appears raised in the new style. In all her finery, Jane looks as well as she ever has and, she fears, can ever expect to.

Once they arrive in the courtyard of the Angel Inn, James opens the carriage door and lunges for Eliza's hand, leaving Jane to take Henry's arm as she steps down from the carriage. She doesn't mind: Henry is resplendent in his military uniform, and Jane would rather be seen on the arm of a soldier, or even a sailor, than a clergyman any day of the week—particularly on a Sunday.

From the way in which Henry stiffens and glares at Eliza's back as she sashays up the twisting staircase and into the assembly rooms on their elder brother's arm, Jane senses he is not as satisfied as she is with their pairing. Eliza's shot silk overdress shimmers every time she moves her hips. Henry's always been besotted with her. Now that he's in his mid-twenties, the ten-year age gap has closed between them, and Jane senses something dangerously carnal in his obsession with their glamorous cousin.

By lamplight, the Angel Inn appears an altogether more reputable establishment. Jane bounces on tiptoe as they enter, scanning the crowd for Tom. The ballroom is a large, square space, with plenty of room for dancing, and the air is thick with the fragrance of cloves and citrus. Around the edge of the parquet floor, the finest families in the county convene at circular tables covered with white linen and set with silver-plate candelabra entwined with ivy. The families—Chutes, Digweeds and Terrys—are covered with powder, jewels and a light sheen of perspiration. On a raised dais, beneath a gleaming brass chandelier, the orchestra plays a waltz. Tonight, there is a full complement of strings, woodwinds and brass, as well as a grand pianoforte. The beauty of the music revives Jane's spirits.

From across the polished dance floor, Jane's friend Alethea extends a long white arm, encased in its ivory glove, and waves frantically. She has piled her auburn hair high on her head and ornamented her coiffure with ostrich feathers. Her father, Mr. Bigg-Wither, has acquired one of the best tables, close to a window for ventilation and overlooking the dancing. Alethea jiggles in her seat. Her ears and throat sparkle with diamonds, and the muslin of her ethereal gown shimmers with gold and silver sequin swirls. She smiles widely as Jane and her party approach, patting the empty seat next to her and batting her eyelashes at Henry and James in turn. "Oh good, you brought some men."

James colours, clinging to Eliza's arm for dear life, while Henry releases Jane to hover at Eliza's elbow. It seems both of her brothers would use their cousin as a shield against any predatory females. They need not worry about Alethea. Jane is quite sure her friend's interest in James and Henry extends only to the parameters of the dance floor. There are around a hundred people present. Discounting those who are not disposed to dance, there should be enough to form at least twenty-five couples.

Jane takes out her pencil and pocketbook to note her observations. "Don't be so gauche, Alethea. You'll frighten the delicate things off."

Alethea pouts. "But we're too many ladies, as usual. Look around, we outnumber them by two to one. Mark me, Jane, we'll be taking turns to play the gentleman by the end of the night."

Jane continues to survey the crowd for Tom. Usually, she'd be content to pair up with Alethea, but tonight she longs to be engaged—in both senses of the word.

"What are you doing?" James gestures toward Jane's pocketbook. "Must you really?"

"I'm making notes for my next project. There's a ballroom scene. As an artist draws from life, cannot a writer?" It is only a half-lie. Jane is plotting her next story, and she wants to include a spectacular ball at the assembly rooms in Bath. Having yet to visit the city, she'll need to draw inspiration from her present surroundings. But she's also making a list of all the gentlemen present so that she may put a simple tick or cross against their name to indicate if they wear a signet ring inset with an intaglio.

James flicks his fingers at the book. "It's unseemly. People will think you're writing about them. Put it away."

Jane's face burns as she's censured by her elder brother in public. "I'll make a list of dances instead. Will that satisfy you? Alethea, you can begin with James. You'll find him much improved. We've been putting him through his paces."

Alethea titters. "How clever! I must start training my little brother."

"And when the Lloyds get here"—Jane points her pencil at James—"you must stand up twice with Mary."

"Why should Mary get two?" Alethea slips her hand into the crook of James's arm, tugging him toward the dance floor.

Eliza quickly withdraws her grip on James's opposite arm, leaving him without a post to cling to.

Jane tilts her head. "Who else will dance with Mary, given her affliction?"

"Don't be so vicious, Jane." James frowns. "Her pox scars are really not so bad."

Jane shrugs. "It's you who's picking at her pockmarks. I was referring to her character." James turns beetroot as the rest of the party snigger behind their hands. "Now, Henry—"

Henry wraps an arm around Eliza's waist, steering her away. "Don't you dare. I can make my own arrangements." Henry and Eliza are both so devastatingly attractive that they cut a swathe through the milieu as they move toward the refreshments table, where a scrubbed-up Mr. Toke is serving punch from a giant silver tureen. Jane can only pray that, in her finery, the innkeeper will not recognize her as the impudent young lady he previously expelled from his premises.

A polite cough sounds at her shoulder. She spins around, and comes face to face with a familiar ivory coat. The scent of bergamot and spice cologne fills her nostrils, and her cheeks flush. Tom greets her with mock solemnity, bowing low and pressing her hand to his lips. His mouth scorches her skin through the fine kid leather of her glove. "Miss Austen. May I have the honour of claiming the first dance?"

"You may, sir." Jane curtsies as he refuses to release his tight grip on her hand.

Tom's lips curl into a sensuous smile. "And the next?" He steals the breath from Jane's lungs. "And very possibly the one after that?"

She giggles as he leads her onto the dance floor. With every step, Jane is mounting the clouds.

Jonathan Harcourt and Sophy Rivers, whose engagement has now been formally announced in *The Times*, are invited to open the ball. They stand, opposing each other at the top of the line of dancers. Sophy's eyes are as hard as flint above the brilliance of her diamond choker, and her grim countenance bears little resemblance to the portrait on her cameo necklace. She should be in her element, dancing a jig over her ascent to the *haut ton*. Instead she looks more like a warrior, forming a shield-wall with her ostrich-feather fan. Jonathan stares at her slippers. He is a lanky fellow, taller than both of his parents. He stoops a little, as if apologizing for his unexpected height.

Eliza and Henry are next in line. They blush and steal glances at each other, looking to all the world more like young lovers than the officially betrothed couple. Jane wonders if her cousin realises the effect she has on Henry. If she does, it is most irresponsible of her to continue to taunt him.

James and Alethea join them, with a giddy Mary Lloyd, who has somehow hooked the dashing Mr. Fitzgerald as her partner. The musicians take up their bows to play an allemande. Jonathan and Sophy set the steps and, one by one, all the couples repeat them, until the entire line is alive with motion.

For that one dance, Jane's world is light, bright and sparkling. Her insides thrum with pleasure as Tom takes her hand and spins her into a pirouette. He leans in so close, his hot breath tickles her neck. "A pity there's no glasshouse here."

"Why, Mr. Lefroy, what are you suggesting?" Jane colours at the memory of their reckless flirtation at the Harcourts' ball, before the evening turned sour. In front of the whole Steventon party, Tom had had the audacity to ask if she was chilly and compared her to a "hothouse flower left out in the cold." A spark fired up inside her when he followed his comment with a subtle wink. That was how Jane had known he would be waiting for her in the glasshouse. He is the only man she has ever met who can keep pace with her lively wit.

"I'm suggesting that I'd give anything to be alone with you right now," he murmurs. Jane cannot tear her eyes from his soft lips. "Meet me tomorrow. In front of your father's church at noon?"

She nods as her pulse quickens. Tomorrow is New Year's Day. What could be more appropriate for settling the details of one's new life? If not for the tight swaddling of her gold sash, Jane's heart would burst from her chest.

The music stops. Jane and Tom break apart, a beat later than the other couples. They beam at each other across the line as they applaud the musicians.

Tom clasps her hand and leads her to the refreshment table. Jane lingers at the edge of the throng, out of Mr. Toke's direct line of sight. Sir John elbows past, carrying two goblets of punch. He wears no ring, but his fingers may be too swollen for one. Jane retrieves her pocketbook and marks a cross next to his name.

The baronet makes a beeline for his wife, who sits beside Mrs. Rivers on a sofa near the orchestra. Lady Harcourt is ramrod straight as she trains her hawklike eyes on her son, standing silently before a sombre Sophy. Sir John rests one goblet on a pedestal beside a vase of dried flowers and retrieves a small glass vial from his waistcoat, slipping a few drops into the other goblet.

Jane's insides tighten as he hands the corrupted punch to his wife. She cannot be sure, but she thinks Lady Harcourt does not know her husband has laced her drink with what Jane strongly suspects is black drop. When Tom hands Jane her punch, she gulps it to settle the disquiet growing in her stomach. The mixture is potent, but Jane gives the brandy and rum little time to register on her tongue. Too many people are nearby for her to share with Tom her observation of Sir John's furtive act.

Again on the dance floor, Jane cuts into the line of dancers so she is standing shoulder to shoulder with Sophy Rivers. She rises on tiptoe and leans close to whisper in Tom's ear. "Can you grant me a favour?"

He leans back on his heels. "Depends . . ."

"Can we interrupt?" She jerks her head toward Sophy and Jonathan.

The opportunity to quiz Jonathan on his father's odd behaviour is too good to miss, and the punch has made Jane bold. She'll try probing Jonathan as to the ugly dynamic between his parents, to develop a greater understanding of the baronet's character. Sir John's casual disregard of his wife's health, and his propensity for welcoming fallen women into his home, not to mention bed, are making Jane suspicious as to what else he might be capable of. She'll have to let go of Tom eventually, if she's to carry out her objective of inspecting the fingers of every gentleman in the room—she may as well start now.

"I don't much like your favours. Not when they carry me away from you."

Jane pouts. "It's important. I'll explain why later," she adds.

Tom huffs. But instead of reaching for Jane's hand when next they meet, he takes Miss Rivers's. Jane latches on to Jonathan. He startles, then visibly softens, seeming almost relieved to be dancing with his old schoolmaster's daughter, rather than his fiancée. "Miss Austen?"

"Mr. Harcourt. Do forgive me for interjecting, but I haven't had the pleasure of standing up with you since you returned from your grand tour." Jane smiles sweetly as they face each other, waiting for their turn to dance again.

"No. But I enjoyed your recital at my coming-home party," Jonathan replies, with no hint of mockery in his light blue eyes. He is dressed all in black, with only a white shirt and cravat to break up the darkness. Even his jet-black hair is scraped back into a queue, and tied with a black ribbon.

"Thank you, that's very generous. But I do realize there were far finer talents than mine on display that day. Tell me, how is your mother? She must be so pleased to have you home."

Jonathan blinks. "My mother?"

"Yes. It must be such a comfort to her to have you back, and about to be married. Are her nerves improving?"

A flicker crosses his pale lips, before he sets them into a thin line. "My mother is as well as ever, thank you. How are your family, Miss Austen? I was so sorry to hear about Georgy. I hope and pray the matter is resolved, and he is released soon."

Jane flounders, imagining her brother languishing in gaol while she is ingratiating herself with the *beau monde*. How odd that Jonathan, of all people, should be the one to remember him. "That's kind of you to say. My family are . . . bearing up." She stalls, searching for a way to interrogate him without exposing herself. She can't ask Jonathan if he's aware his father is bedding the staff, slowly poisoning his mother, and may very well have been responsible for the murder that ruined his betrothal ball. "You went to study art, didn't you? I remember the amusing caricatures you would draw when you were my father's pupil."

Jonathan extends his hands to her. It is their turn to make an arch for the other dancers to pass through. "I did, yes."

As she grasps his papery fingers, she feels the tremor in his grip. It is as if she is holding him up. "Remind me of where you went again, won't you?"

Jonathan swallows and waits for another couple to pass before answering. "Brussels."

Jane's blood roars in her ears. The scene around her blurs as she focuses intently on Jonathan. "Brussels?"

He went to the Continent to study art.

What else did Jonathan do there? Meet Madame Renard, and sire her child?

His face is slack, and his eyes are vacant. "The Royal Academy. That is, until the French invaded." The other guests duck and glide beneath their outstretched arms. Jonathan's features are so devoid of emotion that he is reminiscent of Hastings immediately before his seizure.

Jane's breath quickens. If only it were possible to see directly into another person's mind, to tell exactly what they are thinking. Jonathan's welcome-home party, when Sophy humiliated Jane at the pianoforte, was in September, meaning he could have met and impregnated Madame Renard in Brussels in July. Jane knows because she wore her cornflower-blue gown. A few weeks later, she spoiled it by getting it so filthy at the harvest festival that Sally had to soak it in lemon juice and leave it in the sun to dry, washing out the lovely bright colour.

But Jonathan isn't the kind of young man to ruin a young woman and leave her destitute. Is he? Could he really have seduced Madame Renard, giving her his ring as a promise, then abandoning her to return to England and marry his heiress? He was always such a gentle soul.

But men change. Boys grow up into entirely different creatures. And Jane knows, from the bruised and battered women who occasionally turn up at the rectory's rear door, seeking the vicar's assistance, that a man's countenance behind closed doors can be very different from the congenial face he presents in public.

She gulps for air. "I expect you miss it?"

Jonathan's tone is clipped with bitterness. "I do." Jane drops his hands and takes a step backward. The final couple passes through without their arch. Jonathan continues to stare at her, his dark eyebrows drawn tightly together. "I wish to God I'd never, ever, set foot back on these shores."

Jane flinches at the vehemence of his words. The dance ends, and the other couples make their applause before drifting away from the dance floor in pairs. Jonathan raises his hands and continues his slow, limp claps. On the smallest finger of his left hand, he is wearing a gold signet ring with a reddish-brown stone.

Jane cannot tear her eyes away from it. Jonathan was in Brussels at the time Madame Renard fell pregnant *and* he wears a ring with an intaglio. She swallows to moisten her tight throat—the discovery is threatening to strangle her. He stares at her mournfully, evidently noticing her discomposure. She stumbles backward, not ready to confront him. Jonathan, a young man she has known all her life, cannot be embroiled in Madame Renard's downfall. It is unthinkable.

CHAPTER FOURTEEN

More carriages have arrived, and the ballroom is heaving with people. Jane trembles, bumping against bodies and peering over shoulders as she pushes through the swell, searching for Tom. She needs an ally to confide in, someone who will not accuse her of letting her imagination run away with her. Jonathan did not shift about or blush with guilt—yet Jane cannot ignore his revelation about living in Brussels, or the signet ring glinting on his little finger.

The tang of fresh perspiration and tobacco smoke clogs her throat. She raises herself on tiptoe. Tom is at the far end of the room, talking to his aunt and uncle. Mrs. Lefroy wags a finger at him and her husband, George. She is clearly scolding them. Perhaps she caught them sneaking off to the card tables. Mr. Lefroy pats his wife's upper arm, calming her, while a surly Tom stands with his legs apart, hands perched on his slim hips.

Jane catches Tom's eye, but with a deft shake of his head he warns her not to intrude. Deflated, she weaves through the crush toward Mr. Toke and his punch bowl. She's so thirsty, from the exercise and the disquiet of her encounter with Jonathan, that she tips the cupful down her throat and holds it out for more—no longer caring if the landlord recognizes her. He can hardly expel her in front of the entire county. It would certainly put a dampener on the occasion if he tried.

Nearby, Eliza presses her back against a pillar and flutters a paper fan over her face. Jane stumbles toward her cousin, like a ship in search of dry land. Sir John stands too close to Eliza. His fat-bottomed periwig dangles over his great belly as he brays at her.

Eliza snaps her fan shut. "Really, sir. This is neither the time nor the place. And my uncle, Mr. Austen, deals with my business affairs."

Jane glares at Sir John and links arms with Eliza, attempting to pull her away, but the room is so packed they are hemmed by the press of bodies. Every direction in which they move is blocked by broad-backed gentlemen in swallowtail coats and ladies with towering ostrich-feathered coiffures. The baronet grumbles at the circle of gentlemen next to him without taking his eyes off Jane and her cousin.

Jane cannot share her suspicions about Jonathan's entanglement with Madame Renard within earshot of his father. Instead she'll garner Eliza's opinion of Tom before her beau is back by her side. "So, what did you think of him?"

"He is most impertinent." Eliza glances sideways at Sir John, opening her fan and flapping it vigorously. The paper folds are painted with a bucolic scene: a colourfully dressed shepherd and shepherdess frolic in the French countryside as Eliza cools herself.

"No, not *him*. My Irish friend." Jane tips her head toward the far end of the room, where Mrs. Lefroy has her arm in Tom's and is leading him toward the exit. Mr. George Lefroy follows, a few steps behind. They must be on their way outside for some air. The assembly rooms are increasingly hot and stuffy. Sweat gathers on Jane's top lip and her gown is damp beneath her arms. She prays the dark circles on the muslin will not show. If only Mr. Toke would have his men open some more windows.

"Oh." Eliza swivels her dark eyes across the room to where Tom is draping Mrs. Lefroy's cape over her shoulders. "Why, he's delightful. Extremely charming, and devilishly handsome. And, from what I can tell, he is perfectly enamoured with you. What do you know of his family?"

The skin on the back of Jane's neck prickles. "His family?"

"Yes." Eliza eyes Tom as she speaks. "He's very young. Not yet twenty, you say? And a lawyer just starting out in life. Without a patron, I imagine it would be many years before he could afford to take a wife. So, tell me, what you can, of his family?"

"Well . . ." Jane swallows. A footman passes with a tray of white wine. She grabs a glass and downs the contents quickly. It is warm and sweet, with an aftertaste of vomit. "His father was a captain in the army. But he and Tom's mother are settled in Ireland now."

Eliza closes her fan and taps it against her cheekbone. "Is he an only child?"

"No, he has five elder sisters."

Eliza's eyes widen. "Five? Are any of them married?"

"No . . ." Jane lowers her gaze to the floor, where her pink satin slippers are peeping out from beneath the hem of her gown. With a dash of white vinegar, lye soap and plenty of elbow grease, Sally has removed the worst of the grass stains, but a yellow tinge remains around the toes. "I believe they are all at home."

"So, your Mr. Lefroy will have to support *all* of them?" Eliza opens her fan and uses it to shield her mouth as she speaks. "I wonder, Jane, what would your Lady Susan say of such a match?"

Jane meets her cousin's sidelong glance. "She'd say find a rich, stupid old man to marry—and keep Mr. Lefroy as a lover."

Eliza titters. "Well, there's no need to be quite so mercenary. But I would counsel a little discretion to protect your precious heart."

Jane draws a breath, preparing to argue. Her mother and father had had next to nothing when they started out, but that did not prevent the young Cassandra Leigh from marrying George Austen, the dashing but penniless clergyman who had swept her off her feet. Through hard work and determination, they had created a life for themselves.

Jane has no interest in chickens, or any other kind of farming, but she could run a school for girls. It could hardly be worse than the first school she and Cassandra were packed off to. Jane would do her best to keep her pupils alive, at least. Between their careless schoolmistress, and the prevalence of typhus, the Austen girls were lucky to survive their brief time there.

Eliza straightens, pushing out her breasts and fluttering her fan furiously. Jane follows her cousin's gaze toward Mr. Fitzgerald, who is being harangued by Mrs. Rivers. "Now there's a young man with prospects. I've been doing some investigating into his circumstances, as you asked."

"You have?" Jane remains highly suspicious of Mr. Fitzgerald. He may have been in Brussels at the time Madame Renard conceived. Surely he's just as likely to have sired her baby as Jonathan.

"He's Captain Rivers's only recognized son, and quite the favourite. By rights, he should be in line to receive the bulk of his father's enormous fortune. But, as Mrs. Rivers mentioned, there is a legal impediment to overcome. As it stands, the most he can inherit is two thousand pounds. And no land or property in the West Indies, I'm afraid."

"So, what is he doing here. Really?"

"He's come to see his family."

"The Riverses?" Jane arches an eyebrow. "Why would anyone spend time with them, unless they absolutely had to?"

Eliza grimaces. "You're right about Sophy. She really went for you, didn't she? I always thought you were being oversensitive about her because she's so much better at everything than you—a touch of the green-eyed monster."

"She is not better at *everything* than me. And why should I be jealous of her?"

"Well, I can think of thirty thousand reasons. Can't you?"

"Hmm . . ." Jane stares at sour-faced Sophy, who is dancing a minuet with Jonathan across the room. She's always been a harridan, but she was vicious in her rebuttal of any connection to Madame Renard. Had Jane's enquiry touched a nerve? And why isn't she bragging about hooking the heir to a baronetcy? Are the flames of her triumph doused with guilt for the sins she committed to achieve her exalted position? Or does she suspect her fiancé is as inconsistent as his lecherous father? Jonathan may be able to offer Sophy status and security but, above that, every woman wants to be loved and cherished.

Sophy's hard gaze is directed toward her mother, who continues to berate the extraordinarily well-heeled Mr. Fitzgerald. The fibres of his peruke gleam in the candlelight. There really must be some silver thread intertwined with the horsehair curls. "Mr. Fitzgerald must be here to ask his relations for money," says Jane. "He has an appetite for travel and, by the look of him, burns through his funds as quickly as the rest of his profligate family."

"Not necessarily. There may be another reason."

"Such as?"

Eliza fans herself at the rate of a hummingbird in flight. "Isn't it obvious?"

"Not to me."

"Come now, Jane. You said you weren't a dolt. He's a single man, in expectation of a good-enough fortune. I expect he's on the lookout for a wife."

"I'm not *quite* sure that follows, Eliza."

"Oh, fiddle-faddle. It's as Mrs. Rivers said. If he wants to be accepted into the English gentry, he must make himself agreeable and find a suitable young lady to marry. Even if he's never able to claim his father's wealth in its entirety, the portion he's already been allotted is enough to set him up in life. He's educated, accomplished, not to mention dashing. You should look upon him seriously, Jane. What with your father's connections, I'm sure he could help secure Mr. Fitzgerald a very decent living . . ."

Mrs. Rivers gestures fervently toward Jane and Eliza. With a slump of his broad shoulders, Mr. Fitzgerald bows to his aunt and turns toward the ladies. Jane locks her smile in place, as she answers Eliza through gritted teeth. "I'm trying to catch a murderer, not a husband."

"Can't you do both at the same time? It would be most efficient."

"No. Besides, you know my affections lie elsewhere."

"Yes. Unfortunately I can see that they do."

Jane is prevented from defending Tom's suit, as Mr. Fitzgerald stands before them and bows. "Miss Austen, may I have the honour?"

"Me?" Jane touches a hand to her bosom.

Has she heard him correctly? How can Mr. Fitzgerald have noticed Jane in the orbit of Eliza's brilliance? Perhaps Eliza is right, and Mrs. Rivers has sent him over to woo her. It's true: Jane has more connections to the Anglican Church than she cares to count. Eliza digs the heel of her hand into the small of Jane's back, propelling her forward so quickly that Jane must grab Mr. Fitzgerald's arm to prevent herself from toppling over. As he sweeps her onto the dance floor, she notices he does not wear any rings on his long, elegant fingers—but that does not necessarily prove his innocence. He may simply be wary of flaunting in public anything that might connect him to Madame Renard.

When Jane glances over her shoulder toward Eliza, she can tell by the crinkle of her cousin's eyes that she is laughing behind her painted fan. Henry appears at her side with two goblets of punch. He dips his head, as if to whisper in Eliza's ear, but instead he presses his lips to the pulse-point of her neck. Eliza's eyelids close, her features softening in rapturous delight. What does he think he's doing? As for Eliza, how much punch has she already ingested?

The orchestra gives up any attempt at sophistication and breaks into a more popular ballad, fit for an English country dance. Jane will not be surprised if they strike up with Mr. Beveridge's Maggot before the end of the evening. Fortunately Mr. Fitzgerald is an excellent dancer, making even the most humdrum steps look elegant. He leads Jane in spins and turns with a gentle confidence that calms her ruffled spirits.

She tips her head back and stares up at him, determined to get to the truth of why he is here. "Are you enjoying your visit to Hampshire, Mr. Fitzgerald?"

His voice is rich and deep. "Indeed. I like your country dances best of all."

Beside the orchestra, Mrs. Rivers is squawking while Sophy wrinkles her nose, as if she's knee-deep in a pile of rotten fish.

Jane tilts her head toward them. "The rest of your party seem less amused. Do our country dances not satisfy their more refined tastes?"

Mr. Fitzgerald peers down at Jane from his great height. "Sophy? I expect she hasn't been as fortunate in her choice of dance partners as I have." His thick black eyelashes curl as perfectly as if Sally has been at them with curling irons.

Jane leans into Mr. Fitzgerald's arms, as he circles her waist and they chassé together to the end of the line. "But who could Miss Rivers prefer over Mr. Harcourt? Of all the gentlemen here, there's only his father who outranks him. And I doubt she'd want to dance with Sir John."

The baronet lingers at the pillar, barking at the group of elderly gentlemen. It is odd that he remains in the ballroom so late. Most gentlemen of his age and proclivities are at the card tables by now. Behind him, Lady Harcourt reclines, half comatose, on a sofa.

"Who indeed?" Mr. Fitzgerald smiles, as they reach their destination.

Jane is dizzy. She blames it on the white wine. "Have you heard any more about your living?" she asks, hoping to prompt him to share the exact nature of his financial situation.

A slight crease appears on Mr. Fitzgerald's dewy brow. "Not yet. But my ordination has been confirmed for early in the new year. And, as I said, I would like to see a little more of the world before I settle down."

It's as Jane suspected. He's an idle young man with no consistency, and a taste for the finer things in life. A true Rivers, then, despite the difference in surname. "Touring? Do you plan to return to the island of your birth? I'm sure your parents would like to see you practise your vocation."

He frowns, eyes clouding. "No, Miss Austen. I'm afraid that's out of the question. As much as it pained my mother to send me away, it would break her heart to see me go back."

Jane continues gazing up at him, willing him to go on. "Oh?" She hears Henry's voice in her head. *Growing up in Jamaica can't have been easy.* She never did read that pamphlet—she really should make time to do so.

"It's difficult, you see. There are laws there, new ones introduced with ever more frequency, designed to prevent a man of colour from living a full life. Even with my father's patronage, there is a limit to my privilege—restrictions to the public offices I can hold, how much land I can own, how much of my father's fortune I can inherit. The list grows longer by the day."

Jane is stunned. Any discrimination Mr. Fitzgerald faces in England is likely to be implicit. Even then, his family's wealth and his rank will outweigh most of the prejudice leveled against him. She chews the inside of her cheek, searching for a witty remark to break the tension. "It sounds like being a woman."

"Not quite. And, needless to say, *my* sisters find themselves doubly persecuted." Mr. Fitzgerald swallows before he speaks again. "Do excuse me, Miss Austen." He drops Jane's hand and rushes past her toward Sophy and Mrs. Rivers—who appear to be locking horns on the side of the dance floor.

Jane's cheeks blaze. She has offended Mr. Fitzgerald with her crass comparison. She deserves the public humiliation of being abandoned mid-dance. How can her petty quest for independence compare to his fight for liberty? How much narrower would Jane's life choices be if she was not only a woman but also a woman of colour?

After all, everyone in her supposedly polite, genteel, well-bred circle acknowledges that Mr. Fitzgerald is Captain Rivers's natural son. But no one has deigned to ask the identity of his mother—a formidable woman who will not rest until his fortune is secure. Sometimes Jane could bite her tongue for her tendency to speak in haste and regret her words at leisure.

Before she knows it, another gentleman takes her hand and tugs her gently back into the formation. Jane smiles up at her saviour, only to be confronted with the enormous bushy black and silver eyebrows of Mr. Craven. "What are you doing here?"

He opens his mouth without making a sound. The silk-covered buttons of his salmon-coloured waistcoat strain over his stomach. "I escorted my sister and my niece. I'm staying with them at Deane for the festive season."

"You are?" Jane tenses at the prospect of bumping into the man responsible for Georgy's plight on her daily walk. Despite her regret at offending Mr. Fitzgerald, the punch and the wine she has drunk have loosened her tongue and she cannot prevent it from straying further. "Tell me, do you truly believe my brother capable of stealing that poor woman's necklace and leaving her for dead?"

A sheen creeps over Mr. Craven's forehead. "I haven't accused him of murder."

"You might as well have. If he's found guilty, you're condemning him to a death sentence." Jane draws slow, steady breaths as they dance. She wishes she could lift her skirts and run away. Or, failing that, knock Mr. Craven around the head until he sees sense and releases Georgy. She bristles under the stare of every respectable family in Hampshire and beyond. For Georgy's sake, she must maintain her composure.

Mr. Craven's badger-like eyebrows pull down in concentration. "Miss Austen. I truly am very sorry for the predicament in which your family find themselves, and I *do* understand all this must be terribly upsetting for you. But, as justice of the peace, I can only go on the evidence put before me."

Jane clenches her jaw. "Then I shall get you your evidence, Mr. Craven."

"You saw your brother produce that necklace from his pocket with your own eyes."

"That doesn't mean he stole it. And he definitely didn't kill Madame Renard. He doesn't have it in him."

Mr. Craven tilts his head. "Who?" They are dancing a figure of eight around another couple, who turn out to be James and Mary. Jane is forced to wait until she and Mr. Craven have finished skipping before she can explain. "Madame Renard. I'm sorry, I misheard her name. I should have told you."

"You should have."

"I found a borrowed book in her room at the Angel Inn, and it led me to her reading records at the circulating library."

"That was rather ingenious of you."

It is Jane's and Mr. Craven's turn to remain still while James and Mary skip around them. Jane is thankful for the chance to regain her breath. "Whoever killed Zoë Renard tore that chain from around her neck and most likely planted it on Georgy, precisely because they knew my brother would be unable to defend himself." It takes all Jane's willpower to prevent her voice from warbling. "And I'm going to prove it. Tell me, what would it take for you to set my brother free?"

Mr. Craven takes Jane's hand for the final step in the dance. "Well . . . a physical piece of evidence linking another to the crime, or someone else coming forward with a signed confession, would remove the blame." They turn in circles with James and Mary.

Jane tenses at the prospect of James giving her another public scolding for her lack of decorum in harassing the magistrate on the dance floor over Georgy's case. But James is not listening. Instead, he's leaping around with uncharacteristic abandon as he holds Mary Lloyd. Shockingly, Mary appears to be enjoying herself, too. When she gazes up at James, her face is girlish and her brown eyes sparkle with such warmth that she looks genuinely pretty.

The music ceases and Jane wrenches her hands free of Mr. Craven's sweaty grasp. "Then that's exactly what I'll find for you. Good evening, sir." She claps so furiously her palms sting, as she glares at Mr. Craven across the battle line of dancers.

4. To Cassandra Austen

Steventon, Friday, 1 January 1796

My dearest Cassandra,

Of course, I wasn't serious about reprimanding Sally for your mixing our blue gowns. What do you think I am? My mother, and therefore our entire family, would be cast adrift without Sally. Forgive me, you'll have to look to Mary for all the gossip from the ball. My thoughts are fixed on who might have killed the hapless ~~milliner~~ lacemaker, Madame Renard. Your own good nature will make this incredible to you, but my full list of suspicious persons now stands at:

- The most incompetent thief in all of England (and very probably the entire British Empire)

- Mrs. Twistleton (was Madame Renard about to expose the housekeeper as a harlot?)

- Sir John Harcourt (did his attempt to silence the lacemaker over his whoring turn awry?)

- Sophy Rivers (could Madame R have known something that would keep Sophy from her title?)

- Jack Smith (I can't bear to contemplate it either, but how did Georgy get hold of that necklace?)

As for the furtive father of Madame Renard's unborn baby, I believe he's a gentleman who spent time in Brussels over the summer and owns a gold signet ring. Which points to:

- Douglas Fitzgerald (I haven't seen a ring, but you know how the Riverses love to shine)
- Jonathan Harcourt (I can't imagine him ruining a plate of petits fours, let alone an innocent young woman. Can you?)

Yes, it is most generous of Neddy to insist the lawyer's bill be sent straight to him, but it's not as if he will have to go without to settle the expense. Is it? There's no need to canonize him. You or I (but especially you, as you never were any good at tallying up) would give away our last sixpence and more besides if it would help Georgy's case. But I have said too much, as usual. Cut this letter into pieces and use it to mulch Mrs. Fowle's rhubarb. God willing, my bitterness will save next year's summer puddings from the frost.

Yours very truly,
J.A.

Miss Austen,
Rev. Mr. Fowle's,
Kintbury,
Newbury.

CHAPTER FIFTEEN

The next morning, when Jane finally surfaces, Sally is clumping around the kitchen in her wooden clogs. The maid clatters the crockery and rattles the cutlery, as if railing against every injustice in the world. In the family parlour, Anna shrieks as Hastings knocks a pile of spillikins across the tiled floor. Mr. Austen sits in his battered leather armchair before the fire, rustling his newspaper. At the table, Eliza titters, Mrs. Austen scrapes her plate and James breathes audibly. Jane groans as she slumps into a hardbacked chair. She leans her elbows on the linen tablecloth and places her face in her palms, deeply regretting her decision to alternate between Mr. Toke's punch and the sickly white wine all evening.

Henry pushes a tureen toward her. "Have some scrambled eggs with plenty of salt." For the first time since Eliza's arrival, he's come down to breakfast dressed in his shirtsleeves, without shaving. "It'll help, I promise you."

"Just looking at them turns my stomach." Jane must pull herself together. It is after eleven and she is due to meet Tom within the hour. She is so nauseous, she couldn't even be bothered to pick out a nice outfit and wears her fawn-coloured morning gown with flannel petticoats. It is hardly an ensemble worthy of a seminal moment in a young lady's life. She hopes the thrill of Tom finally making his proposal of marriage will blot out any remembrance of her shabby attire.

James scrapes the blunted blade of the butter knife across his own blackened bread. "Toast, then?" Crumbs scatter across his plate and onto the pristine white tablecloth. Jane shakes her head. The motion causes the dull ache trapped inside her brain to bounce against her skull.

"Tea, and plenty of it." Eliza picks up the pot and pours. As usual, she is immaculately groomed, in a pretty mink-grey morning gown. Her dark eyes sparkle and there is even a hint of warmth in her cheeks. Jane's cousin is more accustomed to a life of sociability. She will have learned to pace herself as a debutante in Paris. Either that, or she's performed some cunning sleight of hand with her French cosmetics. "Some sugar might help, too. Shame we don't have coffee. It's much more effective at reviving the spirit."

Mr. Austen shakes out his newspaper. "Coffee? This isn't Godmersham, you know." Godmersham Park is the luxurious Kent country estate that Neddy is due to inherit from his adoptive mother, Mrs. Knight. None of the Austens have been invited to visit yet, but in their imagination it is the land of plenty.

Jane slides the cup and saucer toward herself with trembling hands. "Tea it is, then." She places the crook of her finger in the handle, but she is shaking so violently she must clasp the cup with both hands to prevent spillage. When she sets it down, there is as much of the dark brown liquid in the saucer as there is in the cup.

Mrs. Austen exhales loudly. "Well, I'm glad you all had a good time."

Henry smirks, leaning back in his chair and folding his arms over his broad chest. "I should say so. Jane most of all. She must have danced with every eligible bachelor in the room. And plenty of ineligible ones, besides."

Jane's head spins at the memory of twisting and turning in time to the music. She never did find Tom again. Harry Digweed told her the Lefroys had left, as Mrs. Lefroy was suffering from a headache. Then Harry had asked Jane to dance with him instead, and she could hardly say no as by then he knew she was free to accept.

Harry doesn't wear any rings, and he was late to the Harcourts' ball at Deane House on account of a very amusing incident involving a determined grouse, two of his brothers and a splinter of shotgun pellet. Jane can't remember the details, but the anecdote had her screaming with laughter at the time.

Mrs. Austen pats her daughter's hand. "Oh, my dear, there's hope for you yet . . ."

Jane tries to scowl, but her tongue is too swollen. "If only James had been more liberal with his attentions. I told you to dance twice with Mary Lloyd, not to let her monopolize you all night."

James examines his fingernails. "Well, Mary's an excellent partner." He is fastidiously dressed in his clerical attire, as usual. Only the sheen of perspiration, forming on his brow, and his red-rimmed eyes betray quite how much fun he had last night.

Jane huffs. "So is Alethea. Yet after the first dance you snubbed her entirely."

"Mary said Alethea would be perfectly happy dancing with Miss Terry."

"That's not the point," says Jane. "Every lady should enjoy at least a couple of sets with a gentleman before she's forced to endure the indignity of pairing up with her own sex."

Mrs. Austen brightens. "Leave him alone, Jane. If he was happy dancing with Mary, he should dance with Mary. You should call on her, James. Take Anna with you. I have one of her mother's tins

I must return, and you could take some of my cottage cheese as an offering. I've just finished a fresh batch."

Jane wonders if her mother is distracting herself from her sorrow over Georgy by planning for the next generation of Austens. God help James if she is.

He colours as he sips his tea. "Steady there, Mother."

"Tell me, how did Jonathan and Sophy look together?" asks Mrs. Austen.

"As complacent as ever." Henry flashes Jane a teasing grin. "Actually, Eliza and I thought Jonathan had a little more spark when he was dancing with *you*, Jane."

Mrs. Austen's eyes grow wide. "You danced with Jonathan? Oh, what a shame Sophy got in there first. You could have been very comfortable up at Deane House."

"Mother!" Jane shudders. If Jonathan really does take after his licentious father, it's possible he seduced Madame Renard while studying in Brussels—leaving her heartbroken and saddled with their love child when he returned to England. Surely such a lax approach to morality would rule him out of the running as a potential suitor, even by Jane's mother's standards.

Mrs. Austen covers Jane's hand with her own. Her fingers are long, cool and slightly callused from the amount of time she spends in her garden. "But just think of it, dear. With a man like Jonathan for a husband, you'd never run out of ink or paper or sugar. You could employ an army of nurses to help raise your children. And you certainly wouldn't have to bloody your hands wringing the necks of your chickens."

Then again, perhaps her mother could be persuaded to turn a blind eye to a wealthy son-in-law's extramarital dalliances. Even Jane can see the allure. It would indeed be bliss to send to

Basingstoke for fresh bottles of ink, instead of having to forage for ingredients and brew it herself.

In the cold morning light, Jane concedes that running a boarding school for girls would be torture—never mind being permanently tethered to her own children by her apron strings. She adores little Anna, but she lives for the quiet moments in her day. Whenever she's been among company for long, Jane craves the solitude of her dressing room, where she can scrape her mind clean of domestic drudgery by running her fingers over the black-and-white keys of her pianoforte, and inscribe stark lines of words across an empty page. "Thank you, Mother. Your point is made."

"I wouldn't be so sure of the Harcourts' fortune," says Eliza.

"Whatever do you mean?" asks James. "They're one of the best-established families in all of Hampshire."

"Far be it for me to speculate on the state of their affairs . . . and I wouldn't want to provoke any rumours . . . but Sir John spent most of the night pestering me for a loan."

Despite her protests, it's clear Jane's cousin is in her element. What a shame her time in King Louis XVI's court was cut short.

"He did?" asks James.

"It's true." Henry sets both hands flat on the table. "And very persistent he was about it. I had to step in, and tell him to leave Eliza alone."

James tosses his toast onto his plate. "But why might Sir John need a loan?"

"He said to invest in a particular opportunity," continues Henry. "Didn't have the ready funds himself, but promised to make a spectacular return for Eliza."

Jane shudders at the prospect of Sir John clamouring to get his swollen fingers on the remainder of her cousin's fortune.

Could money worries explain how a dead woman came to be found in the Harcourts' linen closet? "How brazen of him. You won't agree, will you?"

Eliza laughs, but without amusement. "If only I had the choice. As you know, a good portion of my fortune is quite literally sunk in France." Captain de Feullide had used Eliza's dowry to irrigate his estate but, as he was found guilty of treason, the French Republic confiscated the newly arable farmland, meaning Eliza is unlikely to see any return on her investment. Thankfully, Mr. Austen refused to release all of Eliza's money, so she maintains at least some of the ten thousand pounds settled on her by her extraordinarily generous godfather, Warren Hastings.

Henry curls his hand into a fist, slamming it onto the table. "You'll have it back. We'll put down this insurrection, restore the world to its proper order—even in France. Then Hastings will inherit everything that should be his by right."

Eliza's smile is tight-lipped. "Of course. But until then, I intend to be extremely cautious with whatever funds I have left. I shall be a complete miser and save every penny to set up my darling boy in life." She tickles Hastings under his chin, as he reaches for a slice of her toast.

Mrs. Austen squeezes Eliza's forearm and they exchange a strained smile. "Very wise, dear."

Mr. Austen harrumphs from his armchair. "My dear niece, I'm afraid you're the last person on earth who could ever be considered a miser. Your idea of frugality is to have one bottle of champagne with dinner instead of two."

Everyone laughs, Eliza most heartily of all. No one says what Jane is sure they are all thinking: just like Georgy, it is doubtful that Hastings will ever be able to provide for himself.

Eliza will shoulder the responsibility of caring for her son for the rest of both their lives.

Jane scrutinises Mr. Austen's profile. "Did Sir John ever pay you, Father, for burying Madame Renard?"

He fixes his eyes on his broadsheet as he speaks. "Not yet, but I'm sure he will. You know that people believe clergymen live on prayers and good wishes. The richer they are, the more trouble I have in extracting tithes from them."

Jane turns to Eliza, who raises her eyebrows. Could Jonathan be so desperate to shore up the family finances by marrying heiress Sophy that he'd murder his pregnant lover if she dared to obstruct him? Surely not. The Harcourts' money worries cannot be so dire. They have so much land, and Lady Harcourt is rumoured to have brought a significant sum with her into her marriage to Sir John. Then again, financial problems would explain why she's exchanged the diamond baguettes in her tiara for paste.

Jane gulps the last of her tea and rises from the table. "I think I shall go out for some fresh air."

James looks up. There is a subtle glimmer in his grey-hazel eyes. "Are you walking up to Deane perchance? If so, would you like some company?"

"No, thank you." The last thing Jane wants is her brother tagging along on her romantic liaison. She presses a hand to her temple and rubs it firmly. "I need peace and quiet."

It is bitterly cold, with a clear blue sky and an arctic breeze. Jane is thankful it is dry. Her fingers will be clumsy in her mittens, but there is no need for her to totter around in her pattens. The tea has worked its magic. The butterflies in her stomach are set in motion by the prospect of resolving her future with Tom, rather than by the excess wine and spirits she ingested the night before. She fastens her cloak and pulls up the hood. With any luck, by the time she meets Tom, the chill will have brought some warmth to her complexion, and he will not notice her tired gown.

As she traipses through her mother's garden, the vegetable beds lie empty of all but the most persistent weeds. Frost sparkles on the nettles. Throughout the farmyard, galinies and bantams ruffle their bronzed feathers as they claw at the hard ground, flicking clods of earth behind them in their relentless search for a tasty treat. In the stable block, Greylass and the other horses blow steam through their noses and kick against the gates of their stalls. The pony will be missing Cassandra. Jane resolves to take her a carrot. Even as she thinks it, she knows she'll forget and berates herself for her lack of care.

At the Austens' private entrance to St. Nicholas's churchyard, at the top of the small hill, a scattering of ice crystals glitters on the rusty scrolls of the iron gate. The hinges creak and the latch sticks as Jane opens it. Inside the graveyard, all is quiet and still. Tangles of ivy escape over the flint wall. Moss and lichen in subtle shades of green and grey mottle the weathered granite tombstones. Jane reads the words carved into the granite as she passes. Grand Lord and Lady Portal lie side by side in their matching sarcophagi, while generations of Boltons are snug beneath one flat slab. They are people Jane has never met but regards as old friends.

Tom stands in front of the church, his head down and his hands stuffed into the pockets of his frock coat. Jane's heart fizzes as she studies him before he notices her. A lapis-blue woolen scarf encircles his neck, its tasseled ends flapping in the wind. Which of his five sisters knitted it for him?

He beams when he meets Jane's eyes. "You came."

Heat infuses her shivering body. "And you're here." She skips toward him, and their white-cloud breath mingles in the air.

He closes his eyes and leans toward her, his sandy lashes meeting his chiseled cheekbones. "I'm here," he murmurs, as he kisses her. His lips are warm but the tip of his nose is like ice. "I'm so sorry about the ball. My aunt—"

"Had a headache. I know." Jane threads her arm through the crook of his. "It doesn't matter, we're together now."

He places his gloved hand over hers and they set off down the lane. "So we are."

Jane is content to let Tom lead the way. She doesn't care where they go, so long as they remain in step. They meander through the woods, latching onto the path toward Popham. The old track crosses fields of woolly sheep and glossy dark-brown cows. Tom holds her hand as she climbs over a stile. She jumps down into his arms and they kiss again, and again, until Jane is dizzy with delight. As they ramble, he is uncharacteristically quiet, staring at the path with a crease in his brow.

He must be nervous, with so much hinging on a simple question. Surely he knows she will say yes. She will say yes, won't she?

If only the question wasn't so loaded, and they could have a sensible conversation about it. *Would you like sugar in your tea? Yes, please, I like it sweet. Shall we get married? No, thank you, I prefer the single life.* All done, no hard feelings either way.

In a bid to break the tension, Jane reveals Madame Renard and Jonathan Harcourt might have met and become lovers in Brussels. "You see, they both have a connection to the city. And, what with the ring, it must be more than a coincidence. Don't you think?"

"And so you imagine he killed her?"

"Well . . ." Jane flounders. She didn't go that far, but Tom is peering at her as if she has accused Jonathan of sacrificing newborn babies on the altar of St. Andrew's Church and supping with the Devil in the dining room of Deane House each night.

"It's all conjecture, don't you see? I'm afraid such a tenuous accusation would never stand up in court. You don't even know if they were in Brussels at the same time. Or if they met at all."

"But what about the ring?"

Tom grips the fingers of his glove between his teeth, and pulls out his left hand. "A gentleman's ring with an intaglio?" He is wearing a very similar signet ring to Jonathan's, only Tom's gemstone is black while Jonathan's is brownish-red. Jane removes her mittens and clasps his fingers in her own as she examines the ring. It's an onyx, engraved with a Huguenot cross and a dove.

"Great-uncle Langlois gave it to me. It saves me hunting for a seal. Are you going to accuse me of bludgeoning Madame Renard to death, too?"

"Don't be silly." Jane shoves his arm away. Beneath his many layers of clothing, his muscles are pleasingly firm. "For one thing, that frightful tailcoat of yours would have been drenched in blood." Their eyes meet, and Tom bursts out laughing. No doubt he's imagining himself once again in the place of his literary namesake, white coat ruined after defending Miss Weston's honour to a company of drunken soldiers.

Before either of them replaces their gloves or mittens, Tom takes Jane's hand, squeezing her fingers. He presses his bare palm to hers as he pulls her along. They emerge from the trees into a field, rising to a steep hill. Jane is reluctant to push her point about Jonathan any further, lest Tom thinks her foolish. Trying to catch a murderer may be silly, but Georgy's predicament is deadly serious. And, with his legal training, Tom should be the ideal companion in her quest to prove her brother innocent. "Since you're the expert, tell me, how does one win an argument in court?"

"Well . . ." Tom halts, resting a hand on his hip. He smiles ruefully, as if bemused to be having this conversation with her. "To convince a jury, the most important thing is to establish that the defendant had the means, motive *and* opportunity to commit the crime. Most acts of violence are senseless, but that doesn't stop a jury wanting a reason. Otherwise, it's difficult for any morally upstanding person to conceive of. Has anyone asked your brother where he was on the night of the ball?"

"He was at the cottage by himself. Jack was running errands, and Nan was called out to deliver twins. They don't usually leave him alone, but Georgy was asleep and it was an emergency . . ."

"What do you know about this Jack Smith fellow?" asks Tom. "Running errands sounds like a bluff to me. Could he have been involved, do you think?"

"That's what I said, but my father and brothers are loath to press him for a more rigorous explanation."

"And he's Georgy's keeper?"

"He has been since he was a boy."

"There you go, then. He must want a proper job, and his own life. It can't be easy for him, having to follow the whims of another all the time. You could understand it if he came to resent such a burden."

Jane picks at the loose threads of her cape. "There's something else. Jack's been trying to raise the money to invest in his own livestock. Only a sow to breed, but it obviously meant a lot to him. He asked my father to advance his pay until Lady Day, but he refused."

"So, he's got reason to hold a grudge against your family. It sounds plausible that *he* carried out the robbery, bungling it and killing his mark in the process. Your brother must have stumbled across the spoils before Jack could flee."

A picture of Jack and herself as children rises in Jane's mind. They are hand in hand, splashing through the stream that runs behind the back of Dame Culham's cottage. Sunlight glints off the wet pebbles and from Jack's rich brown eyes. Dame Culham sits on the bank, her feet and ankles dangling in the cool water, while Georgy rests with his head in her lap.

Jane swallows. "But if Jack *did* do it, he'd hardly be likely to insist on going to gaol himself, would he?"

"Perhaps he wants to keep an eye on your brother. Make sure he carries the blame. I expect he's still got the ring squirreled away. He'll be off as soon as the trial's over. Those jewels would have raised enough cash to allow a man like him to start afresh somewhere."

Jane's head spins as she stares at the surrounding countryside. She cannot bring herself to imagine a world in which her brother's companion could betray him so completely. All around her, the fields roll away until they meet the horizon. Only occasional church spires punctuate the sprawling green hills.

In an attempt to regain her equilibrium, she fixes her eyes on the Terrys' timber-framed barn at the base of the hill on Winchester Road. It's known locally as "the red barn" because the plaster glows crimson at sunset. Now, in the pale winter light, it is rather the "dingy grey barn."

"Is that the sort of motive it takes to convince a jury?"

Tom crosses his arms over his chest, staring at the lead-grey clouds gathering on the horizon. "Yes. Isn't that what everything comes down to in the end? Love or money. It's usually one of the two."

It is on the tip of Jane's tongue to tell Tom that Zoë Renard was pregnant. To explain that, if Jonathan Harcourt was the killer, his motive for killing the lacemaker might have been fiscal, too. If Jonathan's lover exposed the fact he'd sired her baby, it would have obliterated his chance to marry heiress Sophy and claim her thirty-thousand-pound dowry. And with Sir John pestering Eliza for a loan and Lady Harcourt trading her diamonds for paste, the chances are they are in financial difficulties.

But it all sounds so far-fetched. Jane has learned the hard way it is one thing to have these flights of fancy in her head, quite another to set them free into the world. No doubt Tom will laugh at her for daring to imagine such a scenario. Madame Renard might have been a respectable widow, carrying her husband's child and killed in a random attack by a witless thief.

At the bottom of the hill, beside the Terrys' farm, a young lady in a maroon riding habit trots along the lane on a chestnut gelding. When she reaches the barn, she slides gracefully down from her horse and hooks the reins over a fence post before slipping inside. Jane shields her eyes from the glare of the silver sky with her palm. "Was that Miss Rivers?"

Tom squints into the distance. "I believe it was."

"What's she doing in the red barn?"

"Maybe her horse has thrown a shoe. We'd better see if she needs assistance."

"Her horse didn't *look* lame to me."

Steel-clad hoofs crash against stone, as another rider tears along the lane from the opposite direction. The man wears a greatcoat, with a three-cornered hat. He pulls his black hunter to an abrupt halt as he reaches the barn. The animal whinnies and rears, waving his forehoofs in the air. Unperturbed, the rider leaps to the ground, secures his horse beside Sophy's and glances both ways, revealing his face.

It's Mr. Fitzgerald. There can be no mistaking him. He pulls up his collar as he follows Miss Rivers inside the barn.

Jane's stomach drops. It's so obvious—the Riverses are social climbers. Mr. Fitzgerald's father sent him to England to become "a gentleman." If he discovers his son has been fornicating with a merchant, he'll be furious—furious enough to cut him off, and desist from his attempts to challenge the laws of Jamaica that bar Mr. Fitzgerald from inheriting his enormous fortune. Zoë Renard must have followed Mr. Fitzgerald to Deane House, looking for his support—but *he* killed her to keep their affair quiet, and he tried to steal her necklace, too. He needs money. If Sophy Rivers is in that barn, as bejeweled as ever, she might be his next victim . . .

"Oh, my goodness. I have it all wrong." Jane sprints past Tom, bolting down the hill.

"Jane, stop."

But Jane cannot stop. The gradient forces her legs to move faster, gaining momentum as she runs. It's like rolling down the slope at the back of the rectory.

"Cowper!" she cries, into the wind. It can be no coincidence that Madame Renard favoured the same poet as Mr. Fitzgerald had chosen to read aloud.

"I really don't think . . . ," Tom calls from somewhere over her shoulder.

Jane slams both hands onto the rough-hewn wooden door of the barn to stop herself falling. With a thwack, it springs wide open.

CHAPTER SIXTEEN

Jane staggers into the barn. Between two teetering stacks of hay, Mr. Fitzgerald has hold of a limp Sophy. Their faces are pressed together. Jane could not save Zoë Renard, but she will rescue Sophy. "Let her go, you scoundrel!"

Mr. Fitzgerald springs upright. Sophy's bosom heaves under the half-undone buttons of her riding jacket and her cheeks glow red. "Jane? Whatever are you doing?"

Mr. Fitzgerald turns his back to Jane. His hat lies abandoned on the hay-strewn floor, beside Miss Rivers's gloves.

Jane reaches for Sophy. "Sophy, where is your necklace?"

Sophy glances down at her exposed chest. "I didn't think it went with this outfit. What business is it of yours?"

Were Sophy and Mr. Fitzgerald *embracing*? "Stay back from Mr. Fitzgerald. You can't trust him. How well do you even know him?"

"Really, Jane. By now, I'd have thought that was obvious."

"Jane." Tom crashes into the barn, sliding across the flagstones on the loose hay. "Miss Rivers, Mr. Fitzgerald." He takes Jane's arm, tugging her toward the door. "We should leave."

So they *were* kissing, and most passionately indeed. Jane stands her ground, pointing to Mr. Fitzgerald. "But it was *him*. He's the murderer. That's why he was so composed when we discovered her corpse. He already knew she was there. He seduced Madame Renard on his journey to the Italian Alps. She must have followed him to Hampshire, so he *had* to get her out of the way in case Captain Rivers found out and disinherited him."

Mr. Fitzgerald spins to face Jane, an expression of abject horror writ large across his features. Sophy sidesteps in front of him, shielding his body with her own. "How dare you?" Her voice quivers. "Douglas hasn't been out of the country since he arrived here as a boy, and he *certainly* hasn't murdered anyone. If he was composed, that's because he's an excellent priest."

Jane falters. "But his painting of the mountain vista?" Tom is still trying to pull her away by her elbow.

"Scafell, Miss Austen," Mr. Fitzgerald protests. "It's in Cumberland. As I told you, I was visiting my father's connections to see about a living there."

"But what about the *gelato*?" Jane asks, remembering Mr. Fitzgerald's unusual turn of phrase. Even as she says it, she knows she's grasping at straws. She is so desperate to save Georgy, she'll draw connections where none exist.

Sophy's top lip curls. "Douglas is an educated man, Jane. He is fluent in several modern languages, as well as the classics."

"Yes," adds Mr. Fitzgerald. "And there's a very nice Italian confectioner next door to my university college in Durham."

"If you're going to make loathsome accusations, I can account for Douglas's whereabouts before the ball." Sophy trembles with rage. "We were together in my chamber—doing exactly what we were doing before you so rudely interrupted us."

Jane's entire body cringes. She has made the worst mistake of her life. Of anyone's life. Of several hapless lifetimes strung together. She is an utter clown. How she ever thought she was clever enough to solve the murder and save Georgy is a mystery. "Oh." She holds up her hands. "I'm so terribly sorry . . ."

Sophy stands tall, gripping tighter to Mr. Fitzgerald. In her riding habit, with her flaxen hair and red cheeks, she looks far more striking than she did in a ball gown. "I will not be made to feel ashamed. This is not some sordid affair. We are betrothed."

"Betrothed?" Jane echoes, in confusion. "But what about Mr. Harcourt? It's only been a few hours since we were toasting your engagement to him."

"Last night I had to go along with my mother's attempts at browbeating me into marrying Jonathan Harcourt. But, as of this morning, I've dissolved the arrangement and I don't care who knows it."

"This morning?"

"Yes." Sophy releases Mr. Fitzgerald, edging toward Jane. "Do you still not understand? And everyone says you're *so* clever. Let me be clear . . . How was your birthday, Jane?"

It is New Year's Day—Sophy's birthday. And Sophy is almost exactly a year older than Jane. "You turned one-and-twenty!"

"Indeed. As of this morning, I reached my majority. Which, according to the terms of my father's will, means my entire fortune is at my disposal. I shall no longer tolerate being dictated to"—with each word Sophy steps closer to Jane, until they are nose to nose—"by a small-minded nasty little bigot."

Jane clamps both hands over her treacherous mouth, waves of shame crashing over her and threatening to topple her off balance. How much easier it was to accuse the outsider, Mr. Fitzgerald, of murder than to contemplate that one of her own childhood companions might be responsible for such a horrific crime. "Sophy, Mr. Fitzgerald, forgive me."

Mr. Fitzgerald dismisses her apology with a flick of his wrist—which, given that Jane has just accused him of debauchery and cold-blooded murder, is far more gallantry than she deserves. She shuts her eyes as she plunges into previously unexplored depths of mortification. Tom wraps his arm around her waist, pulling her away. "As you said, Miss Rivers, it's really none of our business."

Sophy returns to her lover's side, softening her voice. "As soon as Douglas has been ordained, we'll away to Scotland and be married there."

Mr. Fitzgerald places a hand over his heart. "But, my darling, you deserve so much more than a tawdry elopement."

"Douglas, *you* are the only thing that is vital for my happiness. If that means severing ties with the rest of our heinous family, so be it."

Mr. Fitzgerald takes Sophy's wrist, pressing her hand to his lips and kissing her fingers. Their eyes lock, and Jane is shocked by the intensity of the look that passes between them.

"Well." Tom coughs into his fist. His cheeks are blotched with vermilion. "We're very sorry to have disturbed you. Aren't we, Miss Austen?"

"Yes, indeed. More so than I can ever say." Jane stares down at the toes of her walking boots as Tom steers her toward the open door. "Really, couldn't be any sorrier."

"Tell whoever you want," Sophy calls after them. "Go straight to your little friend, Mary Lloyd, if you wish. Or make an announcement in the *Hampshire Chronicle.* I'm sure it amounts to the same thing."

Jane turns back. "Honestly, Sophy. I would never—"

"And don't pretend to be such a prude. The whole county knows what you two were up to in the glasshouse on the night of the Harcourts' ball."

Jane gasps.

Tom picks her up by the waist and carries her out of the barn. "Exactly. None of our business. We won't be saying a word."

Tom continues to laugh at Jane all the way back to Steventon. Jane is a good sport, but by the time they retrace their steps through the woodland, she's running out of patience. "I don't see what's so funny." She crosses her arms over her chest and pouts as they halt beside St. Nicholas's Church.

He is bent over at the waist, holding onto the knees of his breeches for support. "It's just your face."

"Did you know what was going on between them?"

"Well, I knew something wasn't right. She must have been the most unenthusiastic bride-to-be I've ever seen." He grins up at her, with mocking blue eyes. "I hope you're not going to say anything. It would be so unfair, after you burst in on them like that. And it would only rebound on us."

Jane is losing track of the number of secrets she's keeping. There's Zoë Renard's pregnancy, Sophy Rivers and Mr. Fitzgerald's clandestine engagement, not to mention her own furtive affair with Tom. "Certainly not. For one thing, I can't let my mother find out Jonathan Harcourt is on the marriage mart again." Tom's face drops. "Otherwise, she'll have me up at Deane House, playing the pianoforte in my finest muslin faster than you can say 'Gretna Green.'" Jane spins on her heel and stalks off through the churchyard.

"Wait!" Tom calls after her, but he is laughing too hard to catch up before she slips through the gate and onto the Austens' private land.

While it's true Jane has behaved most recklessly and heaped an inordinate amount of well-deserved scorn upon herself, at least she can erase two names from her list of suspicious persons.

Neither Mr. Fitzgerald nor Sophy killed Madame Renard. They clearly have an alibi—and the secret they were guarding so carefully was their devotion to each other. Which means, in her own roundabout way, Jane is two steps closer to apprehending the true killer.

5. To Cassandra Austen

Steventon, Friday, 1 January 1796

My dear Cassandra,

Two letters in one day, what a spendthrift your sister is! Forgive the enforced expense but, through the process of vigorous enquiry, I must tell you I have eliminated two of my previous suspects. It wasn't Sophy—the ice queen does have a heart. Neither was it Mr. Fitzgerald—his money worries are over. Are you sure you want to get married? Tell me what's it like being shut up with Mr. Fowle in Kintbury. Do you ever wish you could purloin a carriage and speed home to your watercolours and our convivial fireside? Rip this letter to shreds and use it to line the cage of Mrs. Fowle's canary.

Yours very affectionately,
J.A.

Miss Austen,
Rev. Mr. Fowle's,
Kintbury,
Newbury.

CHAPTER SEVENTEEN

In the late afternoon, when dark shadows and the silvery moon replace the weak sunlight, Jane searches the rectory for Eliza. With her sister away in Kintbury, she has come to rely on Eliza's ebullience to keep her afloat. She may not be able to share all her mortifications with her cousin, as she would with Cassandra, but Eliza's vivacity buoys her dejected spirit. Jane finds her alone in the back bedroom, standing in her dressing gown, her hair arranged in a long plait over her shoulder. A tallow candle flickers on the dresser. The glow casts Eliza's elongated shadow diagonally over the sprigged wallpaper as she folds linen and places it inside the open jaws of a valise. Jane creaks the door open just enough to slide her slender frame through. "My mother says you're leaving us tomorrow. I'd hoped you would stay for much longer."

Eliza clutches one of Hastings's shirts to her chest and studies the row of neat stitches at the neckline. "We've been invited to stay with some old friends in Brighton. The sea air will be good for Hastings. And your parents have so much to cope with now. I wouldn't want to outstay my welcome." Her voice is strained. As usual, Eliza is trying her best to sound gay—but this time she cannot quite manage it.

Jane slumps into the armchair beside the bed. "But I shall miss you." She hasn't bothered changing out of her fawn calico gown. Mud cakes the hem, and she leaves a trail of brown flecks wherever she goes.

Eliza lifts her face to the candlelight. "And I you, *ma chérie*." Her eyes are red-rimmed and her cheeks are wan. "How was your walk?"

Jane stares at the valise, avoiding her cousin's eye. "Very refreshing," she lies, still cloaked in shame over her outburst. It clings to every pore of her skin like a cold, damp nightgown. She may be desperate to save Georgy, but Mr. Fitzgerald did not deserve to be treated so shamefully. Panic over her brother's impending trial is making Jane sloppy. It was lazy of her to assume the mountain range Mr. Fitzgerald had visited was in Europe. And it seems everyone reads Cowper. After flicking through the collection of verse she found in Madame Renard's room, Jane is beginning to understand why.

To her mortification, it is clear she succumbed to her own prejudice. She is no better than Mr. Craven, who had swallowed Sir John's story about a gang of trespassers, because that was more convenient than pursuing the truth. And Sophy was there to witness it all. The most detestable thing about Sophy Rivers is that she is everything Jane wishes she could be: handsome, rich and betrothed to an attractive, witty, honourable young man to boot.

Eliza cups her cheek, forcing Jane to meet her gaze. "And your Irish friend? You may fool your father and your brothers, my sweet, innocent little cousin, but I'm the mistress of intrigue—and I know a fellow coquette when I meet one."

Jane twists her lips, pursing them to avoid giving anything away with a sour expression. "If you must know, he was fine."

"Just fine?" Eliza refuses to let go of Jane. "You didn't come to an agreement then?"

"No, we did not." It was petulant of her to rush away while Tom was laughing at her. Jane knows that now. But she was in no mood to entertain a serious conversation about their future when he had been so irksome. What would it be like to be married to him and unable to walk away? She shudders.

"Good." Eliza tucks Hastings's shirt inside the valise and picks another from a pile of fresh laundry. "I was your age when I married Captain de Feuillide. I thought I was a woman, ready to love and be loved. Looking back, I was no more than a naïve little fool." She shoves the carefully folded shirt into the bag, rumpling the fabric and undoing her meticulous efforts.

"Do you regret it?" Jane has never dared be so bold with her cousin, yet she's long suspected Eliza was never as content as she pretended to be with her French count.

"No." Eliza shakes her head so vigorously her plait slithers over her shoulder and down her back, until it reaches the base of her spine. "How can I, when he gave me my beautiful boy? But I do wish I'd spent more time getting to know my own mind before I accepted him. Once it's done, there's no easy way to escape a marriage. Enjoy these years of liberty, *ma chérie*, before it's too late. Better yet, enjoy your flirtations. The memory of them will sustain you well into your matronhood when the pickings are slimmer. Or so I'm told."

Jane laughs. Eliza smiles, too, but it does not reach her eyes. "May I ask you something?"

"Anything." Eliza tilts her head. "As long as I'm not compelled to answer."

"Why did you ask Mr. Martin if Zoë Renard purchased a tincture that might restore her courses?"

"Because she was in such a wretched predicament. A young woman, alone, hundreds of miles from her family with a child on the way. No one would have blamed her for wishing to bring on an . . . accident. And yet, from everything you and Mrs. Martin have said, Zoë Renard seems not to have been desperate at all.

Yes, she pawned her jewels, but she soon found the money to retrieve them. She was learning English. And subscribing to the circulating library indicates she had leisure time. She was building a life for herself here."

The curtains are open and a smattering of stars glitters across the black sky. Jane recalls Madame Renard's nonchalance over whether or not she purchased the hat. While Jane preened herself in Madame Renard's looking glass, and quibbled over the price, the merchant maintained a mask of composure. Never once did she look away, or offer to drop the price. Zoë Renard acted as if she was entirely her own mistress—not a ruined woman with a shameful secret. Her life was simple, but she was proud of her accomplishments and resolute in her purpose.

"You are right. She did not behave as though she was short of money or confidence. What does it mean?"

"Perhaps that she wasn't quite as alone as we assumed. That someone *was* taking care of her." One corner of Eliza's mouth turns up into a sly smile. "You know how we women like to keep our secrets."

Jane nibbles at her thumbnail. "Someone in Basingstoke, or nearby, who gave her the money to retrieve her jewels from the pawnbroker, but clearly didn't want anyone else to know of their relationship?"

Eliza's delicate features crumple into a frown. "Perhaps. You won't give up, will you?" She lifts another shirt from the pile. Her valise is almost full. The bedroom will be sad and empty without her lotions and potions scattered across the dresser and Hastings's toys piled up on the bed.

"Absolutely not. There's no way I can stand by while Georgy suffers for something he didn't do. Added to that, Madame

Renard's spirit deserves to be at peace. And I truly don't think it can be, not without seeing her killer served justice."

"Good. Don't ever become too biddable, will you? There's only so far a woman can bend before she breaks."

But intuition tells Jane that Madame Renard's skull may have been caved in precisely because she wasn't biddable enough. She swallows bile, forcing the image of poor Madame Renard's bloodied face from her mind.

The next morning, Jane and her family line up in front of the rectory to bid Eliza and Hastings adieu. James climbs into the driver's seat of the carriage, wearing his father's greatcoat. "Thank you, thank you, my Steventon darlings." Eliza kisses Mr. and Mrs. Austen on both cheeks. "You are charity personified, to have offered such fine hospitality to Hastings and me while you nurse your own sorrows."

"You are a balm to our troubled souls, niece," says Mr. Austen.

"Think nothing of it," adds his wife, "and promise you'll come back to us before another year is out." She jiggles a wailing Anna in her arms. The red-faced baby stretches her chubby arms out helplessly for her playmate. Jane squeezes Eliza's tiny frame tight and blinks back tears when she lets her go.

Henry scoops up Hastings, ruffling his golden curls as he deposits him inside the carriage. Afterward, he stands to attention, so that Eliza must stretch up on tiptoe to peck him swiftly on his jawbone. He glowers down at her, clenching his teeth so tightly that a blue vein ticks in his neck. He is the only Austen to receive just one kiss. Even Sally, to her utter bemusement, received two.

As the carriage wheels creak and turn, he storms inside the rectory, slamming the front door so hard that the rose-covered trellis around the doorframe threatens to collapse.

"What ails him?" asks Mrs. Austen.

Jane shrugs. "Who knows?"

But it's obvious Henry's foul mood has everything to do with Eliza's hasty departure. Jane has no desire to discuss the complexities of Henry and Eliza's relationship with her mother. She'd prefer not to dwell on it herself. Surely he cannot have imagined she would take him seriously as a *suitor*? She follows the carriage into the lane. Piles of dead leaves rest at the base of the bare and thorny hedgerow. Immediately after the vehicle rounds the corner, a brown-cloaked figure emerges.

Janes holds her palm flat over her eyes and squints into the morning sun. Mary Lloyd's pot hat is silhouetted against the dazzling sky. "Was that your cousin leaving?" asks Mary. "Why is James driving her rather than Henry? Or your father?"

Jane halts, waiting for Mary to reach her. "My father says he's too old to go gallivanting in this weather. And I think she and Henry have fallen out."

Mary remains in place, staring mournfully at the bend in the road.

The leaves crunch beneath Jane's feet and the cold wraps around her toes through the thin soles of her leather walking boots as she plods to meet Mary. "What are you doing out unchaperoned? I thought your uncle had you under lock and key."

Mary turns her gaze to Jane. Her eyes are unnaturally bright. "Uncle Richard has been called up to Deane House. That's why I'm here. There's a great hullabaloo—I came to fetch you. Apparently they're going to arrest *him*."

"I knew it!" Jane cries, in relief, startling Mary. "I *knew* he killed her."

Mr. Craven must have followed the same clues as Jane to connect Jonathan Harcourt to the dead woman. His investigation will have uncovered proof they were both in Brussels at the same time and that Madame Renard pawned Jonathan's ring. Georgy will be set free and returned to his family immediately. This nightmare will be over.

CHAPTER EIGHTEEN

"What a lurid imagination you have, Jane." Mary tuts as she and Jane trudge up the hill to Deane. The lane is dirty and the mud clings to Jane's skirts, weighing her down as she tramps along. Really she should have gone back to fetch her pattens to protect her walking boots, but she's in far too much of a hurry to get to the Tudor manor—where, according to Mary, Sir John is about to be arrested for defaulting on his debts, rather than his son for being implicated in the death of Madame Renard.

"Oh, do stop crowing. Can you just start from the beginning and tell me everything again, please?"

Mary hangs onto Jane's arm, staggering up the slope in her clumsy footwear. "But what made you think Mr. Harcourt would be arrested for the murder? It must be all those Gothic novels you read. I keep trying to get through the latest one you and Martha are always gushing over. The one set in the Black Forest? But it's altogether too confusing. And it can't be Christian to dwell on necromancy, wizards and whatnot. No, I much prefer your brother's verses."

Jane takes a deep breath, forcing down her ire. "Do I need to remind you, Mary, that it was you who suggested Madame Renard's spirit would commune with us over the identity of her murderer?"

"That was different."

"How?"

"It was sanctioned by my uncle."

Jane's blood is reaching boiling point. "In that case, can you please return *The Mysteries of Udolpho* to Mrs. Martin's circulating library so that somebody more appreciative can read it. Now, I beg you, stop prattling and tell me everything that happened."

"I've already told you. We were having breakfast when one of the grooms from Deane House knocked on the side door, shouting for the magistrate. Apparently, Mr. Harcourt begged my uncle's pardon to come directly—as old Mr. Chute and his bailiff were threatening to arrest Sir John and carry him off to the Marshalsea."

"So Mr. Chute must have loaned Sir John money. A lot of it, too, if he's after having him thrown into gaol." Jane bounces on the balls of her feet as she suppresses the urge to break into a run. If Mr. Chute guards his wife as closely as he watches over his shillings and pence, Henry was lucky to escape any repercussions of his dalliance with her on the night of the Harcourts' ball. Was the money Sir John owed to Mr. Chute the real reason the baronet wanted to get his hands on Eliza's fortune? The scoundrel would rob Peter to pay back Paul.

"I don't know. My uncle told me to stay at home until he got back. But I thought if I fetched you, we could go there together and try to eavesdrop. Then, if I'm caught, I can say you forced me."

"What a faithful friend you are." Jane berates herself silently for leaping to conclusions. It was foolish of her to hope the authorities had identified the real culprit. The lethargic colossus of English law will not rouse itself to seek justice for an ordinary young woman, no matter how swift it is to act when preserving the interests of a wealthy gentleman.

"I still don't understand. Why would you think Mr. Harcourt killed the milliner?"

As Deane House comes into view, Jane shakes off Mary's grip and strides ahead. "Lacemaker. And I'm not saying that exactly, only that I've a hunch there must have been some connection between them." She will ruin her boots, and her hem may never recover, but without the encumbrance of pattens she's more fleet of foot than Mary.

Did Sir John kill Madame Renard because she was blackmailing him over his arrangement with Mrs. Twistleton and he could no longer afford to pay for her silence? Perhaps Madame Renard simply knew too much about the debts Sir John had amassed on those card nights at the Angel Inn. Both Sir John and Mrs. Twistleton seemed to be as horrified as everyone else when her corpse was discovered, but they might have been feigning it, and covering for each other. Or was it Jonathan? Did he murder his mistress to prevent her from jeopardizing his lucrative marriage to Sophy? Could the threat of financial ruin tip an ordinarily mild-mannered man into performing the most atrocious act?

As Jane approaches the gates of the garish Tudor mansion, a luxurious barouche, attached to two perfectly matched grey horses, sits empty in the driveway. Beside it, Mr. Chute's bailiff stands guard over a post chaise, imprisoning Sir John. Mrs. Twistleton dabs her face with a handkerchief. Her eyes are puffy, and her usually attractive features are haggard. Sir John leans out of the window at a precarious angle to squeeze her hand. Without his periwig, he looks smaller and far less imposing. Thinning hair lies in wisps around his head, except at the rear of his skull, where a small circle of exposed skin makes him appear especially vulnerable. Neither of them notices Jane hastening by.

Angry shouts drift from the open doorway of the house. Jane pauses to the side of the threshold, and peers into the gloomy oak-paneled entrance hall. Mary trots up the steps behind her, her pattens dangling over her arm. She must have kicked them off and broken into a run to catch up. Together, they stand in the shadows, straining to watch the unfolding drama without being seen by those inside.

"Gentlemen, please . . ." Mr. Craven stands directly beneath the weighty brass chandelier, stretching both hands aloft, as if separating a clash of bloodthirsty pugilists.

Lady Harcourt perches on the sofa under the carved staircase, clutching a small glass bottle of smelling salts to her beaked nose. Beside her, Jonathan Harcourt rests one hand on the newel post and rakes his fingers through his lank hair. "Take my father." He is in his shirtsleeves, an ivory linen waistcoat cut tight to his rangy frame. "But I beg you give me a week, a few days at least, to meet the repayments. Please, sir." He presses his hands together, interlacing his fingers as if at prayer. "If you call in everything now, the vultures will descend. Our tenants will be ruined as well as us, and it's hardly fair on them."

Mr. Craven drops his hands to his sides and inclines his head. "What do you say, Mr. Chute? Give the lad a chance, eh? He's right. If you make this known, all of Sir John's creditors will charge in at once and you'll be forced to fight over every scrap. You stand a much better chance of recouping the debt if you allow Mr. Harcourt a short reprieve."

On the far side of the entrance hall, Mr. Chute narrows his rheumy eyes and grasps the handle of his gold-tipped cane. "Very well. I am satisfied." His velvet frock coat and matching breeches are embroidered with a garden of flowers in a rainbow of silk threads. Even the buckles on his shiny black shoes sparkle with diamonds and rubies. "But as for Sir John, he'll not be leaving the Marshalsea until every penny I'm owed is back in my coffers. Do you mark me, boy?"

"No. You can't take him. I won't let you." Lady Harcourt rises from the sofa, wringing her hands. Her voice quivers, like a string about to snap. "It's not fair. I've already lost my son." She glances toward the bust on the landing. Marble Edwin surveys the scene blankly with his milky-white death stare. "And now you would take my husband, too. I won't stand for it, I tell you."

Jane swallows. When Mr. Craven carted Georgy away, she pictured herself running after the wagon, screaming and crying, while tearing the hair from her head by its roots. Instead, she forced down those primal urges, did exactly as her former nurse instructed and scrambled off to alert her father like a good girl.

"Mother, please . . ." Jonathan inserts himself between Lady Harcourt and Mr. Chute. "Why don't you go and lie down? Take some of your medicine?" There are sweat patches under the arms of Jonathan's shirt and his pallor is ashen. He turns to his adversary. "I understand, thank you, sir. I'll arrange an auction immediately. Every piece of plate and pewter—anything we can sell to raise the cash—will be sold. You have my word."

Mr. Craven rubs his hands together. "Excellent. May I propose you shake on it, gentlemen?" Mr. Chute strokes his chin, before grasping Jonathan's palm and giving it one firm shake. "Very good. Very good." Mr. Craven sticks a thumb into his lapel as he glances at his pocket watch.

Jane pinches her lips together. The magistrate hasn't raised the possibility of a connection between Madame Renard's murder and the Harcourts' enormous debts. He's more concerned with keeping the peace between two well-heeled neighbours than with finding her killer and clearing Georgy's name. She cannot let this opportunity to press Jonathan pass by.

"Is that all?" She strides out of her hiding place and into the entrance hall.

"Miss Austen, what are you doing here?" Mr. Craven's gaze travels from Jane's face to her muddy boots and back up again. "Mary? Is that you, child, hiding in the doorway? I explicitly told you to remain at home."

Jane's legs turn to jelly as she stands face to face with the magistrate. "A gentlemen's agreement? A handshake, and then you'll let him get away with it?"

"Miss Austen, what the devil are you talking about? You can't just burst in here like this."

Jane points a shaky finger straight at Jonathan. "It was *you*, wasn't it? You murdered that poor woman, right here, and abandoned her body in your laundry closet."

Jonathan's chest caves as he curls in on himself.

"Are you in your right mind?" Mr. Craven's jaw hangs open.

Lady Harcourt shrieks hysterically, lunging for Jane's face.

Jonathan's pale eyes shoot open. "Mother!"

Lady Harcourt swipes at Jane. Her talons are so close, a breeze sweeps across Jane's cheek and ruffles her curls. Jane staggers backward, but Mr. Craven catches Lady Harcourt by the waist before she can reach her.

Jonathan surges forward, bundling his mother into his arms. "Come, Mother, upstairs to bed. It's been a terrible shock, but there's no need to fret . . ." He half drags, half carries her up the carved staircase. "Mrs. Twistleton! Prepare Mother's tincture immediately."

The housekeeper springs out from somewhere behind Jane. "Hush now, ma'am." She grabs her skirts in her fists, revealing clocked silk stockings as she scrambles up the stairs behind Jonathan and his mother.

Over her son's shoulder, Lady Harcourt twists her neck to sneer at Jane. Venom glitters in her beady eyes. Every nerve in Jane's body jangles.

"Miss Austen, really!" Mr. Craven draws close. "Have you taken leave of your senses? What on earth could have provoked you to make such an accusation?"

Mary brushes Jane's hair out of her face. "Are you all right? The old crone almost took your eyes out."

Jane bats Mary's hand away, a little too roughly. She lifts her chin to Mr. Craven. "It is you who is out of your senses. Can't you see?" Her head is pounding, making her dizzy. "Sir John's debts *must* be connected to the murder."

"I can assure you, Miss Austen, this is a business matter between Sir John and Mr. Chute. It has nothing to do with the dead woman. I've already settled that incident. It was one of the trespassers intruding on Sir John's estate."

"You still believe that? Even after you know there's no evidence of any vagrants?"

"Miss Austen, as I told you last night, I have *not* charged your brother with murder . . ." He lowers his voice to a whisper, his eyes softening as he steps closer to Jane. "Please, don't force me to do so . . ."

With sickening clarity, Jane sees that Mr. Craven is not fooled by Sir John's accusations any more than she is. He truly believes Georgy is guilty, not just of stealing Madame Renard's necklace but of taking her life. Rather than being negligent, he's acting out of compassion. He will not investigate further because he is afraid of what he might find. He knows that, as terrible as it would be for Jane and her family if Georgy was hanged as a thief, it would be even worse if he was condemned as a murderer.

Georgy would be denied the most basic of Christian rights—to be laid to rest in consecrated ground. Instead, after he was hanged before a jeering crowd in Winchester town square, his body would be taken to Deane, wrapped in chains and publicly displayed from the nearest gibbet as a macabre warning to any would-be murderers. It could take years for the birds and maggots to pick his clothes and flesh clean away. Only then would the Austens be allowed to cut him down to bury his skeleton. Even then they could not take him home to rest in St. Nicholas's churchyard. Georgy would lie beneath the crossroads, with a stake through his heart, his soul marked as unworthy of redemption, even on the final Day of Judgment, and doomed to roam the earth for all eternity.

If the grief did not kill Jane's parents, the ignominy surely would.

Mary slides her arm around Jane's waist, saving her from toppling over beneath the crushing weight of her realization.

"I'll be on my way." Mr. Chute breaks the tension by tipping his cocked hat to the ladies and shuffling toward the exit.

Mr. Craven lifts his hand, calling after him, "And you're certain you won't let Sir John remain here? You're well within your rights, of course, but . . ."

"That braggart has been taking me for a fool." Mr. Chute whips his cane in the air. "A dose of debtors' prison will teach him I'm not a man to be trifled with."

"As you wish." Mr. Craven ambles outside. Mary follows, sweeping a still-dazed Jane along with her.

In the driveway, Mr. Chute nods to his man and steps into his barouche. The bailiff mounts one of the draught horses tethered to the post-chaise and taps his crop. With a whinny, both animals toss their manes and lift their forehoofs. The carriage groans and Sir John turns his head toward Deane House, visibly struggling to maintain his composure as he takes a last look at his ancestral seat.

Once both carriages are out of sight, Mr. Craven holds out his arm to Jane. "Please, Miss Austen. Won't you let me escort you home?"

Jane stares at his elbow, unshed tears clouding her vision. "Thank you, sir, but I'll manage on my own." She removes Mary's hand from her waist, and places it lightly by her friend's side. As she limps off down the driveway, she can feel Mary and Mr. Craven's gaze heavy on her back. Despite the enormous weight of their judgment, she staggers on, desperate to keep the pieces of herself together. For Georgy's sake, if nothing else, she cannot let this latest setback destroy her.

CHAPTER NINETEEN

When Jane arrives home, Lycidas, Mrs. Lefroy's impeccably behaved gelding, is tethered to a fence post outside the rectory. Mrs. Lefroy has tried relentlessly to persuade Jane to ride the horse. Jane invariably refuses. Instead, she watches with her heart in her throat, as her friend leaps him over waist-high hedges. The prospect of being at such a dizzying height from the ground, entirely reliant on another being, ties Jane's stomach into agonizing knots.

To master a horse, one must relax into the saddle and use the superior power of the human mind to bend the animal's will to one's own. After her fall, Jane lost the childish arrogance it took to place such complete faith in herself. She strokes the white star on Lycidas's head and lets him nuzzle her shoulder before going inside, hanging up her cloak and hiding her ruined boots in the vestibule by the back door before her mother can chide her.

Her parents and Mrs. Lefroy are cosy and serene, taking tea and pound cake in the best parlour. Jane joins them, hoping Tom has, at long last, sent his aunt to broker the topic of their betrothal with her parents. It really could take some time to convince Mr. Austen of the merit of the match. It is true that she and Tom could not afford to set up house immediately, but Jane is confident she can bring her father round. Her pairing with Tom may not be perfect, but they could make each other happy—if only they were given the chance.

A good fire blazes in the grate as they drink from the blue-and-white willow-patterned china. The Austens' finest tea set was a wedding present from their affluent Knight relations more than three decades ago. The teapot remains serviceable, despite the tiny chip in the spout, but there are only five cups to six saucers and the milk jug is long gone. Jane pours herself some tea, takes up a fat slice of cake and regales the company with the details of her afternoon. In a desperate attempt to keep the mood light, she does not mention that she accused Jonathan Harcourt of murder before the county magistrate.

Mrs. Lefroy is elegant as ever, in her striped redingote, with her powdered hair piled high on her head. "Darling Jane, you really do know how to recount a tale." She perches on the edge of the wingback chair, one leg crossed over the other, as if unwilling to make herself completely at home. "I can't believe Mr. Chute actually went through with removing Sir John to the Marshalsea. How mortifying for the baronet."

Mrs. Austen shakes her head. She has left off her pinafore, for once. "Neither a borrower nor a lender be. Not if one can help it, at any rate."

Mr. Austen balances his cup and saucer on his knee, his white hair forming a halo around his genial face. "And so the ever-turning wheel of fortune rotates for the Harcourts. Well, I never."

Jane licks the crumbs from her fingers. "Quite a fall, eh? Sir John must have been desperate not to let it get this far. I expect this is why he approached Eliza for a loan. It's hard to imagine what such a proud man might do to protect his standing in such circumstances."

Mrs. Lefroy places her empty cup and saucer on the mahogany side table. She stands, peering at the dusky haze outside the window. "The garden looks pretty. Jane, will you give me a tour?"

Mrs. Austen creases her brow. "But we've just ripped everything out. I've plenty of fresh chicken manure to go in the beds, but . . ." She turns to her husband, who shrugs in reply.

Mrs. Lefroy shoots Jane a pointed look. "Well, I could do with some fresh air. Shall we, Jane?"

"Of course." Jane abandons her half-drunk tea.

In the vestibule, she hastily dons her cape and the mud-encrusted walking boots before stepping out of the back door. It is twilight. The evening star twinkles fiercely in the violet sky. Silvery light splits the moon into two perfect halves, bathing one side in its brilliance while leaving the other to lurk in darkness. Hampshire's rolling hills hem the Austens' land on all sides. The crooked branches of the oaks stand out as if they have been sliced from a black card with a scalpel. Jane leads her guest past the empty vegetable beds, while Mrs. Austen presses her nose to a windowpane and frowns.

Mrs. Lefroy turns up the collar of her redingote and tucks her arm into the crook of Jane's. "Not very good at taking hints, is she, your mother?"

Jane laughs. Her breath comes out in wispy white puffs, like those of a spent dragon. "I wouldn't say it's one of her strong points."

Mrs. Lefroy's features remain stern. "It was imperative I saw you alone as . . . well, I'm afraid I must talk to you about a rather delicate matter."

Jane's fingers and toes are numb. "How intriguing." The farmyard is deserted. The galinies and the bantams are shut inside their coops, safe from ravenous foxes prowling the countryside.

"Yes. But . . . before I begin, you must know that I'm asking this precisely because you are so dear to me." She squeezes Jane's arm. "I treasure you with as much love and care as I would any niece, and it is *your* happiness that is uppermost in my mind."

"Oh?" Jane's stomach plummets with every word her friend utters. She fixes her eyes directly ahead as they walk. "That's very kind of you. You know I adore you in return." She tries to smile, but the muscles in her face are frozen.

Mrs. Lefroy holds on to her elbow, forcing Jane to face her. "I'll come straight to it . . ." In the violet light, Mrs. Lefroy's complexion is ashen. "Has my nephew made you a proposal? Because, if he has, I fear he may have misrepresented himself to you."

"Misrepresented?" Jane's mouth is so dry, she struggles to enunciate the word. She's been so close to Tom that his warm breath tickled her neck, and his heart beat against her breast. How could this man, who shares her secret world of joy and excitement, ever conceal anything from her?

Mrs. Lefroy sits down on a tree stump, as if it were a stool. "You see, having been so recently driven out of France, none of the Lefroys has had a chance to establish themselves. Tom's parents live a very modest life. As you know, he's the youngest of six. The rest are all girls, with little to recommend them."

Jane nods, the motion causing her to stumble. A heavy weight is pressing on her chest. So heavy, it could be one of the mottled limestone slabs from the churchyard above.

"Uncle Langlois is the only one with any resources—but they're far from unlimited. It was he who put Tom through university, and he'll be sponsoring his place at Lincoln's Inn. So, you can understand, the expectation has always been that Tom will do whatever he can to further cement his position in the world through . . . well, through . . ."

"Marriage." Jane's voice is flat.

It's the ugly truth she's been running from since the first time she looked into Tom's bright blue eyes and her foolish heart fluttered at the reflection of herself—or, rather, the fashionable young wife and mother she could be—in his enlarged pupils.

Cassandra has hinted at it in her letters, and Eliza warned her, but Jane has been trying her best to outpace it.

At last it's caught her in its vicious jaws, like a hungry steel mantrap—Tom Lefroy, the ambitious young lawyer from Limerick, can ill afford to pledge his troth to a penniless clergyman's daughter from Hampshire, however much he might wish to. It would be ruinous for both of them.

Mrs. Lefroy presses the heel of her hand against her diaphragm. "I'm afraid so. He'll be de facto head of his family, you see. They're all dependent on him. I'm so very sorry. I wish it were otherwise . . . but it's not." The lines in her forehead twist and carve deeper. "So, I'll ask you again, Jane. Has my nephew made you an offer of marriage?"

A throbbing lump blocks Jane's throat. "No. Nothing of the sort. It's just a silly flirtation." She's trying so hard to sound light that her voice screeches. She places her hands on her hips and tries to steady herself as the world spins past too quickly.

And it's true: Tom hasn't made her an offer of marriage. Not explicitly, anyway. Perhaps he never meant to, and it was purely Jane's imagination that placed the intention behind every word of love he uttered, his every fond glance at her and every scorching kiss he pressed to her lips.

"Oh, that's a relief." Mrs. Lefroy sways, as she clears her throat. "I was afraid he might have raised your expectations unfairly."

"Not at all. No harm done." Jane wipes scalding tears from her cheeks with the back of her hand. "Would you mind seeing yourself back to the house? I'm in the mood to walk on a little further." She lurches toward the iron gate, clinging to the tangles of ivy covering the flint wall.

"Jane . . . ," Mrs. Lefroy calls from behind her.

Jane darts into the churchyard. She ducks under the sprawling branches of the yew. Concealed by its evergreen needles, she cups her hands over her mouth and fights to prevent her anguish escaping in angry words she will not be able to retract.

"Jane?" Mrs. Lefroy emerges through the gate and peers around the lonely graveyard. "Jane, please." She picks her way over the grass, searching behind the weeping angels and the Portals' twin sarcophagi. Bats squeak as they explode between broken tiles out of the church roof. Their silhouettes swoop across the purple horizon, soaring one moment and diving toward the ground the next. "Jane. What will I say to your mother?" Finally, she shakes her head and disappears through the gate, back onto the Austens' private land.

Only when Jane is certain she's alone does she fully release her breath.

It rushes from her swollen throat in choking sobs. With blood screaming in her ears, she flails at the rough red bark of the yew. Tears blind her as she slams her fists into its mighty trunk. She kicks and lashes out, sending twigs sprawling only for them to spring back and whip her face. Two giant tombstones trap her heart, crushing her ribs and grinding every last gasp of air out of her lungs.

Marriage is a bargain, a compromise of compatibility and circumstance. Jane is a fool to have entertained the notion it could be anything otherwise. For weeks, she has allowed herself to be deluded by Tom's charm and her own desire. The hot secret of their mutual attraction, bound and held tight to her chest, tricked her into thinking that—for her—marriage could be something different: a true partnership of minds and hearts entwined.

With her reckless display of naïveté, she's no doubt made herself the laughingstock of the county. She is no better than Mary, openly pining for James, or Henry, drooling over Eliza. She is a stupid, hapless young woman—with no wealth to recommend her and no power over her own destiny. She grabs fistfuls of sharp needles, tearing them from the branches and squeezing them between her naked palms.

Encased in her green cell, she howls. Her fingernails rip and her knuckles bleed. She scuffs the tips of her leather walking boots and stubs both of her big toes. Her fists throb, her knuckles sting and her throat is seared.

Exhausted, she wraps her arms around the centre of the tree, and slides to the foot of its ancient trunk. With a thud, her knees hit the cold, damp earth. Jane slumps forward, pressing her pulsing forehead into the jagged bark as her body heaves with guttural sounds.

When her limbs shiver, and her teeth chatter with such ferocity that they rattle her skull, she untangles herself from the branches and rolls out from beneath the tree's embrace. She pushes herself onto her hands and knees, staggers to her feet and drags herself homeward.

An incongruous flash of colour catches her eye.

She limps toward the fresh mound where Zoë Renard lies buried. The hair on the back of her neck rises as if she has walked over her own grave.

Three cherry-red flowers are balanced along the ridge of recently disturbed earth.

The petals of the compact blooms resemble the points of a tiny crown, and are in such perfect condition they might have been modeled from wax. Jane cradles one in her shaking hand, inspecting it by moonlight. They are camellias, exotic flowers that Neddy once sent Mrs. Austen from the orangery at Goodnestone House, the magnificent Kent country estate belonging to his wife's family. But Jane has never heard of a camellia bush growing in Hampshire.

She wraps the flower in her pocket handkerchief and tucks it inside her cloak, stumbling toward the glowing windowpanes and smoke-billowing chimney pots of Steventon Rectory. So, Jane is not Madame Renard's only mourner. In death, as in life, the lacemaker is being furtively cared for. Someone is bringing her flowers, rare and expensive blooms, and artfully arranging them over her grave. But who is it? And why have they not come forward to claim her?

6. To Cassandra Austen

Steventon, Tuesday, 5 January 1796

My dearest Cassandra,

I thank you, beloved sister, for your vitriolic outburst on my behalf at my Irish friend's removal. Never would I have thought your sweet tongue capable of such vile curses. Where did you even learn such a foul turn of phrase? Is this the result of your being in such close quarters with a seaman? Whatever the origin of your new, coarser manner, you must allow the flames of your fury to settle into a more dignified flicker of irritation. I promise you faithfully, every part of my person, including my reckless heart, remains entirely intact. If you truly desire to spare me pain, I beg you do me the kindness of refraining from mentioning the pitiful affair ever again. I'm already made weary by hearing it whispered about everywhere I go. Please, Lord, let some other young lady hereabouts make a fool of herself for love soon enough so that I may be released from my ignominy.

Back to the far more pressing matter of who, and what, sealed the fate of the hapless ~~milliner~~ lacemaker, Madame Renard.

– Jonathan Harcourt (did he ruin Madame Renard, then cast her aside to save his family from ruin?)

– Sir John (did he kill Madame Renard to clear the way for his son to snare the heiress?)

– Mrs. Twistleton (if her protector went bankrupt, she could no longer count on him)

– Jack Smith (is he selling us a pig in a poke?)

I confirm I already settled your account with Mrs. Martin. Really, there was no need for you to fret. Sir John's debts were several thousand times your own, and the librarian could have no reason to want to see you packed off to the Marshalsea in disgrace for your overdue fines.

Yours ever,
J.A.

PS Please screw this letter into a ball and use it to knock the cobwebs from the rafters of Mr. Fowle's barn.

Miss Austen,
Rev. Mr. Fowle's,
Kintbury,
Newbury.

CHAPTER TWENTY

Beeswax candles flicker in their scalloped brass sconces as a liveried butler leads Jane and James through the grand chambers of Manydown House. Jane would give anything to be at home, rather than venturing out to a party at this frigid and inhospitable time of year. Following the debacle of her ill-fated romance with Tom Lefroy, she has no desire to face her friend Alethea, or anyone else who will be in attendance at Mr. Bigg-Wither's annual Twelfth Night celebration. But solitude, and indeed pride, are luxuries Jane can ill afford if she is to save Georgy's life. Someone in her community knows more about Madame Renard than they are letting on. That same someone who likely gave the lacemaker the money to retrieve her jewels and deposited flowers at her grave. And, no matter the cost to herself, Jane will find out who that person is.

The discovery of the camellias has left her with the niggling feeling that she has missed something vital. She is determined to speak again to everyone who was at Deane House that night—starting with Hannah. Jane's early meeting with the maid turned up the murder weapon and Madame Renard's time of death. What more might she have discovered if she hadn't been so tactless as to make the poor girl ill? And if Jane had but known that her own brother's life would depend on the fruitfulness of her interrogation? Like one of her mother's hens, Jane will scratch and claw at the same patch of bare brown earth until she turns over the tiniest of grubs with which to feed her investigation.

The butler bows, then grasps the twin brass knobs and opens both doors to Manydown's magnificent ballroom. Beneath a glittering crystal chandelier, a handful of families stand awkwardly in the conspicuously empty space. All heads turn to appraise the newcomers. Jane clings tightly to James as she surveys the room for Hannah. As she should have expected, the maid is nowhere to be seen. Only the footmen, in their smartest livery, are on display. James, sensing her discomposure, pats her hand without looking down.

After their mortifying encounter, Mrs. Lefroy sent Jane a note to let her know, with her impeccable sense of propriety, that she and Mr. Lefroy would be taking their nephew on a tour of the neighbouring county for the remainder of his visit. Judging by the expressions of curiosity and sympathy on the guests' faces, the news of his removal from Hampshire, and from Jane, has traveled even wider than the buzz of excitement over their initial infatuation. Jane checked the gap behind the loose flint in the wall of St. Nicholas's Church every day until Tom's departure was certain, but there was no word from him. The scratches on her hands and the bruises on her toes may be healing, but the pang in her chest grows sharper by the day. She raises her chin, determined not to betray her mortification to the party. To match her mood of defiance, she's wearing her storm-grey satin gown over her pink Persian petticoats.

As Sally remains cold and sullen, Jane styled her own hair. She left a few natural curls to frame her face, while pinning most of her chestnut locks into a tight, impenetrable chignon. Mrs. Austen swears she gave Sally a generous purse on Boxing Day, and insists that Jane is imagining the girl's ill-humour.

But Jane can feel the coolness emanating from Sally every time they pass each other. Perhaps, like Jane, she would rather retreat into herself than be forced to abide the well-meaning enquiries of others.

Arm in arm, Jane and James step onto the waxed parquet floor of the ballroom as one. A row of Corinthian-style columns stands at either end of the luxurious room. Jane knows, from knocking on these columns at previous celebrations, that they are constructed from wood. However, with their grey- and white-painted swirls, they do their utmost to convince the casual observer that they are hewn from marble. Around the high ceiling, above many levels of cornicing, an Etruscan frieze depicts the great men of the ancient world, lounging on sofas in togas and being fed bunches of grapes by their slaves. The plasterwork is so delicate, it could be crafted from sugar. The silk drapes and paneling are tasteful shades of apricot. Jane suspects Mr. Bigg-Wither chose the colour scheme deliberately to complement his offspring's redheaded complexions.

Indeed, Alethea is as polished as ever as she glides toward the new arrivals. "Oh, is it just the pair of you?"

Jane forces her shoulders back and pastes a smile onto her wan face. "Thank you, Alethea. We're delighted to see you, too."

With January ticking by, and Georgy's trial at the February assize drawing ever closer, none of the Austens can raise much cheer. James's missives to the lawyer are becoming increasingly fraught. Henry skulks around the rectory like a caged bull. To the outside world, Mr. and Mrs. Austen are models of Christian stoicism, but Jane senses her mother and father sinking deeper into dejection with each passing day.

Alethea pouts as she surveys the sparsely populated room. "Forgive me. It's just that we're a rather dull party."

It's true. There are so few people, they could all squeeze into the Austens' best parlour. Mr. Bigg-Wither's grand piano keeps its lid shut tight and refuses to make a sound. Alethea is not diligent enough with her practice to play in public and, like Jane, none of the guests are in the mood for exhibiting. The carpets have been removed for dancing but, as there is no music, the floor is empty. Every sound echoes, and gooseflesh crawls along Jane's exposed upper arms. A dining table groans under the significant weight of a buffet of the richest, heaviest seasonal fare. Platters of sliced beef, roast chicken and mince pies sit untouched. Jane's stomach turns at the sight of it. She hopes the servants are hungry. Otherwise, it will be wasted.

Alethea places one hand on her hip and juts out her chin. "Where's Lieutenant Austen?"

"Moping at home. He has been since New Year," replies Jane. Despite the flurry of letters that arrived for Henry from Brighton, in Eliza's unmistakable hand, he has not regained his usual cheer. Eliza is equally tight-lipped about what passed between them. In her letters to Jane, she ignores any enquiries as to the reason for her abrupt departure. Instead she presses for updates on the progress of Jane's investigation. While Jane confides in Cassandra without discretion, she is too mortified to admit the depth of her blundering to Eliza. Just as she is too ashamed to own that Eliza was right to warn her of the dangers of devilishly handsome young lawyers from Limerick.

James tugs at the collar of his new shirt. He begged Jane to finish sewing it in time for tonight. "We're not sure what's got into Henry, but he's in a foul humour. Trust me, you wouldn't want him here."

"Everyone has deserted us. The Lefroys have gone into Berkshire. For a 'holiday.' At this time of year! Would you believe it?"

Alethea's eyes soften as she turns to Jane. "But I suppose you already know that."

James coughs into his fist and steps away. Jane is resolute she'll remain as silent as Mr. Bigg-Wither's pianoforte when it comes to the topic of her Irish friend. If she refuses to fan the flames of gossip by betraying her emotions, they will burn themselves out soon enough.

"What happened?" Alethea slips her arm into Jane's. "We all thought you two were destined for the altar. But Mrs. Lefroy said Tom will go straight to London when they get back, and we're unlikely to see him again before he does."

Jane lowers her eyes to the floor and shrugs. The yellow-stained toes of her pink satin slippers stare up at her reproachfully.

"Come on, you silly thing. You know I'm only asking because I worry. Why don't you let your friends take care of you?" Alethea steers Jane toward one of the four Carrara marble fireplaces dotted around the room.

As Jane settles into a wingback chair, Alethea snaps her fingers at a footman. He dutifully hands Jane an enormous crystal goblet of claret, while Alethea balances a gilt-edged plate of twelfth-cake on the arm of her chair. Mary Lloyd plants herself on a sofa opposite. She is wearing her usual cream muslin gown and shawl, but there is something different about her appearance. Unless Jane is very much mistaken, Mary has applied the faintest hint of rouge to her cheeks, and has drawn a thin line of kohl where her eyebrows should be.

"Why did you leave James unattended?" Mary frowns. "Look, Mrs. Chute has hold of him now. We'll never get him back."

James is, indeed, pinned to a faux-marble pillar by a merry-looking Mrs. Chute. The newlywed twists a string of pearls around her finger and thrusts out her breasts, while James hides behind the mask of his sermon face—chin up, eyes fixed into the distance as he performs to his audience.

Alethea perches on the free arm of Jane's chair. She points her toe at the fire, letting the heel of her slipper fall away from her slender foot. "I was nursing Jane."

Mary whips her head around to face Jane. "Are you ill? You shouldn't have come if you're sickening for something. And you really should cover your chest. Here, take my shawl."

"No, I'm not ill." Jane turns away from Mary's fussing. "Alethea, stop it. There's nothing wrong with me."

"Of course not." Alethea traces small circles on Jane's back with her ticklish fingers. Jane wriggles, catching Alethea mouthing "Tom Lefroy" at Mary.

"I said stop it! I'm not a jilted bride." Jane bats away Alethea's hand. "I met a mildly interesting young man. We enjoyed a brief flirtation and now he's gone. That's all."

Alethea dips her chin. "Oh, you're so brave."

"There's no need to put on a show for us," says Mary. "We were as desperate as you for him to do the decent thing and propose."

"That's quite enough from you, Mary. Am I never to hear the end of it? From this day forward, I forbid either of you to mention the pitiful affair, whether in or out of my company. I never want to hear that the name 'Tom Lefroy' has been used in concert with 'Miss Jane Austen' ever again. Do you hear me?"

Now their dalliance is over, Jane is encouraging any doubts she hitherto suppressed about throwing in her lot with Tom to push and shove their way to the fore. She is not a patient woman. She could not, like Cassandra, sit around smiling sweetly while it took forever and a day for the object of her affection to amass enough money to marry her. Neither can she pretend she was looking forward to years of drudgery and servitude as the wife of a penniless lawyer. As Mrs. Austen says, "When poverty walks in the door, love flies out of the window."

Mary nods mutely, while Alethea sticks out her bottom lip. "If you think that would help?"

"Ugh." Jane gulps claret. The rich floral notes warm her insides, providing a temporary relief from her turmoil. "Where's Hannah? I can't see her. Will she be in the kitchen?"

"She's had to go back to Basingstoke to look after her brothers and sisters. Her mother's been struck down with the putrid throat," says Alethea. "You see, even the servants are avoiding our party. I don't know what's happened. Usually all the county are begging for an invitation. This year, no one wants to come."

Jane taps her glass with a finger. If she fails to question any of her witnesses, she might have spared herself the humiliation of appearing in public while everyone is clearly still whispering about her ill-fated romance. She consoles herself that by next Christmas her small circle will have moved on to discussing someone else's tragic tale of woe. The short dalliance between Miss Jane Austen and Mr. Tom Lefroy is so entirely unremarkable, it's sure to be forgotten soon enough. "When will Hannah be back?"

"I don't know," says Alethea. "When her mother's better? Or when the old woman's . . ."

"Dead?" supplies Mary.

Alethea grimaces. "I suppose so, yes."

"Putrid throat's no trivial matter," continues Mary, warming to her theme. "I've known strapping young farm labourers carried off by it in less than a fortnight. Hannah could fall prey to it herself. You should start making a list of alternative girls, Alethea."

Poor Hannah, her luck is as wretched as Jane's. It is unlikely her mother will have the means for a doctor. Which may be just as well: Jane is not convinced leeches are effective. A trip to Bath would be much better, but she supposes that is out of the question. As Mary and Alethea prattle on, comparing remedies, Jane eyes the half-empty room and considers who else to interrogate. It seems she must resign herself to waiting until, God willing, Hannah returns to Manydown before she can question her again. A small cluster of guests gather beside each of the four fireplaces. There are so few people, they could have a footman each to attend them. Mr. Bigg-Wither wanders from guest to guest, trying to persuade someone to play the pianoforte.

"Are the Riverses not coming?" Jane interrupts Mary and Alethea's debate as to the efficacy of barley water versus ginger beer. If neither Sophy nor Douglas Fitzgerald is the murderer, Jane must find out if either of them saw or heard anything that night which might lead to the true culprit.

Alethea shakes her auburn ringlets. "No. Apparently, the dashing Mr. Fitzgerald has gone to Canterbury for his ordination. The rest of them remain here with head colds."

Jane frowns. "A shame. On both counts."

Alethea titters. "Really, Jane, what have you against clergymen?"

"Nothing. I've enough of them already to last me a lifetime. That's all."

"A head cold? Is that what Mrs. Rivers told you?" says Mary. "Only I'm sure I saw Sophy, out alone, galloping across the fields behind Deane Gate Inn this morning. And even she wouldn't go out riding if she was unwell, surely."

"Are you certain it was her?" Why is Sophy lying and sneaking around? Could she be on her way to elope with

Mr. Douglas Fitzgerald? Perhaps Mrs. Rivers declined the social invitation while attempting to minimise the scandal. Jane wouldn't put money on her recovering her errant daughter. She can picture Sophy galloping her chestnut gelding all the way to Gretna Green.

Mary smooths her skirts over her thighs. "Absolutely certain. She leaped the boundary—and she's the only lady I've ever seen do it. Even Mrs. Lefroy says it's too high to attempt."

"That little snake," says Alethea. "You can't claim you're not fit to attend your neighbour's party when you're well enough to jump a six-foot hedge."

Jane continues to survey the room. "Where are the Digweeds?"

"We didn't invite them. By heavens, we're not that desperate for company."

Really, Jane knows she should confront Jonathan. She doesn't want to go blundering in, making a fool of herself and offending an innocent party, as she did with Mr. Fitzgerald, but she has little time for delicacy. She swills the dark wine in circles in her glass. "What about the Harcourts?"

"Ugh, what a nightmare they've been through." Alethea sighs. "I did try to persuade Jonathan to come, but he was worried it would appear disrespectful toward his father. When I told him Sir John wouldn't begrudge his son a drink at Christmas, he said he didn't want to give the impression he was reveling when they came so close to losing everything, dragging their tenants down with them. Poor fellow."

Jane runs her fingertip around the rim of her glass. "Why didn't you marry him, Alethea?"

Alethea chokes on her claret. "What sort of question is that?"

"Oh, I see. It's perfectly acceptable for my affairs of the heart to be everyone's favourite topic of conversation, but God forbid I should question yours?"

"Don't be so touchy. I was only asking about Mr. Lefroy because I care about you. I'm your friend, Jane."

Jane considers. Why would Alethea and Sophy hesitate in accepting Jonathan? On the surface, he is the perfect catch—handsome enough, well-mannered and heir to a baronetcy. Is there something about the Harcourts that draws people, then repulses them? And might it have anything to do with why a dead woman was found in their linen closet? "In that case, why can't you tell me what really went on between you and Jonathan Harcourt?"

"Nothing 'went on.'" Alethea's voice is tart. "If you must know, I didn't think it would be fair of me to accept Jonathan's offer of marriage. Edwin had only just died. The whole family was still reeling from the shock. He proposed only because he thought it would ease his parents' grief. They both favoured Edwin, you know. After the tragedy, Lady Harcourt wouldn't get out of bed and Sir John almost drowned himself in drink. Dear Jonathan thought he could rectify matters by settling down and assuming responsibility for running the estate. But I told him he mustn't let his brother's death deprive him of his dreams. His father could live for many years yet, and you know Jonathan's always wanted to be an artist."

Jane pictures schoolboy Jonathan bent over his desk at Steventon Rectory. A fearful boy at first, the butt of others' jokes, he soon learned to enact vengeance on the rowdier pupils by lambasting them with his caricatures. "Are you sure there wasn't something about him that made you uncomfortable? You know him better than any of us. If there was, you must say."

Alethea narrows her eyes as she dabs the claret-spotted neckline of her gown. "No, Jane. Jonathan Harcourt is a sweet, kind man, and my dear friend. I certainly don't think he'd murder a helpless woman. If that's what you're suggesting?"

"Is there anything you two haven't been gossiping about?" Jane glares at Mary.

"What?" Mary's jaw drops. "It's not as if you've been particularly quiet about your suspicions."

"Given Alethea's history with Mr. Harcourt, I didn't think I could trust her to be impartial."

"And I suppose you can be?" Alethea's voice is so sharp that several guests turn and stare.

Jane locks eyes with her friend. In their polite society, there are things one can and cannot say. Jane and Alethea have already crossed the line.

"Try the twelfth-cake, Jane." Mary slices through the tension. "It's really very good."

Alethea juts out her chin and flares her nostrils. "I don't see why a lady should feel compelled to accept an offer of marriage, just because she's asked. I enjoy a gentleman's company, as much as the next flirt—but there are other things I value more, such as my independence."

Jane takes in Alethea's proud features. Mr. Bigg was already a wealthy man when he inherited Manydown from his Wither relations and added their surname to his own in gratitude. He will bequeath the house and its lands to his son but, unlike Mr. Austen, he has plenty of money to leave his daughters well provided for, too. Alethea will not be forced to make a loveless marriage—or be kept apart from someone she adores because the numbers don't tally. "I concede your point there. If only every lady could afford the luxury of choice."

"Exactly. I know I'm privileged. And it's precisely because my circumstances are so blessed that I intend to enjoy my good fortune. I simply don't require a husband to share my life. Or, God forbid, my bedroom."

Jane looks askance at Alethea's reticence—sharing a bedroom with Tom does not feature in her list of suppressed doubts, only the inevitable *consequences* of sharing a bed. It's not that Jane doesn't like children. She adores Anna, Hastings and Neddy's brood, but she's noticed that aunts get to enjoy the fripperies of child-rearing, while mothers are wearied by the more vital aspects of keeping their offspring alive.

"Ooh, Mr. Chute's come to drag his wife home." Mary practically vaults over the sofa, making a beeline for James.

Alethea leans back in her chair until she sits shoulder to shoulder with Jane. "Well, there aren't nearly enough couples for dancing. We may as well play cards. Shall we have a hand of vingt-un?"

"Very well. But keep the stakes low. Unlike you, I can't afford to lose." Jane lifts the gilt-edged dish, taking a bite of her cake. Finding something hard on her tongue, she spits it into her palm and wipes it clean with her napkin. It is a dried pea.

Alethea smiles. "Oh, lucky you. You're our queen of Twelfth Night. I wonder who your king will be?"

A smattering of applause drifts from the other side of the ballroom. Mr. Craven stands at the centre of a circle of admirers, which includes a beaming Mary, who has latched onto James's arm with the adhesion of a limpet.

Beneath the bushy frame of his overgrown eyebrows, Mr. Craven smiles proudly, holding a slice of cake in one hand and a dried bean in the other.

"Oh, yes." Jane lifts her goblet into the air. "Lucky, lucky me."

CHAPTER TWENTY-ONE

A few days later, Jane enlists James to drive her to Basingstoke, under the guise of fulfilling an urgent errand for their mother. If James asks what it entails, which is highly improbable, Jane will utter the magic phrase "Mr. Martin's apothecary shop." He will redden and request no further details. Before Jane departs, she tucks Madame Renard's receipt safely into her pocketbook. She vows to show it to every pawnbroker in the small town until she finds whoever wrote it; if Madame Renard really was being kept by a gentleman, he might have accompanied her to reclaim her jewels. He might even have retrieved them himself. Jane is hoping one of the Basingstoke pawnbrokers can provide a description of such a man. If it *was* Jonathan Harcourt, he might even have been recognized, as a member of the local nobility.

While James tethers the horses to the carriage, Jane fastens her cape and hurries to the churchyard. Last night, as she walked home from evensong, three creamy white camellias were lined up along the ridge of earth marking Madame Renard's grave. This morning, the flowers are in the same position, but they have been changed to rose pink. Jane twists one of the flowers by its stem. "Where did you come from? And who put you here?"

It is a simpler form of camellia, with a single row of petals and a yellow stamen. She places it carefully back where she found it. She cannot risk letting whoever is leaving the flowers know she is watching. But she is watching, and she will discover who cared so very deeply for Madame Renard that they bring fresh flowers to her grave every day.

The sexton is sweeping fallen leaves from the entrance of St. Nicholas's Church. He doffs his hat as Jane passes.

Jane halts, turning to face him. "I wonder, sir, have you seen anyone visiting that area of the graveyard of late?" She points to Madame Renard's plot.

"You mean the murdered woman's grave?" The old man removes his hat, making the sign of the cross. "No, miss. Not a soul since they buried her. Apart from you, that is."

"And you're here every day?"

He straightens, leaning his weight on the broom handle. "Every day, from sunrise to sunset, you can find me hereabouts."

A shivery spider scuttles down Jane's spine, tickling each of her vertebrae with its eight hairy legs.

The floral tribute might have nothing to do with the murderer. It might have been left by children from the village, or by a woman moved by Madame Renard's plight. Then again, children would hardly be likely to bring such an exotic bloom, and a woman would come during daylight. "Will you keep an eye open for me? Let me know if anyone comes?"

The man nods, holding his hat tight to his chest. "Certainly, miss."

A vast expanse of dirty-white sky presses down on the rolling green hills as Jane sits alone inside the carriage, shivering, while James drives ten minutes up the narrow lane to Deane. For wont of a better accomplice, Jane has invited Mary Lloyd to join her in her search. It is not a choice she made willingly. Henry is still licking his wounds. Eliza and Cassandra have abandoned her. James will not allow his youngest sister to wander unchaperoned in the vice-ridden streets of Basingstoke, and Jane cannot ask Alethea as she is clearly blind where Jonathan Harcourt is concerned. Mary will have to do.

The front door of Mrs. Lloyd's cottage opens and an incandescent Mary steps out in her usual pot hat and mud-brown cloak. She skips along beside James, chirping like a feathery tit until they reach the carriage. James opens the door, and a blast of Siberian air hits Jane in the face.

Mary tips her head, gazing dreamily at James. "Actually, Mr. Austen, I was hoping I could sit on the driver's bench beside you. It's such a lovely day."

The harsh gale snaps saplings in two and swirls dead leaves into tiny tornadoes. Jane pokes her head out of the cab. "What are you twittering about, Mary? It's freezing cold. We'd likely lose the use of all our limbs if the horses went lame and left us stranded for the night."

Mary clutches at her chest. She's wearing new gloves, the colour of daffodils. "Yes, but at least it's dry. And I was hoping to hear more of your brother's wonderful verses."

James brushes the brim of his hat. A slow smile spreads across his proud Austen features. "Would you really? Which one were you thinking of?"

"I believe it was about . . . nature?" Mary fidgets with the ribbons of her cape.

"Ah, yes. I am so very inspired by the natural world." James squares his broad shoulders, before offering his elbow to Mary. "But Jane is right. It's far too cold for you to sit beside me. If we get back early enough, I'll come in for tea."

As Mary climbs into the carriage, she leans her slight frame far too close to James, throwing herself into his arms. "Oh, that would be delightful. Mother would be so pleased. She's always cheered by your visits."

James gives Mary a bashful smile as he clicks the door shut. Jane folds her arms under her cloak and shoots sly glances across the carriage. Mary sits opposite, squirming on the leather bench and smiling stupidly out of the window. She is thrumming with happiness.

Jane manages to hold her tongue until they are on the main road. "Don't think I don't know what you're about, Mary Lloyd. Setting your pot hat at James for all to see."

"Me? Hah! What about you? Trying to get your claws into my uncle."

Jane splutters. "What on earth are you talking about?"

"Getting yourself crowned queen of Twelfth Night beside him as king." Mary stares at her.

"That was hardly my doing. How was I to know my slice of cake contained the cursed pea? Believe me, the only thing I want from your uncle is for him to drop the charges against my brother."

Mary pulls at the ties of her hat, loosening the bow around her throat. "That's a shame." She places it on the bench beside her. "Uncle Richard is very taken with you."

The motion of the carriage is making Jane feel ill. "Well, he shouldn't be. I didn't give him my permission to be taken with me. Tell him to put me down wherever he found me."

"What's wrong with my uncle?"

Every rattle of the carriage and creak of the wheels grates on Jane's nerves. "For one thing, I'd be related to you."

Mary swivels her face to the window and blinks furiously.

Jane has gone too far this time. She regrets the words even before they're fully out of her mouth. Mary looks as if her mother has slapped her hard across the cheek. For a terrible moment, it seems she's going to cry. Despite the biting cold,

Jane is hot beneath her cloak. She waits for Mary to return her piercing jibe with a slight of her own. But, for several painful moments, Mary's gaze remains fixed on the fields passing outside the carriage. She takes short breaths until Jane can bear it no longer.

"What are you about in Basingstoke?" Jane asks, to dispel the tension.

Mary sniffs, wiping her cheek with the back of her hand. When she removes it, there is a brown watermark on her new glove. "I wanted some green muslin, to make up a shawl for the spring. Although you'll probably say it makes me look even plainer—compare me to a blade of grass or something amusing, and have the whole shop laughing at me."

Jane's arms and legs are leaden as she sinks into the padded seat. She needs Mary's help. She can't afford to alienate her, not today. Why is her own mouth constantly set on betraying her? How much easier it would be if she could conduct all her interactions by correspondence instead. She shouldn't have been so insensitive to Mary's feelings for James. But Jane has neither the time nor the sense of diplomacy to placate her. February draws ever closer, and she is running out of ideas for how to save Georgy.

"I'm going to catch a murderer," Jane blurts out, before she can stop herself.

Mary cannot resist turning her head to gawp. "What?"

"Before she died, Madame Renard pawned a gentleman's signet ring with her necklace. I found her receipt for reclaiming both items in her library book. We know what happened to the necklace, but the ring is still missing. I need you to accompany me to every pawnbroker in Basingstoke until I find whomever she spoke to, in the hope they can provide a description of the gentleman the ring belongs to. It's my last hope of saving Georgy. I'm begging you to help me, Mary."

Mary recoils, giving herself an extra chin. "But, Jane, we can't go into a . . ." she whispers, ". . . *pawnbroker's*."

Beneath her heavy cloak, Jane continues to perspire. Pools gather under her arms, making the undersides of her sleeves horribly damp and cool. "We can, and we will. We just need to get rid of James. Obviously, he'd never agree to it."

"But we're . . ." Mary grimaces, ". . . *young ladies*. It wouldn't be proper for us to be seen in such an establishment."

"I know. But I have to, Mary. Don't you see? If there's the slightest chance the ring could lead to the killer and prove Georgy innocent, I must take it. My brother's life is at stake. You know I wouldn't ask *you*, of all people, unless I was desperate." Jane falters, wary of offending Mary again. "Please, say you'll do it? Unless, like your uncle, you think Georgy deserves to go to the gallows."

Mary sags, inclining her head to the side. "Jane, how can you say that? You've watched me sew Georgy's shirts and darn his socks while you read to us. I make him a plum pudding every fortnight. I visit him in Dame Culham's cramped cottage, which always stinks of mutton fat, and I force down her disgusting dandelion and burdock concoction while I enquire after his welfare." The carriage shakes, making Mary's voice wobble. "You may have many reasons to dislike me, but disloyalty toward your family is *not* one of them."

Jane's heart somersaults in her chest. It's as if James has driven over a humpback bridge. "So, you'll do it? You'll help me?"

"I don't know. Have you told James, or my uncle, about the receipt? They'd be much better placed to investigate. Shouldn't we leave it to them?"

"Just as you're leaving it to my brother to notice you?"

Colour infuses Mary's cheeks, as she fights to suppress a guilty smile. "Very well, I'll do it. But only if you promise to help me."

Jane is filled with a sudden lightness. She knew Mary would accompany her—she'd be too intrigued by the drama to refuse. "Help you with what?"

Mary twists her hands in her lap, crushing the smooth kid leather of her gloves. "James. If he starts thinking seriously toward me, promise me you won't object? Or make fun of the notion so thoroughly that you put him off?"

"Mary Lloyd, you cunning little vixen. I never knew you had it in you." Jane looks to Mary with renewed respect. If Mary can make James happy, Jane is determined to be happy for James. And Anna, the poor child, needs a mother. Jane nods. "Why did you think I might object? You'd be perfect for each other."

Mary brightens. "Do you mean it?" The glimmer of hope lighting up her dark eyes plucks at Jane's heartstrings.

"Yes. James thinks he's wonderful, and so do you." Mary's chest deflates, but Jane can't have Mary thinking she's gone soft. "Besides, the sooner he remarries and stops cluttering the rectory the better. At least with you as a sister-in-law, I know what I'm getting. Have you no shame? Fluffing him up by praising his terrible poetry as if he's the Bard. I bet you can't quote a single word of it."

Mary straightens, arching her back so that it doesn't touch the seat. "I can."

"Go on, then." Jane crosses her legs, wrapping both hands around one knee.

"Er . . . I think there was a line where he mentioned . . ." Mary glances out of the window, ". . . the sky?"

"The sky?"

"Yes, the sky." Mary clamps her mouth shut, pressing her lips together, but that doesn't hide the merriment plumping her cheeks.

Jane collapses into giggles, followed by Mary. For the rest of the journey, they can scarcely look at each other without losing all composure. At one point, Jane thinks she has hold of herself but when Mary mouths "the sky," Jane laughs so much she slides off the leather bench into the footwell.

It is not yet noon, but merchants and working men pack the Angel Inn, crashing their pewter tankards together and puffing out the foul odour of tobacco as they spill onto the cobbles. Jane steps closer to Mary as they wait. James returns from stabling the horses and carriage, stamping his feet and rubbing his hands together. "We'll meet back here at three o'clock." He flicks open the silver case of the pocket watch he inherited from his maternal grandfather. "And not a minute later. I must be at the church in good time for evensong."

Jane, who was never in line for such a serendipitous inheritance, arches an eyebrow. "Would that be market time, or should we go by the clock at St. Michael's?" The clock in the marketplace has neither ticked nor tocked since the Mote Hall burned down in 1656, and the vicar of St. Michael's refuses to wind his. An antique sundial dictates the schedule of services at the Tudor church—which would be practical, if only Basingstoke had a more temperate climate and the sundial was not situated within the confines of an overgrown walled rose garden.

James snaps shut the pocket watch and tucks it inside his black frock coat. "Very droll, Jane. Just make sure you're here before it starts to get dark."

"Don't fret, Mr. Austen." Mary slides her arm into Jane's. "I'm a meticulous timekeeper and I shall make sure we return at three o'clock sharp. Mother would be so disappointed if you didn't have time to call in on your way back to Steventon."

Jane rolls her eyes but Mary, to give her her due, is an excellent taskmaster and clearly pays more attention to shopfronts than Jane does: she gabbles a list of every pawnbroker in Basingstoke and leads Jane through the crooked streets of the medieval town so that they call on each in the most efficient manner. The distinctive trio of golden spheres suspended from a gold bar greets Jane every time she rounds a corner.

Inside each shop, Mary prowls the shelves, poking at curiosities, while Jane shows the receipt to the proprietor. No one will own to writing it, and all of the pawnbrokers deny dealing in any seed-pearl necklaces or gentlemen's signet rings over the last few months. Until at last, in a cramped, fusty establishment opposite Mr. Martin's apothecary on the London road, a Mr. Lipscombe scratches his bald head under his tangled periwig and squints one bloodshot eye at the slip of paper. "That's definitely my writing. Was she a Frenchie perchance?"

Behind him, a dusty wooden dresser is crammed with swords, spoons, forks and tankards—all items that can be lifted and spirited away easily by light fingers, before the rightful owner notices and gives chase. Mr. Lipscombe's is by far the most down-at-heel establishment the ladies have visited, and the stench is overpowering.

Jane holds her breath as she speaks, giving her voice a nasal quality. "Well, she was from Brussels, actually. But we made that mistake, too."

"Little woman?" He holds his hand flat before Jane's nose. She pushes down the instinct to recoil from his grubby fingers. "Dark? Quiet."

"That sounds like her." Was poor Madame Renard reduced to entrusting her jewelry to this trickster for pennies? She must have been desperate.

"She didn't pinch it from you, did she?" Mr. Lipscombe jabs a dirty fingernail at the smeared glass top of his curiosity cabinet. "This here's a reputable business."

Jane very much doubts Mr. Lipscombe's assertion. When she arrived, he was arguing with some poor wretch over the worth of a golden watch. When the woman complained the amount was far too low for an outright sale, the pawnbroker grinned and said the price would match the gold well enough once it was melted down. "No, nothing like that." She winces.

Every corner of the shop is littered with items of questionable provenance. Unfashionable hairstyles, curled and beribboned, hang from hooks, like the scalps of fallen French aristocrats. Mismatched sofas and chairs, beyond repair, block the path to the door. A rack of secondhand clothes, from filthy rags to disheveled silks and furs, reeks of sweat. If Mrs. Austen knew Jane was here, she'd be most alarmed.

Then again, if her mother caught a whiff of what she was up to, she'd bar her from leaving the rectory at all. But lately Jane's mother has been far from her usual interfering self. With every day that draws closer to Georgy's trial, Mrs. Austen retreats further into her tough shell. It is as if the formidable matriarch is shrinking before Jane's eyes.

"She . . ." Jane hesitates, not wanting to relive the horror in repeating the details of Madame Renard's violent death.

"You must have heard about the woman found murdered at Deane House?"

Mr. Lipscombe leans forward, resting his weight precariously on the chipped glass. "That was never her?"

Jane takes her handkerchief from her pocket and presses it over her nose and mouth. "I'm afraid so, yes."

He lets out a whistle. "Sweet Jesus. And she being such a gentle one, too."

"It was terrible. We're trying to—" Jane breaks off. Call her a cynic but she doesn't quite trust Mr. Lipscombe. If she tells him she's trying to catch Madame Renard's killer, he might refuse to be involved. "We're trying to track down all her acquaintances, so we can be sure they've heard the tragic news. Was she alone when she visited your establishment? Or was her . . ." Jane coughs into her handkerchief, ". . . was her gentleman friend with her?"

Mr. Lipscombe scratches his temple beneath his wig. "Gentleman friend?"

"Yes. The man who owned the signet ring." Jane points to the receipt.

"Just her. Both times. I remember because it was such an unusual chain. I was hoping to get a good price for it. But she came back after just a few weeks." He rubs at his nape. He probably has lice. The entire shop is no doubt infested with them. With so many people coming and going, and leaving their personal possessions, it's inevitable. "I told her, if she ever wanted to pawn it again, to come to me. But she said she wouldn't need to. I thought that meant she was moving on somewhere, and that was why I hadn't seen her."

"Oh." Jane itches all over. Next to her, Mary is scratching herself frantically. "What about the ring? Can you remember what colour the stone was? Or what was carved into it?"

"My mind's not what it used to be. I wish I could help, but I've already told you everything I know."

Jane is weary as she steps out of the shop and onto the paving slabs. Mary squints at the opaque sky. "What now? We still have at least an hour, by my reckoning."

"I don't know. It's beginning to look hopeless. Perhaps we should just take some tea, while we wait for James?" Never before had Jane conceived how easy it would be for a thief to dispose of Madame Renard's jewels.

Perhaps it really was a botched robbery. Tom is right: the money raised on the necklace and the ring combined would be enough for a man like Jack Smith to start a new life on his own terms. He could go to the new world, maybe open a lumberyard there. Why not? Jack might have fooled her parents into believing he's content with his lot, but Jane knows he's capable of so much more. Her father has taken far stupider boys and turned them into Oxford scholars. Boys whose families could afford to set them up well in life.

As unbearable as it is to contemplate, if Jane is to satisfy her conscience that she's done everything she can to save her brother, she must subject her childhood playmate to the same scrutiny as any other suspect. She considered employing a ruse to search Jack's room at the cottage for Madame Renard's missing ring. But Dame Culham is not an easy woman to fool, and Jack would not have hidden a stolen ring where his eagle-eyed mother could find it.

No, if Jack took the ring, it will be in the woods, at the base of a tree, hidden under a stone that only he, or possibly Georgy, could recognize.

So, Jane cannot pick the scab of her suspicion until her father or one of her brothers escorts her to visit him, with Georgy, inside Winchester Gaol. Despite their promises to let Jane go with them, Henry and James have taken to visiting Georgy on horseback—claiming not to have time to take the carriage. Jane knows it's a lie. They are trying to protect her, but they will not be protecting her if they fail to prove Georgy's innocence and the last Jane sees of her brother is his writhing body, dangling from a rope in Winchester's market square.

Mary pinches her features. "You cannot give up at the first sign of difficulty, Jane. You'll never get anywhere with that attitude. Have you considered that if Madame Renard didn't have the ring when her body was found, the thief likely got away with it? We should see if anyone's been trying to sell such a ring since she was murdered."

"But Mr. Lipscombe told us everything he knows, and none of the other pawnbrokers will admit to dealing in a gentleman's ring. I don't know what to do. I've exhausted every lead I have. If I can't expose the real killer by the end of the month, then . . ."

It is impossible for Jane to discuss Georgy's trial without breaking into sobs. Her brother will not understand a word the judge or barristers put to him, and he'll be so frightened. Jane will do anything she can to protect him from such a fate. Maybe it's time she raised the possibility again of having him committed to an asylum—but even considering it makes her feel as though she's guilty of high treason.

Mary taps her foot on the cold slabs. "Calm yourself, Jane. Pawnbrokers aren't the only fellows who buy and sell jewels. Are they?"

Jane is jolted from her grim imaginings. "You suggest we try the goldsmith?"

"No, I was thinking about a 'fence.' If the murderer escaped with the ring, he'd have wanted to sell it quickly. We could go into the tavern, or the coffee shop, and ask about. That's where disreputable types congregate. Isn't it? They do in novels, anyway."

Jane peers at Mary, whose features are alive with unfamiliar animation. "For one who was so reluctant to help, you're getting awfully carried away, Mary Lloyd."

"I was never reluctant. I don't know why you have such a low opinion of me. All you had to do was ask . . ." As Mary prattles on, a bell sounds across the road.

A small round figure steps out of Mr. Martin's apothecary shop, and Jane's heart scrapes itself up from the filthy pavement.

CHAPTER TWENTY-TWO

"Wait!" Jane strides straight into the path of an oncoming carriage. Mary grabs her elbow, jerking her backward. The carriage rattles by so close that Jane can taste the horses' sweat. Across the street, Hannah stands before the bow-fronted windows of the apothecary's shop. She lifts the hood of her tawny cape and jiggles her wicker basket until it rests in the crook of her arm. Hannah could be Jane's last hope of discovering the truth about Madame Renard's murder and saving Georgy. She will not let her get away.

"Hannah!" Jane cries.

As soon as the road clears, she wrestles her arm free and hurries across the cobbles. Their eyes meet and recognition flickers across Hannah's features, but the girl turns and marches into the wind. Jane darts after her. She can almost touch the tail of Hannah's cape fluttering in the breeze. "Hannah, please. It's Miss Austen. We met at Manydown."

Hannah's shoulders rise and fall before she turns to face Jane. "Miss Austen." She bobs in greeting, but her mouth remains in a thin, straight line.

Jane hesitates. Hannah is certainly not pleased to see her. And, as her tactless questions upset the girl so much that she was sick the last time they met, Jane can hardly blame her. "How is your mother? Miss Bigg mentioned she was suffering from the putrid throat."

Hannah lowers her eyes to her basket. In her own clothes, with her mouse-brown hair tumbling free over her shoulders, she looks even younger. "She's on the mend. Praise be to the Lord. I've just been to fetch her another poultice."

"From Mr. Martin?" Jane imitates the tone Cassandra uses with their father's parishioners: cheerful and friendly, without being overfamiliar. "He's very clever, isn't he? We're fortunate to have such a skilled apothecary so close at hand. My mother relies on his medicines for her . . . Well, I'm sure you don't really want to know."

"Good day to you, Miss Austen." Hannah spins on her heel.

"Wait, please . . ." Breathless, Jane does her best to remain in step. "I wanted to say how sorry I was for upsetting you the last time we met. You'd just had a tremendous shock, and I don't suppose I was very kind. Asking all those questions, so soon afterward."

Hannah gives Jane a sidelong glance from beneath her hood. "Thank you, miss. It was very distressing, I must say."

"But I would appreciate it if we could talk again. I'm sure you must have seen or heard more than you think you did that day. And if you could take me through it, just one more time, I might be able to pick out something important."

Hannah looks to the row of cottages at the end of the London road, where the mill workers live. "I told you everything I know last time, and I should be getting home to my mother. She'll be expecting me back, and I need to make the little ones' supper."

The bitter wind whips at Jane's face. "Please. I'll buy you a bun."

"I don't want a bun! I want that monster caught and punished, the same as you do." Hannah's voice is shrill. "Trespassers, the justice said. As if that explained everything. But let me tell you something, Miss Austen. If there was anyone desperate enough to camp in those woods behind Deane House—and I'm not saying for a moment I believe there was—chances are, they'd be after snaring hares or scavenging for firewood. Not braining you and leaving you for dead."

Jane flounders. An image of Zoë Renard's brutalized body flashes in her mind. Her stomach churns at the memory of the dark, sticky blood spattered all over her face and dress, a lake of it pooled around her on the floor. Pints and pints of blood, which must have taken Hannah hours to scrub clean. "I never meant to patronize you. You're right, we do want the same thing. I just have a rather clumsy way of going about it."

Hannah's chin quivers. "If it had been one of you young ladies from the ball, they would have left no stone unturned to catch whoever did it. But seeing as she was one of ours, an ordinary girl trying to make an honest living, what does it matter if someone caved in her skull, casting her body aside like she was rubbish?"

"Please, Hannah . . . if I expressed myself poorly beforehand, then I must apologize. I don't think Mr. Craven investigated that poor woman's death properly either. I've been doing everything I can to find out who killed her. And I'm getting closer, I can feel it. If you'd just talk to me, one more time?"

Hannah's eyes flash, but she doesn't walk away.

"Please?"

Finally, Hannah gives a curt nod.

Footsteps sound as Mary catches up. Jane places her hand tentatively in the crook of Hannah's arm. "Mary, this is Hannah. She's a parlour maid at Manydown. She was working at Deane House on the night of"—Jane gulps for air—"on the night of the murder. She's agreed to come with us to answer a few questions about what happened."

Mary's face falls. "I take it this means we're not going to question any ruffians at the tavern."

"No, Mary. We'll take Hannah for some tea and a b—" Jane cuts herself off before she can offend Hannah again. "For some tea, and a serious discussion as to how we can bring this villain to justice."

Hannah pouts, shifting her weight from one foot to the other. "Well, I might have a bun, too. Seeing as I'm joining you."

Mrs. Plumptre manages the bakery on the ground floor of her shop while her daughters attend to the customers in the tearoom above. It is one of the very few establishments in Basingstoke where a respectable lady may dine unchaperoned. It is so popular that today there is a queue of maids, goodwives and ladies under the green-striped awning, waiting to purchase bread and cakes out of the brick oven. After requesting refreshments, Jane leads the way up the narrow, winding staircase to the tearooms. Or the "tearoom," as the establishment should more accurately be referred to. Every time Jane passes the painted sign, her fingers itch to correct it.

Five wobbly tables are squashed together in the cramped space, overlooking the London road. Jane selects a small circular one beneath the sash window. The others are littered with dirty crockery. The dinnertime rush is over, but the cleaning is yet to begin.

As Jane adjusts herself in the shallow seat of an uncomfortably upright chair, a heavenly combination of cinnamon, yeast and warmed milk fills her senses. Her stomach rumbles and her mouth waters. Opposite her, Hannah hunches, her cloak still wrapped around her shoulders and her basket on her lap. Between them, Mary flicks crumbs from the tablecloth onto the floor.

One of the many indistinguishable Misses Plumptre clatters up the stairs to bring them a steaming pot of tea and three mismatched cups and saucers. Jane holds the table still as Miss Plumptre sets out the tea-things. The serving girl struggles to fit everything onto the table, and drips tea onto the gingham cloth. Hannah stares into her lap, her flat cheeks burning red. The maid is probably more accustomed to visiting Mrs. Plumptre's bakery than her tearoom, if she can afford to frequent the place at all.

When the trio are finally alone, Jane folds a napkin and wedges it under one of the table legs to keep it steady. "This is nice." She smiles. Small talk has never been her forte. But she is too wary to dive into her interrogation, as she did previously, lest she makes Hannah ill again. Instead, she remains quiet, waiting for Hannah to speak.

When she does, Hannah's voice is barely more than a whisper. "I can't stop thinking about her. Every night, as soon as my head hits the pillow, all I can see is Madame Renault's face. No matter how worn out I am, sleep won't come for the thought of her. Lying there dying, all alone, in that black closet."

"Renard," says Jane. "She was actually called Zoë *Renard*, and she was a lacemaker from Brussels. She had such a thick accent, I'm afraid I misheard and gave everyone the wrong name."

Hannah nods, absorbing the new information. "A lacemaker, from Brussels."

"Yes. A very good one, at that." Jane warms her hands on the earthenware teapot.

Hannah lifts her head. "Why did she come here, of all places?"

The teapot shakes in Jane's hands, and it takes all of her concentration to pour the liquid into the cups, rather than drench the tablecloth. "I don't know, but she seemed to be making a life for herself. She hired a stall in the covered market, and she was learning English. She even subscribed to the circulating library. But we have been unable to trace any of her acquaintances—or discover why anyone would want her dead."

Mary adds cream to two of the cups. Jane draws hers close, before Mary can pollute it.

Hannah stares at Jane, her broad features impassive. "They say your brother's been sent to gaol over it. Not the soldier who found her. The mute boy who lives with his nurse?"

In the polite society Jane mixes in, no one would dare raise the topic of Georgy's incarceration outright. People express their sympathy for the "difficult situation" the Austens find themselves in and ask after Georgy's welfare. They do not speak of crimes and gaols, innocence or guilt. She would be a fool to believe the same courtesy applied behind her back.

"Not for the murder." Jane rushes to Georgy's defence. "For the theft of her necklace. He got hold of it, somehow. Or someone gave it to him. He's rather hampered in his comprehension, you see. And he can't explain because, as you said, he doesn't speak."

"I got a cousin similar." Hannah sniffs. "Sandra, her name is. My aunt married so late, she didn't dare hope for children of her own. When Sandra came along, she was so happy. Now she's always fretting about what will become of her daughter if she dies before Sandra does. Sandra wouldn't survive a day on her own." Hannah's eyes are misty. "She works at the mill with my aunt. She can talk all right, but she's never developed any guile. My aunt needs to keep an eye on her at all times, otherwise she'd do herself mischief. Too trusting is our Sandra. Such a sweet little thing."

Jane reproaches herself for judging her mother so harshly for failing to live up to Eliza's impossibly high standard of motherhood. Her parents may not be outwardly doting, but they would cheerfully work their fingers to the bone to ensure all of their children are well taken care of. Throughout his entire life Georgy has been cherished and protected. Until the day he was arrested, he never had a serious care in the world. Countless times, Jane has heard her father extract a solemn oath from each of her brothers that if anything happens to him, they will club together to make sure Georgy continues to be provided for.

Mr. Austen probably makes them swear the same thing about Jane, behind her back. What a horrifying thought, having to rely on the charity of her siblings to cover her expenses. "You understand then?"

Hannah nods slowly as she gazes down into the dregs of her tea. "It wasn't a robber or a simpleton who didn't know his own strength that killed her. It was a vicious devil, with nothing but malice in his heart."

Jane wants to probe further, yet is terrified of upsetting her again. "Why do you say that?"

"The bed-warming pan . . . it was covered in gore, as if whoever had done it had worked themselves up into a right frenzy." Hannah stares into the basket on her lap. Jane and Mary's features fall slack with horror. "Plus, there's all sorts tucked away in that closet. If it was a thief, he would have made away with so much more. All those copper kettles and pans, they'd be worth a small fortune. Not to mention the linen."

The room shakes as Miss Plumptre climbs the narrow, winding stairs with an overloaded tray. She frowns at the table, as if willing more space to appear. Jane shuffles the teapot, cups and saucers until there is just enough room for her to set down three small plates of buns. The butter dish balances precariously on top of the milk jug, and Jane must hold her cup and saucer. "The last time we met, you admitted you didn't like going to Deane House. Do you think you could tell us why?"

"It's just . . ." Hannah frowns. "At Manydown, we're never made to feel ashamed if, say, a teaspoon goes missing or if someone drops a glass. Mr. Bigg-Wither is ever so polite. His daughters are the same. Why, even young Master Harris is a kindhearted boy. It's not like that at Deane House."

Mary splits her bun in two and covers it with butter. Jane watches. She hasn't eaten since breakfast and wants to do the same, but since Hannah hasn't touched hers, she fears it would be rude. Instead, Jane picks a currant off the top of her bun. "What is it like? I promise whatever you say won't go any further," she says, realizing her error in inviting the biggest flibbertigibbet in the county to sit in on her secret investigation.

"That's just it. You can never predict what it will be like there. You may as well try guessing the weather from one day to the next. Sometimes, if Sir John is at home, all will be quiet. Lady Harcourt might be napping in the parlour, while Mrs. Twistleton is left to get on with things downstairs. But at other times, Lady Harcourt will be on the rampage, finding fault with everything the servants do—especially Mrs. Twistleton."

"Lady Harcourt lacks faith in her housekeeper?" Jane pictures Sir John furtively tipping drops of laudanum into Lady Harcourt's wine at the New Year ball. Does he drug her when they are at home, to keep the peace between his wife and her staff?

"Yes. And it makes everything so difficult for the rest of us. That's why the servants are always leaving. There's nothing worse than having two mistresses. If Mrs. Twistleton tells you to build a fire one way, Lady Harcourt will be upon you five minutes later, saying you've done it wrong and ordering you to restack it immediately. She won't even give Mrs. Twistleton her own set of keys. How can she be respected as housekeeper without those?"

Jane is well versed in the politics of servants and masters. At Steventon Rectory, they go through maids faster than loaves of sugar. Mrs. Austen lives in constant dread of a girl's head being turned by another position. The process of hunting down a trustworthy maid and training her is exhausting. That is why Jane is so anxious about Sally. She still hasn't got to the bottom of what's upset her. Something is clearly on the girl's mind. Sally no longer hums to herself as she bangs about in the rectory kitchen and, these days, she won't even meet Jane's eye. Whatever it is must be truly troubling. Mrs. Austen always chides Jane to leave the maids be. Regardless, Jane resolves to speak to Sally again as soon as the opportunity arises. Perhaps the issue can be mended with an afternoon off or a hand with the cooking whenever they have visitors.

"Why doesn't Mrs. Twistleton move on? Or, for that matter, why doesn't Lady Harcourt dismiss her if she's not happy with her work?"

Spots of colour rise in Hannah's moonlike cheeks. "Don't know, miss."

Mary leans forward, gripping the edge of the cluttered table. "It's Sir John, isn't it? He has an arrangement with Mrs. Twis—"

Jane kicks Mary under the table.

"Ouch." Mary scowls, rubbing her shin.

"Don't put words into Hannah's mouth."

"I couldn't possibly say anything about that, miss. But I do know"—Hannah eyes her companions warily, as all three of the women's heads bend together—"that before she was housekeeper at Deane House, Mrs. Twistleton used to spend a great deal of time entertaining customers at the Angel Inn . . ."

So, Jane was right: Mr. Toke *was* being oversensitive when she asked if Sir John kept a room at the inn. He clearly tolerates more vice on his premises than he's prepared to divulge.

"I told you," says Mary. "She's no better than she ought to be."

"Try not to judge her too harshly. Deborah, that is Mrs. Twistleton, wasn't always like that. We were neighbours, see. Deborah married young, and she and her husband, they had a child. A sickly child. He died just before his fourth birthday. And afterward, Deborah lost her way a little . . . or, rather, she kept finding it at the bottom of an empty gin glass. There was a time she'd do *anything* for her next drink. Mr. Twistleton had no patience for it. He left. Gone to London to make it on his own, so they say."

"Poor Mrs. Twistleton. That's very sad," Jane murmurs. She knows the Austens, constantly beset by difficulties as they are, have been unusually fortunate in regard to their lack of close family bereavements. It is almost unheard of for a mother, of any rank, to raise all eight of her children to adulthood as Mrs. Austen has done.

"I suppose she and Sir John had their grief in common when they met. It was just after the tragedy with the Harcourts' elder boy. The baronet was in Basingstoke every day, trying to drink and gamble away his sorrows. Before long, everyone knew he and Deborah had formed an acquaintance. Deborah was proud of it. She said it was only right she comfort him—Lady Harcourt turned cold after their son died. And a man like that will only stand being spurned for so long."

Mary leans back in her seat, folding her arms across her chest. "You see? She's a brazen hussy."

"Hush, Mary. Go on, Hannah."

"After a time, Deborah quit her job at the mill and went to live in a room at the Angel Inn. Everyone knew the baronet must have been paying for her keep. And then she left Basingstoke altogether. The next time I saw her, she was Sir John's housekeeper. Gaining his affections seemed to pull her back from the brink. I don't think she drinks at all now. She'd do anything to keep him happy."

Jane sips her lukewarm tea. Poor Lady Harcourt, it must be mortifying for her to be forced to keep such a woman in her home. No wonder she lost her temper and lashed out when Sir John was arrested. She is clearly under much strain. "Where was Mrs. Twistleton, in the hours before the ball?" A thrill shoots through Jane's abdomen as she speaks.

"Where wasn't she?" Hannah scoffs. "All the household was so anxious that the evening went as it should. Mrs. Twistleton flitted between the house and the hall, supervising matters. Every time I turned round, she was behind me, chiding me to work faster and to put more care into what I was doing."

Jane taps her fingernail against her empty teacup. "And the family?"

Hannah shrugs, staring at the untouched bun on her plate. "They were in their rooms, getting ready. They didn't come down until just before eight, when the carriages began to arrive. Us maids were allowed a glimpse of them all, in their finery, before we were packed off downstairs. With the great hall decorated, it really was a sight to behold."

"I still can't believe I missed the whole thing." Mary slumps in her chair. "Mother and I had to wait for Mrs. Lefroy to send her carriage back to collect us. By the time we arrived, Mrs. Chute had made her ghastly discovery and the celebrations were called to a halt. My uncle leaped out to investigate, and I wanted to see, too, but he told the driver to turn around and take us straight home again."

"How unfortunate for *you*, Mary." Jane forces down the urge to lash Mary even harder for her lack of compassion.

But Jane knows she has no right to the moral high ground. Her own heart still aches at the memory of the evening's promise. The splendour of the great hall really was beguiling—but it was Tom, with his fair-haired good looks and out-of-place ivory coat, who dazzled her. How quickly their secret games turned to tears. She should have known to be on her guard. What is tomfoolery, but an anagram of "O Tom Lefroy"? The mournful self-reproach with which she'll be forced to beat herself about the head for the rest of her days.

Hannah produces a spotless pocket handkerchief and wraps her bun. She nestles it carefully inside her wicker basket, next to the packages from Mr. Martin's shop. "I've told you everything I know. Now I must get back to my mother. She'll be fretting about where I've got to. Thank you kindly for the tea."

Jane chews her bottom lip. "You'll send word, through Miss Bigg, if you think of anything else, won't you?"

"I will." Hannah hesitates. "And I'm very sorry about your brother, Miss Austen. For his sake, as well as Madame Renard's, I hope you find out who really killed her."

Tears prick Jane's eyes. "Thank you, Hannah. That's very kind of you to say."

The ladies peer out of the window until the maid emerges onto the street below. She looks all around before pulling up her hood, drawing up her shoulders and walking directly into the blustery gale.

"So, what do you think?" asks Mary.

Hannah's figure grows smaller. The wind billows her cloak behind her. She keeps her head down and presses on into it.

"I don't quite know what to think . . . except that there's something very rotten going on at Deane House." Jane stares at her uneaten bun, wishing she'd given it to Hannah to take home for her mother so they wouldn't have to share. She's lost her appetite now.

7. To Cassandra Austen

Steventon, Tuesday, 12 January 1796

My dearest Cassandra,

I am glad to hear you're gratified by my spending time with Mary Lloyd. Perhaps you'll be so good as to consider my penance sufficient, and hand me back my Martha. It is most selfish of you to hold onto my dearest friend for so long. Especially since your easy nature means you are appreciated instantly, by all, everywhere you go, whereas my sophisticated wit is more of an acquired taste. Despite my continued investigations, I still cannot say, with any confidence, who killed the hapless ~~milliner~~ lacemaker, Madame Renard. All I can tell you is that I would give anything for an honest conversation with:

- Jonathan Harcourt (how much pressure was he under to clear his father's debts?)

– Sir John Harcourt (was he counting on Sophy's dowry to save him from the Marshalsea?)

– Mrs. Twistleton (was she worried Lady Harcourt would throw her out on her ear if she discovered what kind of woman she was?)

– Jack Smith (how else could Georgy have got hold of Madame Renard's gold chain?)

I regret I cannot give you any more information as to how dear Georgy fares as, despite my continued protestations, my father and my brothers find ever more excuses to prevent them from ferrying me to Winchester. I, too, pray they are to be believed when they say he is bearing up well. Or, failing that, as well as can be expected. Tear up this letter and use the pieces to line your pattens to save your toes from the winter frosts. The weather will turn bitter soon, I am certain of it.

Yours,
J.A.

Miss Austen,
Rev. Mr. Fowle's,
Kintbury,
Newbury.

CHAPTER TWENTY-THREE

It takes more than two hours to reach Winchester from Steventon—slightly longer than usual as it rained heavily overnight. Dense fog obscures the view as the carriage lurches through the Hampshire countryside. The roads are boggy and the carriage wheels are forever getting stuck and hitting half-submerged tree roots. Jane's stomach flips with every jolt. With a mere fortnight left before the February assize is set to begin, James and Henry have finally conceded and are allowing her to accompany them to demand that the barrister does more to help Georgy's case.

Afterward, Jane's brothers will chaperone her inside the gaol to visit Georgy. And Jack Smith, of course. Jane will finally be able to interrogate him thoroughly as to his whereabouts on the night of Madame Renard's murder. It is sickening to contemplate that the person the family trusts most with Georgy's welfare may be responsible for inflicting such suffering on him. But in her desperation, Jane cannot afford to be squeamish. If it will save her brother, she must not shrink from investigating even the most disturbing of possibilities.

James drives while Henry sits, morose, beside Jane inside the carriage. She baits him with titbits from Eliza's letters, but Henry remains stubbornly taciturn. If only James had accepted Henry's offer to drive and accompanied her inside the carriage instead. She could have distracted herself from her worry over Georgy by making great sport of James's growing affection for

Mary. Since the trip to Basingstoke, James has accompanied Jane twice to call on the Lloyds. Jane has been true to her word and has not said anything nasty about Mary to James. She has, however, said all manner of silly things about James to Mary and, while the pair were making love in the garden, she took great delight in catching Mary's eye and pointing to "the sky."

Jane is surprised to find herself genuinely happy for James. Her eldest brother might be a prig, but he is always there when any of the Austens need him. And James remarrying is the best possible outcome for Anna. Mrs. Austen is too old to keep up with a little child, Cassandra will not be at home for much longer and Jane . . . well, as her mother says, the Lord alone knows where Jane will be.

"Are you sure you wish to do this?" James had asked that morning, as he held open the carriage door for Jane to climb inside.

Jane had looked him squarely in the eye. "Georgy is as much my brother as he is yours. That is all there is to be said on the matter."

As they draw closer to Winchester, and Jane stares at the ragged procession of pilgrims and countrypeople making their way toward the city gates, her bravado is wearing thin. Has she the stomach for the task ahead? Already, she can taste bile at the back of her throat and her body trembles from lack of sleep.

She wraps her cloak tightly around her shoulders and grasps her willow basket. Inside it are Georgy's favourite treats, including Mrs. Austen's cottage cheese, Mary's plum pudding and an eye-wateringly strong batch of Sally's gingerbread. It will bring Georgy cheer, she hopes, rather than cause him to long even more poignantly for home.

Once through the gates and into the heart of the medieval city, they leave the carriage at a bustling inn on Great Minster

Street overlooking the magnificent Gothic cathedral. Its pointed turrets and ornate arches stretch to the heavens, dwarfing every other construction in sight. The ancient place of worship marks the origins of Christianity in Britain, but underneath the limestone foundations lurks an older, wilder, pagan past.

Jane grips James's arm as they make their way under the eaves of the timberwork buildings through the crooked lanes. It's Wednesday, market day. People and animals pack the narrow streets. Piles of dung and straw scatter the cobbles. Farmers drive pigs and sheep into makeshift pens to be sold and slaughtered. Over the cacophony of grunts and bleats, calls of "Mind your backs!" startle Jane, as porters drive barrows laden with goods. At the butter cross, Jane spots a stallholder selling the type of green muslin Mary was looking for. She scolds herself for remembering fripperies at such a time.

The barrister, Mr. William Hayter, greets them in his chambers on the first floor of a lopsided building above a silversmith's on the high street. Jane is reminded of his son and namesake: the schoolboy, William, was forever eating earwigs out of her mother's garden and giving himself diarrhoea. Mr. Hayter Senior is portly, with a florid complexion and bulging eyes. He wears a black gown over his silk waistcoat and breeches. An ineptly combed horsehair periwig sits askew on his head, as if arranged in haste when he heard them coming up the stairs.

A generous flame burns in the grate and the small dormer window is shut, partially covered with a pair of ruby velvet curtains. Mahogany bookcases rammed with weighty legal tomes line the walls, and bundles of cream-coloured documents, tied with scarlet ribbon, teeter on every surface in the long, narrow room. After the freshness of the carriage ride, the barrister's apartments are hot and stuffy. James and Henry stoop under the slanted ceiling, but Jane comes through the doorway without having to do so. If her bonnet were more ornate, with an ostrich feather perhaps, she might have dusted the beams—they are certainly in need of it.

James removes his shovel hat and presses it to his chest. "Mr. Hayter. This is my brother, Lieutenant Austen, and our sister, Miss Austen."

Mr. Hayter does not look at Jane. Instead he takes James's and Henry's hands, shaking them vigorously before gesturing to the two oxblood-leather armchairs in front of his ebony desk. The only other seat not entirely obscured with papers is a three-legged stool beside the door. It is currently occupied by a silver tray littered with gnawed chicken bones and an empty pewter tankard, which reeks of ale.

Jane picks up the tray and looks for a clear surface to rest it on. Failing to find one, she places it on the floor beside the chair and crouches gingerly on the edge of the low wooden seat.

James leans forward, hands grasping his knees. "Please tell me you've made some progress since we last met."

The barrister squeezes his bloated stomach behind his desk and takes a bundle out of a black leather wallet. "Yes, yes. I've been looking at the details of the case very carefully." He waves the papers. "Let me see. Ah, yes, I remember. Now, gentlemen, since you pointedly refuse to avoid a trial by declaring Mr. George Austen insane, my advice would be to enter a guilty plea. I shall press your brother's mental deficiencies and make an appeal to the judge for leniency. There are no guarantees, but with perseverance, and testimony of his previous good character, I'm optimistic the sentence could be commuted to transportation."

Jane closes her eyes, a heavy weight pressing on her chest. If Georgy pleads guilty to grand larceny, the only alternative to the gallows is transportation to Australia. Even Jack Smith could not follow Georgy that far. It would be a slower, crueler way for her brother to die. But even Tom, with his supposedly brilliant legal mind, had failed to come up with a better strategy.

"Leniency?" Henry sits bolt upright in his chair. "That's the best you can come up with? How much are we paying you again?"

James runs his palm over his lightly powdered hair, flattening the curls. "With all due respect, sir, we've been over this before." His voice is clipped. He's as angry as Jane has ever seen him, but she doubts anyone outside their family would notice. "My brother wouldn't survive a day in Botany Bay, never mind fourteen years. You must understand, he suffers from a serious medical complaint. He requires constant attention from a physician, as well as general supervision of his welfare. He is incapable of taking care of himself, especially not under such extreme circumstances. He would be a magnet for the vilest forms of abuse and exploitation."

Mr. Hayter's red face is visible between their two sets of broad shoulders. Jane raises a finger in the air to gain his attention, but Mr. Hayter does not heed her. He drops the papers onto the surface of the desk and rolls his palms upward. "Has either of you gentlemen found a credible explanation for why Mr. George Austen was in possession of the victim's necklace?"

James drops his forehead into his hands and rubs his temples with his thumbs. "We think he must have found it discarded somewhere. Either before or after she was killed. He could not have taken it from her. They never met."

Henry straightens, pulling his scarlet jacket into place. "Or the killer might have given it to him, to throw the authorities off his own scent. I'm afraid our brother is completely lacking in guile. It would be typical of him to accept such a thing without question. He has no concept of money. It simply wouldn't occur to him to be suspicious."

Mr. Hayter's lizard-like eyes alternate between James and Henry. "And can you prove either of these suppositions?"

James turns his hat in his hands and lowers his gaze to the plush carpet, while Henry folds his arms across his chest and stares out of the window. The barrister draws a breath. "Then I'm afraid leniency is the very best we can hope for."

Jane chews her lip. "If I may, sir. I've been making some enquiries . . ."

The three men do not hear her. Mr. Hayter draws his eyebrows together, looking grave. "As the necklace was in Mr. George Austen's possession, and that fact is undisputed, any jury would automatically assume the worst. Truth be told, your brother is fortunate that he is charged with theft alone—and not murder."

Jane jumps to her feet. Her voice comes out in one long screech. "But he didn't do it."

Henry and James turn and stare as if they've never seen her before in their lives. Mr. Hayter's chins wobble as he coughs into his fist.

"Georgy can't plead guilty because he *didn't do it*. He was nowhere near Deane House at the time of the murder."

Mr. Hayter turns to Jane's brothers, refusing to meet her gaze. "Gentlemen, your sister is becoming hysterical. Why have you brought her here? A barrister's chambers is no place for a woman."

Jane marches toward the desk. "If you'll just listen to me . . ." She stands three feet away, barred from getting any closer by her brothers in their comfortable armchairs. "The owner of Deane House, Sir John, was in dire financial difficulties. He's since been arrested and imprisoned in the Marshalsea. His son, Mr. Harcourt, was about to be betrothed to an heiress when the murder took place—a marriage that would have saved the family's finances."

"What is the meaning of this?" Mr. Hayter flicks a hand at her. It's as if he's rammed one of his gnawed chicken bones down Jane's throat. She is desperate to spit it out before it chokes her.

"They were *lovers*," Jane shouts. James gasps while Henry twists about in his chair and peers up at her quizzically. "Jonathan and Madame Renard were lovers. They *must* have been—they were in Brussels at the same time. I think Mr. Harcourt might have killed her to—"

"Stop," Mr. Hayter roars. The tendons in his face strain to hold on to his eyeballs, as a sluglike vein pops up in his forehead. "You had better have a valid reason for making such an accusation. Or you're committing slander—a serious criminal offence."

Jane lifts her chin, peering down her nose at him. "Madame Renard was expecting Mr. Harcourt's child. The midwife who laid her out confirmed she was pregnant."

Mr. Hayter's lip curls into a sneer. "For your brothers' sake, Miss Austen, I shall pretend I didn't hear that." He jabs a finger toward Jane. "And if you really want to save Mr. George Austen's life, you won't repeat it to another living soul."

"But why?" If only Mr. Hayter would understand the Harcourts had good reason to want Madame Renard and her baby out of the way, she's sure he'd look more closely at the case. With his authority, he could question the whole family, and Jack. All it would take to prove Georgy innocent would be for someone with an enquiring mind to go over the details. "It's proof of their connection, don't you see? What if she threatened to expose Jonathan as a rogue, and ruin his marriage prospects? That could drive a man to kill—"

"Because, *miss*"—Jane's skin crawls as Mr. Hayter sweeps his bulging eyes up and down her frame—"it will be difficult enough persuading the justice to show leniency for theft, when by rights your brother should be on trial for murder. If there was any suggestion the victim was with child, it would be damn near impossible." He slams the flat of his hands on his desk, rustling his papers and startling Jane. "Now, gentlemen, I believe we've finished. Don't you?"

Jane chokes, looking between her brothers' horrified expressions. This is impossible. The law has Georgy tied in a knot of rope and every move she makes to untangle it binds him even tighter. She must save him, before it closes at his throat.

Jane weeps into her pocket handkerchief as the trio slink defeatedly out of the medieval city centre toward the newly established gaol. James wraps an arm around Jane's shoulders and pulls her close, tucking her head beneath his chin. "We know you were only trying to help. And there's no harm done. It was very obliging of Mr. Hayter to say he'd pretend he never heard you."

Jane sniffs. "I'm not crying because of that, you blockhead." She gulps air, choking on her tears. "I'm crying because I'm so angry he wouldn't listen to me."

James frowns but holds Jane even tighter.

Henry places his hands on his slim hips and exhales loudly, looking up at the forbidding yellow-brick prison building. It is set behind a row of tall, spiked iron railings and runs almost the entire length of the unusually straight Jewry Street. A triangle pediment stands between two squat towers. Bath-stone quoins reinforce each of the barred windows and clothe the sharp corners, making the building impenetrable. Winchester Castle houses political prisoners, West Gate is home to debtors and the Bridewell holds vagrants; only those accused of the most heinous crimes, theft or murder, reside within the gaol's fortified walls.

Henry's easy features contort into an ugly grimace. "Are we really going to escort our little sister into this hell?"

Jane blows her nose and crumples her handkerchief into her pocket. "Is Georgy in there? If so, do not try to keep me out."

The brothers exchange a glance of masculine complicity, further fueling Jane's rage. She wriggles out of James's grasp.

"Come. Let's get it over with." James turns a shade more ashen and his shoulders slope as he approaches the gate. On seeing him, a guard tips his hat in recognition and unlocks the first gate of the fortress. James slips his hand inside his worn frock coat and hands over a silver coin. He repeats the ritual several times, as he leads Jane and Henry through more gates, guarded by more guards, and hands over yet more coins.

Jane's father has already explained that, as Parliament refuses to allot the governor enough funds to run the prison, the livelihoods of the turnkeys depends upon extracting bribes from prisoners—the cost of which is placing a considerable strain on the Austens' finances, even with Neddy's unbridled generosity. The only way Mr. Austen can ensure Georgy's gaolers take good care of him is to demonstrate that he comes from a well-to-do family who are willing to invest in his welfare. It is most disconcerting to wonder what happens to those unfortunate wretches who are not so blessed.

Jane was expecting prisoners to be hanging out of the windows and lining up outside, in the courtyards, being drilled as if they were recruits at the naval academy Frank and Charles attended at Portsmouth. Instead, the solemn, confined spaces are empty of all but the guards, and the windows are too high for anyone to see out. She can hear the inmates, though. They moan and wail in rhythm, like the bow of a ship crashing against the waves. She shadows Henry, stepping on his heel as he stops short at the governor's house, in an annex sitting perpendicular to the main cellblocks. James raps the brass knocker of an imposing glossy black front door. There is a small semicircle of unbarred glass above it.

After several repetitions, an elderly man with a fluffy white beard unlocks the door. "Mr. Austen. Back already?" He opens the door halfway and grins, revealing two brown teeth in his inflamed gums.

James shuffles inside. "Indeed, Mr. Trigg, indeed." Jane and Henry follow. The old man peers at Jane curiously with rheumy eyes. James explains Mr. Trigg is the gaol's former governor, and father of the current post-holder.

Mr. Trigg walks with a stick and leans one gnarled hand against the dark green wall as he goes. He boasts that his whole family live within the prison's walls. Three generations of Triggs, male and female, keep Hampshire's thieves and murderers safely stowed away from honest folk.

"Our gentleman lodger will be pleased to see you, I dare say." Mr. Trigg smacks his lips together, in a semblance of a smile. "I'm afraid he hasn't had a good night. Those blackguards in the cells were making a racket until all hours. Some commotion about a spoon gone missing. There's no honour among thieves. Don't you go believing there is. Like rats, they are. They'd eat each other, if they could." He jerks a thumb in the direction of the main prison block. "I'll be glad when the next assize is over, and they're all cleared out."

Jane's heart shrivels to the size of a desiccated pea. Clearly, Mr. Trigg has grown so accustomed to his "gentleman lodger," he forgets Georgy is as likely as any other man here to be damned at the February assize. A wave of dizziness sweeps over her, as she stumbles through the sequence of dark, sparsely furnished rooms, following the old man who would send her brother to his Maker.

Finally, Mr. Trigg shoves the foot of his stick against one last door and a rush of warm stale air spills out. "Visitors, Mrs. Trigg. Make yourself decent."

Jane's eyes take a moment to adjust to the dim light. The dank space is as musty as the rectory store cupboard, which floods in a storm.

A fair-haired young woman in a mobcap stands at a fireside, jiggling a fat-limbed child on her hip. From the way the woman's plump cheeks flush, and she adjusts her shift around her bodice, Jane realises they have disturbed her in nursing her infant.

"Goodness me." The woman smiles genially. "A young lady come to see us. I wasn't expecting such an honour."

James doffs his hat. "Good day to you, Mrs. Trigg." As a clergyman, James is used to seeing things that Jane is not. She admires his ability to maintain his composure, while her instincts are screaming at her to turn and flee. "Indeed, this time we've brought along our sister, Miss Austen. Jane, this is Mrs. Trigg—young Mr. Trigg's good lady wife. She's been doing an excellent job in caring for our Georgy."

"How do you do, Mrs. Trigg?" Jane's voice is too high-pitched and she doesn't know where to fix her eyes.

Above the fireplace, a drying rack displays the family's undergarments proudly, as if they were their regimental colours. A wooden playpen incarcerates two more fair-haired half-dressed infants. One child wails and shuffles along on his bottom, while the other clings to the bars and shrieks as he takes exaggerated bouncy steps. They are so similar, in size and form, to the babe in Mrs. Trigg's arms that they could be triplets rather than brothers. Or sisters. With their tangled curls and loose pinafores, it's impossible to tell.

Mrs. Trigg nods enthusiastically, jiggling her baby. "Very well. Always well, we Triggs are. But do sit down, Miss Austen. I'm sure your brother will be most glad of your company." She jerks her head toward a long rectangular oak table across the room.

Jack half stands, showing his palm in greeting. His face is pale, and his dark, curly hair stands on end—as if he's been running his fingers through it constantly.

Beside him, a large figure remains seated on a wooden bench, hunched over, his hands wedged between his thighs. His waistcoat and breeches are loose, and his sleeves and collar are grubby. A few days' worth of stubble grows on his jaw. He sits on his haunches as he rocks back and forth.

A lump so hard and bulky, it could be a loose tile from the roof of St. Nicholas's Church, lodges in Jane's throat.

The figure is Georgy, but he looks more like the living ghost of James in the dark days immediately following the sudden and unexpected death of James's young wife, Anne. Poor Anne. One moment she was hale and hearty, enjoying her supper, the next she was overcome with a headache and laid her cheek on her pillow—only to slip out of this realm and into the next as easily and swiftly as a hound taking a nap at his master's feet.

Jack taps Georgy lightly on the shoulder. "Look, we got visitors."

Georgy lifts his eyes without moving his head. When he sees it's his brothers and sister, he gets up out of his seat, waving his arms and making unintelligible sounds. In his agitated state, he forgets his signs. He grunts and moans, desperate to make himself understood.

James places both hands on Georgy's shoulders and guides him back into his seat. "There is no need to be upset. We're here, and we're not going anywhere. Take your time."

Georgy blinks as Jane and Henry crowd around him. Each of the Austens takes it in turns to squeeze his hand and rub his upper arm until he settles. Jane's cheeks ache from the strain of forcing a smile for him. Once Georgy has calmed down, he asks with his fingers if they've come to take him home.

Jane's heart cracks as James tells him, "Soon."

"Mother sent a basket." Jane places it on the long table.

Georgy barely glances at it, but Jack rummages around for a piece of gingerbread. "He's lost his appetite since we been here. Mrs. Trigg makes a lovely stew and dumplings, but Georgy won't eat more than a few mouthfuls."

Jane places one hand on Georgy's knee and another on his cheek, forcing him to look at her. "You've got to keep your strength up."

Georgy shakes his head, shoving Jane's hand away. He stares at his lap, curling his spine as he continues to rock back and forth.

The firelight hits Jack's face as he yawns, illuminating the purple shadows beneath his eyes. "That's what I keep telling him. You'll waste away, Georgy."

A shiver of disquiet runs through Jane as she studies Jack from beneath her lashes. She's vowed to treat everyone she comes across as a potential murderer, until she has good reason to believe otherwise. It is difficult to maintain the same level of rigorous impartiality now that she is in the same room as Jack. He was her first friend, and his easy manners are as unaffected as ever. But the only person Jane will accept, without question, did not murder Madame Renard or steal her necklace is Georgy.

Besides, Jack is a grown man now. His shoulders are broad and powerful, and there are tufts of dark hair above the knuckles on the fingers of his mighty hands. The value of Madame Renard's jewels provides a clear motive, and Jack is without doubt strong enough to have delivered the blow that killed her. The knowledge that Mr. Austen refused to advance his pay only days before the incident took place sticks in Jane's craw.

Mrs. Trigg takes the basket, examining the contents eagerly. "I'll spread some of your mother's cottage cheese on a slice of bread. That usually tempts him." A moment later, Mrs. Trigg's children fall silent. All three are lined up in their pen, happily sucking a piece of Mary's plum pudding, while their mother gets on with boiling water in a copper kettle suspended on a chain above the fireplace.

At least Mary has bought Mrs. Trigg a moment's respite from the demands of motherhood. Jane won't say *peace*, for within the stifling domesticity of the Triggs' kitchen, she can still hear the constant chorus of shouts and bangs from the main gaol. Jane pictures heavy iron doors slamming and weighty padlocks being fastened, as desperate men in leg irons wail against their plight.

What a ghastly place for Mrs. Trigg to rear a family. She looks like a woman of sense. What could have possessed her to accept Mr. Trigg's proposal? Surely living here is too much of a sacrifice, even for a love match.

Henry paces up and down the cramped space between the hearth and the table. "What's that racket? It's like Bedlam in here." Henry is altogether too big, too bright and too brash for this confined setting. His nervous energy makes Jane, and everyone else, all the more anxious.

Mrs. Trigg serves up a tray of weak, milky tea in delftware dishes. "We're used to it. Hardly notice it any more. Do we,

Father?" She addresses Mr. Trigg Senior, who sits in a rocking chair.

The old man creases his face, so that his nose and mouth threaten to disappear into one wrinkly crevice. "You might not, my girl, but I'd say it's the Devil's own torment." He bites the stem of a long, white clay pipe and sucks until the tobacco glows red.

Mrs. Trigg wipes her hands on her greying apron, mumbling something unintelligible as she faces the wall.

The tea tastes vile. Not wishing to cause offence, Jane does her best to drain it as she tries to entice Georgy to talk with his fingers. She tells him she's missed him and asks if he's missed her.

Georgy folds his arms and dips his chin to his chest. The only sign he makes is to put his fist to his heart and move it in a circle—"Sorry."

"Oh, Georgy," Jane whispers, as she grasps his hands and raises them to her lips. "Believe me, we know you've nothing to be sorry for."

Jack makes irritating attempts at small talk. "He keeps asking if we can go walking. Not much walking in here, is there, Georgy?" Jack walks his fingers across his other palm. "Sometimes we go out into the yard, but I fear turning round and round in circles only makes him more restless."

Jane swallows, sensing what may be her only opportunity. "You must miss getting out into the fresh air too, Jack?"

Jack slaps his drum-tight stomach. "I should say. I'll run to fat cooped up in here. I do my best to help Mrs. Trigg with the daily tasks, but there's mornings she fights me tooth and nail to get to the grate before I can sweep it for her."

The hint of a blush creeps into Mrs. Trigg's cheeks. "Now, now, Mr. Smith. You're our guest. I shouldn't be using you as a servant."

Jane's chest tightens. Jack has clearly charmed the gaoler's wife with his seemingly gentle bearing. She grits her teeth. "I've been intending to ask you, Jack. Where were you on the night of the Harcourts' ball?"

Jack's features remain vacant. "What?"

"Jane," says James, in a low tone of warning.

Henry hugs his elbows tight as he stalks past. "Let her speak, James. We'll never get any peace otherwise."

James, Henry and Jack stare at Jane. She feels small, and very far away. "Where were you, exactly, Jack, on the night Madame Renard was murdered?"

"Well, as I said at the time, I was out, running a few errands."

Jane gathers her skirts into her fists. "Yes, but what errands, specifically?"

"Let me think. I delivered some firewood to old Widow Littleworth, out on the lane to Popham. She's on her own, as you'll know. And the chill was setting in."

"Did you speak to her?" Jane struggles for breath in the dank, airless room.

Jack scratches his temple. "No. It was late, and I didn't want to disturb her. I stacked it in a pile outside her cottage for her to find in the morning."

Jane half hopes Jack can come up with a credible alibi. It might not help her solve the case, but it will erase the pain of having to doubt her childhood playmate. "Did anyone else see you?"

"That's enough, Jane," says James. "He's told you where he was."

This time, Henry does not intervene. It is as far as her brothers will let her go, before they haul her out of Mrs. Trigg's kitchen, and away from Georgy.

"Not that I can recall. I suppose someone might have seen me leave the village, with the handcart." Jack rubs his jaw between his finger and thumb. His nails are bitten to the quick. "I'm so sorry, Miss Austen. I really am."

"For what?" Jane snaps, glowering at him. She is furious with her brothers for silencing her, and furious with Jack for not having the sense to rule himself out of the investigation. Most of all, she is furious with herself for having neither the strength nor the wherewithal to break Georgy out of this wretched place.

Jack spreads his arms wide, his voice rising in pitch. "For not being there to vouch for Georgy. I don't often leave him. And I would never have gone, if I'd thought Mother would be called out. And as for how he got hold of the necklace, I've been racking my brain, but I've no idea."

James puts a hand on Jack's shoulder. "No one is blaming you, Jack."

"But you should." Jack's eyes are glassy. "It's my job, isn't it? To keep Georgy safe. And I've let you all down."

James lets out a heavy sigh. "No, Jack. If anyone's let Georgy down, it's us. We've tried our best, but it's impossible to mind him all of the time."

Since he was a boy, escaping into nature has been Georgy's best medicine. For all the treatments he suffered at the hands of physicians over the years, it's long walks in the fresh air that proved most beneficial to maintaining the equilibrium of his constitution. Like all Jane's brothers, he's a ball of energy. Try to keep any of the Austen boys inside for long, and they become fretful and ill-tempered.

When they were children, Jane dreaded long spells of inclement weather, during which her mother would insist the children at home remain inside the rectory. The boys would fight mercilessly, scuffing the skirting boards and knocking over the china—until Mr. Austen threatened to take a slipper to their backsides or send them to sea. At the cottage, Dame Culham and Jack indulged Georgy's need for constant movement, as well as peace and quiet. Countless times, Jane has watched from her window as Georgy marched heedlessly into the pouring rain, Jack tramping through the mud behind him.

Tom suggested that Jack had volunteered to remain in gaol beside her brother to make sure Georgy did not implicate him in the crime. But without Jack to interpret, Georgy would find it impossible to communicate with strangers. A burning pain settles on Jane's sternum, as if she's eaten too much bacon. Surely Jack's kindness toward Georgy cannot be motivated by cunning. He would not betray the Austens, betray Jane, so mercilessly.

When it is time to leave, Jane kisses Georgy's clammy forehead and tells him she'll see him again soon. She prays to God she will not be made a liar. Georgy grips her hand so tightly that she has to peel away his fingers. She lingers on the threshold, thanking Mrs. Trigg profusely, but she cannot bear to take one last look at her brother. Her eyes will brim over with tears at the sight of him.

Instead, Jane takes long, steadying breaths as Mr. Trigg sees them out. He opens the front door, and an icy draught hits her face, cooling the scalding tear tracks on her cheeks. James drops a gold coin into Mr. Trigg's hand. The old man grasps it between finger and thumb and jams it into his mouth, crunching it with his two brown teeth. Jane's stomach drops as she pictures Georgy making the same gesture.

She has been an utter fool.

The sign for *biscuit* is easy to remember because its origins are so revolting: sailors, on long voyages, tap biscuits on their elbows, to dislodge weevils, before they eat them. Therefore, *biscuit* is the left arm folded across the chest, followed by two taps on the elbow.

Georgy was not telling Jane he was hungry when she found him scrabbling around in the bushes outside Deane House on the morning after the murder. He was telling her that he had found *gold*. If only she had paid attention, really paid attention, to what he was trying to tell her, she might have spared him, spared them all, from this agony.

CHAPTER TWENTY-FOUR

By the time Jane arrives in Steventon, her head throbs and her eyes sting as if she's sat too close to a smoking chimney. The sky is an inky black. James rides on cautiously through the darkness, to his own bed in Overton. Inside Steventon Rectory, Mr. and Mrs. Austen remain ensconced in the family parlour, wrapped in their dressing gowns and nightcaps, anxious for a full report on the day's events. Jane drops into a hardbacked chair beside her parents. She rests her elbows on the table and cradles her face in her hands.

Sally tiptoes into the room with a tray of bread and cheese.

Neither Jane nor Henry makes a move to touch it. Jane's stomach is twisted with guilt, while Henry sips Mr. Austen's port wine and mutters darkly at the dying embers in the grate. Once the family are alone, Jane explains, through rasping sobs, how she misinterpreted Georgy's attempt to communicate that he found Madame Renard's gold necklace in the shrubbery outside Deane House. "It's all my fault. If I'd thought about it properly, I'd have known he wasn't signing *biscuit*."

"Jane, you cannot blame yourself for this." Mr. Austen removes his spectacles and massages the bridge of his nose. "You are no more or less guilty than the rest of us. We all have a duty of care when it comes to Georgy, and I'm afraid each and every one of us has let him down. His father most of all."

But Jane is sure, if she hadn't been so distracted with Tom, she would have realized this weeks ago. "Don't you see? *I* told Jack that Georgy was hungry. Then Jack mentioned Mrs. Fletcher's pies, and of course Georgy forgot what he was trying to tell me. He went off in happy expectation of his dinner. If only I'd been less dismissive, he would have shown us the necklace and we could have gone to Mr. Craven together and explained where he found it. I expect it would have been a different matter entirely if *we'd* handed it over."

The skin beneath Mr. Austen's watery blue eyes is loose and puffy. "What's done is done, my dear. There's no use—"

"You must write to Mr. Hayter, immediately." Mrs. Austen fiddles with the lace edge of a pocket handkerchief, turning the trim through her fingers as if joining two crusts of pastry.

"And I will." Mr. Austen pats his wife's restless fingers.

"Will it do any good?" Mrs. Austen dips her chin, frowning at the liver spots on the back of her husband's hand.

Jane's heart sinks. It's too late, and she knows it.

"Well, it might . . . ," says Mr. Austen.

Henry glowers at the fireplace. The log has burned to charcoal. It retains its shape, but one hard stab with the poker and flecks of soot will scatter into the air while the embers dissolve to a pile of ash. "No, it won't. There's no kindness in giving her false hope, Father."

Mrs. Austen chokes back a sob. Mr. Austen takes his wife's hands, as he narrows his eyes at his son.

"It's as Jane said." Henry switches his focus back to the grate. "It would have been another matter entirely if we'd realized where Georgy had found the necklace at the time. But now, well, we can't prove anything. It looks like we're inventing reasons for the magistrate to release him. Which, of course, we are."

"But it's the truth." Jane rubs her temples with the fingers of both hands. Even the dim glow of the fire and the faint circles of light from the candles hurt her eyes. "The murderer must have dropped it as he made his escape."

Henry finishes his port and immediately reaches to replenish it. Mr. and Mrs. Austen exchange a frown, but neither dares to challenge Lieutenant Austen over his drinking. He fills his tumbler to the rim, not bothering to replace the stopper in the blue glass bottle. "So, there was no need for you to put the thumbscrews on Jack Smith, after all."

"Oh, Jane. You didn't, did you?" Mr. Austen's tone is uncharacteristically sharp. "I told you to leave that notion well alone."

Jane's head throbs even more forcefully. "It doesn't mean Jack definitely didn't do it. Only that if he did, he dropped the necklace while running away. Then Georgy found it in the shrubbery—rather than among Jack's things."

A strangled cry comes from outside the parlour.

Jane and her family all turn and stare at the door. It is ever so slightly ajar.

"Was that Sally?" asks Jane, rather unnecessarily. If it wasn't Sally, she finally has proof that the rectory is haunted.

Mrs. Austen lowers her voice to a whisper. "I'm beginning to think you may be right, Jane. Something's bothering her. I hope she's not thinking of moving on after Lady Day."

"I'll go and speak to her, find out what is the matter." Jane lifts the untouched supper tray with both hands.

In the kitchen, Sally stands with her back to the door, wiping cutlery with a cloth before throwing it into the press. Wisps of dark hair escape from her plain mobcap. Jane edges the tray onto the scrubbed-pine table, pushing aside a precarious pile of clean crockery to make room. Sally sniffs and wipes her face with the back of her hand.

"Thank you for saving us supper, Sally. I'm sorry we didn't eat any. It's been a trying day and I, for one, have lost my appetite."

Sally turns away. The gesture is so cutting that Jane can see the outline of her shoulder blade beneath her woolen gown.

"I've been meaning to talk to you," continues Jane. "I wanted to ask if you're well. You seem to be rather . . . out of sorts, of late."

"Fine, miss," Sally mumbles, clattering the forks and spoons onto the shelf without bothering to separate them into the different compartments.

Jane reaches for Sally's arm.

Before she can touch it, the girl flinches and pulls away.

"There is something wrong. I know there is. Whatever it is, Sally, you know you can always talk to me," Jane insists, but Sally dips her chin to her chest, letting her wispy hair fall over her face. "Has my mother said something to upset you? I know she can be rather tactless at times . . . but she's very appreciative of your work. We all are."

"Your mother?" Sally hisses, eyes darting to Jane from beneath her cap. "It's not your mother who's going around accusing . . ."

Jane startles at Sally's vehemence. She takes a step backward. "Sally, what is it?"

Sally shakes her head. "Nothing, miss."

But it's *not* nothing. Jane can see it in every part of Sally's bearing. She's like a frightened hen, wings tucked tight to her breast and crouching in the dirt to play dead. Jane swallows. She must tread carefully to avoid frightening Sally away. "You know something, don't you? If it's about the murder, you must tell me. This is important—Georgy's life is at stake."

Sally meets Jane's gaze, taking short, quick breaths.

"I promise you won't be in trouble. We just need to know."

"I don't know nothing, miss. Except, that is . . ." Sally clutches her polishing rag tight in her fist, ". . . I know who definitely *didn't* do it. Who couldn't have done it, because he was here with me, from late in the afternoon and all the night through."

Jane stares expectantly.

In the silence, Sally wrings the cloth between her hands and peers at Jane earnestly. After a few moments, she mouths, "*Jack*."

"Jack? Jack Smith?" Jane repeats as Sally nods. "Jack Smith was here, on the night of the Harcourts' ball? Then why didn't he say so?"

"Because he doesn't want to get me into trouble with your father . . . for sneaking a *young man* into my bedroom."

"Oh!" Jane's hands fly to her mouth as at last she catches Sally's meaning. Jack Smith spent the *night* with Sally. All night. In the same little room, under the eaves in the Austens' attic. With only one tiny bed.

"I was putting the hens away for the night, see, when Jack happened to pass by at dusk. He was on his way down to Widow Littleworth with a cart full of firewood. He's so good like that, taking care of everybody without ever needing to be asked. So, I told him to call in on his way back, and I'd have a jug of ale waiting for him. And then, well, since everyone was going to be out, and your ma and pa only wanted a cold supper"—Sally takes a deep breath, drawing herself up tall—"I invited him to stay the night."

"Oh." Jane flaps her hands around her cheeks to cool her face. Jack under the same roof as Jane, all night, with *Sally*. "I didn't even realize you two were acquainted?"

"Acquainted? How many times have you walked in on us canoodling in the kitchen? Jack and I have been stepping out together for months. It's no secret. The whole village knows. Us domestics do have our own lives to live, Miss Austen, although you might consider us so low as to be beneath your notice."

Jane gasps. "That's hardly fair. My mother taught me it was rude to pry into the servants' private business."

As Sally lifts her chin, the glimmer of defiance grows in her dark eyes. "Well, you have the truth out of me, at last. And I'm not sorry. Jack Smith would never harm anyone. And he definitely didn't kill that woman up at Deane House because, as I said, he was taking firewood down to Widow Littleworth and after that he was here with me. All night. He didn't leave until dawn. And if you dare accuse him"—she jabs a finger in Jane's direction—"I swear I'll vouch for him at the assize. Even if it means losing my place and my good name."

"Heavens, Sally, why didn't you say something sooner?"

"Jack sent a message, telling me not to. He knows I can't afford to be sent packing without a letter of recommendation. We've got plans, see, both of us, for a better life. We want to have our own home one day. Start a family. So, I can't stand idly by while you accuse such a good, honest, gentle man of committing such a vile crime."

Jane grabs the handle of the press and leans against it. Jack must have asked Mr. Austen for a loan to buy Squire Terry's sow because he is courting Sally, and is planning to provide for a family of his own. "Sent packing? Sally, I'm not going to tell anyone what you told me."

"You're not?"

"Of course not." Jane presses her palm against her forehead. "Besides, you could have a string of sweethearts queuing at the kitchen door, and I'm sure my mother would turn a blind eye if it meant she didn't have to go through the ordeal of finding a new maid."

"Oh, that's a relief." Sally's shoulders drop. "And you'll leave off saying Jack had anything to do with that woman's murder?"

Jane nods. "I never truly thought Jack capable of such a heinous crime. You're right, he is a good man. The best. It's just . . ." Jane recalls Jack's panicked face when she asked where he was that night. It was wrong of her even to suspect him. Jack has been a faithful friend to her brother all his life, and Jane has left him believing the Austens blame *him* for Georgy's terrible predicament. "I'm so desperate to save my brother, I must keep turning over every possibility. It's the way my mind works, you see. I have to spin all these different stories to understand how and why something might have happened."

"Hmm . . . If I may be so bold, miss," Sally eyes Jane suspiciously. "I'd say that was your problem. Perhaps you could try giving your mind a rest and letting your heart or your body do some of the work."

"If only I could, Sally. But I'm afraid my mind is like a spinning wheel that's never still. No matter how hard I try to stop it, it just keeps on turning out this never-ending thread of thoughts. The only way I can prevent myself from becoming tangled in them is to write them down." Jane takes out her pocketbook, as if to prove her point. Every page is criss-crossed with notes about the murder.

Sally regards Jane's unintelligible scrawl with disdain—until Jane feels such a fool that she folds the book closed and tucks it away. She says goodnight, promising Sally several more times, on pain of death, that she will never reveal to anyone the maid's secret assignation with Jack Smith under the Austens' roof.

As Jane reaches the landing, a fresh wave of mortification breaks over her, and she's forced to clutch the newel post for support.

Cassandra has been teaching Sally to read. Jane hopes the maid never takes it upon herself to dust Mr. Austen's office at St. Nicholas's Church. For if Sally decided to browse the parish records for amusement, she'd discover that once, when Jane was very young and silly, and quite carried away with imagining all the different paths her life might take, she had picked up a pen and used the practice page of the marriage register to transform herself from "Miss Jane Austen" into "Mrs. Jack Smith."

How utterly mortifying. Jane must remember to ask her father's permission to tear out the page and burn it in the morning, lest her foolishness be preserved for all posterity.

Over the next couple of days, Jane rises earlier and earlier, hoping to catch whoever is leaving flowers on Zoë Renard's grave. This morning, when Jane dashes downstairs to the family parlour, she finds Mr. Austen already dressed in his clerical robes. "Where are you off to?" She grabs a slice of toast from the rack on the table as she appraises her father's uncharacteristically smart attire for the time of day. He usually relaxes in his banyan, reading yesterday's newspaper, until breakfast is finished and cleared away.

Anna sits in her high chair, red-cheeked and gnawing at a bone teething ring, whittled for her by Frank. Mrs. Austen is staring into space. Unlike her husband, she remains in her nightgown, a nightcap covering her long silver hair. She grasps a bowl of porridge in one hand and a spoon, paused midway between the bowl and Anna's mouth, in the other.

Mr. Austen stands, brushing the crumbs from his black coat. "Church, of course." He guides his wife's hand, with the spoonful of porridge, gently to Anna's mouth. The baby opens her lips briefly, refusing to release the teething ring, so she ends up with both implements between her teeth.

Jane nibbles the crust of her toast. Her heart is lighter since she scratched "Jack Smith" from her list of suspects. Now there are only three names left and they are all intrinsically bound: Sir John, Mrs. Twistleton and Jonathan Harcourt. Are they in on it together? Did Sir John and Mrs. Twistleton spread rumours about strangers camping in the woods to protect Jonathan? Or are they guilty of murdering Jonathan's lover to cover their own indiscretions? Jane must find the loose thread in their cloak of deception and wear away at it until she unravels their lies.

"It's too early for a midweek service." Jane strokes Anna's downy head as her father prepares to leave.

"True, but I've a marriage to solemnize." Mr. Austen adjusts his Geneva bands and snatches his shovel hat from the stand.

"I don't remember any banns being read?"

Mr. Austen's eyes twinkle as he rams his hat over his powdered queue. "Ah, that's because the couple have a licence. Why don't you come? It might restore your faith in true love. Also, I may need a witness. I can't ask the sexton again. He spilled mud all over the register last time."

"Why should my faith need any restoration?"

Neither Jane's mother nor her father has mentioned the sudden disappearance of her Irish friend, but she has caught them looking at her with unusually soft eyes and downturned mouths. She expects one of her brothers has filled them in on the mortification of her heartbreak. Being rejected is bad enough, but being pitied is even worse.

"Oh, my dear Jane." Mr. Austen places his hand on his wife's shoulder, as he leans down to peck her softly on the forehead. "Just now I'm afraid we could all do with a sign that the good Lord has not forsaken us."

Mrs. Austen keeps her eyes trained on Anna. When she speaks, her voice is barely more audible than a whisper. "Perhaps he should enter a guilty plea."

"No," Mr. Austen snaps.

Without looking up, Mrs. Austen scrapes the remainder of Anna's breakfast onto a spoon. "But, my dear, even Botany Bay must be better than the alternative."

"Are you going to send me to the colonies with Georgy?" Jane asks, in an attempt to lighten the mood.

"No. With our luck, they'd send you straight back." Mrs. Austen shakes her weary head. "Neddy will pay, but James is the one who'll have to go."

"I said no," says Mr. Austen, so brusquely that Jane startles.

Mrs. Austen, meanwhile, is too far away to react. As her mother stares mournfully at Anna, Jane can almost see the ruthlessly pragmatic calculations she is making in her mind. She knows her mother is right. Neddy would pay and James, bless him, would go without question. As her father's curate, he's the only one of her brothers who could be sure of being released by his employer. But never, in all her days, has Jane witnessed her parents disagree on something so fundamental. Please, God, don't let their love for Georgy be the straw that finally breaks them.

Jane grips her toast between her teeth as she follows her father into the vestibule. He waits patiently as she slips her feet into her walking boots. They appeared spoiled beyond all repair, but Sally brushed them free of mud and buffed the leather, daubing the scuffed toes with homemade blacking.

Perhaps it's a sign that the maid has forgiven Jane for slandering her sweetheart's good name. Either that, or she's still worried Jane will tell her father that she's been entertaining her paramour at the rectory. Jane throws her cape over her shoulders and pulls on her bonnet, without bothering to tie either. Her father unlocks the back door, and she steps outside.

The sun splashes Jane's cheek as she follows Mr. Austen through the garden and into the farmyard. The weather must have dipped below freezing overnight: the grass is hairy with frost and the bitter chill reduces the brambles to a tangle of glittering ropes. Mr. Austen walks ahead, narrow and straight-backed. He is getting old, three score and five. His calves, in his white stockings, are as frail as spindles and his shoulders slope.

Mr. Fitzgerald is waiting at the main entrance of St. Nicholas's Church, bundled up in his greatcoat and three-cornered hat. He blows puffs of steam into the chilled air and stamps his feet, clapping his hands together in their leather gloves. His hunter is secured to the lich-gate. The horse stretches his neck to the ground and nibbles at the icy grass growing along the verge.

Jane offers Mr. Fitzgerald a tentative smile, mouthing, "I'm sorry," behind her father's back. Mr. Fitzgerald returns a deadpan expression, which Jane sincerely hopes is a sign he's forgiven her for accusing him of murder. Not to mention debauchery. So much forgiveness, where would Jane be without the Christian clemency of her acquaintances? Expelled from the village and forced to live as a hermit in the woods, probably.

"Congratulations, sir." Mr. Austen takes the younger man's hand and claps him on the back. "You're one of us now, eh? Welcome."

Mr. Fitzgerald's smile broadens into genuine pride, as Jane's father enthusiastically pumps his hand. His clerical collar, with Geneva bands, peeks over the top of his greatcoat. It is bright white and perfectly starched, whereas Jane's father's is yellowed and softened with age. Mr. Austen unlocks the heavy oak door, and Jane enters through the Romanesque archway.

The men bow as they approach the altar, while Jane slides into a pew at the rear of the nave. Together, the two clergymen kneel in prayer, before they light the enormous beeswax candles, in their gleaming silver candlesticks, and arrange the King James Bible on the altar in preparation for the ceremony.

Jane presumes Mr. Fitzgerald is present to serve as the second witness, as well as to observe her father officiate before being asked to conduct such a ceremony himself. She stares at the jewel-bright panels of the stained-glass windows, remembering what a performance James made of taking his own services immediately after ordination. To watch him, you'd think he was auditioning to tread the boards at Drury Lane.

Unlike her father, James preaches a new sermon every week, sometimes disregarding his notes and daring to improvise from the pulpit. But James has always had a theatrical bent, ever since he was a twelve-year-old boy with the audacity to open his own theatre in the family barn. Jane was too young to make the cast. Instead, she sat mesmerised while Eliza stole the show.

The door sounds. Sophy Rivers rushes in, dressed in her riding habit as usual. She must have spotted Mr. Fitzgerald's stallion tied to the lich-gate and be hoping for a clandestine meeting.

But no: Clara and the rest of Sophy's giggling sisters follow hard on her heels.

The four Rivers girls are extremely close in age and almost identical in appearance, like a string of paper dolls. They tumble into the aisle, behind Sophy, as she lifts the black netted veil of her sugarloaf hat.

"Douglas." Sophy's eyes sparkle and her cheeks flush with warmth.

Jane catches her breath, wondering how Sophy will react when she realises Mr. Fitzgerald is not alone. Mrs. Rivers glides into the church behind her daughters, letting the heavy oak door swing shut behind her. Surely Sophy cannot have brought her mother and all her sisters to a chance dalliance with her lover.

"Sophy." Mr. Fitzgerald steps down from the altar and strides briskly along the aisle.

They meet halfway, clasping hands and gazing into each other's beaming faces. A sunray hits the stained-glass window, and the couple are silhouetted against the kaleidoscope of dazzling multicoloured light.

Jane places a hand to her lips as she realises that, far from being a chance passerby and a ready witness, Sophy and Mr. Fitzgerald are the bride and groom. It's as if she's watching a miracle unfold. A sense of calm floods Jane's veins at the rightness of it. The couple's reunification is a balm to her restless spirit.

As the Rivers women file into the front pew, Sophy and Douglas stand, hands clasped, before the altar, and Jane's father begins the ceremony. It's easy to see from whom James inherited his talent for oratory. Mr. Austen may read aloud from the same tired set of sermons, never daring to improvise, but it is impossible not to be moved by the power of his baritone voice. Sophy's sisters whisper to each other and bounce along the bench as the couple make their vows. When Mr. Austen pronounces Douglas and Sophy man and wife, even Mrs. Rivers takes a handkerchief out of her reticule and dabs it to her cheek.

The generosity of Jane's happiness for the newlyweds takes her aback. Rather than burning with jealousy, she, too, is moved to tears. Her father was right. It warms her soul to know that two people can strive to be together and, through patience, persistence and sheer doggedness, transcend all obstacles of rank and circumstance.

It's simply a case of wanting it enough.

Sadly, Tom seems not to want her, but that doesn't mean it's not possible for love to conquer all. She follows the wedding party outside into the churchyard. The sky is brightest blue, and the sun has melted away the morning frost. Clara gives Jane a handful of rice and she whoops as she joins in the throng, throwing it over the newlyweds.

"Jane?" The new Mrs. Fitzgerald releases her husband's hand and pulls Jane aside by her elbow. "What are *you* doing here?"

"Oh." Jane flounders. It is the red barn all over again, and Jane is intruding on Sophy's moment of private joy. "My father said I should come to stand as witness. I didn't know it was you and Mr. Fitzgerald who were getting married." She lowers her voice to a whisper. "Believe me, I can't apologise enough about leaping to conclusions, and I never said a word . . ."

Sophy lifts her palm in its kid-leather glove. "All is well. No more secrets. What with Sir John's arrest for defaulting on his debts, and my persistent refusal to marry Mr. Harcourt, my mother finally came to her senses and agreed it would be best if Douglas and I married quietly and slipped away."

Jane grins so widely that her jaw aches. "I'm so happy for you, Sophy. For both of you. Really, I am."

Sophy smiles, but her flint-grey eyes remain guarded. "Thank you, Jane. We're hoping that by keeping things quiet the scandal of my brief attachment to the Harcourts won't spoil my sisters' chances of social advancement. Mother's taking them to do the London season, poor things."

Jane glances at the remaining three Rivers girls, wishing her prospects were half as fortuitous as theirs. What she wouldn't give to spend the winter in town, primping and preening and dancing every night. She can think of no better medicine to revive her flagging heart. "Oh dear. How will they bear it?"

Sophy frowns at her riding habit. "I'm afraid you must think me a very dull bride?"

"I've never seen you more radiant." Jane smiles. Sophy stands tall. She holds her head high and her eyes shine with self-assurance. She is a woman who fought hard for the life she wanted and won.

"Douglas and I are dashing straight to Falmouth to catch our ship, you see."

"Ship? Are you going to Jamaica, after all?"

Sophy shakes her head, sending grains of rice scattering to the ground from her veil. "No, Upper Canada. A place called York. We wanted a fresh start, and Douglas has been offered a position with the Anglican mission there."

Jane reaches for Sophy's hand. "How wonderful. I've heard the scenery is spectacular." Secretly, Jane cannot help but wonder how Sophy can willingly exile herself from her sisters. Jane is only just coping with Cassandra being three counties away. If an entire ocean lay between them, it might prove enough water for Jane to drown in her own despair.

With a shudder, Jane realises, if she'd been fool enough to elope with Tom, before they could afford to set up home together, she may very well have been shipped off to Ireland while he pursued his career. Jane could not raise his children while living in shared rooms at Lincoln's Inn. If or, rather, when she fell pregnant, living with Tom's family would have been her only option. Jane can only just stomach deferring to her own worthy matriarch. How would she have softened her sharp edges enough to rub along under the same roof as Tom's mother, let alone his five sisters?

Sophy nods, then withdraws her fingers from Jane's grasp and returns to her new husband's side. Mr. Fitzgerald is laughing with Clara. He wraps his arm around Sophy's shoulders, drawing her tight and planting a kiss on her forehead. Sophy buries her face in his lapel.

Jane leaves, not wanting to intrude any more than she has done already. She traverses the churchyard, nearly forgetting to check Zoë Renard's grave. When she remembers, and tiptoes over to Madame Renard's plot, she places her hand over her heart and catches her breath. Three exotic orchids sit at intervals along the ridge of the raised mound of earth. The strange creamy-white flowers are speckled with brownish-purple spots—the colour of dried blood.

An icy shiver runs through Jane's frame. There is only one place in Hampshire that she's ever known exotic orchids to grow: the glasshouse at Deane House.

Sir John couldn't have left the flowers, as he is locked away in the Marshalsea. Lady Harcourt rarely leaves home, and if she had done, Jane or her family would have heard her coach from the rectory. Mrs. Twistleton is unlikely to come alone at night. It's a fair trek from Deane to Steventon and, as far as Jane knows, Mrs. Twistleton doesn't ride. No other servant would dare to cut and remove such rare and expensive blooms.

It must be Jonathan Harcourt.

What is more, it would be just like Jonathan, with his artistic bent, to select the three most perfect blooms from his glasshouse every day. In her mind's eye, Jane can see him perusing the rows of plants lined up along the shelves in their terra-cotta pots, deliberating on the very best specimens. He'd compare each flower for its depth of colour, and examine every petal for defects before snipping his choice from its stem with a pair of sharp silver scissors.

With his long white painter's fingers, Jonathan would wrap his offering in a handkerchief and tuck it into his pocket, taking great care not to crush the delicate blooms. Then, once he'd reached Madame Renard's plot, he'd get to his knees, with no thought for the grass stains on his nankeen breeches, and take his time thoughtfully arranging the three flowers along the earth as if he was preparing the composition of a painting.

Jonathan Harcourt is leaving the flowers. Which means Jane finally has proof he was Madame Renard's lover and the father of her unborn child. She is not grasping at straws or letting her imagination run away with her. He's the only person with access to orchids and the means to visit the graveyard alone at night—arriving on horseback and placing the flowers unseen. She was wrong to let Tom dismiss her suspicions about Mr. Harcourt so casually.

But it's still not enough to save her brother. In order to drop the charges against Georgy, Mr. Craven wants a physical piece of evidence, linking the true culprit to the crime, or a signed confession. If Jane took the magistrate a flower, he'd likely make plans to have *her* committed. She might be able to demonstrate a link between Mr. Harcourt and Madame Renard, but Jane has no evidence that he killed her. As Eliza foretold, Jane will have to work harder than that if she is to catch a murderer.

8. To Cassandra Austen

Steventon, Friday, 22 January 1796

My dearest Cassandra,

I am more certain than ever that Jonathan Harcourt was Madame Renard's lover, but how am I to know if he killed her? With every hour that passes, and we draw closer to February, my spirit plummets. I have been to Winchester. Dear Georgy is bearing up as well as can be expected. Don't ask me for more details, as I cannot lie to you. Jack Smith has an alibi. You would not countenance it, even if I told you, which I cannot, as I'm sworn to secrecy. I can, however, tell you that Sally's scatter-brained mismanagement of our wardrobes is likely due to a severe case of lovesickness. It was wrong of me to doubt Jack. He has been a constant friend to dear Georgy all his life. My heartfelt apologies for the tardiness of this correspondence. I know you will have been waiting many days to hear from me, but I am rendered useless by my own despair. I shan't attempt to hide the depth of my dejection from you, beloved sister. You will no doubt scoff when I tell you that lately I have even found myself staring at the tidy stitches of your sampler hanging in the family parlour, and wondering if I were to trust in the Lord with all my heart, would he show me the answer? I hope this missive reaches you before the weather turns for the worse and the roads are blocked. Write back to me soon, if you can.

I remain your affectionate sister,
J.A.

PS Burn this letter, won't you?

Miss Austen,
Rev. Mr. Fowle's,
Kintbury,
Newbury.

CHAPTER TWENTY-FIVE

At dusk, Jane sits in her dressing room, scribbling in her tiny sloping handwriting. *Lady Susan* needs a conclusion, but Jane can't find one. She cannot bear to marry her villainous heroine off to a man unworthy of her vicious wit. And what man could ever be worthy? So, instead, Jane lets Lady Susan dally with her lover while her friend distracts his rival. She uses the ink she made herself from sloeberries, adding some gum arabic to aid the solution's adhesion to the page. It is dark purple, rather than the satisfyingly stark Japanese black she used to write the first section. Jane fears the marks will fade, but it's all she has to hand.

Madame Renard's exquisite lace hatband and the original wilted cherry-red camellia Jane plucked from her grave stare at her from the dresser, reproaching her for her frivolity. The morbid tableau makes Jane's fingers itch to begin a new composition about a girl whose mind is as fixed on ghosts and ghouls as her own, and who sees murder and violence in every passing shadow.

As Jane dips her quill into the inkpot, she looks up from her writing table and out of the window. White rings of pipe smoke hover in the lavender sky. The concentric circles drift up from the direction of the stables, lingering above the farmyard before dispersing into the wind. There's only one person who would be smoking tobacco in the Austens' stableyard—Henry. Sensing an opportunity, Jane sprinkles setting powder on her work, blows it dry and places it safely inside her writing box.

She slinks downstairs, pulls on her cloak and steps out into the garden, following the obvious distress signals to the tack room.

In a small cell attached to the stables, at the end of the line of stalls, Henry is slumped on the floor, blocking the open doorway. Usually the tack room smells of leather and beeswax. Tonight Henry pollutes the earthy aroma with strong spirits and tobacco smoke. His long legs are stretched out in front of him. A taper, in a brass holder, flickers on the floor at his side as he clutches a bottle to his chest and pokes a white clay pipe between his downturned lips.

"Is that Father's port?" Jane coughs as she steps over him.

He draws on the pipe, blowing the smoke directly into Jane's face. "What if it is? Will you tittle-tattle?" His eyes are red, and there is at least two days' worth of stubble growing along his jaw. The brass buttons of his military jacket are undone and his cravat is missing. He was meant to return to his regiment and his college as soon as they came back from Winchester. Instead, he sent a message saying he was ill. Jane is quite sure that any malady he is suffering from is entirely self-inflicted.

She wafts away the smoke, wrinkling her nose. "When have I ever done that?" Greylass's saddle rests on a three-legged stool. She lifts it with both hands and dumps it on the floor, before taking a seat. It's been years since she handled any tack and the padded leather saddle, with its iron stirrups, is far heavier than she remembered. "I wish you'd talk to me."

Henry glowers. "I wish you wouldn't insist on talking to me."

Jane ignores his hostile air. "Did you hear Sophy Rivers married Mr. Fitzgerald this morning?"

A flicker of animation passes across Henry's features. "Well, huzzah for them." He takes a swig of his port. "A toast to the bride and groom."

Jane kicks Henry's calf with the toe of her walking boot. "Out with it."

He rakes a hand through his chestnut hair, making a fist and pulling at it from the root. "What are we going to do, Jane? Our brother, our sweet, harmless brother, is headed for the gallows for a crime he didn't commit, and none of us can come up with a way to save him."

A pang shoots straight through Jane. Deep down, she knows every member of her family is equally tormented by Georgy's fate, but their near-religious commitment to stoicism makes it nigh impossible for any of the Austens to express extremes of emotion. It is testament to Henry's wild streak that he can occasionally let his mask of composure slip. "Mother seems to have joined the campaign for Georgy to plead guilty."

"Father will never stand for it. They'd brand Georgy a thief and banish him to the colonies."

"I know." Jane folds her arms across her chest.

"It's not a metaphor, Jane. They'll sear the letter *T* into his thumb with a red-hot—"

"I know!" She cuts him off, unwilling to hear more. "Perhaps we really should think about having Georgy committed. An asylum can't be as bad as all that, can it?"

"Worse." He glares at her. "Next time you're in town, I'll stand you the penny to get into Bedlam, and you can see for yourself. Father's right. Georgy would be denied any shred of dignity."

"And is there any dignity in dancing the Tyburn jig?" Jane shudders. Sometimes her jokes are too black, even for herself. "Dear Lord! Henry, they won't really hang him. Will they?"

Henry stares out into the encroaching darkness.

"What is it? What are you not telling me?"

"Last year, at the Winchester assize, two fourteen-year-old boys were executed as pickpockets."

"But it's not fair."

"It's the law, Jane. It's not meant to be fair—it's meant to be so horrifying that a man would starve rather than lift a loaf of bread." Henry closes his eyes and weeps softly.

Jane turns her face away. If she watches Henry cry, she'll start, too. "We've got to do something. We can't just sit here, waiting for the judge to condemn him."

Henry cradles his bottle of port, as if he's Anna cuddling one of her rag dolls. "We've already tried everything. That lawyer's bleeding Neddy dry and he's worse than useless."

"So we must discover who *really* killed Zoë Renard. And prove it, before it's too late. But, no, by all means, carry on sitting here, sulking over the state of your romantic affairs, and wailing like an infant, if that's what you'd prefer."

"You don't understand."

Jane swipes the bottle from his hands. "I might. Why did you and Eliza fall out? Is it your plan to join the regulars? You should listen to her. She knows far more about what it's like to be caught up in a real war than you do."

"It wasn't that. I . . . ," Henry takes a ragged breath, chest heaving ". . . I asked her to marry me."

Jane splutters a mouthful of port. "You did what?" She can't believe Henry would go so far. Surely Eliza would laugh at him.

"Don't look at me like that. I'm a grown man, making an independent living. What's wrong with me proposing to Eliza?"

Jane wipes her mouth on the sleeve of her gown. "You mean other than that she's our first cousin?"

"Mr. Fitzgerald is Miss Rivers's first cousin."

"I suppose he is, but that's different."

Henry arches a sardonic eyebrow. "Why?"

"Because he's not my brother, and she's not *my* first cousin." Jane tuts, realizing she's as guilty as her brothers of wanting to keep Eliza to herself. "Besides, Captain de Feullide has only been dead a short time."

"It's been almost two years."

"Has it? That went by quickly."

Henry snatches the bottle back out of Jane's grasp. "Eliza never loved him, you know. He was Aunt Phila's choice."

"He was the father of her child."

Henry leans forward, staring up at her from beneath his thick dark lashes. He reminds her of a newborn foal, struggling to stand. "I love her, Jane."

Jane raises her eyes to the cobwebbed ceiling, resisting the urge to kick him again. "We all love her. She's Cousin Eliza."

"Not like I do." Henry tips his head back and takes a long swallow of port. "Well, I've a feeling James might."

All of Jane's life she's watched her brothers vie for their glamorous cousin's attention. When Henry was younger, there seemed to be such an enormous age gap between him and Eliza that his boyish infatuation was ridiculous. Holding tight to his fixation into adulthood seems downright pathetic. "What did she say?"

Henry rests the base of the bottle on his knee, staring at it instead of meeting Jane's eye. "She said she loves me, too, but she isn't ready to be married again. She isn't sure if she'll ever be ready."

It was cruel of Eliza to indulge her coquettish nature by encouraging Henry. She should have put him out of his misery, so that he could learn to let go of his childish fantasy. "I'm sorry . . . but if you really want to get married, why can't you find yourself a nice, suitable young lady? Instead of always chasing women you obviously can't have."

"I don't know, Jane. Why can't you find yourself a nice, suitable young man?"

All of the breath in Jane's lungs rushes out of her. She crumples, slumping forward. It has been more than three weeks since she heard from Tom. She dearly hoped he'd have the decency to write and let her know that their flirtation was over, but apparently not. The searing pain has settled to a dull ache. Sometimes she thinks it might be gone but when she pictures his handsome features, or passes one of the paths they trod together, the agony returns. It's like the lingering pang of a wobbly tooth, always there but smarting when prodded. She wishes she could find a way to wrench it out completely and be done with it.

"That was rather harsh. I shouldn't have said it. What did happen with Lefroy? You seemed to take to each other, but the next thing we know, he's fled the county."

"I can't say." Jane grabs the bottle, taking a large gulp. It tastes of blackberries and green peppercorns. A warm fuzzy feeling spreads from her mouth down her throat and into her chest, numbing her bruised heart. "Unlike you, I'm not a grown man, making an independent living. These things are beyond my control."

Henry turns his head away from the bitterness in Jane's tone. They fall silent for a few moments. She sniffs, blinking away hot, shameful tears. He puffs on his pipe and blows languid smoke rings out of the open door into the frigid night air. "Do you want me to punch him for you?"

"Don't you dare. I already have one brother in trouble with the law. The last thing I need is another. So, no more flirting with Mrs. Chute, either. I've witnessed her husband's wrath when crossed. Believe me, he's not at all the forgiving type."

"Elizabeth Chute! Don't remind me." Henry covers his face with one hand, grimacing at her through his open fingers. "If it wasn't for her, Georgy wouldn't be in this fix. I wish to God I'd never picked that lock."

Jane's mind whirs. On the night of the murder, she'd assumed anyone could access the laundry closet. The number of guests, servants and tradesmen who might have nipped inside it that day is incalculable. But, as Hannah pointed out, the closet is full of valuables that the family would have guarded closely. "You picked the lock?"

"Yes. I'm rather good at it, actually. Elizabeth didn't believe I could do it, but two minutes with my penknife and I had the mechanism sprung."

Jane wants to grab Henry by the lapels and shake him until his stupid head rolls off. "Why didn't you tell us at the time?"

"I thought I did. Why? Is it important?"

"I should say so, yes. Don't you see? Madame Renard is hardly likely to have locked herself into that closet. Is she? If the door was locked, it means someone—most likely her killer—locked her in. And for that person to have the key . . ."

"The killer really *must* be someone from Deane House." Henry scrambles to his feet. He grabs a bridle, looping it round his neck, and picks up a saddle, then staggers out of the tack-room door.

"Where do you think you're going?" Jane pinches out the taper, burning her fingers, and scrabbles to her feet to follow him.

"Deane House, of course," Henry shouts over his shoulder.

By now, the sky is black and the cold cuts Jane to the bone. In the distance, candles burn in the windows of the rectory and white smoke billows out of the clay chimney pots in the red-tiled roof. As Jane passes Greylass's stall, the mare blows steam through her nose and kicks at the door with her front hoofs. Jane ignores her, making instead for Severus's box. Inside, Henry holds a steel bit to the stallion's closed mouth. The animal twists his neck, swishing his tail and presenting Henry with his piebald rear, forcing his master to step backward.

Jane stands at the threshold, too afraid to enter. "Wait." She reaches for Henry's arm, catching the cuff of his jacket. "You can't just march in there."

"Why not?" Henry frowns. He's deadly serious. The only other time Jane has seen Henry looking so severe was when he was standing guard over Madame Renard's slain corpse.

"Because I have tried confronting the family with it, which took me nowhere. They're not going to admit it."

"Jonathan will, when I show him my sabre."

"A confession obtained through torture will hardly be worth anything. And we don't have enough evidence to prove it was Jonathan."

"But it must have been. As you said, she was his mistress. He wanted her out of the way so he could marry Miss Rivers for her fortune."

"But that doesn't necessarily mean he killed her."

Henry shakes himself free of Jane's grasp. "Who else would have done it?" He plants both hands on Severus's rump, leaning his weight on the horse as he tries shoving him round. Severus remains resolute. The only movement the horse makes is to swish his tail disparagingly.

"What about Sir John?" says Jane.

"What reason would he have had to kill her?"

"The same as Jonathan? To get his son's pregnant lover out of the way, in case she ruined his chances of marrying an heiress. Sir John must have had a hand in Jonathan's pursuit of

Sophy, don't you think? He needed her dowry to save the estate from ruin."

"But you saw the baronet that night. He was just as confounded as the rest of us."

"But people don't always act according to the truth. Do they?" It is not Sir John's face that comes to mind as Jane says this but Tom's. Will she ever forget the sparkle of his bright blue eyes and the curve of his seductive smile by moonlight? She shakes her head, willing the vision gone.

"I suppose you're right."

"And then there's Mrs. Twistleton."

Henry scoffs. "That's hardly likely, is it?"

"Why not? I told you she's having a liaison with Sir John." Jane pinches her lips together. "You don't think a woman can be capable of murder?"

Henry walks backward out of the stall. He slides the bolt, slinging the bridle over the door. "Not generally, no. Mrs. Twistleton may be a harlot, but that does not make her a cold-blooded killer."

"But what if she did it to protect Sir John? People say she'll do anything for him. She might have been afraid she'd lose her protector, and her place at Deane House. Or perhaps Madame Renard learned of their arrangement and tried to use it to extort money from them both."

Henry snorts. "This isn't one of those novels you and Eliza are so fond of, Jane." Behind him, Severus rotates, poking his head over the half-door and nibbling his master's shoulder. Henry bats him lightly on the cheek.

"I know that," Jane responds. "And, hypocrite, you're just as fond of Mrs. Radcliffe's work as we are, if not more so. Either way, you can't just burst into Deane House frothing at the mouth. They're likely protecting each other, and they'll close ranks to deny it—leaving you looking like a raving madman. We should be clever about this, gather evidence if we're going to make it ring true in court. Mr. Craven said another party confessing to the crime would be the best way to exonerate Georgy. We must persuade the real killer to come forward with the truth."

Henry rests one hand on his hip. Severus continues to nuzzle his cheek. Jane can feel her brother's temper cooling, leaving him curious. Dear Henry, he's too good-natured to remain vexed for long. "If you're so clever," he says, "what is our plan?"

Jane fights to repress a sly smile. This is the moment she's been waiting for. "Well, actually, there is something I've been pondering." She pictures Cassandra's tidy stitches: "Trust in the Lord with all thine heart; and lean not unto thine own understanding." Jane is not too pigheaded to know when she needs help. She may not be able to save Georgy on her own, but with the Almighty, and now Henry, on her side, she may find a way.

The following Sunday, silver ice crystals cling to the edges of the ivy covering the flint walls of St. Nicholas's churchyard, transforming the evergreen leaves into sparkling five-pointed stars. Jane and Henry stand shivering beside the carriage, as their father shakes hands and converses leisurely with each of the parishioners filing out of the arched doorway. With the Reverend George Lefroy still in Berkshire, James and Mr. Austen are taking turns to cover his services at St. Andrew's, as well as fulfilling their own duties. On this particular Sunday, it is Mr. Austen's turn to lead worship at Ashe, which is most serendipitous as Jane's plan to induce the Harcourts to confess to murder relies on the compliance of a preacher who is not wont to improvise.

Mr. Austen rubs his hands together as he tentatively crosses the icy path in his glossy heeled shoes. "All done. Now I must be off to Ashe."

"Brrr." Henry tilts his clean-shaven face up to the white sky. "It looks like Dick Snow is on his way. Shall I drive you up there in the carriage?" He pats Severus, who is conveniently tethered to the carriage beside Mr. Austen's own horse.

Jane smiles. "I thought I'd come, too. It's not often you conduct the service at St. Andrew's." She pulls her cloak tighter with her mittened hands.

Deep vertical lines carve into the papery skin of Mr. Austen's cheeks. "I led worship there on Tuesday, and on Thursday evening."

"Yes, but those were midweek services. Sunday is special." Jane takes her father's twiglike arm, tugging him toward the carriage by the sleeve of his woolen frock coat.

Henry opens the door. "Let me help you up."

As Mr. Austen mounts the step, the strap of his black leather satchel falls down his arm. Henry takes the bag, passing it behind his back to Jane. She pulls off her mittens and reaches inside, discreetly switching her father's tattered papers for several crisp new sheets bearing her own handwriting, then shoves the satchel back at Henry.

"There you are." Henry hands his father his bag.

Mr. Austen eyes his son warily as he takes his seat. Jane tucks the stolen papers inside her cloak before climbing into the carriage beside her father. He shuffles along the bench, making room for her beside him. "Pray tell me, what have I done to deserve such thoughtful children?"

"Are we not always thoughtful, Papa?"

"No." Mr. Austen peers up at her from beneath the wide brim of his hat.

"I'm sorry to hear you say so." Jane interlaces her fingers and sets them in her lap primly. "I assure you, you're always first in our hearts."

"Hmm." Mr. Austen clutches his satchel tight to his breast as Severus whinnies and the carriage wheels creak into motion.

Snowflakes dance in the frigid air as the Austens arrive at Ashe. Henry ties Severus to a post while Jane scrambles down from the carriage. The siblings make a dash for the oak door of the church, abandoning their elderly father to disembark by himself. They burst inside and charge up the aisle toward the front benches, directly in front of the altar. St. Andrew's is almost identical to St. Nicholas's. The only difference is that Ashe is a more prosperous parish than Steventon, so a few more silver candlesticks gleam from the altar and the scent of beeswax is more pronounced.

The service is later than usual and most of the villagers are waiting for their priest to arrive. Harry Digweed and his brothers bunch up together to accommodate Jane and Henry in their family pew.

The Harcourts, as the other foremost family in the vicinity, are stationed across the aisle. Mother and son sit straight-backed and stare directly ahead. With her husband in debtors' prison, Lady Harcourt has adopted widow's weeds and is head to toe in black bombazine and rabbit fur. Jonathan's complexion is ghostly. He smooths his hair away from his forehead and there's a haunted expression in his pale eyes.

A couple of rows back, Mrs. Twistleton sits at the end of a public pew beside the Harcourts' butler. Her dark eyebrows draw tightly together, and her ash-blond hair is swept back into her cap. Beside the ladies' finery, her emerald cloak, with its fox-fur trim, is rather shabby. She fiddles with a matching green velvet reticule in her lap.

Jane taps her foot against the cold tiled floor as her father reads the liturgy. Beside her, Henry drums his fingers on his prayer book. Several eternities pass before Mr. Austen's knees crack as he climbs into the ornately carved pulpit to deliver the sermon. He fumbles in his pocket for his spectacles, breathes on the glass lenses and rubs them clean with a handkerchief. When he turns to the papers resting on the lectern, a deep V-shaped crease appears in his brow. He picks up the pages, flicking through the small bundle and studying each side carefully, before setting them down again.

The church is silent, apart from a few impatient coughs reverberating through the congregation, as if in conversation with each other. Jane can barely breathe as she waits for her father to speak. Beside her, Henry has turned to stone.

Mr. Austen lifts his head and surveys the congregation. "My fellow Christians, let us take this moment of reflection to examine the very foundations of our faith—the Ten Commandments. And chief among these"—his eyes alight on Jane—"'Thou shalt not . . . murder.'"

A ripple of gasps and whispers tears through the nave. Mrs. Twistleton grips her reticule, curling a finger around the drawstring and pulling it tight. Jonathan swallows, tugging at the knot of the white linen cravat looped around his upturned collar. Lady Harcourt wedges her rabbit-fur muff between her head and the back of her pew, positioning it as a cushion on which to rest her cheek, before closing her kohl-rimmed eyes.

From his elevated position, Mr. Austen scowls down at Jane.

She smiles keenly and nods her encouragement.

"For you'll be familiar with the commandment, and indeed what the law has to say on the matter, but what consequences should follow if it is broken?" Mr. Austen scratches his temple, ruffling his pristine white curls and disturbing his smooth queue. "Genesis is clear: 'Whoso sheddeth man's blood, by man shall his blood be shed.'" He pales as he speaks, stumbling over the archaic language. In his long and esteemed career, the Reverend George Austen is not accustomed to quoting from the Old Testament, especially the more vengeful verses.

Jane's mouth dries as she watches her suspects' every move. Beside her, Henry takes quick noisy breaths and rests his hand on the hilt of his sabre.

Across the aisle, Mrs. Twistleton's almond-shaped eyes bore into the back of her mistress's head. Jonathan squeezes his eyelids shut and his features strain harder with every word that Mr. Austen intones. Red blotches crawl along his neck as sweat soaks his forehead. Only Lady Harcourt is unruffled. Her eyes remain closed and her face is as slack as her bosom, adorned with glittering jet, rises and falls like the tide of the sea.

Mr. Austen clears his throat. When he speaks, his voice is strained, as if he hasn't quite managed it. "And further . . . we may take as the foundation of our earthly laws 'A man that doeth violence to the blood of any person shall flee to the pit; let no man stay him.'" He pauses, his face a reflection of one of the gargoyles carved into the Gothic arches of the vaulted ceiling above him.

Neither Mrs. Twistleton nor Lady Harcourt has moved. In fact, her father's performance seems to be having a soporific effect on Lady Harcourt, which is hardly fair, considering the effort Jane put into composing his sermon. It's no matter: Jonathan has become the sole focus of Jane's attention.

"'Christ Jesus came into the world to save sinners,' of whom I am chief." Mr. Austen exhales loudly, having reached more familiar biblical territory. "So, I say, repent and, though you may be damned on earth, your soul may achieve salvation."

Jane sits forward on the edge of the pew. Her knuckles turn white as she grips the bench. Jonathan draws his shoulders up around his ears. Although there is no sound coming from his mouth, his lips are moving.

It's working. He's moments away from breaking down and making a confession. Jane places her hand on Henry's forearm. Henry covers her hand with his own, gripping it firmly. Together, they lean toward Jonathan.

Mr. Austen rolls his papers into a tight scroll. "That's enough . . ." He removes his spectacles and climbs down from the pulpit, glaring at his offspring. "I'm sure you comprehend the gist."

As he returns to the high altar, the tension evaporates. Mrs. Twistleton swallows, releasing her tight grip on her reticule and leaving the velvet crushed. Jonathan reclines in his seat and opens his eyes. His features slacken as he joins in with the monotonous chant of the Creed. Beside him, his mother remains comatose.

Jane slumps forward as Henry draws his hand away from his weapon. She spent hours carefully crafting three more pages of threats and inducements for the Harcourts to confess, but her father is unwilling to cooperate any further. All she can do is pray he's already said enough to prick the murderer's conscience.

Outside the church, Henry hunches his shoulders and leans against the carriage. "I told you it wouldn't work."

The snow is coming down heavier now, claiming every surface. The church's tiled roof, and the grass of the graveyard surrounding it, are quickly bleached white. Parishioners wrap their cloaks tightly around themselves and keep their goodbyes brief.

"No, you didn't." Jane grits her teeth. "You said it was the idea of a genius. And, furthermore, that if I was a man, I'd be head of intelligence for King George's forces in the Continental war." The snow muffles the sounds of the countryside. It is so quiet she is forced to hiss at Henry to prevent the parishioners overhearing their squabble. "And I have not finished with the Harcourts yet. You'll see, that was only the first part of my plan."

The quick procession of people leaving the church turns the snowy path to grey slush. Mr. Austen thumps through it, glaring at them both. "What on earth was that?"

"I wanted to help you with some new material," says Jane. "You must be getting tired of reading the same sermons over and over again?"

Mr. Austen opens and closes his mouth, like a freshly caught fish. "For God's sake, why didn't you tell me?"

Henry takes his father by the elbow and steers him toward the carriage. Mr. Austen shakes off his son's assistance and lunges inside.

Jane swallows as she climbs in after him. "I thought it would make a pleasant surprise."

"Have you taken leave of your senses?" Mr. Austen opens his satchel, retrieving the offensive pages and flinging them at her. "Would you change the bill of play once the actors are already on stage? Is your way of trying to 'help' stirring up a bloodthirsty mob? And what about Georgy? What will people say, hearing me advocate the death penalty when my own son is in prison, awaiting trial for grand larceny? They'll think I'm condemning him."

Jane screws the rejected sermon into a ball as the carriage moves off. "I'm sorry, Father. I didn't think . . ." How could she have been such a blockhead? Of course, anyone but the murderer would think her father was referring to Georgy.

They make slow progress along the frosted lane. The snow rests at the base of the carriage windows, reducing the view of the white fields and powdered trees. Mr. Austen lays his palm over Jane's hand and presses her icy fingers. "Dear child, if you truly want to try your hand at composing sermons, I'd be happy to deliver them for you. Just give me a little warning—and no fire and brimstone. You'll have me hauled up in front of the bishop."

Jane snatches away her hand, twisting her body toward the window. "Don't fret, Father. I promise I shan't be so foolish as to repeat the experiment."

The snow comes down like a thick woolen blanket. Jane stares out of the rapidly shrinking patch of clear glass. By the time they reach Steventon, banked-up snowflakes cover the window and she can hardly breathe for the sensation of being buried alive.

In trying to save Georgy, Jane has inadvertently made things worse—and may even have signed his death warrant. How will a jury find him innocent, if even his own family are known to condemn him? By attempting to use the fear of God to draw out the murderer, Jane has revealed how inadequate her own understanding is.

CHAPTER TWENTY-SIX

That night, Jane goes to bed in her stays and shift with her woolen stockings still on her feet. She wakes every couple of hours and peers out at the full moon, glinting high in the clear sky, like a newly minted Spanish coin. When the cockerel crows, she knows an hour or so remain before dawn. Thus far, she has failed to catch whoever is leaving flowers on Zoë Renard's grave, but she's never risen so early before. A stirring deep inside Jane tells her the mourner will not be deterred, even in this unforgiving climate. And neither will Jane. She pulls on a second pair of stockings and throws her warmest woolen frock over her head. It is a mourning gown. One of the tired garments she sacrificed to the dreaded black dye when Aunt Phila succumbed to the brutal torment of her final illness.

Jane creeps downstairs, fearful of waking Anna or her parents. The staircase and kitchen are in blackness, no fires burning and no candles lit. But it is so familiar that she can feel her way through the shadows by skimming her hand along the wall.

Moonlight spills through the gap between the curtains in the family parlour, where Henry sprawls on the sofa. He slept in his shirtsleeves, with a patchwork blanket thrown over him. His long legs, in their breeches and stockings, dangle over the arm of the dainty piece. Jane grasps his shoulder, giving it a gentle shake.

Henry rolls onto his side, throwing an arm over his face and drooling onto an embroidered cushion. "In a minute . . ."

Jane kneels, shaking his shoulder more vigorously. Something hard hits her knee. An empty port bottle rolls out from beneath the sofa. "You said you'd come," she hisses into his ear.

Henry pulls up the blanket around his ears and works his lips together. "I will, I will . . ." His breath reeks of strong spirits.

Jane tiptoes to the window and peers out at the moonlit garden. At least Henry fulfilled his promise to dig a path before he passed out drunk. The blizzard lasted all afternoon, laying a thick layer of white over Hampshire. More snow has fallen during the night, but only in light flurries.

In the vestibule, she buttons her cloak and pulls on her woolen mittens. She borrows her mother's pale shawl, wrapping the fine wool around her face, leaving only her eyes exposed. Tentatively, she rotates the key in the iron lock of the back door until the mechanism releases with a click.

She strikes out ankle-deep into the dense frosting covering the back doorstep. By now, it is first light. The sun has not yet risen, but an eerie glow reaches over the horizon. Apart from the tracks of a prowling fox, the only footsteps in the virgin snow are her own.

She shivers as she makes her way up the hill, but the chill does not set into the marrow of her bones until she reaches the churchyard and climbs into the great yew's embrace. Clumps of snow weigh down the tree's sprawling branches, but the earth beneath it is bare. Jane's blood cools. She forces herself to remain silent and still as she carries out her vigil. She pulls her cloak tight and tucks her hands beneath her arms.

Her fingers stiffen and her toes turn to icicles. She wishes she'd slipped on Henry's top boots, instead of her own inadequate ankle-length lace-ups. The hems of her cloak and gown are steeped in snow. Her teeth chatter. Her ears are so cold, they burn.

How ironic it would be for Jane to freeze to death while attempting to catch a killer. If she were to die, would Zoë Renard's murderer be morally responsible? Or could she be said to have died by her own hand for placing herself at the mercy of the elements? Would the bishop refuse her burial within the churchyard, even if the Lord saw fit to take her on consecrated ground?

No one will find her body until the snow thaws, when the carrion crows peck out her eyes. She is becoming delirious. What would Mary say? "Pull yourself together, Jane. You'll never get anywhere, lying dead in the snow."

Somewhere, in the darkness, a pair of tawny owls are courting. The female makes a short screech. After a few moments, the male answers with his more melodious *twit twoo*.

A horse whinnies. Poor Greylass in her stall. Did any of the farm labourers think to cover her with a rug before the frost set in? The pony's dappled white coat is thick, but even she will feel the bite of this bleak winter. Jane cups her mittened hands over her face and blows into the cavity, warming the tip of her nose with her breath.

The horse whinnies again. It is not Greylass: it is too loud and too close.

Jane peers through the gaps in the snow-coated branches. A shadow of a man treads wearily, emerging slowly from behind the flint church. The snowy blanket at his feet reflects the moonlight. He is tall and thin, wearing a dark overcoat with the collar turned up. He pulls a cocked hat low over his brow and rubs his hands together in their leather gloves, blowing out puffs of steam as he crunches through the snow.

The beating of Jane's heart booms in her ears.

The man passes Lord and Lady Portal in their icy beds and the single slab for the multiple generations of Boltons. He pushes on, wading through the calf-high drift in his top boots. Weeping angels and rows of upright crosses are silent and still as his shadow falls across them. He arrives at the far corner—where Zoë Renard lies buried in the frozen earth—and reaches inside his coat.

It really *is* Jonathan Harcourt.

Jane could tell him anywhere, by his lanky gait. Now she can see his profile clearly in the moonlight. Her imagination had not deceived her—he really was Madame Renard's lover and the father of her unborn child. His lips move, but she cannot make out what he is saying. He is too far away, and the snow dampens his words to a low murmur.

What reasonable motive can Jonathan have for skulking around a graveyard in the dead of night? If his association with Madame Renard was innocent, why hasn't he come forward? He *must* have killed her. And now Jane must creep even closer, if she's to bear witness to Jonathan's confession. She crouches, sneaking through the tree, careful not to disturb the powder settled on the branches. Once she is out of the yew's clutches, she moves stealthily across the churchyard, toward him.

There is no path here. Ice crystals crunch with her every step, and she sinks into the snow, which reaches up to her knees. She pulls her hood lower over her eyes and sticks to the shadows of the tombstones. If Jonathan is a murderer, Jane is placing herself in grave danger. She should go back and rouse Henry. But there is no time, and Georgy's life is at stake.

Jonathan crouches, murmuring to himself as he carefully places three reddish-brown orchids on the white mound. They are the only burst of colour in this black-and-white world. Jane is almost next to him. A few more steps, and she can hide behind Lady Portal's sarcophagus. She'll turn to her old friend for protection while she hears Jonathan's confession.

She lifts her foot, planting it gently. The sole of her boot hits ice. She slips, thrashing her arms and landing on her tailbone. The fluffy snow breaks her fall but clings to her skirts. She pushes herself upright.

Jonathan turns.

They are face to face. His eyes grow wide, milky white surrounding the black of his enlarged pupils. His mouth falls open, lower lip curling back, like that of a cartoon villain. He roars, lunging for Jane.

She screams.

Her piercing cry carries through the night, sending birds into panicked flight. Jane was wrong to think Jonathan incapable of deadly violence. He *did* murder Zoë Renard, and now he will kill Jane, too. Her heart hammers so hard in her chest that it hurts. As Jane stares into the face of death, she pictures her writing box at home on her dresser. Lady Susan is imprisoned within the drawer. Sheafs of blank paper cram the vault, and sloe ink fills the pot. If Jane dies here, her Catherine will never make it onto the page.

With trembling limbs, Jane plants her palms in the snow and pushes herself to her feet. She tries to flee, but she cannot move fast enough. She chokes, caught around the neck and dragged backward by her cloak. As she falls, strong arms encircle her waist.

Jane lifts her knee and sends a kick behind her. Her foot connects with Jonathan's shinbone. He yelps, releasing her for a fraction of a second. The world spins. His fingers encircle Jane's ankle with a vicelike grip. "Zoë, please, don't go. Forgive me . . ." Jane trips, landing hard on her knee. Jonathan lies on the ground behind her, both hands gripping her boot. "Zoë!"

Jane flaps her foot furiously.

The guilt of taking Madame Renard's life has driven Jonathan insane. He thinks Jane is a ghost come back from the grave to haunt him for his sins. Her lungs burn as she writhes for air. She cannot breathe. Her arms and legs are too heavy.

A flash of scarlet speeds past. It is Henry, thank God. He is here, at last, just as he said he would be. "Get off my sister!" he bellows, diving over Jane and landing on top of Jonathan.

Jane kicks her ankle, finding herself freed.

Henry and Jonathan tumble over and over in the snow, away from Jane, until they reach the Boltons. Henry pins Jonathan to the ground. Jonathan flings his arms across his face, blocking Henry's blows.

"Henry?" Mr. Austen staggers through the snow in his nightcap and russet banyan. "For the love of God, children. What is going on?"

"Father." Jane pushes herself up onto her knees.

Mr. Austen's mouth gapes as he turns to his daughter.

Henry sits astride Jonathan, fists poised. "I had to, Father. He had hold of Jane." Jonathan puts both hands over his face, groaning in agony at Henry's assault.

Mr. Austen's eyes grow round. "Jane. Are you and Jonathan Harcourt . . . ?"

"No!" Jane shrieks, flushing with indignation at the ridiculous suggestion. She has single-handedly apprehended a murderer—yet her father's first concern is to enquire after her virtue.

"I—I'm sorry." Jonathan curls up on his side on the snowy ground, sobs racking his frame. "I took her for Zoë's spirit."

Henry stands, legs wide, as he points down at his captive. "He's the killer, Father. He murdered that woman up at Deane House."

Jonathan struggles to sit. Snowy powder dusts his overcoat and clumps of ice dangle in his loose hair. "I didn't. I swear it. I would never have hurt her. I *loved* her."

Jane staggers toward her father, grabbing his elbow. "She was his mistress. They met in Brussels and she was having his baby. He had to get her out of the way so he could marry Sophy Rivers for her money."

Mr. Austen takes hold of his daughter with both hands. "What the devil are you talking about?" Swaying slightly, he turns to the others. "Jonathan, is this true?"

"No, it's not." Jonathan rubs his eyes with his fists. "She wasn't my mistress. She was my *wife*."

CHAPTER TWENTY-SEVEN

The frozen fields gleam gold under the dawn sun. In the hedgerow, a chorus of birds chirrups the start of a new day. Jane's father leans on her for support as they trudge through the garden. Behind them, Henry hoists Jonathan's arm around his neck as he half carries, half drags the bruised and weeping man to the rectory.

As they near the back door, Jane's mother peers through the glass, jiggling a sleepy Anna on her hip. She flings the door wide. "Will someone please explain to me what is happening?" Jane's pace slows at Mrs. Austen's fury.

"Henry and Jonathan were engaged in fisticuffs," says Mr. Austen, as he steps over the threshold into the cramped vestibule. "At their age. Would you believe it? I thought we were free of brawling schoolboys. At least until the new term begins. But apparently Jonathan laid hands on Jane."

Mrs. Austen looks at her daughter askance, spots of colour rising in her cheeks. "Jane, are you and Jonathan . . . ?"

"No!" Why must Jane's every move be interpreted through the lens of romance? There is so much more to her, to her potential, than matrimony. Jane stamps into the vestibule, treading snow across the rug. "He thought I was the ghost of Madame Renard come back to haunt him."

"Is it any wonder? Look at you." Mrs. Austen sweeps her gaze from Jane's lace-up boots to her pointed hood. Jane is an ominous, black-cloaked figure, her face completely covered. "If you crept up on me dressed like that, I dare say I'd die of fright. You look like the love child of an Irish banshee and an Egyptian mummy. What were you doing in the churchyard at this ungodly hour? You frightened us out of our wits when we heard you screaming."

Jane lowers her hood and unwinds the shawl, revealing her face. "I was doing what's needed to save Georgy—proving *he's* the real killer." She points to Jonathan.

"But I'm not. I've told you I'm not." Jonathan presses his cheek into Henry's shoulder. Henry stares down at him, clearly bemused as to how their epic fight has transformed into something closer to an embrace.

"Children, this has gone far enough." Mr. Austen rubs his temples.

Sally appears at the door to the parlour, already dressed in her linen smock and wooden clogs. She gawps at Jane, as she takes Mr. Austen's wet banyan and passes him the woolen patchwork blanket. Thank goodness Jane is guarding Sally's secret, or the news of her own misdemeanour would be carried the breadth of Basingstoke to Winchester on servants' lips before the day was out.

Mrs. Austen holds Anna tight to her chest. "Jonathan's not a killer. Look, you've upset the poor boy." Tear tracks mark Jonathan's pale skin and hiccups shake his rangy frame.

Henry dips his chin and looks up at his mother through his dark lashes in his best imitation of an injured puppy. "It was Jane's idea."

"Now who's the tittle-tattle?" Jane suppresses the urge to punch him as she hangs up her sodden cloak. Her mother shoves Anna into her arms. The baby grabs Jane's icy nose with her warm, sticky fingers.

Jonathan limps over the threshold. Mrs. Austen takes the sleeves of his damp overcoat, peeling it down his long arms. "Let's get these wet things off you at once. You're dripping all over the floor." She ushers everyone through to the family parlour, where a new fire is blazing. Sally stands beside it, jabbing the logs with a poker, but not tearing her eyes away from the unfolding drama.

Jane sticks to Jonathan's side, determined to get the truth out of him, despite his distress. "If you didn't kill Zoë Renard, why were you asking her spirit for forgiveness?"

Jonathan slumps into a chair, resting one elbow on the table and cupping his cheek in his palm. "Because she was my wife, and I failed her." His dark hair drips onto the collar of his shirt. "I *knew* you all thought I did it. That's why you gave that sermon, wasn't it? I told Mother, but she said I was being too sensitive—as usual."

Mr. Austen takes his usual place, his back to the fire. With the blanket thrown over his nightshirt, he looks like a medieval king. "Henry, get my port. I should say we could all do with a nip."

Henry grimaces. "Are you sure you wouldn't prefer brandy, Father?"

"Oh, not again." Mr. Austen slaps one hand on the table. There is no cloth covering it, and the sound bounces off the walls. "That was a full bottle."

Jane slides into the seat closest to Jonathan, settling Anna on her lap. The baby is warm, better than any bed-warming pan. Sally takes six cut-glass tumblers out of the sideboard and places them directly on the table. Mr. Austen raises an eyebrow. The maid frowns as she removes the sixth glass and puts it back into the sideboard. Henry produces a fresh bottle of brandy and dispenses a generous measure of the golden liquid into each of the five remaining tumblers.

Jonathan grips his glass between trembling hands and tips the contents swiftly down his throat. "It's true . . . we did meet in Brussels, as you said." He holds out his glass for another. "I loved it there. I wanted never to come back to this place. I was perfectly content, making my living as a portrait painter. And Zoë was so gifted. Her family, the Renards, make the finest lace in the city. They have done for generations."

"And you married?" Mr. Austen places his hand over Jonathan's forearm, to prevent him from shaking.

"Yes." Jonathan gulps. His pale blue eyes are red-rimmed and brimming with tears. "Then we heard the French were on their way, planning to invade. Zoë wanted to stay. It was her home. All her people are there." He takes another swig of brandy. "But I was afraid that, despite the way I was living, they'd somehow find out my rank and I'd be . . . well, you know."

Henry draws a finger across his throat. "Executed."

"Exactly. You must have read the reports. No one is safe from the Jacobins." Jonathan's right cheek and his lower lip grow redder by the second. His face is swelling from the impact of Henry's fists. "So, I persuaded Zoë to come back to England with me. I lost everything when I fled. It happened so quickly—one minute Brussels was my home, and the next I was fleeing for my life. I was forced to abandon my paintings, and my materials. I turned to Mother and Father for support but . . ." His voice cracks.

Mr. Austen rubs Jonathan's arm. "Go on, Jonathan. You know you're safe here. You've always been safe with us."

Jane sips her brandy slowly, remembering the desperate, wide-eyed boy Jonathan was when he first arrived at her father's school. He'd wake the entire household with his night terrors and "accidents," causing the other boys to tease him with the shameful nickname "piss-the-bed Johnny." For the first few months he lived at the rectory he was petrified of his own shadow and—most bizarrely for the Austen children—even more scared of their parents.

Jonathan leans his forehead against the heel of his palm. "They wouldn't accept Zoë as my wife. They said it was because she was a Catholic, but I know that had nothing to do with it. It was because she wasn't from 'the right sort of people.' Zoë's family are merchants, so they deemed her unfit to be their daughter-in-law. But none of that nonsense mattered to me. She was clever, and kind, and so talented." He clamps his eyes shut as a fat tear slides down his cheek.

In all of Jane's musing about the nature of Jonathan's relationship with Madame Renard, it never occurred to her that he might genuinely *love* her. As he screws up his features and fights for every breath, it is so very clear that he did.

Mrs. Austen stands behind Jonathan, resting her hands on his shoulders. "Oh, you poor child."

Jonathan wipes his nose on his sleeve. "They tried to tell me, as we'd married in a Roman Catholic ceremony, it wasn't valid here."

Mr. Austen frowns. "That's not true. A Catholic ceremony is perfectly valid in the eyes of the Anglican Church."

"I know." Jonathan nods eagerly. "And I would never have wished for it to be otherwise. I tried my best to stand my ground against my mother and father, but I was so desperate for their help. I'd escaped with nothing but the clothes on my back. Without my materials, I had no way to make a living. I had to start again. But they would advance me money only if I agreed to marry Miss Rivers. And . . . it's so difficult to explain, but they have a way of twisting things. They always have. It's why I went to the Continent in the first place, to get away from them."

Mrs. Austen hands Jonathan a clean handkerchief. Jane bites her thumbnail as she recalls the words he used at the ball. *I wish to God I'd never, ever, set foot back on these shores.* Not because he was guilty, but because his wife had been murdered and his heart was broken.

"I found Zoë somewhere to stay in Basingstoke while I moved back to Deane House, trying to bring them round. Eventually, my father admitted he couldn't help, even if he wanted to, because of all the debt he'd racked up at the card table. He said that by refusing to marry Miss Rivers, and securing her dowry, I was letting everyone down, that the estate would be bankrupted. All our tenants would lose their homes and starve. And still I'd have no way of looking after Zoë. We'd all be ruined because of my stubbornness. So, I gave in and said yes, just to gain a little time. We"—he chokes on a sob—"we were expecting a child. I needed money to pay for somewhere more suitable for Zoë to live, and for a physician. I don't think I'd have taken part in a wedding ceremony, knowing it to be a sham and stealing Miss Rivers's dowry, but at the time I couldn't see any other way."

Tears sting the back of Jane's eyes as she watches Jonathan convulse with sobs. He is so distraught, he no longer attempts to maintain any semblance of dignity. Henry, unable to bear it, stalks to the fireplace and turns his back to the scene. All this time, the siblings have been searching for signs of guilt, when it was grief the poor man was fighting to conceal.

"The night of the ball, I didn't know Zoë was there." Jonathan blows his nose into the handkerchief and wipes his cheeks. "I never told her my parents wanted me to take another wife, just that they needed some time to get used to the idea of me being married. The first I knew she'd been killed was when Henry discovered her body . . . And I still don't know what happened.

I was so distraught, I couldn't explain why. My father had never laid eyes on Zoë. He didn't understand why I was so upset. He accused me of being hysterical. He had the footmen force Mother's tincture down my throat, before dragging me to my chamber and locking me in . . .

"And when Georgy was found with her necklace, my mother tried to make me believe *he'd* killed her. But I knew that wasn't right, because the chain couldn't have gone missing until *after* they'd discovered Zoë's body. Otherwise they wouldn't have been able to retrieve my ring." He lifts his trembling hand.

"So, it *was* yours?" Jane leans forward to examine the signet ring on his little finger. "You gave it to Zoë, and she pawned it with her necklace?"

"She had to. It was the only way she could cover the rent for her room in Basingstoke. We'd brought her lacemaking materials with us. They were so much more portable than my canvases and boxes of pigments. But it took time for her to build up her stock and gain a reputation." Jonathan withdraws his hand, twisting the signet ring round and round. "It was her wedding band. It got in the way of the bobbins when she was making her lace, so she wore it on her chain. She must have been wearing it when she was killed . . ." He slumps forward, elbows resting on his knees as he makes a guttural cry into his palms. The sound reaches inside Jane, twisting her heart. "B-because *someone* retrieved it, and it was back on my finger when I woke in the morning."

Mrs. Austen kneels beside Jonathan, stroking his dark hair away from his face. "Oh, you poor boy. What have they done to you?"

Jane stands, passing a sleeping Anna to Sally. Her legs shake as she tiptoes to the back door before her mother and father, or Henry, can notice and object. While her family are distracted with grief-stricken Jonathan, Jane must finish what she started. Jonathan clearly did not murder the lacemaker. If Sir John was unaware of who she was, he had had no reason to kill her either. That leaves only one name left on her list of suspicious persons—Mrs. Twistleton—and, after what she's just heard, Jane is more determined than ever to confront her.

CHAPTER TWENTY-EIGHT

Jane deflates as she steps into the garden, ankle-deep once more in fresh snow. Another flurry had hit Hampshire while she was inside the rectory. She was so engrossed in Jonathan's story that she hadn't noticed. The drift has filled in the footsteps from earlier and covered Henry's hard-dug path. In the fields, the snow must be a foot deep. It was difficult enough, staggering up the hill to the church. She'll never make it on foot through the lanes to Deane House in this blizzard. Resigned to her fate, she ploughs through the garden, into the farmyard, and toward the stable block. If she's to save Georgy from the gallows, she must conquer every last one of her fears.

The tack room is unlocked. James is always chiding Mr. Austen to put a padlock on it, but Jane's father possesses far too much faith in human nature to harbour any genuine fear of thieves. She rifles through the numerous leather bridles. Jane has never ridden any of the horses currently residing in the Austens' stable block. The flighty mare she came off is long since consigned to the knackers' yard. She has no idea which bridle will fit Greylass. Except there is one, and only one, with a black-and-brown leather plait across the browband. Only Cassandra could have selected something so saccharine for her pony to wear.

The sidesaddle is easy to identify, designed for a lady. It lies on the floor where Jane dropped it. She drapes the bridle around her neck and hauls up the heavy saddle with both hands. Greylass lifts her head and points her ears forward in greeting. "I'm sorry, my girl. I never did bring you that carrot, did I? But if you help me catch this devil I'll bring you a whole bunch."

As she enters the stall, her stomach hardens at the prospect of being flattened between the mare's dappled rump and the brick wall. Greylass prances across the straw to make space for her visitor. The steel bit is cool in Jane's hand as she presses it to the pony's mouth. Her fingers tremble at the prospect of Greylass's enormous square teeth, but the pony curls her black lips and accepts it immediately. "There. We did it." Jane loops the bridle over the animal's head and fastens it, then heaves the saddle onto the pony's broad back. She prays that she's remembered Frank's instructions for tacking up correctly. She cannot fail, and she must not fall. Greylass whinnies, blowing steam through her nose and kicking the snow with her front hoofs as Jane leads her out into the yard.

"Yes, it's deep, isn't it?" Jane pats the pony's cheek, guiding her toward the mounting block with the reins. "Otherwise, you'd still be nice and snug in your stall, and I wouldn't have to risk breaking my neck. But needs must."

Jane wraps her skirts over her arm and, placing two hands on the saddle, she lifts one foot into the stirrup, closes her eyes and wills herself into the air. "Please, please, please . . ." She laughs with delight as she realises she is standing upright in the stirrup. Jane sits heavily, wriggling in the saddle to find her seat after all these years. She didn't take a crop, but Cassandra's faithful steed doesn't need one. Greylass walks on as soon as Jane is steady. It's as if the pony can sense her purpose.

For the first few steps, Jane is rigid and her stomach lurches. Then, a burst of energy explodes through her body, her muscles relax and her heart expands with the freedom. She is off—dashing through the farmyard at a trot.

The wind kisses Jane's cheek and her skirts fly out behind her. With the snow banked up, the ground is not so very far away. Henry rushes out of the back door of the rectory. "Jane, wait!" He breaks into a run after her, waving both arms above his head.

But Jane is in perfect control of her body as she bounds into the lane. She clutches the reins to her chest and sits back in the saddle. Greylass speeds into a canter. It's as if Jane is flying, as she dashes through the barren whiteness in hot pursuit of Zoë *Harcourt's* killer.

By the time Jane passes through the gates of Deane House, she is more alive than she has ever been. Her cheeks blaze and her heart pounds in her chest. A groom rubs sleep from his eyes as he sweeps the drive. "Here." Jane slides down from the pony, tossing the reins to him. "Go to the Lloyds in Deane, quick as you can. Tell the magistrate that Miss Austen has his murderer, and she's about to get a confession. There's a sixpence in it for you. Now, make haste."

"Right you are, miss." The boy leaps onto Greylass's back and gallops away. Jane fixes her eyes on the shrubbery below the oriel window, where Georgy must have found Zoë's necklace. Consumed with righteous fury, she pounds the solid oak door of the grand Tudor mansion with both fists and calls at the top of her lungs to be let in. After what seems like hours, a crack opens.

The butler pokes his nightcapped head out into the frosty air. Jane jams her foot inside and slides past him.

Mrs. Twistleton stands in the dimly lit, oak-paneled entrance hall in a frilly dressing gown. "Miss Austen?" She takes a step backward, as she lifts a taper burning in a brass chamber toward her wan cheek.

Jane strides across the Turkey rug until they are face to face. "Did you know who she was? Did you meet her in Basingstoke, at the Angel Inn?" Mrs. Twistleton's dark brows shoot upward as she clutches her lapel. "Madame Renard was Mrs. Harcourt, Jonathan's *wife*. Not his mistress, his wife. She must have come here looking for him. And, somehow, she ended up dead and locked in that closet."

"Miss Austen, are you quite well? You're making no sense." Mrs. Twistleton appeals to the butler with her eyes, but he makes no move to intercede.

Jane clenches her jaw. This is her last chance to save Georgy. She will drive out the truth, or it will all have been for nothing. Her brother, the most innocent of men, will die for another's sins. "You must tell the truth. It's the only way to salvation. Hide it, and the sin will forever stain your immortal soul."

Mrs. Twistleton's voice is shrill. "What sins? *I* am not guilty of any."

Beside her, the butler rolls his eyes.

Jane draws a sharp breath. "Other than the adultery, there's falsely accusing others. There haven't been any trespassers lurking in Deane woods, Mrs. Twistleton, and you know it. You're extremely fortunate the search party didn't pick up any vagabonds the day after the murder, or yet another hapless victim might have lost their life through no fault of their own. How many innocents will you watch go to their death to protect your place in this family, Deborah?"

"No!" Mrs. Twistleton clutches her throat.

Jane steps closer, until she can taste the woman's breath. If she's not mistaken, there's the slightest hint of gin on it. "I know who the murderer is, Mrs. Twistleton. And, what's more, I know you do, too. You've already lost Sir John. There's no point in hiding it any longer."

"No, Miss Austen . . . I don't know what you're talking about."

"Don't you?" Jane points toward the closet. "Then open that door."

"I can't." The housekeeper's lips tremble as she stumbles backward.

Fists pound against the front door. The butler jerks it open and an icy blast rushes into the entrance hall. The chill wind douses the flame of Mrs. Twistleton's taper, plunging the hallway into darkness. Henry stands in the open doorway in his full military uniform, silhouetted against the dazzling morning light.

Has her mother sent him to bring her home? Jane darts out of his reach, resting her hands flat against the door of the dreaded linen closet.

Henry charges inside. "Jane?"

Mr. Craven is behind him, his bulky frame blocking the light. "Miss Austen. What are you doing here, again?"

The brass chandelier rattles as Lady Harcourt storms down the ornate wooden staircase, wrapped in a plum-coloured banyan with a matching turban covering her hair. "What is happening down here? I am trying to sleep."

All of Jane's muscles seize, as she readies herself to fight from being dragged out of this place. They will not silence her. She'll kick and scream until she's made her point, if she has to. Her love for Georgy will outweigh any obligation to propriety. "The door to the laundry closet was locked when Henry and Mrs. Chute found the corpse. Did you know that, Mr. Craven?"

"I remember signs of forced entry, yes. It looked as though someone had jammed the lock, inexpertly, with a sharp instrument."

Henry grimaces, looking shamefaced. "Ah, yes. I'm afraid that was me."

Mr. Craven nods, as if to say he expected as much. It's just another secret between gentlemen. How convenient that they can always rely on one another for their discretion.

"So, Mrs. Twistleton. I demand you either open this door, at once, or tell us what really happened that day." Jane's words rush out in a strangled cry as she slaps the palms of her hands against the solid wood.

"I can't." Mrs. Twistleton clamps her hand across her mouth.

"Miss Austen, really," says Mr. Craven. "I've warned you about harassing the Harcourt family before now."

Lady Harcourt halts on the landing, next to the bust of Edwin. "Get her out of my house." Without her usual cosmetics, her face is ashen. She is a reflection of her son's death mask with no warmth in her slack features.

"Fear not, Lady Harcourt, I shall resolve this," Mr. Craven assures her. "Now, Miss Austen, come with me. I must have a serious talk with your father."

Henry holds out an arm, blocking Mr. Craven's path. He inhales deeply, puffing out his broad chest. His eyes are alight with amber streaks. "Mr. Craven, as an officer in His Majesty's Militia, keeping the peace is my jurisdiction."

Mr. Craven nods. "Yes, indeed, sir."

Henry turns, meeting Jane's gaze.

She stares across the entrance hall at her brother, beseeching him not to dismiss her. Silently, she tells him, *Believe in me, Henry. You know I'm right.*

Henry pushes back his shoulders and places his hand on the hilt of his sabre. Wrapping his fingers around the handle, he draws the silver sword from its sheath. Jane trembles as he points the curved blade directly at where she is standing, before the entrance to the linen closet. When he speaks, his voice is clear and deep. "Mrs. Twistleton, ma'am, we're here on the King's business. As such, I command you to do what my sister says and open that door at once."

"Henry!" Jane gasps, her heart flooding with warmth.

As always, Henry is on her side. He might drive her to distraction, but her brother stands with her against the world.

The housekeeper holds on to the sideboard to support herself. "No, Lieutenant Austen. You misunderstand me, sir. It's not that I won't. I *can't.*" She closes her eyes, steeling herself. "I've never been granted my own set of keys."

"I knew it." Jane spins to face Lady Harcourt. "It was you! You killed Zoë. You're the only one who could have done it. She wasn't wearing her necklace when Henry found her, because you tore it from her to get to Jonathan's ring. You were so furious that your son had dared marry without your permission that you murdered your own daughter-in-law."

Lady Harcourt rears backward. "Jonathan had no right to give away that ring. It shouldn't even have been his. We had it made for Edwin."

"But her necklace meant nothing to you so you flung it out of your bedroom window into the shrubbery, where my brother—my sweet, harmless, innocent brother—found it. And you would let him hang for your crime." Jane had not even thought to include Lady Harcourt in her initial list of suspects. But she had as much to lose as Jonathan and his father, and *she* is the only member of the Harcourt family Jane has witnessed lash out in the heat of the moment. And, as Hannah revealed, she alone keeps the keys to Deane House.

"Get out of my house! You're just like her. How dare you pollute my home with your foul presence? You, a nothing, a no one, yet you would take everything from me. You are not fit to breathe the same air as I do. I come from a noble family, a line descended from the bluest blood." Lady Harcourt leans toward the statue, wrapping both arms around the bust, so that its cold stone face is pressed against her bosom. "Is it not enough that my Edwin was taken from me, his lineage too pure for this world? And that my fool of a husband gambled and whored away my fortune?

"And then *she*, that filthy, foreign papist whore, she would take Jonathan, the pathetic weakling, and turn him into nothing more than . . . a . . . a . . ." The word sticks in her throat. "A *tradesman*." She quivers with rage. "I will not have it. Do you hear me? I am wife to a baronet, mother to his heir, and mistress of Deane House, or I am nothing."

Jane's ears ring with the enormity of Lady Harcourt's words. It's an admission that she killed Zoë.

Henry advances toward the foot of the staircase with his sabre drawn. "Ma'am, I'm afraid you must come with me."

Mr. Craven follows, half a step behind. Lady Harcourt wraps her arms around the statue, drawing her shoulders to her ears and lowering her lips to the smooth stone to kiss Edwin's carved curls. Her shoulders heave as she shoves the bust from its plinth with both hands. It topples, careering down the stairs toward Henry and Mr. Craven. Marble Edwin strikes the wooden steps. His nose chips off as he crashes down, bouncing hard on each rung. Henry leaps out of the way, but Mr. Craven is too close behind him. For a split second, both men are suspended in midair.

The train of Lady Harcourt's banyan swishes from the landing, disappearing out of sight as she flees.

Henry and Mr. Craven barrel into each other, tumbling to the floor in one enormous tangle of arms and legs. Henry's silver sabre clatters onto the hardwood. The bust rolls, like a bowling ball, slowing to a halt at the feet of a distraught Mrs. Twistleton.

Jane lifts her skirts, springing over the men to reach the murderess. She bounds up the steps, two at a time. The soles of her walking boots slap against the wooden slats until she arrives at the first floor.

Breathless, she halts.

A multitude of doors lead off the long corridor. Where did Lady Harcourt go? Jane sprints toward the far end, in what she calculates is the direction of the oriel window overlooking the shrubbery. The furthest door is ajar. An empty suit of armour, holding a battle-axe, stands guard.

Jane kicks it open.

Lady Harcourt stands in profile before a coroneted bed, clasping a glass bottle. She sneers at Jane, tips her head back and empties the contents down her throat.

Jane screams, stretching out her hand and grasping the air before her. "No!"

Lady Harcourt presses her thin lips together with grim fortitude. Jane rushes to her side, knocking the bottle out of her hand and sending it smashing against the wall. But it is too late. Lady Harcourt gags, drawing her hand to her throat. She continues to choke, gasping for air as her complexion turns puce.

Jane is so close. But without a signed confession it could all be for nothing. Heavy footsteps come chasing after her. Henry and Mr. Craven crash into the room, followed by Mrs. Twistleton and the butler. They stand at the doorway, staring with open mouths and features contorted in horror. Lady Harcourt drops to the floor, spluttering and writhing on the carpet as flecks of vomit fly from her mouth.

In desperation, Jane sinks to her knees and wraps her arm around Lady Harcourt. She smacks her hard on the back—but she cannot prevent her from choking on her own vomit.

"Jane, stop." Henry crouches before her. "Let her go."

Reluctantly, Jane releases the woman. As she lays her to rest on her side, she places one arm in front to cushion her face. Lady Harcourt's skin bleaches of all colour, her eyes turn vacant and the tips of her fingers are tinged with blue.

After a long while, Mrs. Twistleton creeps forward, one hand clutching her breast. She kneels over her mistress, placing her ear to Lady Harcourt's chest for several moments. Finally, she lifts her head. "Dear Lord in Heaven, have mercy . . . I can't hear her breathing." She places two fingers to Lady Harcourt's throat, pressing hard into her neck. "No pulse either."

Jane grips onto Henry's forearm, staring wide-eyed at Mr. Craven. "But you heard her. You heard her confess. Please tell me you heard her confess?"

Mr. Craven gets down on one knee before Jane. His great bushy eyebrows draw together. "I heard her, Miss Austen. I heard her, and I heard you."

Jane collapses into Henry's arms, sobbing as her brother cradles her. Her body goes limp as she fills her lungs fully for the first time since Georgy was arrested.

CHAPTER TWENTY-NINE

Zoë, 11 December 1795

The stagecoach rolls to a halt outside Deane Gate Inn and Zoë scrambles down from the roof, gathering her chintz skirts to protect her modesty. The catcalls of the working men outside the public house are just the latest of the indignities she has endured since she arrived in this hateful country. A swing door opens, and a serving girl steps out with a wide tray of freshly baked pies between her hands. Zoë asks her for directions to Deane House, and the girl tips her head toward the lane. At the sight of the ornate tiled roof in the distance, Zoë's heart races.

It is the quickening inside her womb that spurs Zoë on. She must confront the Harcourts for the sake of her unborn child. She does not regret marrying her "English lord," as her family call him, but she deeply bemoans leaving her beloved homeland. She has tried to be patient and give Jonathan's mother and father time to accept their marriage. Her own family objected to the match, too, at first. As a successful merchant, Zoë's father had had in mind a far more lucrative union with a fellow bourgeois for his youngest daughter. Even Zoë, with her romantic disposition, never expected she'd be foolish enough to marry for love. She joined the classes at the Royal Academy to improve her sketching, not to catch a husband. Most of the men ignored the new cohort of female students.

When the strange young Englishman kept staring at her, Zoë assumed he shared their arrogant disapproval. Yes, he was handsome, with his lofty frame and his raven's-wing hair, but it was his indisputable talent for capturing the likeness of the sitters that caught Zoë's eye. Then, one day, he leaned across her easel and whispered, "Tell me, please, mademoiselle. How is it, when you're using the same earthly combination of charcoal sticks and white paper as the rest of us, you're able to create such a sublime contrast of light and shade?" And with that, Zoë's heart was lost to Jonathan forever.

After Zoë finally agreed to take him home to meet the Renards, she was amazed to watch him charm them with his quiet, respectful manner. Slowly, her father came around to the idea of their marrying. Her Jonathan might have been born into the English aristocracy, but he was no shirker. During his time at the academy, he stayed on in the studio after lessons to complete pieces for sale, and spent evenings dashing off caricatures in the marketplace. Zoë's father introduced Jonathan to his merchant friends, and the commissions flooded in.

Their future seemed so bright until the moment they received the terrifying news—the French Revolutionary Army was about to march on the city. Jonathan wanted to flee immediately. Zoë's family were nonplussed, but the newspaper reports of the show trials and massacres in Paris told a different story. If the Queen of France was not safe from Madame Guillotine, how could Zoë assure her noble husband that he would be?

Jonathan warned her they'd have to start again, that his parents would not welcome the news that he'd married without their approval. He said his mother was a harridan, his father a coward and a bully—but everyone knows the English are a peculiar race. They have no concept of family and could not profess any feelings for each other. It constantly amazes Zoë how Jonathan, so cold and reserved in public, makes love to her with such wild passion behind closed doors.

With her wedding vows fresh from her lips, Zoë could not forsake the promises she'd made. She'd never willingly separate from her husband, no matter how long it took for his people to accept her.

But Zoë is weary of playing the obedient wife. She has spent three months living as a widow, bearing the humiliation of pawning her jewels, and selling her creations to pay for her bed and board. Now one of her customers, the young lady with the unfortunate smallpox scars, tells her there is to be a grand ball to celebrate the betrothal of the heir of Deane House to a beautiful, wealthy heiress. After everything Zoë has sacrificed to be with Jonathan . . .

She knows her husband is the heir to Deane House, and he cannot possibly betroth himself to another because he is married to Zoë, in the sight of God and by the laws of man. So, she has come here to confront her new family. How dare they treat Zoë as if she were Jonathan's mistress? *Those whom God hath joined together let no man put asunder.*

The black-and-white Tudor manor rises in the distance, but its grandeur does not intimidate Zoë. Jonathan's parents are so deeply in debt, they're at risk of losing the roof over their heads. Pragmatic Jonathan has been trying to persuade them to let the house and move into a cottage on the estate to meet their repayments, but they are too proud and too ignorant to listen. Such is the way with aristocrats: they have no respect for a balanced ledger. That is why their days are numbered, even if they are too stupid to count them for themselves.

Through the gates of Deane House, tradesmen fill the swept gravel drive. A wine merchant unloads crates of Madeira from his wagon. Liveried servants carry chairs and tables to and fro. It is true, then. Zoë's parents-in-law are preparing a ball to celebrate the betrothal of her husband, the father of the child in her belly, to another woman. A rich heiress they would swindle out of her fortune. Zoë grinds her teeth as she traipses toward a middle-aged woman dressed in black silk. "*Excusez-moi, madame.*"

"There you are." The woman's cheeks are red. She's flustered by the effort of directing the various activities. "Her ladyship has been asking all morning whether you've arrived." She ushers Zoë into an oak-paneled entrance hall. "Be careful, mind. She's in a foul mood. Her medicine is finished. She's taking more and more these days. We can't keep up. I've sent a maid into town to fetch more, but she's not back yet. So, don't upset her, whatever you do."

Zoë doesn't know who the woman thinks she is, or what medicine she speaks of. If it means she can get inside the house and confront her new family, she will go along with the ruse.

If Jonathan's mother is ill, he has never told her. Perhaps that is why he is adamant he will not introduce them. As much as Jonathan resents his mother's cruelty toward him as a child, he is too gentle to want to upset an elderly woman on her deathbed. Or maybe he is hoping his mother will die, and he will have only his more rational father to deal with. Surely Jonathan cannot have betrayed Zoë. Not her Jonathan. It will be his parents' doing, she is certain.

As she waits alone in the entrance hall, Zoë examines the portraits lining the walls. It is clear her husband did not inherit his attractive countenance from his ancestors, and he is a finer artist than any of them could afford. And there is the marble bust of his dead brother, Edwin—a grotesque creation cast from

Edwin's death mask. And the English have the gall to accuse Catholics of worshipping false idols.

A beady-eyed dame in a plum-coloured dressing-gown thumps down the stairs. "What is it?" She pinches her shrewish features. "You're not my usual hairdresser. They told me she was here. Where is she? It's getting late."

"Good day to you, Lady Harcourt." Zoë lifts her chin. She reaches into her bodice and pulls out Jonathan's signet ring, resting on her late grandmother's gold and pearl chain. "I think you know exactly who I am, and why I am here."

The stairs groan and the brass chandelier shakes as Lady Harcourt thunders down the rest of the stairs. "How dare you!"

Jonathan had warned Zoë to keep away, promising he would deal with his family. She knows his mother has a temper, that Jonathan is afraid of her. But there are plenty of strong women in the Renard family, Zoë among them. If she and Lady Harcourt can sit down and talk together, she is sure she can make her mother-in-law see how futile her behaviour is. "I've come to put a stop to this nonsense. Whether or not you approve, Jonathan and I—"

Glass bottles clink as the wine merchant struggles to manoeuvre his handcart over the threshold. Lady Harcourt grabs Zoë's arm, digging her clawed fingers into Zoë's soft flesh. "Quiet. Anyone could overhear you."

As Zoë is dragged across the hallway, stumbling over the edges of the Turkey rug, she squirms under Lady Harcourt's vice-like grip. "What if they do? I have nothing to hide. It is you who have reason to be ashamed. Jonathan is your son, your blood. You should be supporting him, helping him to build his studio and his reputation as an artist here in England."

Lady Harcourt whips a chain from her pocket. She jabs a key into the oak paneling, fiddling with one hand until a door opens, revealing a small room. "My son is a *gentleman*. I will not see him touting for business, like some vulgar tradesman."

The space is dark and cramped, but Zoë lets her mother-in-law pull her inside. She will not leave until she has given Lady Harcourt a piece of her mind. Jonathan and his father are wrong in pandering to her. There is only one way to deal with bullies, and that is to stand up to them. "Your son is an artist, a very gifted one. There is no shame in it. The world is changing, Lady Harcourt. Your title and your coat of arms will not protect you from that truth. It's hard work and talent that matters now, not birth or family name alone. Jonathan understands that, and he chose a wife who shares his values."

"You are not his wife." Lady Harcourt purses her mouth. Flecks of spittle gather at the corners of her creased lips. "You are no one, nothing. A miserable foreign wench with no name and no fortune, and I will *never* accept you into this family."

The insults glance off Zoë. This woman is ludicrous. How dare she speak so of the mighty Renards? Zoë draws herself up to her full height. Still, she only reaches Lady Harcourt's earlobe. Zoë might be petite, but she knows God is on her side. "It is not up to you. We are married according to the Holy Roman Catholic Church. It is impossible for you to divide us."

Lady Harcourt wags a gnarled finger inches from Zoë's face. "Now listen to me, you scheming papist whore . . ."

In the dim light, Zoë's eyes adjust. She's not in a small sitting room, as she presumed. Baskets of dirty linen lurk in corners, and a battalion of gleaming copper pans lines the walls. Even now, Zoë's mother-in-law will not give her the respect she deserves and hear her out with dignity. Instead, she takes her into a closet and insults her, as if Zoë were one of her servants.

Heat flashes through Zoë's body. "No. It is time you listened to me." She bats Lady Harcourt's hand away from her face. "If you force your son to go through with this travesty of a marriage, you will make him a bigamist, and any grandchildren he gives you with his new bride will be bastards."

A flash of copper . . . and Zoë staggers backward. A wave of pain splits her skull as stars dance in blackness. Her hands fly to her belly, protecting her beloved child. Her ankle hits something hard, and she struggles to regain her balance. Zoë grabs at the handle of the linen press but misses it by a hair's breadth.

The back of her head smacks against the wooden floor.

Above her, Lady Harcourt curls her top lip into an ugly sneer and wields a bed-warming pan over her with both hands.

Jonathan is right. His mother is a monster.

Too late, Zoë realises she has made a terrible mistake in confronting Lady Harcourt alone. A terrible, terrible mistake.

Where is Jonathan? He will find her. He must find her . . .

CHAPTER THIRTY

12 February 1796

"There you are, Georgy." Jane stands in the garden of Dame Culham's cottage. The weather is uncharacteristically mild for the time of year; soft sunlight warms her face and brightens the rolling hills in the distance. A flock of unruly bronze hens peck at the toes of her walking boots and around her feet, turning over the vegetable beds ready for spring. Jane folds her left arm diagonally across her chest and taps her elbow twice with her right hand. "Enjoy your biscuits."

Georgy grins, holding the package of shortbread from Mrs. Plumptre's bakery to his chest. His chestnut hair has grown so long that Dame Culham has tied it back into a queue with a length of twine. His clothes are still far too loose, but he's regained his appetite and his complexion is warm from walking across the Hampshire countryside with Jack. He's wearing a crisp new shirt, hastily stitched together by Cassandra, with one of Henry's linen waistcoats and a pair of smart black breeches. He looks so much like James it's uncanny.

Jack makes a grab for the brown-paper parcel. Georgy frowns, holding Jack back with one hand while lifting the biscuits out of the smaller man's reach.

Jack chuckles and his brown eyes burn bright in the sunshine. "Georgy, you must share." Jack, too, is looking more like his usual self. He's rolled his sleeves up to the elbow, revealing the sinewy muscles of his forearms, and tied a printed calico handkerchief at the open neck of his linen shirt—almost, but not quite, covering the springy dark curls of his hard chest. He turns to Jane and winks. He really does possess the most open and friendly countenance of any man Jane has ever known. She hopes Sally knows how lucky she is.

Sadly, Jack is no closer to his dream of owning a sow, and the pigsty remains half-built and empty. However, Mr. Austen has turned over a couple of his fields, which are too muddy for his sheep to graze, to Jack to farm. The land has been left to itself for years, so it should be fertile, and a stream cuts straight through it, giving constant access to freshwater. Mrs. Austen suggested growing strawberries, as they are quick to multiply and require little maintenance, but Jack has a strange notion that watercress will prove popular, and he is determined to try his hand at that.

Cassandra takes Georgy's arm, reaching for a biscuit. She passes it to Jack, glaring at Georgy with mock severity. "Yes, you must share, Georgy. We bought them for all of you."

Jane laughs. Judging by Georgy's dour expression, he's far from happy, but his defiance is no match for Cassandra's sweetness. "You'd better get in quick if you want some, Nan?"

"I'll leave 'em to my boys." Dame Culham leans against the open doorway to her kitchen, half smiling as she crosses her arms over her bosom. "We have so much food. Every one of the neighbours has brought something. Even Mrs. Fletcher. I keep telling her we have more than enough, but she won't stop sending fresh pies up from the inn every day. Between you and me, I don't think she's too happy with her husband for putting our Georgy through such an ordeal. I sincerely doubt he'll be volunteering for the role of parish constable next year, not if she has anything to do with it."

Jane smiles, with satisfaction. After she had exposed Lady Harcourt as the murderer, everyone involved in her brother's incarceration was most apologetic. Mr. Craven arranged for the charges against Georgy to be dropped immediately, as it was clear Zoë Harcourt's chain had been discarded rather than stolen.

Since then, Jane and her family have been recovering from their anguish by throwing themselves back into their usual routines. Henry has returned to his regiment and his studies. He sent Jane an amusing letter, saying he'd met and was determined to court an exceptionally suitable, and very nice, young lady. Another Mary, as if one wasn't enough. Henry says he is planning to woo her with his account of single-handedly foiling a murderer. He really is a rascal. James has not yet proposed to Mary Lloyd, but all of the Austens know it won't be long. Jane returned for the green muslin and is embroidering a shawl for Mary as an engagement present, even though it will most certainly make her resemble a blade of grass.

Jane and Cassandra wave goodbye to Georgy and stroll through Steventon village. They nod and smile as they pass women pegging out washing and children playing barefoot outside the thatched cottages. So far, Cassandra has been too distracted by the drama at Deane House, and Georgy's welfare, to make any enquiries as to how Jane is coping with the loss of her Irish friend. But Jane knows she will not be able to avoid the topic forever and is steeling herself to laugh off her heartache when it eventually arises. She is so glad to have her sister home. For a short while, at least. Just until Mr. Fowle returns from making his fortune in the West Indies.

Cassandra wraps one of her golden ringlets around her finger and loops her free arm through Jane's. "Tell me again what Mr. Craven said, after Lady Harcourt confessed to the murder."

Under their open capes, Jane and Cassandra are wearing their matching cornflower gowns. While her sister has been away, Jane has taken so little care of Cassandra's gown that they are almost the same shade of washed-out blue.

"I've told you a hundred times. You must know the story better than I do by now."

Cassandra tugs on Jane's elbow. "But it must have been so satisfying."

"Yes, it was rather." Jane stands taller, pushing back her shoulders. "But not nearly as satisfying as riding to Winchester to fetch Georgy home from gaol."

Cassandra squeezes Jane's arm, grinning. "I'm so proud of you. Will you come out riding with me again now?"

"Absolutely not." Jane scowls. "Unless there's another murderer on the loose."

"I'm so sorry I left you to manage everything all by yourself."

Jane lifts her chin, letting the warming rays relax the tight muscles of her face. "It was hardly your fault. We left you high and dry, stranded in Kintbury."

Cassandra squeezes Jane's arm tighter. "I never stopped fretting about you, all the time I was away. From the tone of your letters, I feared you were losing your wits without me."

Jane shoots her sister what she hopes is a withering glance. "Well, if you're no longer to be an Austen, I'm afraid you must forfeit your part in our amateur theatricals."

"I'll always be an Austen at heart, Jane. When did they realize Lady Harcourt was still alive?"

"When the carpenter came in to measure her for her coffin." Jane's eyes are wide with ghoulish delight. "Apparently, he'd just got his tape measure out when she sat up and gave him an awful fright."

"The poor man. It's a wonder it hasn't put him off his profession entirely."

"No one could have predicted it. Mrs. Twistleton and the butler swore she had no pulse, and Mr. Martin said she'd taken enough laudanum to kill a horse." Jane tuts. "Apparently, she's used it for years—ever since her sons were born. Sir John encouraged it to control her rages. But her consumption has doubled, sometimes even trebled, every month since Edwin died. Mr. Martin also said that such an addiction could make one prone to violent outbursts. He's been warning the family that she needed to wean herself off it, but Sir John didn't want to hear it, as the drug kept her compliant."

"She didn't recover completely, though. Not if Jonathan was able to have her committed to Bedlam."

"No. The Crown physician said taking such an enormous quantity of the opiate had done such damage to her rational mind that she was in no fit state to stand trial. Instead, he advised she be confined to an institution for the insane for the rest of her life."

"Would you rather she went to the gallows?" Cassandra arches an eyebrow. They've reached St. Nicholas's Church. The sharp edges of its flint walls glint in the sunlight.

Jane takes a deep breath. "It is not for me to judge. But I would rather she had not killed Zoë."

Cassandra pulls Jane to a halt, as she gazes across to the other side of the churchyard, where Jonathan stands over his wife's grave. "I expect you're not the only one."

"I should speak to him. He comes every day, you know. He really did love her."

"It must have been terrible to lose her when they were only just starting out on their life together. At least he can grieve her properly now, as her husband." Cassandra tilts her head, her hazel eyes misty.

"Before I forget, you owe Greylass a bunch of carrots."

Cassandra frowns. "Do I?"

"I promised her you'd take her some. You will remember, won't you?"

"Of course. I'll go and see what Mother can spare." Cassandra skips through the rusty iron gate. Jane's sister really is the sweetest, kindest, most gullible of creatures. Jane will be bereft when she's all the way up in Berkshire. She'll go and visit, but it won't be the same. Cassandra will have a husband and very soon, no doubt, children of her own. Jane will no longer lay claim to the central place in her affections. She dreads the day when, instead of celebrating Jane's ridiculousness and lamenting her disappointments as if they were her own, Cassandra's eyes glaze over at the details of her many insignificant trifles.

Jonathan lifts his head and gives a weak smile as Jane approaches. The bruises from the altercation with Henry have faded, but his complexion is as pale as ever. Before him, the mound is almost level, and the grass is creeping over the wound in the earth where his wife lies buried. In another few months, the ground will be compact enough to support a headstone. For now, he continues to mark the burial site with fresh flowers cut from the glasshouse at Deane House every day.

"Those are pretty." Jane stares down at today's offering: three chartreuse orchid blooms on a single stem. She's never needed to ask why he always brings three. She knows there is one for Zoë, one for their unborn child and one for the man Jonathan might have been.

He nods, staring at the ground. "I haven't thanked you yet, Jane. I really should."

"Thank me?" Jane echoes, in astonishment.

"Yes. You freed me." His chest heaves. "Despite trying my utmost, I never quite managed to escape my mother and father. But you found a way to rescue me, and I want you to know how truly grateful I am."

Jane fights the urge to turn away. Jonathan's grief draws the breath from her lungs every time she looks at him. "What will you do?"

"I've been granted power of attorney, so I've appointed a broker to sell off any assets we have left. I'll let the house, if anyone will take it. And then I suppose I'll do my best to keep the estate afloat, protect our tenants and pay back as much as I can of my father's debts." He meets Jane's eye, lips curling into a wry smile. "Perhaps not quite enough to bring him home, though."

"I heard Mrs. Twistleton has gone to London to be with him."

"Yes. They've set up home together and are living as man and wife, inside the Marshalsea. You can do that in debtors' prison."

"How quaint." The complexities of other people's romantic relationships will never cease to fascinate Jane. "And is she . . ."

"Sober as a judge." Jonathan catches her meaning. "She keeps trying to persuade Father to practise abstinence, too, but I can't see her succeeding with that. Still, with her there to keep him in check, perhaps he won't get into too much trouble."

Jane can just imagine Mrs. Twistleton triumphantly wandering the streets of London, with the key to Sir John's cell tied to a ribbon and nestled at her bosom. "I wish them well."

"As for me, I've moved into one of the estate cottages so I can continue to be near Zoë's grave. Do you know, she reminded me a little of you when we first met."

"Me?" Jane puts a hand to her throat. From Jonathan, she knows it's the greatest compliment he could ever pay her.

"Yes. We came to know each other while we were both studying at the Royal Academy. Zoë was a very talented artist, as well as a craftswoman. Some of the other fellows didn't like sharing a studio with the new intake of young ladies, but I thought it was a marvellous innovation." Jonathan smiles, and this time there is a glimmer of light in his pale eyes. "It put me in mind of when your father used to bring you into the schoolroom to read aloud your stories. You'd have us howling. Do you still write them?"

Jane flushes, a little proud and embarrassed that he should remember. "I do, yes."

"Good. I hope you'll let me read them again, one day. I'll never forget the capers your villains and villainesses would get up to. Kicking each other out of windows, getting caught in mantraps, and whatnot."

"I'm working on something with a much cheerier ending now. I think we've all had enough gloom." Jane's new heroine is the most unlikely young lady ever to grace the pages of a novel. Catherine is humble and ordinary, even a little silly. Yet she'll triumph over her demons at the end.

"You're probably right." Jonathan nods gravely.

"What about you? Do you still paint?"

"I have been sketching, yes. Mostly pictures of Zoë. I don't want to forget her face, you see." His voice wears thin as his eyes brim with tears.

"I am so sorry." Jane reaches out her hand, placing it gently on his forearm.

"So am I. If only I'd had the strength to stand up to Mother and Father . . ." His breath is ragged. "But at least I can trust Zoë will be at peace now, thanks to you. And I'll go on until, God willing, we're reunited in Heaven."

"Jane!" Cassandra's voice interrupts. She and James, wearing near identical expressions of concern, stand side by side at the entrance to the Austens' private land.

Jane says a hurried goodbye to Jonathan, then rushes to join them. "What is it? What's happened?" She holds her breath, readying herself for bad news. Surely their family has suffered enough to merit a short period of tranquillity before the next disaster strikes.

Cassandra looks up at James. "Tell her."

James scratches his powdered curls. "It's Lefroy. He came to the house about an hour ago. Looking for you."

"Mr. . . . Tom Lefroy?" Jane hardly dares to believe it. She's tried her best to convince herself she no longer cares. Yet, her knees buckle at the mere mention of Tom's name.

"Yes. He said he was on his way to catch the stagecoach back to London, but he was most eager to speak to you before he left." James peers at her warily. "I can drive you up there in the carriage. If you like?"

Jane shakes her head, the motion making her dizzy. "No, no. It's all right."

Cassandra squeezes the top of Jane's arm. "Go, Jane. See what he has to say, at least."

With that, Jane realises the reason her sister has not asked how she's enduring the loss of her Irish friend is because she already knows the answer is too grievous for Jane to give.

Jane walks alone in the sunshine. Her treacherous heart leaps, still hungry for the meanest scrap of Tom's affection, while her more pragmatic stomach roils with dread. When she reaches Deane Gate Inn, Tom is standing at the crossroads with a leather satchel slung over his shoulder and a battered valise at his feet. At the sight of her, his blue eyes brighten, as if the sun has appeared from behind a cloud.

"You came," he breathes.

"And you're still here." Jane beams at him. Her legs are weak and her insides thrum. She wishes they were deep in the woods, where he could hold her in his arms and kiss away her doubts instead of standing at a polite distance, causing her to feel even more alone.

He glances at the other travelers beside them. "We don't have much time. The coach is due at any moment. I expect you know my aunt is furious with me. She thinks I've been leading you on. And it's true. I've struggled, in vain as it turns out, to repress my feelings for you. That is why I let them take me away. I hoped that, by removing myself, I might sever our attachment. I'm a rational man, Jane. I *do* have to make my own way in the world, and I've my family to think of. Uncle Langlois has always made it abundantly clear he expects me to marry for money."

Tom spreads his arms, giving a half-hearted smile, then smacks his palms against his thighs. "Or, as he would put it, cement my position in life by attaching myself to a woman of good breeding, and even better fortune."

Unable to meet Tom's eye, Jane fixes her gaze on the movement of his soft lips. Her heart drags against the stony ground as her arms and legs turn to lead. Her clever young man was right: in the end, everything comes down to love or money. In this case, not quite enough of either.

Tom places his hand over his chest, his forehead creasing with earnestness. "Dearest Jane, my affection for you is true.

You've only to say the word, and I'll give up those aspirations. I've no doubt there are plenty among our friends and family who will find our connection reprehensible. But, in time, I'm confident they'll come to accept our alliance."

Jane stares at Tom's lapis-blue woolen scarf. She never did ask which of his five sisters knitted it. "Mr. Lefroy . . . Tom." She attempts a smile, but she has lost all control of the muscles in her face. "I want you to know that I wish you every happiness and success in life . . ."

Tom's face darkens. "Say the word, Jane."

Jane steps backward, blinking away hot tears. An image of Mrs. Trigg, the gaoler's wife, with her three wailing infants pawing at her breast, springs to mind, strengthening her resolve. Jane cannot, she will not, brick herself inside a prison of her own making. "And my girlish heart will ever remember you with fondness . . ." She can't utter anything more without her voice cracking.

She turns to flee.

"Jane, I beg you . . . ," Tom calls after her, but creaking wheels and horses' hoofs muffle his cry.

The stagecoach has arrived.

Jane runs, leaping over tree roots in the dusty path. Green leaves are about to unfurl amid the thorny hedgerow, and snowdrops hang their heads along the bank, petals held tight. She does not look back to watch him go.

When Jane arrives at the rectory, Cassandra is waiting in the garden with a deep crease in her brow. "Well?"

Jane sniffs, wiping away the residue of tears with the back of her hand. "He wanted to say goodbye. That was all."

Cassandra continues to peer at Jane, clutching a hand to her breast. Jane brushes past, to reach the back door. She hurries up the stairs, heading straight for her dressing room. She wants to slam the door shut, but Cassandra is only a footstep behind her and she would not risk harming her sister.

Instead, Jane grabs her writing box, flipping it open to retrieve a half-written page of Catherine's story. Jane's heroine is in Bath. She's made a new friend, but friends are not always what we want them to be. With a deep sigh, she sinks into her chair, arranging the writing slope on her lap. She takes her penknife, selects a quill and makes swift, smooth cuts, flicking the blade away from herself.

Cassandra lingers in the doorway, watching her intently. "Sally's made some gingerbread. Shall I see if I can bring some up, with a dish of tea?"

Jane pauses in her work. "That would be nice," she replies, without looking up.

Cassandra remains. "Then I'll cut you some paper. Shall I? You've almost run out, and I can see you're making great strides with this new composition."

Jane lifts her chin, trying to keep it steady as she meets her sister's gaze. "Thank you, Cass. I'm so glad you're home."

Cassandra smiles, sunshine illuminating her pretty features. "And I to be home, silly." She turns, skipping down the steps, eager to retrieve whatever Jane might need.

Bittersweet tears well in Jane's eyes. Her heart is bruised and her pride is stung, but she is free, safe in the bosom of the family who cherish and believe in her, and ready to pour her soul into her writing box.

To be continued . . .

AUTHOR'S NOTE

Jane Austen met Tom Lefroy at Deane House in January 1796. I altered the style of the house, making it Tudor and Elizabethan rather than Georgian. The Harwoods, rather than the Harcourts (who appear in *Henry & Eliza*, from Austen's juvenilia), lived there. The illuminated greenhouse was at Manydown Park.

By 1795, James Austen lived at Deane Parsonage and Mary Lloyd had moved to Ibthorpe in north Hampshire. Anna Austen lived at Steventon Rectory, also in north Hampshire; I have made her younger. As infants, the Austen children were fostered by the Littleworth family of Deane. George Austen Jr. was later cared for by the Culham family at the Basingstoke hamlet of Monk Sherborne. The Prince of Wales was at Kempshott Park in Basingstoke until 1795.

I borrowed many names from Austen's life and work and used them for my characters: Mrs. Twistleton was the adulteress Austen observed in Bath; the Austens employed several maidservants named Sally; and a teenage Jane Austen really did marry herself off to Jack Smith in the sample page of the parish register. Austen mentions the Rivers family in her letters, but Sophy is thought to be fictional. Douglas Fitzgerald is my invention, but his circumstances are based on Austen's contemporaries: the Jamaican-born Morse siblings (who inherited great wealth and married into British high society).

Likewise, I've moved some events to fit within my timeline. George Austen bought his daughter's writing box shortly before her birthday in 1794. Austen began writing *Susan* (*Northanger Abbey*) in 1798. I brought this forward, as this is my homage to that novel.

My greatest liberty is that, despite Austen's genius, interest in the law, acute sense of justice and innate understanding of psychology, I can find no proof she solved any crimes. However, since so few of her letters survive, we cannot say she never attempted to do so. And if she had ever applied her skills in this way, I'm confident she would have been a great proficient.

ACKNOWLEDGMENTS

It is testament to Jane Austen's friends and family that so much of her work survives for us to enjoy. With *Miss Austen Investigates*, I want to celebrate this cast of supporting characters, including those who were deliberately erased from her story, and pay tribute to the life and work of Jane Austen herself. Whenever I've needed her, she's always been there.

In pouring my soul into writing this novel, my heartfelt gratitude goes to my wonderful supporters. Especially . . .

To my incredible agent, Juliet Mushens, and everyone at Mushens Entertainment (Rachel Neely, Liza DeBlock, Kiya Evans and Catriona Fida) for believing in me and my Jane right from the start. To my editor, Jessica Leeke, and Penguin Michael Joseph, for understanding exactly what I wanted to achieve and so expertly guiding me to realise it. I'm so proud of what we have created.

To my fabulous North American agent, Jenny Bent, for carrying my Jane across the Atlantic. To my fantastic team at Union Square & Co, for bringing this story to US readers with such care and enthusiasm: Claire Wachtel, Barbara Berger, Lindsay Herman, Kevin Ullrich, Johanna Baboukis, Scott Amerman and Diane João.

To my writing buddy, Elizabeth Welke (Felicity George), and my mentor, Suzy Vadori, for encouraging me to give this story everything I have. To my writing group for cheering me on all the way: Ceinwen Jones, Joni Okun, Joanna Wightman, Katy Archer, Liz Brown and Trudi Cowper.

To the Austen biographers and scholars whose work is invaluable to me: Susannah Fullerton, Claire Tomalin, Lucy Worsley, Helena Kelly, Devoney Looser, Paula Byrne, John Mullen and the late Deirdre Le Faye. To my early sensitivity readers: Dami Scott (host of the Black Girl Loves Jane Facebook group) and Olivia Marsh for challenging me to do better. To the Janeite community on social media (podcasters, booktokkers, bookstagrammers, YouTubers, tweeters, meme makers, etc.) for making me feel part of something bigger than myself.

To every English teacher I ever had, but especially Jonathan (MPW, London), who in 1995 sent me to the library to borrow *Northanger Abbey* (probably to stop me distracting the class with any further discussion of a certain BBC period drama starring Colin Firth and Jennifer Ehle). To my mum, dad and sister, Kelly, for lauding my ability to daydream away the hours and never once seeking to tether my feet to the ground. To my husband, Stephen, and our daughters, Eliza and Rosina, for accepting my tendency to live half in the present and half in the long eighteenth century.

Finally, to a clergyman's daughter from Hampshire, who made a bold choice about the way she lived her life, and quietly changed the world.